JUST MY LUCK

THE KING FAMILY

LENA HENDRIX

Developmental editing: Paula Dawn, Lilypad Lit

Copy editing: James Gallagher, Evident Ink

Proofreading: Julia Griffis, The Romance Bibliophile

Model cover design: Echo Grayce, WildHeart Graphics

Model cover photography: Ren Saliba

Discreet cover design: Sarah Hansen, OkayCreations

For my fellow women who like the drama fake, but the orgasms very, very real—You're in good hands with Abel King . . .

LET'S CONNECT!

When you sign up for my newsletter, you'll stay up to date with new releases, book news, giveaways, and new book recommendations! I promise not to spam you and only email when I have something fun & exciting to share!

Also, When you sign up, you'll also get a FREE copy of Choosing You (a very steamy Chikalu Falls novella)!

Sign up at my website at www.lenahendrix.com

AUTHOR'S NOTE

Just My Luck deals with a bit of heavy emotional baggage including: a mother and children surviving a house fire (off page), death of a parent (off page/not detailed, but referenced), a mother abandoning her children, suspected child neglect/abuse (off page), an MMC who was in prison, a single mother with a manipulative ex /emotionally abusive ex in her past, and the death of a child via car accident (off page but discussed/remembered).

We all agree that Russell King sucks, but please be kind to yourself when deciding if these triggers are too much for you.

The book also contains explicit, open door sex scenes with a MMC who isn't afraid to get what he wants (is it hot in here?).

ABOUT THIS BOOK

You might think it's reckless for a single mom to enter into a marriage of convenience with her boss . . .

You would be correct.

To make matters worse, Abel King is a grumpy local brewer with a criminal past. He also happens to be my boss and a total stick-in-the-mud. Every time I come to work with a smile and wave, I'm lucky if I can get a grunt in response.

When I accidentally-on-purpose overhear that he's having trouble securing a business loan due to his criminal record, **I hatch a plan to help the both of us.**

The arrangement is perfect—a business transaction and nothing more. Like having a roommate without the hassle of other people bugging you for dates.

I will definitely not be falling in love with him—no matter how many times he says "my wife" and *tingles dance in all the right places*.

Trouble is, as time goes on, things stop feeling like business and start feeling a whole lot like *pleasure* . . . and really, that's *just my luck* . . .

ONE

SLOANE

GETTING under my boss's skin is the second-greatest highlight of my day.

Waking up safely with my twins is the first, of course, but there was just something about knowing I was going to annoy the hell out of Abel King that added a little hitch in my giddyup every morning.

Case in point: I planned to use me running late as the perfect excuse to poke the bear.

"Ben! Tillie! Three minutes!" I called down the hallway of the small, run-down cabin on my granddad's property, rushing to shove lunches into backpacks.

"Don't you raise your voice at those kids, Sloaney." Granddad sat in a recliner that leaned too far to the right and looked dangerously close to collapse. I softened and walked to him, pressing a brief kiss onto the top of his wispy, white-haired head.

"If I recall correctly, you were always quick with an order, and if I didn't hop to it fast enough, a swat wasn't far behind." I crossed my arms and lifted an eyebrow at my granddad.

His bushy brows furrowed as he swatted the air between us. "Ah, what do you know?"

My laugh was bright and quick. Time had softened my grandfather, and we both knew it. My eyes raked over his pajama pants and the rickety TV tray next to him.

It had been over a year since the historic farmhouse Granddad had lived in his entire life burned down while we were sleeping inside. Even so, we'd been struggling to get back on our feet as a family. Both Ben and Tillie had been having issues, and instead of life moving on, I was watching the strongest man I ever knew spend his days rotting in a broken recliner. After the fire we moved into the one-bedroom cabin, and instead of taking the bed, Granddad insisted that he sleep on the recliner.

He had offered us a place to stay after my divorce from Jared, and I brought danger right to his doorstep. My ex and I were kids when we met—some would call us high school sweethearts, but our relationship was tumultuous from the start. If we weren't running around the San Fernando Valley on our parents' dime, we were breaking up for the sole purpose of getting back together. His family had made their money in the entertainment business, while my father made his millions as a financial adviser to the world's wealthiest. When Dad died, it was clear there was no love lost between me and his fourth wife. Other than what Dad had set aside for me, I was cut off. When I got pregnant at twenty-two, Jared's family insisted on a marriage, and for a while we tried to make it work.

I fought the familiar well of tears and shoved down my unspoken regrets to focus on the one man who'd always been there for me.

"Maybe you should head downtown and see what some

of the other old geezers are up to." I opted for a hopeful smile.

"What do I want to hang around with a bunch of old men for?" Granddad's grumble would have been endearing if it wasn't quite so sad.

Resigned, I turned back to the hallway to try to get the kids moving again. "Chickens! Let's move!"

Tillie was the first to appear in the hallway, coming from the bathroom. Because of the tiny nature of the cabin, the kids and I shared a room, and if we wanted any privacy, we had to change clothes in the tiny bathroom.

Just be thankful you have running water.

I closed my eyes and tried to feel gratitude. Things could have been so much worse, but mornings like these were draining. It was hard to feel like we'd ever get our lives back on track.

After the fire was ruled arson, any progress on rebuilding the farmhouse had come to a screeching halt while both legal and criminal investigations were conducted. In the meantime, we were forced to sit and wait.

"Mama, can you put a bow in my hair?" Tillie was holding up an oversize sequined purple bow. My daughter was still discovering her own personal style—some days she wore baggy overalls and high-tops, others were frilly dresses and hair bows. Her lightly freckled cheeks and thick brown hair reminded me of a tiny version of myself. The only difference was that when I was seven, it was my au pair who'd taken the time to put pretty bows in my hair.

"Of course, baby. Turn around." Tillie smiled and gave me her back while I secured the bow in her half-up hairstyle. I smoothed the straight strands down her back. "Have you seen your brother?"

"He was dancing naked. Again. So I got dressed in the

bathroom." Tillie was unimpressed with her twin brother's fascination with thoroughly grossing her out.

I laughed and squeezed her shoulders. "Okay. I'll get him. Please finish getting your bag together."

Down the hallway, I stopped in front of the room I shared with the kids. I knocked twice but turned the handle to open the door. There was a mattress tucked into the corner and a makeshift bed on the floor. The queen-size bed wasn't quite big enough for the three of us, so I'd made a pallet of blankets and pillows to sleep on to keep the kids from having to sleep on the floor.

My heart hurt just looking into the room.

I tried to push past the shame and infuse my voice with sunshine. "Ready to go, bud?"

Ben turned and his eyes went wide as he took me in. "Mom." His groan had me stifling a laugh. "You cannot drop us off at school wearing that."

I looked down in mock surprise, feeling a zip of accomplishment at my chosen attire. Seeing Abel nearly pop a blood vessel when I showed up for work in sponge curlers and a bathrobe would be enough enjoyment to carry me through the weekend. Not only did fucking with him make me giggle, but I was convinced it was something he needed too. It seemed like everyone in town was afraid of him, and the man needed to lighten up.

It became my mission to do that, and I took it very seriously. If my outfit was enough to get the attention of a seven-year-old, it was certainly enough to ruffle my grumpy boss's feathers.

I opened my arms. "What? It's cozy."

Ben rolled his eyes and yanked his zip-up hoodie onto his shoulders. He shook his head. "You are so weird."

I ruffled his nearly white-blond hair as he grumbled past

me. "I promise I won't even get out of the car. I was just running a little behind today, that's all."

Herding him out of the bedroom and down the narrow hallway, I turned to my granddad. "You can get them after school, right? I took a double shift and have to work until eight."

Granddad nodded. "I can take care of the rascals." He gestured toward them. "Come here."

Enthusiastically, the twins hugged their great-grandfather. He may be grouchy and set in his ways, but he'd always shown up for us. His home was our safe haven after my divorce, and I owed him everything.

I checked my watch. "Okay, we're officially late! Let's go!"

Like herding cats, I rounded up backpacks, grabbed water bottles, and shuffled the twins out the door. True to my word, I didn't get out of the car and embarrass the kids with my outfit. Instead, I smiled the biggest grin I could and waved as they walked into the elementary school building. Tillie was enveloped by a gaggle of girls, while Ben did what he had done every morning at drop-off—turned back for one last smile and wave.

I watched him walk into the elementary school building with a lump in my throat. The house fire had taken everything from us—almost. I would be grateful every single day for Lee Sullivan and for how he'd found Ben huddled in a closet and had saved his life by jumping out of the second-story window.

As it did every single day, driving away felt nearly impossible, but I reminded myself that he was safe and I had a grump to irritate.

≈

I CHECKED my reflection one last time. Biting back a smile, I channeled our lord and savior Miss Taylor Alison Swift by painting on a bold red lip. I flipped up the visor in my car and strode into Abel's Brewery with a little extra swing to my hips.

Fridays meant the craft kitchen opened a few hours early, and patrons would be filling the booths and tables until close. On the outskirts of Outtatowner, Michigan, the brewery was nestled into a large sand dune overlooking North Beach and the vast open waters of Lake Michigan. Abel's Brewery appealed to the upscale tourist vibe in every way. It was a masculine contrast to the soft whimsy of the beach grass and had large wooden beams and iron accents inside and out. The back wall faced the lake and was lined with glass garage-style doors that opened during the spring, summer, and fall months. It was my favorite feature of the brewery. Fire pits with cushy seating dotted the exterior. Inside, a large double-sided fireplace could add warmth during the chillier winter months.

The luxurious, upscale vibe of the brewery was a stark contrast to its somber owner. Abel King was nothing but dark glowers and heavy sighs. Sometimes I worried my antics were taking it a bit too far, but then I remembered Abel's little sister Sylvie had become my best friend, and that protected me . . . at least that was what I told myself.

Instead of using the side entrance designated for employees, I sauntered through the main entrance, hoping to make a splash with my appearance.

And make a splash I did.

Like clockwork, Abel was grumbling behind the bar, wiping off surfaces, washing glasses, and arranging everything the bartenders would need for a busy afternoon and evening of serving patrons.

I sneaked a glance from the corner of my eye. Abel King wasn't just tall; he was massive. With wide shoulders and a tapered waist, most women in town would say he was devastatingly handsome—if they could manage to get past the perpetual storm cloud over his head.

His hair was dark and cut close on the sides, but lately I'd noticed he had let the top grow a little longer than his usual no-nonsense style. Dark eyebrows shadowed his irises, and I hadn't yet dared get close enough to see if they were brown with hints of something like green or caramel or pitch black, as I'd suspected.

Why am I so drawn to dangerous men?

I tamped down the thought, and with my chin in the air I wove around high-top tables and past intimate high-backed booths that lined the outer perimeter.

My hips sashayed as I walked past the bar. "Morning, boss," I singsonged as I slipped past him and reached for a glass.

While I filled the glass with water, Abel's gaze was like a brand on my back. I'd certainly caught his attention. Stifling a giggle, I tightened my grip on the small duffel slung over my shoulder, carrying the work clothes I'd need to eventually change into. Under my robe was nothing but a bra and panties, because when you decide to mess with someone, you commit to the bit.

I took my time sipping the water and acting as if nothing at all was strange about me showing up to work on a Friday looking the way I did.

As I finished my drink, I swallowed with an audible *aah* and clinked the glass into a wash sink. Satisfied that I had left my ever-serious boss reeling, I had moved to exit behind the bar when his hard, stern voice rolled over my shoulder.

"Sloane." The deep rumble in such close proximity made me jump.

I scurried out from behind the bar, but in my haste, the loopy bow of my robe snagged. My forward momentum tugged on the belt, sending it tumbling to the floor. I turned, eyes wide with shock as the cold air tickled my skin.

I looked down to see my robe wide open, revealing my very visible nipples through the lacy mesh bra and thong set. My head whipped up to find that Abel also had a clear view of my barely there underwear.

With a yelp, I gripped the sides of the robe and pulled it closed. Heat burned my cheeks as I nearly ran around the bar and toward the back.

This was not at all how I'd seen this going.

Once safely inside the employee bathroom, I flipped on the light and, for the first time since leaving the house, took in my appearance. I looked ridiculous in the furry robe and curlers.

And Abel almost saw you naked.

A fresh wave of embarrassment rolled over me. The prank was supposed to be cheeky and funny, but instead I had flashed my boss wearing nothing but a minuscule thong and mesh bra that broadcasted the temperature of the room at any given moment.

I coughed out a laugh and held my hand over my mouth to keep Abel from hearing me. I needed this job, and I had been busting my ass for months to save up in order to get our lives back on track. The last thing I needed was to get fired for being a clumsy idiot.

Abel's face had been shocked and embarrassed. Those dark eyes—with flecks of gold, by the way—had pinned to my chest and run all the way down my exposed front for a full beat before flicking back to my face.

Oh, yeah. He'd definitely seen *everything*.

How the hell was I supposed to face him now? I wanted to crawl into a hole and die a slow, mortifying death.

A hard knock on the door jolted me. "Sloane. We need to talk."

Oh, shit.

TWO

ABEL

When the front-entrance door to the brewery had swung open, my jaw nearly fell to the floor. You'd think there was a wind machine and background vocals given the way Sloane flounced through the doorway. Her wavy brown hair was done up in hot-pink curlers, and instead of casual work attire, she was still in a bathrobe and fuzzy white slippers.

What in the actual fuck?

Without a second glance, she floated past me, her scent of baked goods and something sweet hanging in the air.

"Morning, boss!" Humor and happiness laced through her feminine greeting. She refused to call me anything but *boss* no matter how many times I'd told her to call me Abel.

My gaze snagged on the round fullness of her ass as she made her way behind the bar for a glass of water. She swallowed the drink with a flourish before putting the glass in the sink.

"Sloane," I ground out.

The harsh tone of my voice made her jump and she

hurried to leave. And then it happened—a single snag on a rough corner of the bar and her robe fell open.

My blood hummed. Sloane had always been dangerous curves and flirty banter. She was sunshine and laughter. Not even my own frosty exterior seemed to cool her warmth. I had no right, but too often I caught myself leaning into her presence like a flower getting its first taste of morning sunlight.

And now she was exposed, right in front of me.

I was her boss, and instead of looking away, I stared at her tits and followed the smooth line of her stomach to the swatch of fabric covering her pussy.

I felt sick.

And really fucking turned on.

Disgusted at myself, I slapped the rag onto the bar and stomped down the hallway after her. I stopped at the bathroom door, listening to her quiet movements through the wall.

I raised my fist and let it fall heavy on the wooden door. "Sloane. We need to talk."

After a moment it cracked open. One green and gold hazel eye looked up at me as Sloane peeked out of the slit in the door.

"Did you need something?" Her voice was feathery and light.

I bit back a groan. "Sloane, I . . ." How the hell do I navigate this?

I cleared my throat. "I'm sorry if I—" Fuck.

I tried a stern approach. "Casual Friday is—" The words escaped me.

Honestly, I didn't give a fuck what she wore to work, but there'd be no way in hell I could concentrate without thinking about the nothingness underneath that bathrobe. "Damn it."

Her eyes widened and she blinked, a small smile spread across her red lips. Clearly she was enjoying my internal meltdown.

I racked my brain for a single logical thought before giving up altogether. "I'll be in the front if you need me."

I turned and walked away, shaking my head and all thoughts of Sloane's naked body from my mind. Trouble was, Sloane Robinson was a walking, talking pain in my ass. From day one I'd regretted hiring her as a favor to my sister Sylvie. But what choice did I have? I'd never been able to say no to Sylvie. When she looked at me, it was like she saw a better man standing in my shoes. My sister was quiet and often faded into the background of this town despite being one of the most tenderhearted people I knew. After everything that had happened, she was the first person to tell me things would be okay.

I didn't believe her, but the thought was nice.

Now, with Sloane working for me and showing up to confirm my suspicions that she was as gorgeous naked as she was clothed, I had managed to exchange one prison for another.

Once back in the safety of the taproom, I grabbed the rag and continued polishing the wood bar. The white furry belt of Sloane's robe was crumpled in a pile at the corner of the bar. I reached down and ran it through my fingers. A soft, silent laugh pushed out of my nose as I felt a tug at the corner of my mouth.

Sloane had a way of poking at me that was equal parts irritating and endearing—almost like she'd lent me some of her lightness for even the briefest of moments. It was a kindness I rarely received, even in my own hometown.

Outtatowner, Michigan, had been a dream location to grow up. Nestled in the beachy coastline of Western Michigan, we had it all—good fishing, sandy beaches, and enough family money to not take life too seriously. Tourists floated in and out of our town throughout the year, which meant there were always new girls to meet and friends to make.

For most kids, it was a dream come true. But most kids didn't have Russell King as their father. My siblings and I grew up with our dad being detached and absent. His harsh words were swift and cutting, but we'd adored our mother and lamented the days when business would bring Dad back home. That is, until one morning I woke up and my mother was gone.

She left you and she isn't coming back. Maybe if you'd been the man of the house in my absence, she would have stayed.

Four days before my twelfth birthday, my mother vanished, and nothing was ever the same. My father's words sliced through me as I floated through middle school without direction. I was hurt, angry. I found solace in solitude and work. Then one night, years later, my life fractured again.

Driven by anger, stubbornness, and poor decisions, my actions turned my world upside down and took a life.

I scrubbed at the bar top, certain my incessant circles would wear a hole in the wood eventually. My jaw ached from gritting my teeth.

I worked twice as hard to stomp out any ridiculous thoughts of Sloane. She was my employee and my little sister's best friend. She was a mother and had been hit with hard times this year. Her working at my brewery was a favor and nothing more.

Still, for the rest of the day, the memory of her red-lipped smile and bare skin flashed into my head and settled into my gut.

~

WHEN MOST PEOPLE walk down Main Street in Outtatowner, they're greeted with friendly smiles and waves. Not me. Not the man branded a criminal and a murderer.

They wouldn't be wrong either.

It was solely because of the grace of my father and his savvy business sense that I even had a job after prison, let alone a thriving brewery.

I learned early on that Russell demanded results above all else, so I busted my ass to turn a fledgling brewery into a premier taproom and craft kitchen that tourists and townies alike could enjoy. They didn't need to like me in order to appreciate the time and care I put into brewing each flavor profile.

Only after I had proved myself did he offer even a modicum of approval. Irritation rolled through me. At least in state prison I had to worry about only myself. Here I had the weight of the King name pressing down on my shoulders.

The brewery might be named Abel's Brewery, but it would always be his.

The thought grated on me. My dad controlled every-thing and everyone. It had only been in the last year, when my sister Sylvie had defied him in every way, that the threads of our family had started to unravel.

My sister had the audacity to befriend and have a baby with a son of the Kings' most hated rivals—the Sullivans.

Generations of pranks and general chaos between the families defined our town, but Sylvie and Duke's relationship
had slowly begun to dismantle it all.

My father was no longer talking with our sister, but the
rest of us had banded around her. Only then had we fully
begun to see the cracks in Russell King's armor. They were
minuscule, but they were there.

My long legs carried me through the midday sunshine,
and my steps pounded up the sidewalk. Two women
walked ahead of me in the opposite direction. When we
caught eyes, I offered a flat-lipped smile and nod. You'd
have thought I flashed a gun or bared my teeth at the way
the women glued to each other and hurried past me while
sneaking wary glances in my direction.

Everyone knew I had done time, but few knew the
details. Had they known, I wouldn't just be an outcast; I'd
be a pariah. After prison, my consequence was being
shunned by my own hometown.

But I deserved it.

"Abe!" My name caught my attention, and my head
swiveled around to see my younger brother Royal exiting
his tattoo parlor. Younger than me by two years, Royal was
tall and built, like all King men. Tattoos peeked out from
under his short sleeves and ran down past his wrists and
over his hands. Ink even bled out above his collar. Had he
not run a lucrative tattoo shop, I'm sure our father would
have plenty to say about his appearance.

Royal's sharp features carried a dangerous edge to him
that could cut a man down with a single look. That is, until
he opened his mouth.

"Out of the cave scaring tourists already?" His shit-
eating grin spread wide as he leaned against the brick wall
to his shop.

A silent stare was my only response.

Royal laughed, unfazed by my brooding. "Figured. Where are you headed?"

My jaw ticced. My plan was still in its infancy, and I wasn't ready to share it with anyone, since it likely wouldn't go anywhere. "Out."

"Whatever." Royal rolled his eyes. "Syl texted about a dinner on the farm tonight. MJ is off work, so she'll be there too. You in?"

A dinner at my sister's house meant playing nice with her husband, Duke Sullivan. He probably wouldn't be too happy if he knew I'd helped source the glitter that was stuffed into the air vents of his truck. While Sylvie made us all promise we'd get along for her and little Gus, it didn't mean we couldn't have a little fun fucking with them.

Still, seeing my little sister as a mom did something to my chest. August was adorable, even if he was half-Sullivan.

"Yeah, I'm in," I said.

Royal grinned. "Good. And text her back. She worries about you."

Shoulders slumped, I nodded and headed in the direction of the bank.

The Outtatowner bank was on the far east end of town and a long fucking walk. Sure, I could have driven, but getting behind the wheel was still a challenge, even after all this time. Instead, I took the mild weather as an opportunity for a long walk to think.

The lobby of the bank was drab and soulless. The familiar scent of coffee clung to the air, and the hushed shuffle of paperwork greeted me, creating an odd mix of anticipation. It was a risk even going to the bank for fear someone would casually bring up my presence to my father.

Still, something needed to change.

"Mr. King?" a polite receptionist called into the tiny waiting area.

I unfolded myself from the too-small wooden chair and watched as her eyes went wide and she craned her neck to meet my stare.

"Um," she stammered. "Right this way."

Like a dog with his head hung low, I followed her to the glass wall of offices in the back corner of the bank. The receptionist opened the door and gestured inside. "Mr. Lowell, your two thirty is here."

The office was filled with heavy oak furniture and framed diplomas. Stephen Lowell stood from behind his desk and extended his hand. "Mr. King."

I gripped his hand and shook. "Abel, please."

With a nod, Mr. Lowell sat behind his desk and eased back in his chair. "What can I do for you, Abel?"

As I settled into the chair, my hands involuntarily tightened on the armrests. "I'm seeking a business loan." The truth tightened in my throat, but I forced the words. "I am looking to buy out my father's share in the brewery."

Mr. Lowell's eyebrows raised slightly. He nodded, tapping his fingers on the desk as his lips pursed. "Buying out a business is a significant endeavor."

I nodded, well aware after hours and hours of time spent researching.

Mr. Lowell cleared his throat and tapped a few keys on his keyboard. "Let's go over some details."

Hope swirled within me as the conversation progressed. He asked some general questions and then shifted to information regarding the business. When he requested profit and loss statements, I produced a slim folder with information I had been prepared to present. The possibility of realizing my dream felt tangible, and my mind wandered to the future.

"So, Mr. King—Abel," he corrected. "I've gone through the financial history of the brewery, and everything seems in order. In fact, it's quite impressive what you've done in its infancy."

I nodded, his veiled compliment making my shirt feel too small.

"However"—Mr. Lowell pulled his glasses from his nose and folded his hands over his desk—"we do have to consider other factors."

I leaned forward, eager for the final confirmation as doubt and fear swirled in my brain. "What factors?"

You know damn well what factors.

Mr. Lowell hesitated, and an icy chill ran down my spine. "Your criminal record, Mr. King."

The words hit hard, a gut punch I half expected but prayed wouldn't come. My gaze dropped to the floor briefly before meeting Mr. Lowell's eyes again. "I served my time. Paid my dues," I muttered, the bitterness of my past choices lingering on my tongue.

Mr. Lowell sighed, his expression sympathetic but stern. "I understand, Mr. King, but as a result, you do have a disrupted credit history due to your period of incarceration. Additionally, there's the issue of collateral. A lack of substantial assets is a barrier for approval."

My throat went tight, my back rigid. I knew this would be the outcome, but having it spelled out in plain terms was a tough blow.

Mr. Lowell sighed. "It's a risk the bank is not willing to take at this time. You see, we have to consider our investors, our reputation. Approving a loan for someone with a criminal history such as yours, well, it's not seen favorably."

I clenched my fists, fighting the surge of frustration. The burden of my past weighed heavily, not only on my conscience but on my aspirations. "I've changed," I argued, desperation creeping into my voice.

His expression softened as he nodded, acknowledging my plea. "I don't doubt that, Abel, but it's a complicated situation. And, if I may be frank, there's another factor at play here."

I frowned, my brow furrowing. "What do you mean?"

Mr. Lowell hesitated again, choosing his words carefully. "Your father is a significant figure in this town. His influence extends beyond the brewery. Going against his wishes, especially in a matter like this, could have real consequences."

A bitter taste filled my mouth. I'd hoped to distance myself from my father's shadow, carve out my own path. Yet there I was, faced with the harsh reality that his name carried more weight than my aspirations. The denial of the loan wasn't just about my criminal record—it was about a power play in a town where my father's influence was a force to be reckoned with.

Dejected, I shook Mr. Lowell's hand and excused myself, tail tucked between my legs. On the long walk back, I didn't bother looking up and acknowledging any of the tourists or townies I passed on my walk back to the brewery.

I had known better than to chase dreams I didn't have any right to hold.

THREE

SLOANE

THE BUZZ of a packed evening at Abel's Brewery pulsed with life as I navigated through the boisterous crowd. Laughter and the clinking of glasses melded into a friendly hum, creating an atmosphere that was invigorating and alive. The scent of hops and malt wafted through the evening air floating out of the open garage door that faced the beach. I soaked in the comforting embrace that wrapped me in the familiarity of this small town I was learning to call my own.

"Hey, Sloane, we could use another round over here!" Tall Chad's voice cut through the chatter, and I shot him a playful salute before making my way to the taps. In Outtatowner, it seemed the majority of people who'd grown up there held random nicknames, but it only added to the small-town charm.

I dried my hands on my hips and slipped behind the bar. The draft poured smoothly into the glasses, creating a cascade of amber as I bounced to the beat of the music and rolled the stiffness from my shoulders.

Layna, the first friend I ever made in Outtatowner, sat

at the bar, strumming chords on her acoustic guitar. The twang of sad country songs floated above the din of the crowd, blending seamlessly with the hum of conversation. I couldn't help but smile as Layna caught my eye, her playful wink acknowledging our shared connection to the rhythm of the town.

After Tall Chad picked up his drinks, I walked toward Layna, sidestepping the other bartender who was serving with me that night.

I smiled at my friend. "You're giving the Grudge a run for its money tonight."

The Grudge was Outtatowner's downtown honky-tonk, and if people weren't at Abel's, they were there. Layna grinned, fingers still strumming. "Someone's gotta inject some life into this joint. But if I get a gig at the Grudge, I'm gone."

We laughed, sharing a moment amid the lively ambiance. Layna's music added a layer of warmth to the brewery, the familiar country tunes resonating with the patrons who swayed to the rhythm. It was these connections, these shared experiences, that made this town feel like more than just a collection of people—it was a place of shared stories and laughter.

As the song ended, Layna set her guitar aside. I moved quickly to slide her a fresh beer, and she leaned in. "So what's new? I feel like if I don't see you here, I never see you."

I rolled my eyes, playfully nudging her. "You know how it is. I'm just the purveyor of good vibes and well-poured pints. Flying solo with two kids doesn't make a social life that easy."

She smiled, an understanding softness in her eyes. "You're doing a great job with those kids."

A knot formed in my throat. Most days I was white-knuckling it through life, but if I had my best friends fooled, maybe I was doing something right.

The front entrance swung open, and Abel stormed through the doorway. Mischief glittered in my eye as a zip of excitement ran through me. I'd been thinking of other—less naked—ways to needle him since this morning's incident went awry.

"Jesus, he's scary." Layna's voice was barely a whisper as she leaned in. Together we watched the owner skulk and disappear down the darkened hallway of the brewery. Like it always did, his brooding presence stood out amid the lively patrons.

My brow furrowed. There was a sharper edge to his demeanor tonight, a heaviness that hadn't been there before. Something weighed on him, and my mischievous instincts sensed this wasn't the time for playful banter.

My shoulder lifted as I aimlessly wiped down the bar top. I thought back to how endearing it had been when he'd tried to apologize for staring at my boobs. "Sometimes he's not that bad."

A disbelieving scoff escaped my friend. "He did hard time in prison, you know."

My back tightened. "Yeah, I heard." I'd quickly learned that rumors were just as much a part of small-town Michigan life as the gossip in LA. The commonality was that Abel had served jail time, but the reason varied greatly —drug trafficking, espionage, and my personal favorite, smuggling chickens across state lines.

Like, what the fuck?

Layna looked around and leaned in to whisper. "Russell King did everything he could to keep it under wraps, but there are some things you can't completely hide. He killed a kid."

My stomach plummeted as my mind raced to catch up. "What?"

With wide eyes, she shrugged. "That's the rumor I heard, at least. The records are completely sealed, so no one really knows the truth."

My eyes flicked back to where Abel had disappeared down the hallway toward his office.

He had harmed a child?

My mind didn't want to believe it. Sure, he was surly and antisocial, but I would have never guessed he would actually hurt someone, let alone a child.

And your track record makes you an awesome judge of character?

I tamped down the judgmental voice inside my head and focused on my friend. Layna pulled the guitar strap over her head and went back to playing as though she hadn't just dropped a bit of universe-tilting, bombshell news.

The brewery hummed with the joy of community, a stark contrast to the struggles Abel faced in fitting into his own town. The melodies shifted, the tempo of Layna's music adapting to the ebb and flow of the night.

Eventually I found a moment to slip into the back hallway, my sanctuary away from the energetic chaos of the brewery. Addressing the previously dim area, Abel had installed a few more overhead lights after catching one too many customers fooling around in the darkened space.

At the far end of the hallway, Abel's office door was slightly ajar. After looking back over my shoulder, I quietly tiptoed closer to the door.

Abel's rough voice quietly spilled into the hallway. "I

tried, Syl. He wouldn't budge. Said I was a liability to the bank."

I knew eavesdropping was wrong, but I was pinned in place by the urgency—the *sadness*—in his voice.

"If I want to buy Dad out, the money will have to come from somewhere else. It's that or I walk away. I'm not sure I can do this much longer."

For heavy moments, Abel was silent, presumably listening to his sister on the other end of the telephone. I knew from Sylvie that Russell King was a hard man to have as a father. Sure, he put on the appearance of a kind and benevolent businessman, but those close to him knew the truth—he'd give up his own children to maintain his pride. I hated him for how he had treated my friend, and to hear the sadness seeping from Abel, Mr. King had officially planted himself into enemy territory.

I was a loyal friend and just petty enough to hate him on principle.

Abel's solemn sigh was heartbreaking. "Yeah, I'm leaving now. I'll fill you in on the rest at dinner. I have some news from the private investigator too."

Private investigator? What the hell?

Hearing the conversation was a peek into a vulnerable side of Abel that I suspected few were privy to. I couldn't help but feel a pang of sympathy for the man who bore the weight of his past and present struggles.

Why did he need a PI? Had he really killed a child?

Sylvie was my best friend, and she'd never spoken a word about any of it. My brain couldn't wrap itself around the idea that it was true. I carefully exited the dimmed hallway and resumed my duties with a knotted pit in my stomach. The town's heartbeat thrived in the brewery, each interaction a testament to the interconnected lives that shaped this close-knit community.

All the while I considered Abel's unspoken burdens and wondered if the rumors were true. At some point I realized that maybe sometimes the loudest stories were the ones left unsaid.

My shift came to a close, and I never did see Abel slip out to leave. After cashing out, I left the lively atmosphere behind, driving home under the soft glow of the streetlights.

Thanks to Granddad, the kids were already in their bed when I entered the cabin, though they'd waited up for me to finish their nightly tuck-ins of back scratches and cuddles.

I steadied my breath and plastered on a smile before cracking open the door to our bedroom.

Ben and Tillie were too old to be sharing a bed, but we had limited options. They'd constructed a wall of pillows between them and were currently tugging at the shared covers.

"Stay on your side!" Tillie groaned. Ben took the opportunity to fart loudly, and he laughed as Tillie squealed in disgust.

I shot him a serious look. "Benjamin."

He did his best—and failed—to hide a grin. "Sorry, Mama."

I sighed and sat on the edge of the bed. "I missed my chickens today." One hand smoothed over Tillie's brown locks as the other patted Ben's calf.

"Mama, can I join the soccer team?" Ben's hopeful voice rang out. "Everyone is on the soccer team at school."

"Oooh, I want to take dance lessons!" added my daughter, the twins' eyes shining with excitement.

Their requests tugged at my heartstrings as my smile flattened. I wanted to give them everything, but the weight of my financial worries pressed down on me. When I'd fled LA after the divorce, I had no job, and getting the twins enrolled in school was my top priority. Every penny I had squirreled away had been spent on the divorce and on moving us across the country to where we could have a fresh start. The burned-out husk of the farmhouse and crumbling state of my grandfather's cabin only added to my growing list of concerns about how I was going to continue making ends meet.

"Let's talk about it tomorrow, okay? I promise we'll figure something out," I reassured them, leaning in to give each a good night kiss.

With them placated, I tickled their backs and tucked them in, then slipped into the hallway. Before I closed the door, I heard Tillie whisper, "Soccer and dance are too expensive."

My chest ached. They were too little to understand the stressors of money troubles. Hell, my upbringing was a stark contrast to the tiny run-down cabin. As a seven-year-old, I had wanted for nothing. Now I was scraping to get by, and my kids were feeling it.

In the dim light of the living room, Granddad sat in his well-worn chair, staring into the distance. His once-lively eyes now held a hint of sadness, and the lines on his face had deepened.

"Granddad, are you okay?" I asked, my voice a gentle murmur.

He sighed, his gaze lifting to meet mine. "I'm just tired, Sloaney. Tired and feeling the weight of time. But don't you worry about an old man like me."

His words hung in the air, and I couldn't shake the feeling that the threads holding our world together were beginning to fray. The challenges ahead seemed insurmountable, but as I sat beside my grandfather, I felt peace.

"I can fix this," I promised, sitting on the arm of the recliner and folding my body over his with a hug.

My grandfather's creases deepened with concern as he patted my hand. "Nothing to fix, Sloaney."

His words were meant to comfort me, but instead I could feel the resigned sadness in his tone. I had to figure something out—for the sake of my children and the fading light in my grandfather's eyes.

Unable to slow my mind, I sat at the small kitchen table and worried as I doomscrolled through social media. The soft glow of my phone illuminated the room, casting an ominous glow on the rustic surroundings. Frustrated with myself, a plan started to form in my mind. It was a long shot, but there was a chance it could work.

With a sense of determination, I closed out the social media app and opened my email. Tapping away, I fired off a quick inquiry to the bank holding my trust fund, wondering whether there was any way to unlock those funds now that there was some time and distance between Jared and my divorce.

In that moment, with the quiet hum of the cabin around me, I felt a flicker of hope. Maybe, in the midst of life's twists and turns, there was a chance not just to rebuild my granddad's farmhouse but to shape a brighter future for my kids and me.

SUBJECT: Inquiry about Trust Fund Access

Hi Mrs. Cumberton,

I hope this email finds you well. My name is Sloane

Robinson. We've spoken before regarding a trust fund with your bank. I was wondering if there's any possibility or process to access my funds for a significant life event. I understand there might be certain criteria or steps involved, and I would greatly appreciate any guidance or information you can provide.

Thank you for your time and assistance.

Warm regards,

Sloane Robinson

As I HIT SEND ON that email, a mix of emotions swirled within me. The very notion of navigating the complexities of my trust fund, a result of my father's hard work and savvy business decisions, often stirred resentment. After my father's unexpected death, my stepmother cut all ties with me. She was irritated enough that his entire fortune didn't automatically transfer to her and made no qualms about her concerns with my then-husband.

At the time I had been married to Jared, and I ventured a guess they both saw the signs I had chosen to ignore. Jared was nothing but impulsive decisions and reckless actions. Now that I was a bit older and finally free of him, there had to be a way to use the money my father had set aside for me to get us out of this shithole.

In the quiet darkness of my granddad's cabin, a quiet pride emerged as I set aside my shame and reservations. The email marked a tiny step toward independence, a choice to carve my own path beyond the weight of family history and the poor choices of a defiant young woman.

A small smile played on my lips as I stared at the screen. Venturing into the unknown, I embraced the possibilities ahead, recognizing that taking charge of our destiny meant confronting the shadows of my past.

I had already done hard things and, damn it, I'd do them again.

FOUR

ABEL

"THIS BATCH IS ABSOLUTE SHIT." My brewer went by the name Meatball despite the fact that he was thin as a rail. He stood about five foot four with dark hair and a thick black mustache. Maybe the nickname was because he looked vaguely Italian? You never knew with this town, and I was still trying to figure that one out.

Tuesday mornings were quiet. The brewery didn't open until the afternoon, which meant I could spend my time working on recipes, checking batch fermentation, or equipment sanitation without interruption. I enjoyed the solitude and quiet hum of the machines. Meatball was the only person I had to interact with, and that suited me just fine.

In the brewhouse, brew kettles and large fermenting tanks took up much of the area, but I'd tucked a small desk into the space. It allowed me to work alongside the batches in peace. Above the desk I'd even installed a shelf, and on it were jars of ingredients I was tinkering with—lavender, candied orange, new varieties of hops.

I swiveled in my chair to face him. Meatball was direct and never looked at me the way the rest of Outtatowner seemed to. It was the main reason I'd pushed to hire him to be my assistant brewer despite his lack of experience. He was a hard worker, and that meant more to me than his lack of skills. Skills you could learn.

When I didn't respond, but only glanced his way, he continued, "It's close, but there are notes of . . ." He rolled his tongue, smacking it against the roof of his mouth to taste the sample. "Licorice, maybe? Something bitter and off-putting."

My eyes narrowed, and I gestured for him to come closer. "Let me see."

Meatball used a sanitized pipette to get a fresh sample and deposited it into a tasting glass. He passed the glass to me. I held it up to the light, examining the color and meniscus as it clung to the sides of the glass. I sniffed and it held notes of berry and a hint of herbs. I placed the sample to my lips and took a small taste.

Jesus, fuck.

My face pinched and I set the glass down.

"I don't think it'll get better with conditioning." Meatball frowned, crossing his arms.

I shook my head. "No, you're right. It's off. Scrap it."

His eyebrows lifted. "The whole batch?"

I turned back to my desk. "You said it yourself—it's shit. Scrap it."

Meatball nodded and worked to clean the area before taking steps to dump all ten gallons of the test batch down the drain. "You got it, boss."

I flinched at his words as Sloane's throaty voice hammered into my memory. She may not realize it, but she got under my skin anytime she called me boss. It sounded different coming from her. The word rolled around in my head and clung to my ribs.

Distracting myself from a particularly irritating brunette, I pulled a three-ring binder off the shelf and flipped to the recipe page for that specific batch of beer. Something was off, and it was my job as the brewmaster to figure it out. Any number of things could alter a brew, from oxidation to contamination to something as simple as an odd combination of flavors. My gut told me the combination of blueberry and basil would be a hit around here, given everyone's obsession with blueberries in this region.

I couldn't blame them. Because of the acidic soil and coastal climate, there was nowhere else in the country where you could get berries as delicious.

Unfortunately, the best blueberries in the state were from Sullivan Farms, but my father's hard-on for hating the Sullivans meant sourcing from them was out of the question. Dad nearly had a coronary when I'd suggested reaching out to Duke Sullivan, owner of Sullivan Farms, for a collaboration. He'd thrown a tantrum and insisted that we source the berries from any number of other farmers in the area. What he hadn't anticipated was the farmers' loyalty to the Sullivans. As a result, our only option was to obtain berries from outside of Michigan—frozen ones at that.

They were absolute trash.

He may pride himself on being a skilled businessman, but Dad didn't know beer. Only the best ingredients would translate into the best-tasting beer, and that meant berries from Sullivan Farms.

I slashed a thick black line in permanent marker across the berries listed on the recipe and above it wrote "Sullivan berries." I'd swallow my pride for the benefit of the beer and would see about getting some from Duke for a new batch.

What my father didn't know wouldn't hurt a damn thing.

"Hey," I called out to Meatball. "We're going to try this recipe again, but I'll need a few days to get some ingredient variants."

He nodded and continued cleaning the equipment. Another fantastic quality was he kept his mouth shut. I eyed my assistant.

He's getting a raise.

I went back to my work, hunching over the recipe and mentally calculating again to adjust for fresh versus frozen berries. My gut had rarely been wrong about a recipe—I didn't want to give up on this one so quickly.

With the next step of conditioning the new beer grinding to a halt, I found myself with a free afternoon. It was a rarity, and I hated not having something to do. Tucking a small notepad into my pocket, I sneaked out of the brewery, avoiding the front bar altogether. People had already begun filtering in, spending afternoons here grabbing a post-work beer or pre-beach snack. I didn't have the energy for their sidelong, wary glances.

Instead, I set off on foot, walking down the beach toward Main Street, notepad in hand. In it, I often noted smells or tastes that seemed interesting or appealed to me in some way. It didn't matter how obscure or seemingly random they appeared; everything went into the notebook.

Corn dog (fried corn). Misty air. Beach grass. Coconut oil.

I underlined *coconut* and mulled over that idea as I walked.

Coconut and chili pepper. Cardamom? Lemongrass?

Most ideas were random thoughts that would never come to fruition, but I knew inspiration could strike at any time and I would be ready. I tucked the notepad back into the front pocket of my jeans as I approached the sidewalk that would take me east through downtown. I paused to consider my destination. South Beach was already full of tourists soaking up the late spring sun. Downtown was slowly shifting from day-trippers and shopping to coastal nights out on the town. Gawking stares and fearful eyes held little appeal.

I'd decided to turn back and head north toward the brewery to head home when Sloane's rusted navy-blue car caught my eye. It was parked outside of Wegman's Grocer, an overpriced convenience grocery shop for tourists too hurried to head a few blocks over to the grocer the rest of us used.

Curiosity got the best of me, and I shifted directions, pounding up the pavement toward downtown. When I reached the storefront, patrons were milling around inside. I didn't recognize anyone outside of the checker working the register. Despite my anonymity, wary glances still melted over me as I walked down the aisles.

I pushed a cart, aimlessly assessing the overpriced items. *Why are you even here?*

I tossed a box of cereal into the cart and a can of ranch-style beans before rounding a corner and coming to an abrupt stop. At the end of the aisle, I spotted Sloane hunched over a small figure—her son, I presumed—while her little girl stood next to her, silently bawling her eyes out.

I scanned the store—*was no one else seeing this?*

Despite Sloane's obvious crisis, not a single person was stopping to ask whether she was okay or needed help. Indecision gnawed at me. The Sloane I knew was confident and a spitfire. She didn't need some asshole coming to her rescue. Hell, she probably didn't even need help in the first place.

I slowly made progress toward her, keeping my gaze

impassive and discreet. Sure enough, the little girl had hot tears streaming down her face as one hand covered her mouth to muffle her sobs. The young boy was in the fetal position, gently rocking on the floor as Sloane rubbed his back and whispered to him.

"Please, baby. We have to get up. You're safe." Her voice was rough and thick with unshed tears. "I need you to get up, Ben. You're too big for me to carry."

Sloane's shopping cart was haphazardly stopped, blocking the aisle. It was plumb full of what I assumed was their food for the week. The young boy continued to cry, his wails getting louder and drawing more and more attention.

My heart hammered against my ribs. Sloane looked around, her eyes pleading. Her attention returned to her son as she wound her arms around his middle and attempted to pick him up. The kid wasn't big, but Sloane was unable to get his deadweight to budge.

A sorrowful sob escaped her and ripped my chest open. Without thinking, I abandoned my cart and closed the distance between us. As my footfalls drew closer, her eyes whipped up, rimmed in red.

I paused in front of the boy. "Can I get him?"

Shock flitted over her petite features before her eyes went wide and she nodded. I took the single dip of her chin as permission and bent to scoop the boy in my arms. He was light, and I adjusted him against my chest.

"You're all right, man. I'm just going to help your mom get you to the car." Soft muffled tears were his only response. I turned to the little girl, whose face was splotchy and red. She looked at me, not with fear, but with awe. Something shifted, tight and uncomfortable under my skin, but I held out one hand.

Without hesitation, the little girl slipped her hand into

mine. I didn't look back as I walked the children straight toward the exit, Sloane right behind me.

As I neared the checkout, I caught the eye of the checker. "Sloane's cart is in aisle seven. Bag it up and send the bill to the brewery. Have the groceries delivered to the Robinson place."

The wide eyes of the checker stared back at me.

"Got it?" I asked with irritation.

"Yep. Yes. Got it," the checker stammered.

Without looking back, I walked through the automatic doors of the grocery store and toward Sloane's car. The boy in my arms clung to my neck, and the little girl's hand was tiny in mine, so I tried my best to keep my grip firm but gentle.

When we got to her car, Sloane moved around me to unlock the door and open the back seat. I offered the little girl a flat smile that I hoped wasn't a grimace. Her tears had dried, and her sad smile tore at my heart. She climbed over the seat and settled into the back. I placed the boy on his feet. He didn't look up from the concrete, so I simply gave his shoulder a gentle squeeze and turned.

About to walk away, Sloane's voice called to me. "Wait."

Cautiously, I looked over my shoulder, bracing for a quick poke or witty response from her. Instead, she tucked her son into the car, fastened his seat belt, and gently closed the door. I watched her every move. In two steps, she surged forward, wrapping her arms around me.

My arms were pinned to my sides by her hug. Her small stature was dwarfed by my mass, but she squeezed. "Thank you."

The broken sadness in her voice nearly killed me. I bent my head down, reluctantly accepting her gratitude and stealing a whiff of her hair.

When she released me, I cleared my throat. "Yeah."

Unsure what to do, I turned and fled down the sidewalk in hulking steps toward the safety of the brewery. When I was out of sight, I finally slowed and pulled the notepad from my pocket. I scribbled down exactly the way Sloane smelled so I wouldn't forget.

Honey. Biscuits. Home.

FIVE

SLOANE

THE DRIVE back to my granddad's property was a blur of panic, sadness, and confusion. What had started as a quick grocery trip after school had turned into a literal mess of Ben crumpled on the floor. My grip tightened on the steering wheel as I fought back the helpless feeling that threatened to overtake me.

One minute we'd been negotiating the nutritional merits of Pop-Tarts, and the next Ben was frozen with panic. He'd melted to the floor, and I'd lost him to whatever all-consuming emotions had overtaken him. Poor Tillie was collateral damage as I did anything I could to get Ben off the linoleum floor.

My eyes flicked to the rearview mirror. Ben's gaze was unfocused as he looked out the window. Tillie was doing her best to lighten the mood by jabbering away and filling the silent car with anecdotes about her day. She wasn't looking for a response, but simply grasping for a sense of normalcy amid the crisis we'd all just experienced.

Bless that sweet girl.

"We're almost home, bud. You doing okay?" I was proud

how strong and sure my voice sounded despite the worry gnawing at my stomach.

Ben nodded but didn't respond.

"Who was that man?" Tillie bravely asked.

That man.

A flash of Abel's strong arms lifting my son and effortlessly carrying him through the grocery store was no match for how sweetly he'd gripped Tillie's hand. She'd accepted it as though it were the most natural thing in the world.

My chest caved in.

I'd needed help, though it sucked to admit it. In the most public, mortifying way, Abel had appeared out of nowhere and, quite literally, saved the day. How could that be possible if he really was someone who'd harmed a child? The two warring versions of Abel King tussled in my head as I drove the quiet country road toward my granddad's property.

"That man is my boss, sweetie." I attempted to keep the conversation light.

"Is he your friend?" she pressed.

"Um . . ." I hardly knew anything about him, but the way he'd shown up for me spoke volumes to his capacity for friendship. "Kind of." When that didn't sit right with me, I lifted my shoulders and accepted the truth. "Yes, he's my friend."

"He's *big.*" In the mirror I could see Tillie's eyes go wide as she emphasized the word.

My brows lifted. "Baby, we've talked about how it's impolite to comment on someone's size. That's an inside thought."

Her little brown eyebrows tipped down. "I didn't mean *fat.* He's, like, a giant."

I suppressed a laugh. She wasn't wrong. "Yes, Mr. King is very tall."

And built. And handsome in that broody kind of way . . .

"And *strong*," Tillie added. She bumped her brother's arm. "Did you see how he picked you up like you weighed nothing?" Ben shrugged off his sister and continued to stare absently out the window.

The conversation drifted back to Tillie reminiscing about her day at school. I knew it was her way to reassure us, and I loved her even more for it. When we turned into the long gravel driveway, I averted my gaze. The blackened wood of the farmhouse was a painful reminder of the house fire we'd survived. If it were up to me, I'd find another way in, but driving past it was the only way to reach the cabin.

Our only saving grace was that the farmhouse was on Tillie's side of the car and not Ben's. I was sure that his most recent meltdown stemmed from the trauma of the fire. We unloaded ourselves, *without groceries*, and I suggested the twins play for a bit before starting on any homework. I needed a minute to catch my breath anyway.

Tillie ran ahead, tossing open the cabin door seemingly without a care in the world. Ben was slow moving, and I stepped up beside him, gently placing my arm around his shoulder. He leaned into my affection, and a tiny spark of hope grew brighter.

"I love you, Benny," I whispered.

"Love you more," he answered.

"Love you *most*," I countered as we made our way toward the front door.

"Love you moster, toaster, chicken roaster." A small smile tugged at his mouth, but immediately it fell. After a moment Ben found his voice again. "I saw him."

Confusion clouded my brain and my brow furrowed. I crouched to be eye level with my son. "Saw who, baby?"

Worry knotted in my gut as fear flickered over my son's face. "Dad . . . at the grocery store."

My eyes searched his. The twins hadn't seen their father since the divorce. Despite our custody agreement, Jared was unreliable and absent. Despite my efforts, after one too many no-shows and disappointed children, I'd given up on trying to force a relationship with him. When our verbal arguments escalated further, I ran.

However, my suspicions that Jared wasn't just mean but dangerous peaked when the house fire was ruled arson. There was only one person I knew who would ever want to harm us, and it was Jared.

My father and stepmom had both warned me when we were dating that they had concerns, but I was too stubborn and foolish to accept it. They saw what I wouldn't—Jared was a spoiled kid who'd grown into a man who couldn't handle not getting what he wanted.

"Are you sure?" I gripped Ben's hand, not wanting to believe Jared was here.

He nodded, tears welling in his eyes.

I steadied my breath. *How the hell was I supposed to navigate this without losing my shit or traumatizing him more?*

"I believe you." I wrapped him in a hug. "I will keep you safe. You don't have to worry. Your dad is upset at me, not you. Everything is going to be okay."

My words were reassuring, but I wasn't entirely sure they were true. Jared was a wild card, and I wouldn't feel safe unless I knew for sure whether he was lurking around Outtatowner.

Determined to salvage our evening, I plastered on a

happy face and went through the motions. All the while, worry gnawed at me.

How the hell was I going to get through this?

UTTERLY EMOTIONALLY EXHAUSTED from an evening of pretending everything in my world wasn't crumbling around me, I collapsed onto the pile of blankets on the floor. Ben had fallen fast asleep, and Tillie and I cuddled a few minutes longer than usual. She put on a brave face, but I had a sneaking suspicion her people-pleasing ways were a defense against the fear and worry she carried.

I grabbed my phone from the nightstand and adjusted the brightness in order to not wake the kids. I pulled up my email and sent a quick message to the children's therapist, explaining the incident today and asking for help. Hopefully a professional could do more than me. Still, it was hard to not feel like I was failing my kids.

A new message was waiting for me in my inbox. I recognized the bank's email and opened it up while holding my breath.

SUBJECT: RE: Inquiry about Trust Fund Access

Dear Ms. Robinson,

It was a pleasure to hear from you. Per our previous discussions, there are specific provisions attached to the trust in your name. I am happy to discuss those in detail, but for the sake of clarity, a substantial life event would include marriage, birth of a child, private school tuition for the children, or college tuition for one or both children.

Outside of those parameters, the funds would be available to you as equal, lump-sum payments on your thirty-fifth and forty-fifth birthdays. Again, I am happy to make an appointment to discuss the details further. Please reach out to my secretary at your earliest convenience. I have attached her contact information below.

Regards,

Regina Cumberton

I READ the email at least five times.

Marriage? Nope.

Birth of a child? Hell no—I'd have to be having sex for that to be even a remote possibility.

Private school? No way. The nearest private school was across the state, and I couldn't imagine sending my kids away.

College tuition? Jesus, I needed to get them through second grade. I couldn't bear to think about either of them moving away for college. College also wouldn't help Granddad.

Dejected, I closed out of my phone and stared at the ceiling.

Anxiety crept over me in the darkness like an icy blanket. I worried my gut was right and Jared had been responsible for the fire. I had hoped the ensuing public investigation would be enough to keep him away.

What if he had come back for us? What if he'd never left?

I'd wasted years of my life not seeing the signs that Jared was a twisted and dangerous man. He'd manipulated and controlled me, and I'd been a willing participant. Once we'd gotten pregnant with the twins, his jealousy over his own children was astounding. He'd been convinced I could never love him as much as I would love the babies.

He was right.

When I realized my sham of a marriage was over, I spent my days in secret, plotting and planning my escape. It wasn't until we had disappeared to my grandfather's coastal small town that I ever felt safe. Still, he found us.

I wouldn't be controlled. I couldn't. Trouble was, with mounting debt and no way to access the trust that would be our lifeline, I was drowning.

That night I dreamed I was floating away. Ben and Tillie stood on the shores of Outtatowner's beach, waving as I struggled to swim to them. The tide took me out—farther and farther from them. I screamed and rioted against the crashing waves as they dumped over my head. My arms and legs were leaden. Water choked me and burned in my lungs. My feet thrashed as a dark figure loomed over my children in the shadows. I screamed, and still no one came. I fought.

Then suddenly a faintly familiar grumble and a strong hand gripped my arm and hauled me ashore.

SIX

I DIDN'T HAVE many gifts, but avoiding people was one of them. It had been a week since Sloane's wardrobe malfunction, and I'd spent those days with my head down, escaping any and all interactions with my employee.

What I couldn't escape was the memory of Sloane's smooth skin or the curve of her breasts. It was like once I'd seen it, the image lodged in my brain and refused to leave. Even a flash of it running through my mind and my cock would get rock hard.

The incident at the grocery store didn't help me feel any better about the fact I was obsessing over my gorgeous employee.

A rapid series of knocks pounded at my office door.

I scrubbed a hand over my face and sighed. "Yeah?"

The knob turned, and one of my bartenders, Reina, popped her head in. "We're swamped out here. Ken was a no-show." She shot me an irritated look. "Again."

Frustration grated at my nerves. It was the third time this month Ken didn't show up for work, and I was definitely going to have to fire the guy. "On my way."

I looked at the mountains of paperwork I had been going through and let irritation roll over me. I was still desperately looking for a loophole in the brewery's ownership contract, but I'd have to leave that headache for another day.

I walked down the hallway toward the taproom behind Reina. "Hey," I called to her. "Can you serve?"

She shot me a flat look. I knew she preferred to be behind the bar, but my ass would only scare more customers away, and she knew it.

"The tips are yours," I added to sweeten the deal.

Her black eyebrows shot up. "Seriously?"

I nodded. I didn't need the tips from the bar, and not having to be out on the floor was worth giving up the money to her.

She grinned, shoving a fist toward me. "You've got yourself a deal."

Unsure what to do, I gripped her fist and shook it. "Okay."

She laughed and sauntered into the busy taproom. Abel's Brewery was comfortably busy—not so frantic that we were swamped but welcoming a steady rhythm of customers. A late spring breeze floated off the lake, and I was pleased to see people enjoying the open garage doors and outdoor seating.

Groups of people mingled and laughed. A few had taken board games from the community game shelf and were playing over a few beers. It was the quiet sense of community that drew me in—a community I wasn't even allowed to be a part of, but enjoyed all the same.

My attention immediately found Sloane. With her back to me, I watched as she effortlessly gathered up used glasses and smiled at our customers. She had a natural and engaging way about her that people were drawn to. Her laughter was light, and her smiles were genuine.

I stood behind the bar and pointed at the man waiting to order. "What do you want?"

He bristled at my clipped question.

I guess I should work on that.

He ordered but cast a wary glance before leaving a few singles on the bar top. I swiped them up and dropped them into the large jar for tips behind the bar. Tending bar was steady and mindless work, so I was careful to allow myself to watch Sloane from only the corners of my gaze.

A low whistle from the corner of the bar caught my attention. My younger brother Royal was perched on a stool with a beer in his hand.

I walked over and extended my hand. "What do you know?"

Royal shook it, then grabbed his beer and laughed before taking the last sip. "I know you're in way over your head with that one." He gestured toward Sloane.

Blood drained from my face, and I busied my hands with drying a pint glass. "I don't know what you're talking about."

Royal's flat, playful stare burrowed under my skin as he smirked. "You've been eyeing her since you walked out here."

I ignored him, mostly because it annoyed me he'd seen what I had been trying so hard to hide. "Are you staying? If you're going to bug me, I'm making you pay tonight."

Royal grinned and stood. "Wish I could, brother. Just popped in to say hello, but I've got work." The tattoo business meant Royal worked odd hours. We shook hands one last time, and I watched as he exited the brewery. Eager eyes followed him toward the door. The friendly waves and happy handshakes were a stark contrast to the way people scattered when I walked by.

Just the way it goes.

I continued working behind the bar, all while sneaking glances in Sloane's direction. Though she was efficient and friendly, I couldn't help but think something seemed . . . *off*. Her shoulders bunched, and I nearly broke a glass in my grip when I saw her flinch at a casual touch from a tipsy customer. Instead of rounding the bar and beating the shit out of him, Sloane had effortlessly slinked away and successfully avoided his attention. Still, I watched him like a hawk.

Her face was pinched in a smile, but her eyes were dulled, flicking to the entrance as though she was expecting someone to walk through the door—that, or she was looking for an escape. Something was definitely up with her, and I couldn't ignore the gnawing feeling that it was likely my fault. First I'd gawked at her and then inserted myself between her and her kids. I should have just left her alone, but for some reason I'd been compelled to help her. Gone was the defiant woman who radiated sunshine, and in her place was a mother who was struggling with her son's very public meltdown.

I couldn't not help her.

I sighed as I wiped spilled beer off the bar top.

I thought I was doing the right thing, but I swear if she quits, this place is screwed.

A loud crash sounded in the busy taproom, and my head whipped up in time to see Sloane nearly jump out of her skin. Her eyes were wide, and unexpected tears brimmed at their corners. It was only a busted beer glass that had been elbowed off a high-top table—it happened all the time.

I rounded the bar, swiping the mop and bucket as I went. "Reina," I called, sliding the bucket and mop toward the spill. "A little help here?"

She nodded. "On it."

I turned toward Sloane. "My office." When she flinched at my tone, I softened. "Please."

She barely nodded, but she moved past me and hurried across the room and down the hall to my office. I entered behind her, closing the door to give us a bit of privacy.

I raked a hand over the short hairs on the back of my head. "Sloane, is something—you seem . . . look, if this is about the other day—"

"What?" Her eyes darkened as her eyebrows furrowed.

Jesus, she's going to make me say it.

I gestured between us. "You seem uncomfortable, and if it's because I saw you . . . you know . . ."

Realization flickered over her features before she barked out a laugh. "What? No. Oh my god. No."

I paused, not expecting that reaction. I searched the ground, fumbling for what to say next.

"They're just boobs." Her laughter was directed at me, but I preferred it over the near-tears version of her from earlier. "It's really okay, boss."

"Don't call me that." I gritted my teeth. They were definitely not just boobs. I'd seen enough pairs to know that Sloane's breasts were the perfect size and shape—so much so I'd even jerked myself off to the thought of how they might fit in my palm.

Fuck, I need to get myself together.

Sloane ignored me and folded her arms over her stomach. "I'm just off-kilter tonight." Her neck rolled to stretch. "I can feel it."

"Is everything okay?" I hoped my question came across as supportive and not like the prying jerk I was.

She huffed out a breath and tipped her face to the ceiling. I took the opportunity to steal a glance at the slender column of her neck. Her pulse thrummed at the base, and I imagined running my tongue over that exact spot.

"No. Not really." She looked at me. "The other day—at the store when you helped me? My son saw my ex."

She didn't offer any more explanations, but I was able to fit the pieces together. I breathed a sigh of relief that she saw my intervention as helpful. An odd sense of pride swelled in my chest, and a protective ache followed closely behind.

I risked a look at her. "Are you okay?"

Her hazel eyes searched mine. "I'm not sure. I think so? I haven't seen him, but Ben swears he did. I want to believe him, but I mean—why would he come here? Just to fuck with us?" She sighed. "I don't know. I'm just stressed about it. Every time the door opened, I worried it was him."

Rage bubbled dangerously close to the surface. I didn't know anything about her ex, but if he was the type of man who'd put this kind of fear into a woman who'd given him children, he was immediately on my shit list.

I'd known a whole host of scary men, but her ex had never met me. "What does he look like?" I ground out.

Her face pinched as she thought. "Um . . . blond hair, blue eyes"—she held her hand only a few inches above her own head—"about this tall? A pompous air about him that makes you want to punch him in the face?"

A humorless laugh escaped me at that last part. "A picture would be helpful. That way we can make sure everyone knows he's not welcome here."

I was lost in the greens and browns of her eyes as they went wide. "You'd do that for me?"

I nodded. Protecting Sloane felt like the simplest thing in the world. "Of course."

For the second time in a week, Sloane surged forward and wrapped her arms around me in a hug. Her body pressed against mine as she tucked her cheek into my chest.

Instead of freezing this time, I shifted and held her close, pulling in the sweet smell of her shampoo and letting it brand itself into my lungs. Her soft frame was dwarfed by mine as I held her.

Slowly, she shifted and tilted her head back to meet my eyes. I couldn't look away. The air buzzed with electricity. Blood surged beneath my skin, settling low between my legs. Sloane's breasts pressed against my chest as my arms banded us together. Her soft breath tickled my neck, and my eyes fell to her lips.

Blood whooshed between my ears, and time stood still. My right hand smoothed up her back, settling between her shoulder blades. Sloane's head tilted as if she was granting me access to those tempting, plush lips.

My muscles flexed, every inch of me rock hard and coiled tight. If I snapped, I'd devour her and incinerate us both.

A reckless part of me didn't care. I was drawn to her in ways I couldn't explain. Her fingertips toyed with the hem of my T-shirt, skating across the skin at my back as a finger dipped below the hem.

I lowered my head, ready to plunder, and fuck the consequences.

As I pulled her closer, a sharp knock at the office door jolted me upright, nearly pushing Sloane away from me.

Without hesitation, Reina's face burst through the doorway. "Abel, what the hell? I'm drowning by myself out here!"

"Yeah!" I grumbled. "One minute."

With an exaggerated eye roll, Reina pulled the door shut, enclosing Sloane and me in the charged atmosphere of my small office.

"Abel, I—" Sloane's hand brushed her bottom lip as if we hadn't been interrupted and she could feel the kiss that almost happened.

Irritated—either by the fact we were interrupted or that Sloane made me weak, I wasn't sure—I shouldered past her toward the reprieve of the taproom. "I've got to go. It's busy tonight."

Without looking back, I flung the door open and stomped toward the front of the brewery, hating myself and my inability to articulate the riot of emotions I was feeling.

Minutes later, Sloane appeared, her smile perfectly in place, as though I hadn't nearly mauled her in my back office. If Reina hadn't interrupted us, I imagined hauling her onto my desk and stripping her bare before sliding my cock into what I could only guess was the tightest pussy on the planet.

I pressed my thumb and forefinger into my eye sockets and willed my hard-on to go away before someone noticed I was pitching a gargantuan tent behind my jeans.

Jesus Christ, I'm losing it.

Reina was right in that it was another bustling night. I found myself working tirelessly behind the bar, pouring pints and being an outsider to the witty banter that defined our small town. Despite the lively atmosphere, an undercurrent of tension lingered in my neck and shoulders.

Memories of my past mistakes played like an unwelcome reel in my mind, especially when Sloane's kids popped into my head. The shame I harbored resurfaced, whispering that I was forever defined by a single dark moment, marked by my own shortcomings.

The door opened, and Bootsy Sinclair's familiar face sauntered in. Bootsy, a simple soul with a loyalty that ran deep, worked for my father. It was his innocence that made him dangerous, as his loyalty was unquestioning, and his curiosity was often a subtle form of espionage for Russell King.

"Abel," Bootsy greeted with a wide grin, sidling up to the bar. His innocent eyes sparkled, but there was always a lingering sense that he was sniffing around for information.

"Bootsy." I returned his greeting with a curt nod. "What brings you in tonight?" My tone remained neutral, though resentment simmered beneath the surface. His allegiance to my father grated on me, a constant reminder of the complex dynamics within my own family.

"Just thought I'd drop by for a cold one," Bootsy replied, seemingly oblivious to the undercurrents surrounding him as he fumbled for crinkled dollar bills that spilled from his pocket and onto the floor. "How's everything going?"

"Busy as always," I replied, pouring him a pint. "You know how it is." I slid the pint toward him and waved away the cash. "On me."

"Appreciate that." He nodded with a grin. As Bootsy took a sip, he glanced around the brewery, his eyes always observant. The regulars engaged in conversation, and the atmosphere was relaxed despite the underlying tension in my own neck and jaw.

Bootsy leaned in, his tone conspiratorial. "Heard anything interesting lately, Abel?"

I raised an eyebrow, not fooled by his feigned innocence. "Just the usual, Bootsy. What's on your mind?"

He chuckled, his simple demeanor masking a shrewdness that unnerved me. "Oh, you know, just curious about the town gossip. People talk, and I like to listen. Matter of fact, people been talking they seen you at the bank." He sipped and his eyes watched me over the glass.

A greasy knot tightened in my stomach. I looked around, and Sloane caught my eye from across the room. Her eyes narrowed as she finished with her table and made her way toward the bar with a tray of empty glasses.

I couldn't let Bootsy's probing go unchecked. "Just regular business. Nothing exciting around here lately."

He shrugged, seemingly unbothered. "Just doing my job, Abel. Mr. King likes to stay informed."

The mention of my father irked me, but I kept my composure. The brewery, with its eclectic mix of patrons, was a melting pot of stories and subtle alliances. It wasn't as divided as the Grudge—where Kings sat on one side and Sullivans on the other—but old habits died hard. I couldn't afford to let Bootsy's loyalty to Russell King disrupt the fragile balance I was trying to create.

To my surprise, Sloane marched up to the bar, settling next to Bootsy. "Hey, you're the guy who sells jewelry on the beach, right?"

I slid her tray toward me and made quick work of cleaning the dirty glasses, all while listening in to their conversation.

Bootsy chuckled, taking another sip. "You've got me pegged, young lady." Bootsy was proud of his creations, and Sloane was feeding right into it. "That's me."

"Wow." Sloane angled her body so Bootsy paid attention to her and forgot all about the probing he was attempting only moments earlier. "You know, I'd love something simple. Maybe something matching for my daughter and me."

"Oh yes. I have something perfect." Bootsy rifled around in his pockets, depositing old receipts, gum wrappers, and bits of sand and trash on the bar top.

Sloane glanced over with a sly smile and winked.

It was a wonder she didn't hear my visible gulp.

Bootsy, lost in the attention Sloane was giving him, held up two not-at-all-matching bracelets made of broken shells and what looked like bits of plastic trash.

"Oh!" Sloane fawned. "That's perfect. I'll take them."

Bootsy stated his price—far too much for beach trash if you ask me—and Sloane slipped a bill from her apron to pay for the bracelets with her tips.

High off her attention, Bootsy all but forgot his reason for digging up dirt in my brewery.

I wiped down Sloane's tray and pushed it across the bar toward her. I leaned in so only she could hear. "You know that's just broken bits of trash he collects on the beach, right?"

Sloane flicked her wrist, and the pair of bracelets swished and sparkled on her arm. "Some of us can see beauty in what others would call trash. Even something broken can be loved."

With a lift of her shoulder, she reached over the bar to retrieve her tray and walk away with the flick of her ponytail.

As the night continued, I juggled the demands of the bar, the echoes of my past mistakes, and Bootsy's ever-watchful presence, though he'd softened after his exchange with Sloane. Her unwavering support offered a semblance of comfort, but the fear of being forever defined by my past lingered at the edges.

Even something broken can be loved.

My chest was hot and tight as her words rolled around

in my head. The brewery, with its quirky charm and familiar faces, remained a sanctuary of possibilities. The dream of making this brewery truly mine, independent of my father's shadow, burned brighter than ever, fueled by the sunshine lent to me from one irresistible woman.

I'd never believed it before, but a tiny ember of hope sparked to life.

SEVEN

SLOANE

WE WERE SO CLOSE. A few more inches and his mouth would have covered mine and devoured me—that much I knew for certain. Abel King didn't strike me as the kind of man who delivered soft, gentle kisses. No, a man like that took, and I had been ready and willing to give.

In the early-afternoon sun, I dug my toes into the sand as I waited for Sylvie to join me on the beach. She'd called, and we'd agreed to meet up by the water so her son could splash around and we could catch up.

Nerves skittered through me as I wondered if she'd somehow know I'd been fantasizing about her oldest brother. Sylvie was much quieter and more reserved than me, but I still think she'd have plenty to say about me hooking up with him.

I groaned at myself as I looked out onto the water. I worked for the man, and that was a boundary that shouldn't be crossed.

So why was I even thinking of hooking up with him in the first place?

Because he had a big dick, that was why.

My stomach whooshed as I recalled the hard mass that had lengthened between us as he'd held me. Oh yeah, Abel was big all right.

When his arm slid up my back and pressed me closer, I was a goner. His brown eyes went dark, and when his tongue slid over his lip, all I wanted was a taste.

He should have kissed me. At that moment, I didn't care that he was my boss or my friend's brother. Not only would I have allowed the kiss, but I had *craved* it.

My nipples hardened into aching points just thinking about his hulking frame folding over mine, pinning me to a soft mattress and allowing me to steal his warmth. That was also something totally unexpected. Abel ran *hot*—and not just in the tall-and-muscular handsome man kind of way, but as though actual lava coursed beneath his skin.

I soaked up the summer sun and listened to the steady rhythm of water lapping at the shoreline. I let my mind wander to what it might feel like for his rough hands to rake over my naked body. Would he put those massive hands to good use? Was he even a good kisser?

Freaking Reina.

In reality, I didn't blame her *at all* for needing help in the taproom. It was also obvious she knew something was up. Despite me trying to pretend like nothing had happened in Abel's office, Reina kept looking at me with sly, knowing smiles.

Shit.

What the hell was wrong with me? The man barely spoke in complete sentences around me, and when he did, he was usually irritated. In fact, most of the time he was downright rude. Still, there were tiny glimmers where I saw something—someone—different. He cared about his employees, and he loved that brewery. He was soft and gentle with my children. Sylvie always promised there was a soft heart hidden in there somewhere, and that had to count for something, right?

As if I willed her into existence, sand kicked up beside me as Sylvie plopped down with her son August in her arms.

"Hey," she huffed.

Her son was the perfect mix of her and Duke, with sandy-blond hair and light-brown eyes. His pillowy baby cheeks were slowly changing into those of a toddler. I grinned, holding my arms open and opening my hands in a grabby motion. "Give him here!"

Sylvie smiled and hoisted her son into my arms. Her light-blond hair was tucked into the back of a Sullivan Farms baseball cap and tumbled down her back in a thick wave. Her brown eyes were shadowed by the brim, but I could see she'd never looked happier.

"Ooof." I nuzzled Gus's chubby neck. "You're getting huge."

"Right?" Sylvie said as she arranged a beach blanket and deposited a few toys for Gus. "He's a monster."

"No," I said, speaking to the grinning toddler, who blew a raspberry in my face. "Well, a *cute* monster maybe." I squeezed him, and Gus tugged at my ponytail.

It felt like only yesterday the twins were Gus's age. Lately time moved too quickly. I'd always wanted a big family, lots of kids and a house full of sunshine and laughter. I swallowed back a hot ball of regret, shoving the sad thoughts from my mind and focusing on my friend.

"What about Ben and Tillie?" Sylvie asked.

I set Gus down on his blanket and shook a crocheted jellyfish toy to grab his attention. "Granddad took them fishing. He should be dropping them off in a little while."

"That's nice. How is Bax?" My granddad, Norman Robinson, was known around town as Bax—don't ask me why.

I sighed. "I don't know. Sad? Bored? He won't talk about it."

"Men." Sylvie playfully rolled her eyes.

"He won't admit it, but I think he misses the farmhouse. I mean, how could he not? We're in close quarters with me and the twins in that tiny cabin. Plus, he grew up there, and now it's just a burned-up reminder of everything we lost." I picked at the blanket beside me.

"Still no news from the investigation?" she asked.

I shook my head. "It's slow going, I guess." I sighed and looked out at the tourists gathering on the beach. "They did say we could rebuild, but insurance won't do anything until the criminal investigation is complete, and I know I don't have the money to build a whole house. Serving tables at the brewery doesn't pay that much."

I chuckled a dry laugh, but beside me, Sylvie frowned. "I wish there was something I could do to help."

I bumped my shoulder into hers and took a sip of water from my tumbler. "You did. You got me a job in the first place."

"How is Abel treating you? I told him to lighten up a little."

A laugh burst from my chest as I nearly choked on my water. She slid a sidelong glance in my direction, and I grunted to clear my throat. "He's been fine. Kind, actually. The other day he helped me out when Ben had a meltdown in the middle of Wegman's."

She frowned. "Poor Ben."

"I know." My foot wiggled in an anxious jitter. "He said he saw Jared and freaked out."

"He did?" She was as shocked and worried as I was. "Do you think it was really him?"

I lifted a shoulder. "I don't want to believe it but . . . maybe?" I toyed with my lip before deciding to finally admit to my best friend the extent of what had really been going on. "Jared has also been trying to contact me. I'd blocked him from social media, but then he used my money-transfer app to send me some nasty messages."

"Sloane, I am so sorry. That's really scary." Her arm wrapped around my shoulder. When she released me, she let out a frustrated growl. "God, what a prick!"

I swallowed and nodded before the truth came out in a tiny whisper. "I just want my kids to be safe. Sometimes I feel really alone and . . . I don't know—*exposed* in the cabin."

Sylvie frowned. "Do you need to stay at the farm for a while? It's not a fortress like Abel's place, but there are lots of people there, and we can all keep our eyes out for Jared."

I leaned into her. "You're the best, you know that? Right now I think we're okay. But thank you."

Our conversation shifted to Gus and how he was growing like a weed. Not long after, Tillie came running up to us with smears of orange sherbet on her face, and Ben was grinning behind her. It was a relief to see them unburdened and carefree. Granddad wouldn't stay, of course, but I was glad to see him out and about for at least a little while.

Throughout the day, a thought kept nagging me. It stayed with me long into the night as I lay on the floor staring at the cabin's leaky ceiling.

It's not a fortress like Abel's place.

What had Sylvie meant by that?

The fact that I knew very little about my boss and I still wanted to climb him like a tree didn't sit well with me.

Stress from the house; not being able to access the trust fund money; Jared's incessant, manipulative contact despite an order of protection; and worry over how I was ever going to climb out of this hole I'd gotten myself into was overwhelming.

It felt like all my troubles would float away on the breeze if only I could access the trust. There was more money there than I even knew what to do with. With those funds, I could help rebuild the farmhouse, pay for a proper lawyer to end Jared's harassment, give more to the kids. I couldn't let my ex control my life with fear any longer. I needed to be strong.

We could finally start over.

Then, as if I was struck by lightning, the perfect solution came to me. It was wild and ridiculous and completely *feasible*.

With a surge of energy, I jumped off the floor and tiptoed out of the bedroom toward the kitchen table. After firing up my laptop, I reread the email from the bank trustee.

I bit back a squeal when I realized the answer was right there in front of me.

All I had to do was convince my surly boss to marry me.

EIGHT

ABEL

Meatball and I were working in the brewhouse when an intruder's slinky movements caught my eye. I stood and my throat went dry.

Not an intruder.

Sloane was wearing a thin, floaty dress that hugged her curves and nipped in at the waist, accentuating the soft lines of her body. I shoved my hands into my pockets.

"Hi." Her lips were painted bright red. Again.

I couldn't speak, so I only stared.

Meatball turned, and his jaw unhinged when he saw her. "Hey, Sloane. What's up?" The grin on his face had me second-guessing that raise, and instead I wanted to fire his ass on the spot.

"Hi, Meatball. Think you can give me a minute with the boss?" She tossed her head in my direction, and my blood warmed.

Meatball wiped his hands across his jeans. "Sure thing. I think I'll take my lunch." He patted my back as he walked by, and I stared at him as he left me alone with Sloane in the back.

Her hazel eyes blinked up at me. I was at a complete loss for words. I finally landed on a grumbled "You're not on the schedule today."

Her white smile widened, and a soft laugh pushed through her lips. "I'm aware of that."

"Is there something else you need?" My teeth ground together.

Please don't let her quit.

"Actually, yes." Her hips swayed as she moved forward and leaned against my desk. Her ass crumpled a few papers and my fists tightened. "I have a business proposition for you."

My brow creased. "Business?"

"Yes, a mutually beneficial business arrangement, if you will." Her lips rolled inward as she nodded. She held up a finger. "But first I need to come clean."

An image of a hot, dirty Sloane flashed through my mind. I could imagine with perfect clarity what her ass would look like if I bent her over my desk and hiked her dress up. My fingertips could graze up the backs of her thighs before disappearing between her legs.

I adjusted my stance and ignored the magnetic pull toward her.

"A while ago I accidentally overheard you on the phone." I straightened, ready to argue over the invasion of my privacy, but she stopped me. "Now, before you interrupt, it was definitely an accident. But I heard you say something about wanting to buy out your dad but being unable to. You may not know this, but I have money . . ." She shrugged. "Kind of."

My eyes narrowed. I didn't like where this conversation was going. My aspirations for the brewery were supposed to be secret. "Kind of?"

"My father did very well in California, and when he passed away, some of that money went into a trust fund for me." She lightly scoffed. "A lot of money, actually."

"Okay . . ."

"I would like to invest in Abel's Brewery." Her hands went wide in a *ta-da!* gesture that was altogether very Sloane-like. I tried not to smile.

My frown deepened as I let her words roll around in my head. "Invest?" There had to be a catch. None of it made any sense.

"Yes." She smiled and brushed her hand against her collarbone. "I will provide the money you need to buy out your dad and remain a silent partner. The brewery would still be yours."

The brewery would be mine.

The thought alone sent a bolt of energy coursing through me. Still, things weren't adding up. "What's in it for you?"

Sloane's eyes flicked sideways. "Well . . . there's a tiny issue with accessing the trust."

I gritted my teeth and sighed. "What's a *tiny* issue?"

"In order to access the money, I have to incur a *significant life event*." Her eyes rolled and her fingers formed air quotes to emphasize how inconvenient she found that particular clause. "That could be marriage. Unless you want to have a baby . . ."

She scoffed at the last part, but I nearly choked. A feral part of me went wild at the idea of making a baby with Sloane. A man like me had no business being a father and quickly trampled the mere thought. My shoulders tensed.

Sloane's hands went up. "I was kidding." She laughed. "Oh my god, I was kidding."

In a slow, slinky movement, Sloane stepped forward.

Her eyes were locked on mine as she crowded my space. Awareness crackled under my skin, and my cock went hard in anticipation. She was so close I could feel her breath brush across my neck.

My fist stayed clenched at my side, and I watched as Sloane jerkily lowered herself to one knee.

I stared down at her in disbelief as she said, "So . . . Abel King, will you marry me?"

My brain paused, trying and failing to register the question she'd just asked. Her nervous smile wobbled.

Sloane was ridiculous and charming and altogether dangerous. When I regained my senses, I looped a hand under her arm and lifted. "Get the hell off the floor. What are you doing?"

She grinned and flicked a stray piece of hair away from her face and straightened her dress. "Proposing. It's my idea, so I figured I should be the one to get down on one knee."

My arms crossed to keep from touching her again. "I thought this was a business decision."

"It was—it is! You just seem like there might be a romantic hiding in there somewhere." Sloane tapped my chest, and the contact seared through my clothes and into my skin.

This is a very bad idea.

"There's not," I let out gruffly.

"Okay." She nodded and looked around the brewhouse. "Noted."

For a moment we stared at each other. The hum of equipment was the only sound as I contemplated exactly what she was proposing.

Sloane wanted to marry me. There wasn't a world in which a woman like her would ever hitch herself to a man like me—it was impossible. Still, there she was, offering it up like it truly was nothing but a business move.

I huffed. "I don't buy it. You don't even know me."

"You're right, I don't, and I do think there are some things we'd need to talk about beforehand, but . . . come on." She gestured toward the large brew kettles and bounced her eyebrows. "Don't you want this to be *yours*?"

I did. Desperately.

Mentally exhausted, I moved toward my chair and deposited my sorry ass into it with a sigh. "What do we need to talk about?"

With a stifled squeal, Sloane's heels clacked against the concrete floor as she gripped Meatball's chair and dragged it toward mine. She sat facing me and crossed her legs. My eyes stayed pinned to her face despite my peripheral getting a full view of her bare thigh.

"I have questions." Sloane clasped her hands in her lap.

"You got down on one knee and *now* you have questions?" I crossed my arms.

Her shoulders slumped dramatically. "It was a *gesture*. But yes, I have questions." Sloane slipped a small, folded piece of paper from the pocket of her dress. She eyed me as her fingers gently unfolded it.

I lifted an eyebrow. "You came prepared."

"Thank you." I hadn't meant it as a compliment, but her sweet nature didn't seem to register the gruffness in my tone. "First stipulation . . . *if* we move forward with this business deal, I need to know the details of your incarceration—not to pry, and I won't tell a soul, but for my own safety."

My molars ground together. I wasn't sure I'd be able to look Sloane in the eye and admit what I had done. She certainly wouldn't be sticking around if she knew.

Despite my silence, she continued. "Also, we would have a prenuptial agreement preventing you from accessing any additional money once we are divorced."

My brows cinched down. "Divorced?"

She nodded. "Yeah . . . it's not like we would stay married." Her dismissive laugh landed like an anvil against my ribs. "Once we get the money and it's settled, you'll be rid of me. We just stay legally married until the sale is complete and construction on my grandfather's farmhouse is underway."

I pressed my thumb and forefinger into my eye sockets. Sloane was presenting the idea of marriage in the most simple, emotionless way possible.

It almost makes sense.

Still, something was off. She wasn't saying it, but there were reasons other than money that she needed this to happen. I just didn't know what yet.

The chair creaked beneath my weight. "Can I think about it or is this a one-time offer?"

She stood with a triumphant look on her face. "You can think about it, but you know I'm right. This is going to work."

I stood, still reeling from the conversation.

Sloane took one step forward and planted her hand against my chest. My heart hammered, and I prayed she didn't notice.

She smiled and my stomach swooped. "I'm going to be the best wife you've ever had."

She left me slack jawed and staring as she sauntered around the brewing equipment and disappeared down the hallway.

NINE

SLOANE

H**OLY SHIT**, I did it.

I had asked Abel to marry me, and he hadn't said no.

He hadn't said no.

The singular thought zipped through me as I typed the words *Is a fake marriage for a trust fund considered fraud?* into the search engine on my phone. When only a few articles relating to immigration laws popped up, I blew out a quick sigh of relief.

I also cleared my search history . . . just in case.

Walking in the summer sun down Main Street, I mentally high-fived myself.

Girl, you've got this. We're both getting what we need. Besides, Dad would be proud of your entrepreneurial spirit. You'll be married on paper, but no one even needs to know.

A tiny pang of guilt pinched my side when I thought of my friend Sylvie. She'd probably be hurt that I'd married her brother and didn't bother to tell her . . . even if it was just a business arrangement.

The guilt gnawed at me. *Maybe telling* one *person wouldn't be so bad . . .*

I returned the polite smiles and friendly waves as I passed people on the sidewalk.

In my time living in Outtatowner, I was getting better at recognizing the faces of townies and those of tourists spending their weekends and summer months in the small, coastal town. The tourists held an excited glint in their eye as though they were awestruck by the towering dunes and clear Michigan waters.

The townies still appreciated the view but held it more in quiet reverence. The sandy soil and coastal breeze were more like the steady hum of breath or the thump in their chests—always reliable, and always there.

When I passed the Sugar Bowl—the best bakery in three counties and Outtatowner's local gossip spot—and peeked through the large front window, I didn't spot Sylvie working. A small sigh of relief passed over me. I would find a better time to break the news to my best friend that I was considering marrying her mysterious brother in order to get my life back on track.

Abel and I hadn't made any final decisions, so I was confident that talk could wait for another day. With the line to the Sugar Bowl nearly out the front door, I glanced across the street at the little café near the corner. The coffee wasn't nearly as good, and the pastries were almost always stale.

I was grumbling with indecision when a movement caught my eye.

Down the road in the direction of the beach, a man stood wearing sunglasses. He leaned against the light post with one ankle casually draped over the other . . . but not just any man—him.

And he was staring right at me.

Doubts that Ben had seen Jared in Wegman's Grocer evaporated. There he was, standing in the middle of a bustling sidewalk, staring right at me. The blood drained from my face and my knees wobbled. My tongue went thick and fat. I could hardly swallow, and it felt like sawdust lined my throat.

The connection between Outtatowner and me was so slim I had thought it would be impossible to find us. In fact, Granddad was the father of my dad's second wife. He was the grandfatherly figure I'd known as a child, but technically we weren't even related by blood. When I fled California, taking Granddad's last name and moving in with him was a comfort.

After the fire was ruled arson, my doubts that I had actually escaped became more real. Maybe he *could* find us. I simply hadn't wanted to believe a place like Outtatowner wouldn't be safe for us.

My heart squeezed as the world narrowed around me. My breaths sawed in and out of my lungs, and I was struck with fear, unable to move.

"Sloane, right?" The words behind me barely registered, but I blinked in their direction. "Hey, are you all right? You look like you've seen a ghost."

Royal King stood holding the door to his tattoo shop open as he stared at me with bewilderment.

"What?" I replied weakly.

I turned back toward where Jared had been standing, but he was gone. There was no sign of him near the lamppost. I looked up and down the street in panicked confusion.

I know he was there. I saw him with my own eyes.

"Are you sure you're okay?" Royal sounded concerned and slightly irritated.

I tried to answer, but the words tumbled out in a quiet and weak mumble. "Sure. I don't know. I think so."

"I'm calling Abe."

"No! Don't." I turned to stop him, but Royal had already disappeared into his tattoo shop. Behind the counter, his face furrowed as he spoke into a cell phone.

Fucking great.

I sighed and pinched the bridge of my nose. I know I saw him . . . right?

I rubbed my eyes, unsure if my mind was playing tricks on me and it was just some look-alike tourist I had seen or if it was in fact Jared and he was taunting me in my own town.

The bell on the glass door to King Tattoo rattled as Royal pushed it open again. "Hey, come inside and have a glass of water. It's kind of hot out today."

Still in a daze, I followed Royal's orders and walked into King Tattoo before depositing myself in one of the plush leather chairs in the waiting area. A moment later Royal gently shoved a cold glass of water into my hands.

I took a sip and assessed him over the rim of the cup. He was tall and well built, as I had learned all King men were, but where Abel was deliciously thick and massive and JP was lean and long limbed, Royal had a striking presence to him.

The colorful tattoos that peeked out of the collar of his shirt and ran the length of his arms to his knuckles added an edge to him, while the colorful and seemingly random tattoos hinted at a touch of playfulness and whimsy.

Apparently all King men are also walking contradictions. It was the only conclusion for how Abel could be dark and brooding while at the same time have a soft and gentle air about him.

I flinched when the bell clanked against the glass door, then immediately laughed at myself for being so jumpy.

"The hell is going on?" Abel's voice was growly and demanding.

I probably shouldn't have liked it so much.

"I don't know, man," Royal supplied. "I looked up from the desk to see your girl looking like she was about to pass out in the middle of the sidewalk."

"I'm not his girl."

"She's not my girl."

Our voices tangled over each other, and heat scorched my cheeks.

"Whatever." Royal raised his hands before returning to his work.

In two heavy footfalls, Abel was towering in front of me. My eyes slowly lifted to meet his, but instead of being greeted with an angry, annoyed face, his features were soft and concerned.

Abel crouched down, folding his massive frame so that he could be eye level with me. His hand reached out as if it were going to gently land on my knee, but he snatched it back.

"Are you okay? What happened?" His voice was soft and quiet, only for me.

My eyes searched his, looking for any hint of judgment or annoyance in which I found none. I toyed with my lip, unsure of how much to divulge. I didn't want him to think that I was some scattered, paranoid lunatic when in fact that was exactly how I was feeling.

"I'm not sure." My eyes flicked back to his but immediately looked away from the intensity of his deep-brown eyes. "I thought I saw someone and it—I don't know." I swallowed hard. "It rattled me."

"Same as Ben?" My eyes flew to him. In three words he communicated that he understood and believed me.

I swallowed back the lump of emotion that formed in the back of my throat and nodded through a fresh round of tears.

"Will you let me take you home?"

I tried to laugh and make light of the situation, but it only came out as a weak whoosh of breath. "Okay, sure."

I lifted myself from the seat, easing away from Abel to avoid risking a single touch. I worried that with one touch of his warm, protective embrace, I might melt into him.

Abel offered Royal a nod and a silent three-finger salute as we shuffled out of the tattoo parlor. Four steps into the afternoon sunshine, and worry and panic tightened in my chest.

My mind whirled.

Granddad had taken Ben and Tillie fishing before dropping them at library camp for the afternoon. What was supposed to be a free afternoon doing whatever I wanted had suddenly turned into a complete mess.

If that really was Jared and he knew I was here, it confirmed my fears that he knew where I was living, which meant I would be in the cabin alone. The realization that all the fears I'd told myself were irrational were coming true crashed down on me.

My steps faltered beside Abel. "Hey, you know what?" I gripped his forearm to stop our forward progress. His muscles rippled beneath my hand, and I pulled it back. "I'm really not feeling . . . um, I don't know. Comfortable . . . at the cabin right now."

Abel looked at me the way he sometimes did, as though I was some mystery he was working his ass off to unravel.

In reality, I wasn't all that hard to figure out. I was a single mom scared out of her wits, desperate and with nowhere safe to go.

"How about my place? It's quiet, and no one will bug you there. I can bring you back whenever you're ready." The way his gravelly voice rolled over the words *my place* sent tingles humming straight to my clit, but immediate relief flooded my system.

Well, this is a very bad idea.

"I'd love to. Thanks." At ease, I gave him a soft, appreciative smile. "The twins are at a day program at the library. I'm just going to send a quick text to check in on them."

Abel dipped his chin with a no-nonsense jerk of his head. "Okay. My truck is this way."

He gestured down the road to where his rugged gray truck was parked in a small public lot. Without another word, Abel yanked open the passenger door, and I scurried inside. I watched him as he moved around the hood and sucked in a lungful of his earthy masculine scent.

It was like lemon and oiled leather filled the cab of his truck, making it all Abel.

I fired off a quick text to my friend Emily—she was the head librarian at the library, and she assured me the twins were having a great time. I hesitated only a moment, unsure if I should tell her about seeing my ex. Instead, I just insisted that no one but Granddad or I should be picking them up. Satisfied with her reassurance, I settled back against the passenger seat of the truck.

Abel turned over the engine and started driving. I watched as the sinews and muscles rippled in his arms while he shifted gears. "A stick shift, huh?"

A grunt was his only response, but I leaned my elbow on the window, propping my head to continue looking at him, encouraging him to say more.

Under my assessment, he finally sighed and rolled his

eyes. "I like a manual transmission. It keeps you active and alert while you're driving."

I scrunched my chin and nodded. "Makes sense. To be honest, I didn't know if you drove at all. I always see you walking everywhere."

The muscles in his jaw flexed as he shifted uncomfortably in the driver's seat. "I don't like to drive unless I have to."

Realization dawned on me. Today he had to because he was called to come and rescue me.

I swallowed hard. "I appreciate it, really. I'm sure I would have been fine, but"—I shrugged, leaning into the truth—"I guess sometimes I need a little rescuing."

I caught a long side-eye from Abel. "I guess so."

We rode the rest of the way in silence. Abel's house was a short drive, only a few blocks from the heart of Outta-towner. The long driveway was lined with trees, obscuring the view of the road and neighboring houses. The plot of land opened up into a beautiful, well-manicured lawn.

Trees dotted the lawn, but most lined the edges of the property. Lush green grass grew around professionally manicured flower beds. At the end of the driveway stood a ranch-style home that almost looked like a storybook cottage.

The home's exterior was white board and batten and had a front porch that wrapped around one side. I climbed out of Abel's truck, awestruck by how pretty the house was.

It was quieter there, the trees buffering any noise from the road. A coastal breeze gently shook the leaves of massive oaks that lined his property.

I breathed the coastal air in deep and held it in my lungs. My face tipped up, allowing the summer sun to warm my cheeks.

Fear and anxiety slowly faded away as I exhaled.

This is what Sylvie meant by a fortress. Safety.

When I opened my eyes, Abel was looking at me, and my lashes lowered as I glanced away. "Thanks for letting me hide out for a little bit. Abel, this is—" I breathed in deeply and appreciated his property with a smile. "This is so charming."

A tight, flat-lipped nod was his only response.

Clearly he was uncomfortable with my praise, but he deserved to know how beautiful his home was. "Can I get the grand tour?" I asked, hoping to lighten the mood.

Abel reached back and scratched at the base of his skull. "Sure."

I looped my arm through his, and when he didn't pull away, I beamed up at him and let him lead the way.

Here goes nothing.

TEN

ABEL

I COULDN'T FUCKING focus with Sloane's arm looped through mine. Her warm, comforting scent rose up and filled my nose as I unlocked the front door to my house and gestured for her to step inside.

It was strange having a woman in my space. When you spend as much time as I did locked in an eight-by-eight cell, you learn to appreciate your surroundings. My home was my sanctuary, and in the time I'd been back, I'd done everything I could to make it feel complete.

The ranch had been purchased with family money from a retired couple who'd decided Michigan winters no longer suited them. I'd held on to a few of the vintage pieces they'd left behind.

To no one's surprise, I preferred subtle, moody tones and clean lines.

Sloane's grip on my arm tightened when we walked inside. "Oh! Abel, this is gorgeous!"

From the covered front porch, we entered into the vaulted ceiling of the great room, which was open to the kitchen and dining room toward the back.

Sloane clasped her hands in front of her chest. "May I go in?"

Struck by her cute politeness, I smiled and nodded. "Look around."

Sloane smiled at the stone hearth along one wall as she walked toward the heart of the home.

She pointed at an end table that flanked the couch. "I love this furniture. It's so modern but with a vintage feel to it."

I nodded. That had been exactly what I'd been going for. "My brother Whip built those. He's a bit of a wood-smith on his days off from the firehouse."

"I've met him. He makes Emily very happy. Though I didn't realize he had hidden talents." Her pretty hazel eyes went wide, and her eyebrows bounced. "I wonder what yours is."

I shrugged. "Don't really have one."

She playfully harrumphed. "I doubt that."

Heat sizzled up my back. I may be out of practice, but there were a few things, under different circumstances, I wouldn't have minded showing Sloane. Things one might consider talents—at least, no one had ever complained before.

I watched as Sloane went deeper into my home. The kitchen was also an open concept, with raised bar-top seating, a decent-size kitchen island, and doors leading from the eat-in dining area to the backyard.

Adding windows to the home was one of my first projects—I'd never wanted to feel locked in, stifled. I needed the openness the windows provided to feel like I could breathe.

To her right, a hallway led to the remaining bedrooms and bathrooms. She raised her eyebrows expectantly.

I jerked my head and shrugged. "Go ahead."

With a delighted squeak, she padded down the hallway. The rest of the house was no-nonsense, with two spare bedrooms and a primary suite. I tensed, wondering if Sloane would want to look inside the rooms. My blood pressure wouldn't be able to handle seeing her in my bedroom—I knew that for damn sure.

Thankfully she did a quick walk down the hallway and returned to the dining space, which led outside.

She lifted a hand and pointed through the french-style doors. "What's out there?"

I opened one of the doors and gestured. "Just a back porch and my garden beds. I have a few raised beds here, and farther back are some in-ground gardens." Feeling silly, I stuffed my hands into my pockets. "I like to experiment with the beer recipes. It makes more financial sense to grow the ingredients if I'm just going to fuck it up."

Her eyes shone with delight. "How very domestic of you, Mr. King."

I gritted my teeth. "Abel."

"Yes, boss." She brushed past me to take a closer look at the gardens that actively grew lavender, hops, herbs, and a whole host of other ingredients I'd been wanting to play around with.

My blood hummed and my body itched to follow her. Instead, I stayed rooted to the spot. If I couldn't control the incessant thoughts about her, I'd control my body by sheer force of will.

Her hand brushed across the green and purple tips of a lavender plant. She paused as she looked toward the back of the house and pointed. "What the heck is that?"

I angled myself to see what she was looking at. At the back of my home, the primary bathroom opened to the outside through another set of french-style doors. Through the glass, a pristine claw-foot tub could be seen.

"That's, uh . . ." I couldn't place why I suddenly felt nervous. "My bathroom."

Sloane stepped to the house and cupped her eyes to peer through the glass. "That's not a bathroom, that's a dream come true. Abel, it's so pretty!"

A small smile tugged at the corner of her mouth, deepening the dimples in her cheeks.

She turned to me with narrowed eyes. "Do you even fit in that?"

I squared my stance. "I manage."

She pursed her lips. Her eyes roamed over my frame, and a soft little *huh* escaped her. Not one to shy away from a challenge, I held her stare. The woman in front of me was bubbly and curious and a real fucking problem.

Not an hour ago she had gotten down on one knee and proposed marriage. And I'd almost said yes.

My eyes drifted from her face down the column of her neck. My heart hammered as the soft skin peeking from the neckline of her dress tempted me.

Jesus, it's been a long time if someone's neck is that tempting.

I needed to focus on anything other than the way this petite woman was knocking my world sideways. "So what happened today?"

Sloane's face fell.

Real smooth, asshole.

She gently cleared her throat and wound her way around the raised garden beds before plopping down on the top step of the back porch stairs.

She patted the area next to her, and I sat down, but gave plenty of space between us.

"So Ben and Tillie's dad—my ex—we don't have what you'd consider a functional co-parenting relationship. In fact, we don't have a relationship at all." She sighed, and my silence made space for her to continue. "I was only twenty-two when I had the twins. We didn't know what to do after we found out I was pregnant, so we decided to get married. From the beginning it was a nightmare. Jared wasn't inter-ested in growing up. He ran with really shady people, liked to party and do some minor drugs. My dad and stepmom begged me not to marry him, but I was proud and thought I was in love. I had hoped having the babies would change things. Well," she scoffed, "it *did*, but not the things I expected. He was jealous of his own children. Things got manipulative and scary, but I still put up with it. Once, after too much partying, he came home and picked a fight. *Again.* Only this time he pushed me while I was holding Ben, and I nearly dropped him. Things escalated—lots of shouting back and forth. The neighbor called the police when they heard us, and the next day I got a judge to agree to an order of protection and filed for divorce."

Anger bubbled inside me. I'd learned to contain my rage, but the mere thought of someone putting their hands on Sloane had me brimming with hatred. I counted back-ward, tried deep breathing, anything to allow her to continue despite the war raging in my head.

"The divorce went uncontested—he didn't even bother showing up—and I was granted custody. I didn't even seek child support. I just wanted to disappear. Still, I worried that he might try something, so I reached out to my granddad and asked him for a place to stay. But last year Granddad's house burned down."

Storm clouds rumbled inside my head. "You think it was him."

Her warm hazel eyes held me in place. "It was ruled arson."

I scrubbed a hand on the back of my neck. "Jesus. And you saw him today? You should call the police, Sloane."

"I know." She picked at a nail. "I did make a report after Ben thought he saw him. I'll call again."

I had my own feelings about the justice system and its many holes, but there had to be something they could do to protect her and the kids.

A mutually beneficial business arrangement.

Sloane's words from earlier echoed in my mind. The woman in front of me was at the end of her rope, and instead of simply saving herself, she'd devised a way to help us both. The thought that perhaps I could pay my share of the bargain by helping with her dipshit ex rolled around in my head.

"You'd do it again?" I cautiously asked. "Get married?"

She sucked in a deep breath and exhaled. "If it meant that I could fix up Granddad's house? Have a safe place for me and the kids? Absolutely. Getting married is the only way I can access the trust fund right now. If you help me do that, investing in the brewery is the least I can do."

Emotions were trampling my thoughts as I worked through what I needed to say. "And where will you stay while the farmhouse is being rebuilt?"

She blinked up at me. "We're staying at my granddad's cabin."

I frowned. "What about your ex? Is there a security system? Something to make sure help arrives if something happens?"

Sloane scoffed. "No, Abel, there is not a security system on my grandfather's *hunting cabin.* Look, I know it's not ideal, but it's the only way to—"

"No," I ground out.

She reared back with wide eyes as though I'd slapped her. I settled my emotions and tried again. "No, it's not the only way."

I sighed and rubbed my palms together. "If we do this—get married—then I'm not going to have my wife staying at some run-down cabin while her potentially dangerous ex-husband is lurking around town. That doesn't work for me."

My wife.

My chest squeezed. The words had slipped out unintentionally, but now that they were out there, I let them hang in the air.

A tiny furrow formed between her eyebrows. "What do you suggest? That we stay *here*?"

I shrugged as if it were the simplest solution in the world and not completely life altering for me to share my space with her and the kids. "There's plenty of room."

She gave me a flat look. "There are three bedrooms."

I swallowed. "I'll sleep on the couch."

Sloane nibbled her lip as she considered what I was proposing. "I know it's been hard on my granddad to have us all on top of one another. Us being across town would also help him get out of the house a little . . . maybe?" She looked around my property and sighed. "It does feel safe here."

The reality that we might actually be considering getting married hit me like a ton of bricks. My gut twisted. It was becoming a very real possibility that my father would be very unhappy to hear I was interested in buying out his share of the brewery and that I would have the means to do it, thanks to Sloane.

Sloane leaned closer. "What are you thinking about? I can practically see the smoke billowing out of your ears."

I looked at her and sighed. "My father, actually. If he even suspected the marriage was illegitimate, he'd likely do anything he could to stop it. He doesn't like things he can't control."

She nodded in understanding. "Then it won't be fake. The marriage would be very much real. He doesn't have to know the *feelings* aren't real."

But what if they were?

The errant thought had my palms sweating.

I tamped down my feelings and nodded. "If he thinks it's real, he just may go for it. Anything to help my reputation would be good in his eyes. And if you move in, that's two birds with one stone. Your ex can't fuck with you, and my father will believe this marriage is legitimate."

She hummed as though she were playing over the scenario in her mind. "I need to know what happened. You understand that, right?"

I knew she was talking about my incarceration. I didn't blame her. All she knew was that I had done time in prison, and here we were entertaining the idea of getting married.

Seconds ticked by as I hung my head, struggling to find the right words.

Shame coursed through me in thick, choking waves. The air around us thickened and my heart galloped. I knew she deserved answers, but I didn't even know where to begin.

I settled on starting at the end.

"I killed a child."

ELEVEN

I STARED at Abel with wide eyes as the words *I killed a child* hung in the air. A bird chirped in a nearby tree, but all I could do was stare at the side of his face. Thousands of questions tumbled through my mind.

"How?" It was the only word I could get out.

His shoulders slumped as the weight of the truth bore down on the both of us. Finally, after what felt like an eternity, Abel sighed and wiped his hands down his jean-clad thighs. "I had been working as a distribution manager for a local distillery near Kalamazoo. We were short-staffed, so the owner had asked a few of us to stay late, work an overnight shift to try and catch up. I'd been saving every penny to go toward my dream of opening a brewery and wanted the overtime." Abel's voice was low and shaky. "We worked all through the night. By the time we finished, I was exhausted. We cleaned up the shop and called it a night. I wasn't high or drunk. I was just . . . tired."

Pain was etched on Abel's face, and he pinched the bridge of his nose as if he could still feel the fatigue wash over him. "Thing is, I didn't think twice about climbing behind the wheel. I just wanted to get home." He swallowed hard and struggled to continue. "Somewhere along the highway, I nodded off and struck an oncoming vehicle."

I froze with a sharp intake of breath. I hadn't meant to react, but I couldn't help it. My mind whirred. "So it was an accident."

Abel shook his head. "No. I killed him."

"An accident," I repeated carefully. "Abel, you have to know that you went to prison because of an accident."

His jaw flexed. "My lawyer tried to argue that the final positioning of the vehicles suggested I wasn't who crossed the center line, but . . . the prosecutor didn't see it as an accident, and neither did the judge. The penalties for drowsy driving are the same as for charges of driving under the influence of alcohol or drugs. They had to prove that I operated a vehicle intentionally recklessly, with a willful disregard for the safety of others, and they did."

"How long did you have to be in jail?" My words were barely a whisper.

"I could have had up to fifteen years, but the mother testified on my behalf." Abel scoffed. "Can you believe that? A dead child and a broken back, and she'd asked for leniency when I didn't deserve it."

I bit back the tears. *Would I have been so forgiving?*

"I served five years." Abel finally looked at me. His umber eyes were stormy with unspoken emotion. I was sure he was waiting for me to shove him away, maybe scream and run because he saw himself as a reckless killer.

My heart ached for him, and I could barely whisper "Okay."

He frowned in disbelief. "What do you mean, *okay*?"

I nodded. "I asked for the truth, and you gave it to me, even though it was hard for you to do. It's not my story to tell, so I won't share it with anyone, but my worry is satisfied."

His eyes scanned my face as though he couldn't believe my acceptance was that easy. Truth was, I had about a thousand other questions, but I knew in my bones Abel was a protector. He was a good man.

"I still think we can make this work," I said, placing my hand on his forearm.

When he shifted, I let my hand slip off and tucked it into my lap.

Abel's scowl was locked into place. "What will you tell the kids?"

I lifted a shoulder. "Only as much as they need to know. We're friends, and friends help each other. You're helping us while we get started on fixing up the farmhouse. They don't need to know more than that."

When I said it out loud, it seemed easy. Simple. I only hoped that was the case.

He slowly nodded. "Makes sense."

Finally, I tilted my head toward Abel and said, "So are we really doing this?"

He sighed and rested his elbows on his knees, gazing out into the yard with sad eyes. "Looks like we're really doing this."

HOLY SHIT. *I can't believe I'm doing this.*

Five days after Abel rescued me and brought me to his house, I was standing in front of the steps of the Remington County Courthouse. Michigan law required a three-day waiting period after applying for a marriage license before it could be issued and used. We then had thirty days to change our minds.

Since this was strictly a business arrangement, we'd wasted no time in deciding to stand in front of a judge and make things official. After dropping the twins off at the library, I'd offered to drive us both, but Abel insisted that he meet me there.

County law also required that we supply *two* witnesses. When I saw Sylvie round the corner, my chest pinched.

She waved. "What's with the cloak-and-dagger texts?" She offered a quick hug, and her hands stayed planted on my shoulders. "Are you in some kind of trouble?"

I swallowed hard and looked around. "No, not trouble really. But I do have something to tell you. It's going to be a shock, and I hope you're not mad."

Sylvie steeled her spine and lifted her chin. "Okay. I'm ready."

I offered a wary grimace as I said, "I'm marrying Abel today and need you to be my witness." I hoped my words sounded playful and upbeat, but I was fairly certain I sounded like I was going to puke.

"You're what?!" Sylvie shrieked.

My hands came together in front of me. "I know. I know. I should have said something sooner, but I was worried you'd freak out or that he'd back out and I would have told you for nothing. Hear me out. I promise it's not as bad as you think."

"I doubt that." Sylvie crossed her arms. "But I'm listening."

"I have money from my dad that I can't access unless I have a significant life event—like getting married. I need that money. *Ergo*, I need a husband."

"And you're marrying Abel?" Her eyes narrowed.

"Yes. In exchange, I am investing in Abel's Brewery so he can buy your dad out, but we also need him to believe that Abel and I are *actually* married . . . which means I'm also moving in with him?" The end of my sentence rose as if I were asking a question.

In reality, I was just hoping Sylvie would still speak to me after all this.

She exhaled. "What the hell, Sloane?"

"I know." My nose scrunched. "Do you hate me?"

Sylvie pulled me into a hug. "No, I don't hate you. Do I think this is totally out of left field and kind of fucked up? Yeah . . . but who am I to judge? It's just that . . . wow." She laughed as the reality of the situation settled over us. "Wow!"

I smiled at my best friend. "I guess this means we'll be sisters. At least . . . on paper and for a little while anyways."

Sylvie shook her head. "I mean, if you're really getting married, are you sure you don't want your grandfather here?"

I smiled and shook my head. "Definitely not. I've got enough on my plate without my granddad poking his nose into things. He's a romantic at heart and wouldn't understand that this is strictly business. He needs to know as little as possible."

Sylvie nodded once. "Got it. Well . . . I guess you're marrying Abel then . . ."

I swallowed hard and looked up at the courthouse. "I guess so."

Just inside, we waited for Abel, and I tried not to let my nerves get the best of me. I paced across the tile as my fingertips played with the hem of my shirt. Despite their pleading and open dislike for Jared, my dad and stepmom had once paid for a big, splashy wedding—complete with a dress that made me look like a frosted cupcake. I'd grown up and now I knew better. Today was a business arrangement and nothing more. Plus, I was on shift at the brewery later, so I chose to wear a pair of black jeans and a formfitting black shirt that I could swap out for an Abel's Brewery tee later. The outfit was simple and no-nonsense.

I'd chosen it in part to keep my brain from thinking things like: *Why does Abel smell so good? Will he keep saying* my wife *in that gruff tone I seem to like so much? What if this feeling isn't entirely fake? Oh, fuck, am I making a huge mistake?*

When I saw Abel walking up the courthouse steps, my heart sank. Beside him was his aunt Bug.

For the first time in my life, I saw him dressed in a suit that looked as though it had been tailor-made for him. It was nearly black, but in the sunlight I could see the expensive material was, in fact, a beautiful dark gray. His black dress shoes were shined, and the white of his shirtsleeves peeked out from his jacket.

He'd worn a tie.

Shit.

I gulped and looked down at my own outfit. Nerves rippled through me, and I sent a pleading look to Sylvie. With nowhere to go and no time to change, I stood my ground. When he opened the glass doors and entered the corridor of the courthouse, I adjusted the strap to my purse and smiled.

Thank god I remembered lipstick.

"Hi," I chirped.

Abel's eyes floated down my front and back up, snagging on my red lip.

"Morning."

Nervous, I ran an errant hand down his white dress

shirt, noticing he'd even trimmed his stubble. "You sure clean up nice."

Abel leaned away from my touch and tugged at his collar. He angled his body away and held his arm out for Bug. "Aunt Bug, I think you've met Sloane."

Bug King was the standing matriarch of the King family. It was common knowledge that she was stern and humorless. Her assessing eyes moved over me, and I tried not to squirm under her stare.

I let out a surprised squeak when she pulled me into a hug. "Thank you for doing this for him," she whispered in my ear.

I watched Abel over her shoulder as he shifted uncomfortably. It seemed the story he'd told her left out what I was gaining as a part of the arrangement. After she released me, Bug moved toward Sylvie and started chatting, no doubt about the impromptu wedding they'd both been thrown into.

Determined to make the best of this, I smiled up at Abel. "Ready for this?"

A small laugh escaped him. "Definitely not."

I looped my arm into his. "Aw, come on. I told you—I'm going to be the best wife you've ever had."

When I went to step forward, Abel stayed rooted to the spot, and I glanced up at him.

His eyes were soft and warm. "Before we go in . . . I have something for you." He adjusted his stance and reached into his pocket, pulling out a simple silver band.

He held it between us as I stared.

Abel cleared his throat. "It was my mother's."

My hand flew to my mouth. "Oh, Abel . . . no. I couldn't—"

"It wasn't her wedding band or anything." Abel shook

his head. "I remember Mom wearing it on her right hand. She never went anywhere without it. For some reason she'd left it on the dresser when she . . . you know, left us."

His eyes were steady on mine, but they held a depth of emotion I couldn't quite read.

"Anyway," he continued, "I managed to grab it before my dad burned it with the rest of her stuff." Abel shrugged. "I figured this is probably the only marriage I'm going to get, so . . . it just felt like you should have a ring."

My heart thumped and my chest ached for the small, motherless boy he had been.

"It's beautiful." I held out my left hand and allowed him to slip it on my ring finger. "Huh." I smiled and flipped my hand over. "It fits."

His jaw flexed as he stared at my finger. "We should go in."

I steadied my shoulders and tried to ignore the weight that slim silver band added to my hand. "Let's do it."

Side by side we found our way to the appropriate office, Sylvie and Bug not far behind us. The clerk reviewed our paperwork and gestured toward the seats that lined the large office window. "We'll call you when it's time."

In near silence, the four of us sat in the stiff wooden chairs and stared ahead. Only the sounds of creaking wood and the shuffling of paper filled the waiting room.

Finally, after what felt like an eternity, the door to the judge's quarters opened, and a woman filled the doorway. "Sloane Robinson and Abel King?"

We stood before her.

Here goes nothing.

TWELVE

ABEL

Ten dollars plus a few muttered words later, and Sloane and I would be husband and wife.

"Please join hands." The district court judge smiled and gestured for us to face each other. Sylvie and Bug silently stood behind us.

I shifted in my shoes as I took Sloane's delicate hands in mine. Her eyes were a riot of greens and browns, melting into an intoxicating combination of hues. She stared into me, her gaze unwavering and unafraid.

Inside, I was a fucking mess.

Was I ruining her life?

Are we making the right choice?

How am I ever going to let her go?

"We are gathered here in the presence of these witnesses to join Sloane Robinson and Abel King together in matrimony. The contract of marriage is a most solemn one, and one not to be entered into lightly, but thoughtfully and seriously and with a deep realization of its obligations and responsibilities. If anyone can show just cause why this couple should not be lawfully joined together, let them speak now or forever hold their peace."

I glanced at my sister and aunt, who only offered supportive half smiles.

The judge continued. "Do you, Sloane, take Abel to be your lawfully wedded husband?"

My heart tripped when she smiled brightly and without hesitation.

"I do," she said.

"And do you, Abel, take Sloane to be your lawfully wedded wife?"

I cleared my throat. "I do."

The judge smiled and asked, "Are there rings?"

Sloane laughed and held up her hand, flashing my mother's ring to the judge.

The judge nodded. "Very well. Abel, please repeat after me. 'I, Abel, take you, Sloane, for my lawful spouse, to have and to hold, from this day forward, for better, for worse, for richer, for poorer, in sickness and in health, until death do us part. With this ring, I thee wed.'"

My hands clasped hers and I repeated the words, never looking away from Sloane's beautiful eyes.

The judge instructed Sloane to repeat the same, minus the ring part. To my shock, she did it all with a bright smile.

"By the power and authority vested in me by the State of Michigan and as the district court judge for Remington County, Michigan, I now pronounce you lawfully married." She gestured between us and took a single step back. "You may now kiss your bride."

The room tilted. I had known this moment was coming. I'd craved it even. Without hesitation, I stepped forward, wrapping my arm around her waist and pulling her into me as I lowered my mouth to hers.

Seconds dragged on as I was overwhelmed and intoxicated by her. Sloane melted into me, accepting my kiss with soft lips as her arms wound around my waist. I cupped the side of her face and let my fingers thread into her soft brown hair.

My heartbeat throbbed in my skull as I savored her plush, full lips. Her perfume surrounded me and threatened to pull me under completely.

Bug gently cleared her throat, snapping me back to reality, and I immediately broke the connection, stepping back and blinking down at my wife.

Her face was flushed with a mixture of desire and slight embarrassment. She glanced at my sister, whose wide eyes spoke volumes as to the lack of appropriateness of that kiss.

"Congratulations, you two." The judge offered a simple shake of our hands, and we shuffled out of her small office.

Back in the waiting room, I looked at my aunt. She smiled at me, patted the side of my face, and sighed. "I've got to get back to the library, but thank you for allowing me to be here."

My lashes lowered. "Thank you for coming on short notice."

Her hand gripped mine and she nodded.

"Hey, Bug?" Sloane called out. "Tillie and Ben are at camp at the library. Could you pop in and see that they're okay?"

She offered a kind smile. "I can do that."

"I'll walk out with you," Sylvie called to Bug. My sister wrapped me in an awkward hug. She shook her head and smiled at me before shaking my shoulders. "What am I going to do with you?" Her playful tone helped to unfurl the knot of dread in my gut.

I watched the twosome leave as Sloane stepped up

beside me and leaned her head on the side of my arm. I stiffened at the subtle, carefree gesture. "Wow. We actually did it."

I looked down at her. "We sure did."

Sloane sighed. "Well, I should get going. I have work today, and my boss is a real pain in the ass." She shot me a pointed look over her shoulder as she took a step toward the door. I forced myself to not look at how her ass filled out those tight black jeans.

"I think if you asked him, he'd give you the day off. I mean . . . since it's your wedding day and all." A tiny spark that our playful banter remained intact warmed my chest.

Her face scrunched. "I don't know. He's a real grouch. He'll probably dock my pay."

"Go home, Sloane," I demanded. "Pack your shit. You and the kids are moving in."

I didn't miss the sly smile that tugged at the corner of her mouth. I also didn't miss the way my cock enjoyed the flirty bat of her lashes.

"Yes, boss." She offered a playful salute. "I'm going to tell the kids this afternoon and break the news to Granddad. We'll be at your place around dinnertime, if that's okay?"

I nodded and stuffed my hands in my pockets.

Tonight couldn't come soon enough.

"Whoa! Are you freaking kidding me?" Ben's voice echoed from the end of the hallway when he opened the bedroom door.

"Benjamin. Language," Sloane admonished. She sheepishly glanced my way and mouthed, *I'm sorry.*

I shook my head to let her know it was fine. After

following her down the hall, I stood in the doorway to Ben's new room. The space was painted a soft green. It was open and bright. A large window provided a view to the side yard, and there was more than enough for the bed, dresser, and room in the middle for Ben to spread out with his belongings. It was a far cry from the cramped quarters of the cabin.

His butt bounced on the bed. "This is all mine?"

Sloane smiled. "Mr. King is letting us stay here for a while. Isn't that kind of him?"

Ben flopped on the bed. "It's amazing!"

Sloane reached out to pat Ben's knee. "What do we say?"

Ben sat up and smiled. "Thanks, Mr. King."

I crossed my arms. "Abel. Just . . . call me Abel."

"Mom! You have to see my room!" Tillie burst past me and into Ben's room. She grabbed Sloane's hand and tugged her past me and out the door.

Sloane laughed. "I've seen it. Isn't it nice?"

I followed as Tillie stood by the bedroom window that faced the backyard. "The yard is so *big*. I can see the garden and the open grass and the trees, and there was a little squirrel that ran right up that tree!"

Her excitement was infectious. I assumed it would be strange and uncomfortable having Sloane and her two kids move in with me, but in the few minutes they were there, I found the noise and chaos a welcome break from the unrelenting voice in my head.

A soft thud against my leg jolted me back to reality. Tillie had slammed into me, hugging me tightly. "Thank you so much."

I awkwardly patted her back. "You bet, kid."

She giggled and flounced back into her new room to

unpack. Sloane exited, and I followed her to the kitchen like an obedient dog. "They love it, Abel. Thank you."

My throat was dry and tight, so I only nodded. "I'll show you to your room."

Sloane stopped and stared up at me. Her eyebrows pitched down as her face scrunched. "My room?" When realization dawned on her, she shook her head. "No, no, no. I've got the couch. It's more than fine. I promise."

I shook my head, ignoring her ridiculousness, and headed to the primary bedroom. I wrenched open the door but stayed in the hallway. "My clothes are still in here, but the room is yours. You're not sleeping on the couch."

Sloane hesitated, but I knew she was tempted. Her eyes lingered on the king-size bed, and she'd already had a peek at the en suite bathroom. "I don't know, Abel. I—"

"It's done. I've got the couch." Hoping to divert the conversation, I headed toward the kitchen and was surprised when she stopped in front of the hallway bathroom.

She pointed into the room and looked at me. "You keep your shower curtains closed?"

My brows scrunched. "Yes . . . ?" I didn't know what she was getting at.

Sloane smiled. "That's perfect." She moved toward me, walking past and heading toward the living room. "My ex and I used to fight over shower curtains and closet doors." She laughed in dismissal, but my gut coiled. "Well, not really *fight*, I guess. He'd open them all up, and I would quietly close them when he wasn't around. He used to say he liked them open because you never knew who was hiding behind one. I thought he was just being paranoid and nitpicking me. We waged a silent war over the shower curtains and closet doors. It's the silliest thing, but it irked me so bad." I watched as she dismissed her own feelings so easily.

I shrugged. "You can keep the shower curtain however you want it."

Her beaming smile stopped me in my tracks. After staring too long, I finally asked, "So how did Bax take the news?"

Sloane sighed and hiked herself onto the kitchen island. "Granddad is solitary by nature. I think maybe it's because his wife died so long ago. He all but shuffled us out the door."

My forehead creased. "He wasn't worried about . . ." I gestured inarticulately at myself. "You know."

Sloane braced her hands on either side of her legs and tilted her head. "You mean about my new husband?"

Her eyes flicked over my shoulder toward the hallway. She still hadn't told the kids we were married, but I suspected her grandfather knew the truth. At least, most of it anyway.

When I stayed planted on the floor, she continued, "He claims he saw our connection months ago." Sloane laughed and made air quotes, and a knot tightened in my chest.

I had started to dismiss her grandfather's implication when her phone rang. "Speak of the devil." Sloane hopped off the island. "Hey, Granddad, what's up?"

She looked at me and frowned. "Um . . . I don't know about anyone installing a security system. Hang on, let me ask him."

Her eyebrows popped up, and she shot me a pointed stare.

I stuffed my hands into my pockets and shrugged. "It's for his safety."

She shook her head and smiled. "Yeah, it's okay. We just

wanted to be sure you're safe out there all alone." I could hear the old man arguing with her through the phone. "I know, I know. I'm sure it won't take long and they'll be out of your hair. Just . . . be nice, okay?" She laughed at something he said before hanging up.

I swallowed hard when her mossy eyes shifted my way. "You arranged to have a security system put in at the cabin?"

I shrugged it off. The hopeful, wide-eyed look she was giving me was making me uncomfortable. "It's fine. I knew you were worried about him being there alone. Plus, if your ex does try something, it'll be on camera."

Worry overtook her face as her eyes flicked back toward the hallway. "Do you think he will?"

I shook my head. "Only if he's reckless or stupid."

I knew Sloane was worried, but until the police could locate her ex, a security system was the best we could do . . . at least for now. I hadn't told them about Sloane and me getting married yet, but I did rally my brothers and ask them to be on the lookout for Jared too.

This is our goddamn town, and no one was going to come here and scare my wife when—shit.

I scraped the heel of my hand across my chest. Thoughts like that had been popping into my head all damn day. Sure, Sloane was legally my wife, but somehow my subconscious didn't get the message that it was strictly business.

I needed space to think. "Are you hungry? I could cook or pick something up?"

Sloane didn't mention or pay any mind to my total one-eighty in conversation topics. "I'm spent after today. Maybe we can grab takeout or something?" She tossed a thumb in the direction of the hallway. "I've got one that will try anything at all and another that thinks plain white rice is a delicacy."

I offered a flat-lipped laugh to acknowledge her, though I didn't really know a damn thing about kids or picky eating habits. All I knew was that my own upbringing was a far cry from healthy and stable. Dad had employed a full-time chef until we hit our teens, and then we were pretty much on our own. "How about Uncle Mao's in Pullman? I can run out and grab it . . . let you three get settled in here."

Sloane paused, looking at me like she was about to say something, maybe about me offering to drive somewhere. Instead, she only smiled softly. "That's perfect. Anything is fine. And . . . thank you."

I nodded, swiped my keys off the counter and hurried out the door before my mind could think of anything else— like how I had kissed her before and how badly I wanted to do it again.

THIRTEEN

THREE DAYS LIVING in Abel's house and I already felt spoiled.

In that time, I'd learned that despite his size, Abel was unnaturally quiet. He moved through the house as though he were a ghost—the shell of a man I rarely caught glimmers of. Abel was tidy, but he also seemed unaffected by Ben's discarded socks or the pieces of artwork that Tillie hung on his refrigerator.

Jared had never stepped up to be an involved parent, which meant all the responsibility had landed on me. Groceries, laundry, meals, nighttime tuck-ins—everything had been my responsibility from the beginning.

It was odd getting used to Abel clearing the table or sweeping up at the end of the night. More than once I caught myself standing around, wondering what to do once the kids were tucked in for the night and there wasn't a mountain of laundry to be folded.

I still felt completely guilty that the kids and I had taken over every bedroom in his house. I didn't even see Abel sleeping on the couch—I turned in early and he was up before the sun.

Still in bed, I checked my email and was thrilled to see I'd gotten confirmation from the bank that they'd received all the required paperwork. To their shock, I presented the official documents declaring Abel King and me legally married. Given the language in the trust fund documentation, I met the minimum requirements for a significant life event. I wasn't completely draining the trust, but my withdrawal request was still more money than I ever could have imagined, and it would be deposited into my account within a few business days.

A giddy squeal ripped through me.

Once that money was freed up, I could officially invest in Abel's Brewery and begin the hunt for a reputable contractor to assess my grandfather's house and begin reconstruction. With any luck, I'd even have some leftover money to squirrel away into my savings account.

Staring at the large, unused half of Abel's king-size bed, I let my mind wonder how much of that space his frame would consume. I curled into the pillow, and a tiny part of me wished it smelled like him—rich and warm and safe. Something had shifted inside me when we'd kissed at the courthouse. I'd be lying if I said I hadn't imagined kissing Abel once or twice before.

Fine . . . maybe several hundred times. Sue me.

With lips like his, I figured he would be a decent kisser, but I never expected his mouth to be so assertive, yet soft.

Commanding.

Hungry.

I groaned and rolled to my back, hoping to forget just how much I enjoyed that kiss. The comforting smells of coffee and cinnamon seeped into the bedroom. I quickly dressed and walked out to see Abel in the kitchen and the kids plopped in front of the television.

"Whoa. What's all this?" I asked.

Tillie grinned. "Abel is making cinnamon rolls."

"And not from the can like yours," Ben added. I ruffled his hair as I walked past and playfully stuck out my tongue.

My eyebrow shot up as I glanced into the kitchen. "Is that so?"

Abel's gaze flicked to me before returning to the rectangle of homemade dough in front of him. He was barefoot but dressed in jeans and a T-shirt. A comically small black apron was tied around his waist and dusted in flour.

A tiny pull to my heart pinched in my chest. "Morning, boss. What do we have here?"

Abel tipped his chin toward the coffee maker. "There's coffee if you want it. Breakfast should be ready in about twenty minutes."

I glanced at the clock, noting the time. "Chickens," I called affectionately to the twins. "Granddad asked if you would like to visit the marina today. Are you up for it?"

"Yes!" they called without looking up from their cartoon.

I moved into the kitchen, giving Abel a wide berth as I reached for a coffee mug. He grumbled behind me as he smeared the dough with softened butter.

I peered around his massive shoulder. "Cinnamon rolls, huh?"

He didn't stop, but generously sprinkled sugar and cinnamon on top of the butter. "I asked Ben and Tillie if they wanted eggs, pancakes, or cinnamon rolls, and this is what they chose."

"Well, boss"—I hopped onto the island counter next to

Abel to get a better view of him working—"color me impressed."

He grunted and continued to work while I watched. Abel carefully rolled the rectangle into a log and used a sharp knife to cut equal-size disks. An energy buzzed around him as he worked, and his shoulders bunched. I couldn't help but feel as though something was . . . *off*.

I narrowed my eyes at him. "Are you okay?"

He didn't look me in the eye. "I'm fine."

My lips pursed. "You just seem . . . jumpy."

The glass pan rattled as he placed it on the oven rack. "I'm not jumpy. I'm just—" He blew a stream of breath from his mouth and pinched his eyes. "I don't know."

Nerves tittered through me. I lowered my voice so the kids wouldn't hear our conversation. "Look, if this is too much, you have to tell me. Just say it."

His dark eyes whipped to mine. "It's not that. It's not you or the kids. I just—" His shoulders slumped. "Sometimes I bake when I feel out of sorts."

My eyes went wide as realization dawned on me. "Are you telling me you're a *stress baker*?"

His eyes went flat, and he shot me an annoyed glare. "I didn't say that."

I grinned. "Yes you did." I took a small sip of coffee. "If it's not us, then tell me why you're stressed."

Abel leaned back against the counter, his arms crossed.

"I made an appointment to meet with my father to discuss the brewery. I'd like to officially introduce you two."

My face twisted. "You had to make an appointment to talk to your dad?"

Sadness flickered across his face. "Yeah."

"When?" I hid my own nerves by taking another generous gulp of coffee.

"Today. I was going to tell you but needed to work up the sack to do it. If you're too busy or need more notice, it's fine. I—"

"No," I interrupted. "It's totally fine. It's what we agreed to. I'll do it. Granddad was eager to take the twins to the marina, so I am free most of the day."

The muscles in his jaw flexed, but after a moment his deep-brown eyes met mine. "Thank you."

I lifted my eyebrows. "We're in this together, remember?"

Abel swallowed hard. "I remember."

Russell King had a reputation, and clearly Abel was concerned about how this conversation was going to play out. I hopped off the counter and swiped my mug to get ready for the day. "Don't worry, boss. I can show up, shut up, and wear beige."

"Don't." His insistent tone made me pause as his dark eyes raked over me. "Just show up as you."

My innards went gooey. I hid a small smile behind my coffee cup and headed toward the bedroom.

I had taken over a small section of the primary bedroom's walk-in closet. Abel's shirts and jeans hung in tidy rows along one side. My fingers grazed down the sleeve of the suit he'd worn to our wedding, and I smiled. I hadn't realized it then, but the fact he thought to dress up made me feel special.

I glanced down at the slim band around my finger. *I married him wearing jeans.*

Scanning my clothes, I considered the fact Abel wanted me to dress as myself. Being friends with Sylvie, I'd been introduced to Russell King, but only in passing. Even I understood that being officially introduced to him as Abel's wife carried weight.

Instead of my go-to denim cutoffs, I opted for a pair of slim tapered pencil slacks in a mossy-green shade. For my top, I pulled a sleeveless cream-colored blouse with a high ruffle neck and tone-on-tone cream stripes from the hanger.

After tucking my top into the pants and adding a slim belt, I slipped into a pair of sandals and looked in the full-length mirror. It certainly wasn't *all* beige.

I looked at myself from several angles, and once I was satisfied that I looked like me, but a slightly refined version, I fluffed my hair and went in search of Abel.

He hadn't bothered to change out of his dark denim jeans, work boots, and T-shirt. His eyes moved up my body from my painted toes to my face before stopping.

I held out my hands. "I got nervous," I explained. "I opted for Sloane 2.0. You said to be myself, so you get the full Sloane experience."

"It's perfect. Ready?" Abel turned toward the door.

I nodded, rounded up the kids, and herded them toward the door. We arrived at the marina, and Abel walked with us while I met up with Granddad.

After giving the twins enough hugs and kisses to be embarrassing, I left them with Granddad. He insisted on shaking Abel's hand and offering his congratulations. Shame stained my cheeks as I hurried the kids along and made them promise to be good for their great-grandpa.

As we walked back, the late-morning sun was already warming up, and I took a moment to watch Outtatowner come to life. "He likes you, ya know—my granddad."

Abel nodded. "Bax is a good man. He's never treated me any differently."

Warmth and affection for my grandfather filled my chest. "He might be stubborn and he doesn't listen to anybody, but he's always been there for us. He opened his home when I needed it." I bumped my arm into Abel's. "Kind of like someone else I know."

His acknowledgment was a deep grumble that settled between my legs.

Up the road, I noticed the Sugar Bowl already had a line forming, and other storefront owners were busy placing their A-frame sidewalk signs to welcome the guests. In my time here, I'd seen a few storefronts come and go, many catering to the tourists who helped the small town thrive. When I headed toward my car, a new store, Gleam & Glimmer, caught my eye.

When I approached my parked car, I paused. "Hey, do we have time to make a quick stop?"

Abel nodded. "Of course."

I smiled and reached for his hand. I didn't miss the subtle jerk of his wrist, and I shot him a plain look. "Seriously?"

He swallowed. "Sorry."

"Just"—I motioned to my side—"come here."

Next to one another on the sidewalk, I looped my arm into his. "Not bad, right?"

He shifted his shoulders. "It's fine."

I laughed and playfully rolled my eyes. "Fine? We're married, or did you already forget that?"

He glowered down at me. "I didn't forget."

Satisfied, I smiled. "Good. So we need your dad to believe this, right? So . . . you can't act like I'm about to bite you anytime I touch your arm."

He cleared his throat. "Sorry."

I rounded him and planted my hands on his biceps before shaking them out. "Loosen up . . . and don't be sorry. You wanted the full Sloane experience, so you're going to get it."

Once his shoulders relaxed, I slid my hand into his and tugged him down the sidewalk. When we reached Gleam & Glimmer, I motioned toward the door. "After you."

He pulled the door open and waited impatiently for me to step inside. I smiled and slipped past him.

The store was simple and clean. Glass display cases lined the edges of the room, with one large case in the center. A woman stood at the back of the store and smiled brightly as the bell on the door announced our entrance.

"Welcome to Gleam & Glimmer, Outtatowner's premier jeweler." She didn't need to mention it was also Outtatowner's *only* jeweler. "What can I help you two find?"

I straightened and tightened my grip on Abel's arm. "We're looking for a wedding band." My head jerked toward Abel. "For this big guy."

The woman smiled and moved toward a display case on the side. "Certainly. We have a variety of men's wedding bands in various styles and materials. When is the wedding?"

"Already happened! We just couldn't wait, so I cartwheeled to the courthouse and put a ring on this handsome fella before he could get away. Trouble is, I forgot the ring part."

The woman laughed with me as Abel shook his head. Despite his surly demeanor, I caught the hint of a smile on his lips.

I turned to him. "So, husband. What do you like?"

Abel looked at the arrangement of men's wedding bands in the case. "I don't really know."

The woman took his hesitance as an opportunity to shine. "We have titanium, wood, classic white and yellow gold, even rings with diamonds and gemstones if you're looking for something a little more flashy."

Abel shifted his stance. "Just something simple. Traditional."

A flutter rippled across my chest. I looked down at the case and found a simple band similar to the one I wore, only thicker and more suited for a man's hand. "What about that one?" I pointed to it.

The woman followed my finger and plucked the band from its cushion and placed it on a black mat in front of us. "A classic choice."

I held out my own hand. "I thought it matched mine."

Abel stared at the band in stunned silence as if he were staring at another prison sentence.

"Do we know your ring size? It's unlikely it will fit out of the case, but you could try it on and see if you like the style."

When he didn't move, I picked up the ring and slipped it onto his left hand. My eyes went wide. "It fits."

Abel flexed his hand and stared at the ring.

"Do you like it?" I whispered to him.

His eyes caught mine and he nodded. "I do."

A giddy excitement raced through me. "We'll take it!"

Before he could back out, I presented my debit card.

Abel stopped me with a brush of his hand against my forearm. "I got it."

I smiled, hoping the clerk wouldn't see our back-and-forth play out. "No, really. It's the least I could do." I leaned in closer. "Besides, I can take it out of your cut of the trust fund." I winked and Abel softened at my gentle teasing.

"I'm paying."

A flutter erupted inside my chest at his soft, yet commanding, voice.

"Okay." I swallowed hard. "Thank you."

Once the ring was paid for, we hurried out of the store. In the light of day, we were immediately thrust back into reality.

I looked up at the shining sun and exhaled. "Guess we should go break the news to your dear old dad. You ready?"

Abel looked at his ring and flexed his hand again. "I guess there's no turning back now."

I beamed up at him as a flurry of nerves tickled my tummy. "Nope."

FOURTEEN

SLOANE

RUSSELL KING's primary office was miles away in the city of Chicago. When he wasn't traveling for work or in Chicago, he mainly operated from an opulent office in the King family home.

According to Sylvie, Bug King had taken over the residence when Maryann King abandoned her children and their father was too consumed with business to care. Still, Russell operated out of the home when he needed to.

Abel and I bumped along the country roads as we made our way to the King estate. When we pulled down the long driveway, I shielded my eyes from the summer sun.

I'd visited Sylvie and her sister MJ at the King home before. It always struck me as out of place in such a quaint small town, but the Kings never seemed to do anything small. Large steps led to a grand oak door carved with intricate details.

I quietly followed Abel as he opened the front door without knocking. As it always was when I had visited Sylvie in the past, the interior was pristine, with floor-to-ceiling windows casting a golden glow over the tastefully arranged furniture. Every corner exuded money and power, with high ceilings and thick drapes. When we reached a closed door, Abel paused before knocking.

I took a deep breath. If the whisperings about Russell King were true, Abel would have to appeal to his mercurial temperament and business savvy.

"Come in." Russell King's voice boomed through the thick wooden door.

Abel pushed the door open, entering while I followed closely. Sitting behind a grand, opulent wood desk was Russell King. He was dressed in a shirt and tie despite the warm summer heat. Time had not been kind to Russell King. I knew the signs of a drinking problem, with his ruddy cheeks and bloodshot eyes. His paunch and bloated face nearly took away from the striking brown of his eyes—so deep and dark they reminded me of a snake's.

I calmed myself before a shudder involuntarily coursed through me.

In a chair beside the desk was JP King. If memory served me correctly, JP was second to last born and only a few years older than MJ, the youngest. Still, he was immaculately dressed in a well-tailored suit, tie, and shiny shoes. As if he were cast from an identical mold, I imagined JP was the spitting image of a younger, handsomer Russell.

He was tall and lean. His high cheekbones were more angular than Abel's, and he lacked the dark King eyes. Instead, his were an intense shade of blue-green. While Abel's shoulders carried the weight of the world, JP's seemed to have a sharp edge to them. Women in town thought him devastatingly attractive, though his icy demeanor was enough to scare off most.

As Abel and I approached, Russell stood to shake his son's hand. "Welcome. Please, come in."

Russell reached for me, and I slipped my hand into his. His swollen fingers held mine as he brought the top of my hand to his lips. I swallowed a visceral gag.

"Pleasure, my dear." Russell's smile was cautious and questioning, but as slick as oil.

"Thank you." I quickly tucked myself next to Abel, hoping to hide my revulsion.

"What are you doing here?" Abel's glare was directed at his younger brother.

JP's hands went wide. "I was told this was a business meeting."

Abel scoffed and rolled his eyes. "Of course you were."

JP's lips twitched into a half smile. "Is it not?"

I watched the odd exchange between brothers. Finally, Abel gestured for me to sit, and he took a seat in the chair next to me. "It's a family announcement as well as a business meeting."

JP smiled widely. "Then I wouldn't miss it for the world, brother."

Abel cleared his throat. "Sloane and I are married."

I nearly coughed on my own saliva at the abruptness of Abel's announcement. Russell and JP stared at us in shock, though Russell recovered more quickly.

"Why, that's fantastic news!" Russell laughed and leaned back into his leather chair. He pointed at Abel. "I knew you were up to something. Here you thought you could get one over on me."

Ice ran through my veins at his accusing tone.

I slipped my hand onto Abel's arm. "We tried to keep it between ourselves . . . for the sake of my children. At least initially, but they couldn't be happier."

Abel stared at me and I smiled at him, willing him to stop freaking out and just play along. I squeezed his arm.

Russell's eyes landed hard on the slim silver band on my left hand. The room pulsed as I froze.

I managed to grab it before my dad burned it with the rest of her stuff.

"Surely you didn't marry this poor girl with that, did you?" Russell's mocking laughter filled the office as he pointed to the ring.

My fingers curled into Abel's forearm, and the muscles beneath his shirt rippled.

Russell shook his head. "She needs something bigger." He winked at me and my stomach curled. "Flashier. A woman deserves to show everyone how a King spoils his woman."

Abel shifted uncomfortably in his seat. Tension filled the air.

He was about to speak when I cut in. "Actually, I requested something simple. I love that we have matching rings. It's perfect."

Undeterred, Russell scoffed. "Nonsense." He scribbled something down on a pad of paper. "I'll have my jeweler set something up for you. We can't have a King woman walking around with that on her finger."

My back straightened, and I was ready to speak again when JP cut in. "Maybe we should get on to the business portion of this meeting." He glanced at his watch. "I have another appointment."

With a curt nod, Russell shifted gears. His fingers steepled as his eyes zeroed in on Abel. "Yes, of course. What is it that you needed to discuss, Abel?"

Beside me, nerves rolled off his shoulders in waves. I squeezed his arm once and gave him a reassuring nod.

"As you're aware, Abel's Brewery continues to expand and be more profitable than we initially anticipated. You were an integral part of getting the brewery off the ground, and I will always be thankful for that. Moving forward, I would like to buy out King Equities' shares and carry it forward on my own."

Pride swelled in my chest, and I smiled as Abel stared ahead at his father.

JP scoffed lightly to my right. "With what money?"

I resisted the urge to sneer in his direction.

"I've been saving," Abel said. "That, in addition to Sloane's family money, would be enough to outright purchase the brewery."

Russell's index fingers tapped together as Abel's words settled over him. "I don't know, son. A total buyout is a bold move. Maybe the firm should stay on for a while as a minority shareholder . . . just in case."

Abel tensed beside me. It was clear he didn't want his father involved with any part of Abel's Brewery. "When the brewery was purchased, we'd agreed the firm's money was a loan. As the brewery has grown, those repayments have been made regularly."

Russell's chair groaned as he shifted in his seat. "I understand that. You've surprised everyone with what you've done with the business, even me. Still . . ."

"The terms of the loan were clear, Abel," JP interrupted. "King Equities provided the initial loan but remains a partner, even once that loan is repaid."

"You don't want King Equities involved?" Russell sounded deeply wounded, though I suspected it was simply a guilt tactic.

Abel jerked his chin. "It's not that. Land and business acquisition has been the primary goal of King Equities. Now that Abel's Brewery is established, there is no residual value outside of profit shares. I would think it would be far more beneficial to use the buyout to acquire other businesses in the future."

A light *huh* escaped JP, and a tiny twirl of victory zipped through my belly. Abel had done his own research, and I couldn't have been prouder.

Russell's hand moved across the pad of paper as he scribbled more illegible notes. "I'll have to mull this over, of course."

Feeling a skittering of panic, I licked my lips and sat up. I smiled widely at Russell. "Thank you, sir." I leaned into Abel, resting my head against his arm. "Owning the brewery with the man I love has been a dream of mine, and Abel has been doing everything he can to make my dreams come true." I blinked up at my husband's shocked face. "He really is a teddy bear."

JP sneered and Russell laughed. "My, my. I see you've got your hands full with this one, Abel. I'm sure we can work something out. I will think it over and get back to you."

I stood, seeing our exit and taking it. Russell, JP, and Abel all stood. Quickly, I rounded the desk, wrapping my arms around my new father-in-law. "Thank you, sir. I am so honored to be a part of this family."

Russell King's patronizing eyes looked down on me. I knew a man who liked a pat on the ass when I saw one, and Russell King took the bait. His hand dipped far too low on my back as he returned my embrace, and my stomach soured. Still, I beamed up at him before I retook my position beside Abel, who was frozen in place.

His shoulders bunched, and he didn't seem to move as he stared at his father. "It's time to go. My wife and I have afternoon plans."

My wife.

There it was again. Two words that sent a dull ache straight between my legs.

Confused by the sudden darkening of Abel's mood, I leaned into him. His arm wrapped around my waist, pulling me flush against his side. He dropped a soft kiss on the top of my head, selling our farce to his father, I assumed.

Russell smiled in an oily kind of way that made my skin crawl. He sighed. "It's a good day to be the king."

I swallowed back the bile that rose in my throat and clung to Abel as we exited the stuffy, too-dark office.

JP followed us out, closing the door behind him. "Abel," he called, stopping us both in our tracks.

We turned to see JP frowning and pointing his finger between us. "I don't buy this bullshit for a second . . . but it seems he does. I'll talk to him. He's got his eye on a failing law firm office over in Bloom County. The funds from the brewery buyout would clear up some red tape and make a hostile takeover of the building much simpler. It might take a few days to get everything in order, but if I can make it work, I will."

Abel nodded, revealing nothing. "Thank you."

The men shook hands, and Abel headed straight for the door with me hot on his heels.

Once outside, I exhaled in relief and trotted beside Abel as he walked toward my car. Hoping to break the ice, I said, "Your brother seems a little frosty, but kind of nice."

Abel yanked open the driver's-side door for me. "He's not. If there's an angle JP can play, he'll play it. But our hands are tied. We'll have to trust him."

I scurried into the driver's seat and waited as Abel climbed into the passenger side. "Where to?" I asked.

Abel's brown eyes burned into me as my pulse skyrocketed under his assessment. "Let's go home."

FIFTEEN

ABEL

Watching Sloane embrace my father while his hand grazed the top of her ass drove my fury to an all-time high. I'd lived with him waffling between absent and overbearing my entire life, but the minute his hand was on her, I settled into *enraged*. I didn't care that the rest of our small town saw him as a benevolent benefactor or savvy businessman.

He touched her, and I didn't fucking like it.

I tightened my crossed arms and focused on the road from the passenger seat of Sloane's car.

"Are you okay?" Sloane asked from the driver's seat.

I shifted and willed myself to relax despite the bubbles of anger rising from my gut. "Fine."

"Is it . . . am I a bad driver?" She gestured between her and the steering wheel.

Yes.

My molars ground together. "No."

It wasn't her shitty driving that was making me uncomfortable. How was I supposed to explain the complexities of the King family dynamic and that the mere brush of his fingertips across the top of her ass sent me reeling? I wanted to snap his fingers and tear apart his office—but I'm not stupid enough to bite the hand that feeds me. No one crossed Russell King and survived it.

Maybe not even my mother.

The thought darkened my mood further, and I stayed quiet the rest of the ride back to my house. Sloane gave me space to brood, and by the time she pulled down my tree-lined driveway, I had finally relaxed.

She parked, and I exhaled before turning toward Sloane. "I'm sorry I'm . . . in a mood."

Sloane smiled softly. "You're allowed to have emotions, Abel." My chest pinched and she unbuckled.

That was precisely the problem—I was having far too many emotions where she was concerned. Ridiculous emotions like possessiveness and contentment. When I couldn't find the words to respond, Sloane offered a soft smile and disappeared into the house.

I found myself twitchy with pent-up energy and had no idea what to do with myself.

Do I follow her inside? Head to the brewery and give her space?

In less than a week living with Sloane, I'd lost all sense of autonomy and felt like one of those ridiculous dolls with peg legs just aimlessly teetering around.

My phone buzzed and I slipped it from my pocket.

SYLVIE

Bug did a thing . . . don't be mad.

I didn't need to know what this *thing* was to know it was definitely going to piss me off.

Well, what is it?

Three dots popped up and disappeared, then popped up again. I was pretty certain my sister was attempting to find the right words to soften the blow of whatever scheme my aunt had cooked up. Before Sylvie could reply, my phone rang.

I closed my eyes in frustration as I answered. "Hey, Bug. What's up?"

"Abel. How are you, dear?" I knew her too well to know she dropped her hard-ass exterior only when she needed something.

"Fine. You?" My tone was unnecessarily clipped.

Bug clicked her tongue. "Now, is that any way for a brand-new husband to be?"

I really didn't know how a new husband *should* feel, so I stayed silent.

"You should be celebrating. Which is why . . ." She paused, letting her words linger in the air. "I have a surprise for you and Sloane."

I let out a deep, annoyed sigh. "We don't need any surprises, Aunt Bug."

"Oh, nonsense. First you date the woman in secret and then run off to the courthouse. I suspect if you hadn't needed a witness, I still wouldn't know about your marriage."

Well, she isn't wrong.

I let out a disgruntled, half-hearted laugh.

"*Exactly*," she continued. "So . . . your check-in at the Wild Iris Bed-and-Breakfast is at five p.m."

My tongue went thick. "The what?"

"It's nothing, really. A cute little B&B in Star Harbor. I could only swing one night with such short notice, but at least it's something."

"Something?" I was racking my brain, trying to figure

out why my aunt had booked us a stay at a bed-and-breakfast.

"Every woman deserves a honeymoon, Abel," she said with a wistful sigh tacked on at the end.

I audibly gulped. *Honeymoon?*

It was absurd.

I shook my head. "We can't just leave. Sloane has kids."

Her haughty laugh rang through the telephone. "You don't think I thought of that? It's taken care of. Bax will be entertaining his great-grandkids for the night."

I kicked the dirt with the toe of my boot. "Well, we have work."

I could practically hear her eyes roll through the phone. "You're the boss. Give yourselves the night off."

A night alone in some random hotel room with Sloane? No fucking way.

I scrambled to come up with another plausible excuse, but my aunt cut in. "Sylvie already broke the news to Sloane, and I heard your wife is looking forward to it. You wouldn't want to disappoint her already, would you?"

Sloane knew about this? And she was excited? Well, fuck me.

I exhaled. *Why did it seem that my default was always to be an asshole?*

Defeated, I lowered myself onto the front stoop and pressed my fingers into my eyes. "Sure. It sounds great. Thank you for doing this for us."

"Excellent. Now, try to enjoy yourself, Abel. It's about time you made some happy memories."

I hung up without even saying goodbye.

Happy memories? Sure, like that'll happen.

The only memories that would be made tonight were

how painfully uncomfortable I made Sloane while we were forced to share a hotel room.

Behind me the front door opened.

I looked out onto the front lawn, avoiding her eyes. "Looks like we've got plans tonight."

Sloane's soft laugh floated over my shoulder. "Yeah, looks like it. I just got off the phone with your sister. She and Bug sure work fast."

I pressed my lips together and nodded.

Sloane lowered herself next to me, her arms resting on the tops of her knees. "I called my granddad to confirm, and it's already been decided. He's planning to take them to a movie in the park and then have a sleepover here. He's taking them to camp in the morning and everything. The kids will be thrilled."

At least someone is.

I tipped my face toward her. "Do you really want to do this?"

Sloane picked at her nails. "We need to be believable, right?" Her eyes flicked up to meet mine, and she scrunched her nose. "It would seem kind of weird if a newlywed couple refused a romantic night away, don't you think?"

Newlywed or not—any man in his right mind would be a fool to refuse a night away with Sloane.

I nodded.

Sloane slapped her thighs and stood. "Great. I'll go pack a bag."

I WAS IN HELL.

My dear, sweet, scheming aunt forgot to mention that the Wild Iris Bed-and-Breakfast was a boutique B&B

specializing in romantic getaways for couples with *themed accommodations*.

I frowned at the king-size bed in the middle of the room. "Is that leopard-print bedding?"

Sloane's wide eyes surveyed the room. "It appears to be . . ." She lifted something that strangely resembled a wooden club. "Caveman themed?"

She moved to the side table and picked up a brochure. "Wild Iris Bed-and-Breakfast," she read. Her eyes flicked up as she tried not to smile. "Adventure suites. The caveman is a much-loved prehistoric figure, and your room is a whimsical glimpse into his existence. The Caveman Suite has a king bed and will accommodate two primates."

I stomped toward her and pulled the paper from her fingertips. "You have got to be kidding me." My eyes scanned the brochure, and sure as shit, I was in hell. "I'm sorry," I stumbled. "I had no idea. I can't believe this . . ."

Sloane moved around the room, her hands brushing across the stony cave-like walls. I watched as her fingertips danced under the flowing waterfall in the corner of the room. She circled toward me, but stopped at a small piece of animal hide and lifted it.

Her eyes went wide and glimmered with humor. "I think this is your loincloth, husband."

Heat flared in my cheeks, and I swiped the furry fabric from her hands. "This is not funny."

A barking laugh burst from her small frame. "This is *hilarious*. Loosen up a little. Me Jane. You Tarzan." Sloane thumped her chest in rhythm with my clunking heartbeat.

My eyes landed on the lone bed in the middle of the room.

My hand had reached up to tug at the collar of my shirt when Sloane laughed. I pinned her with a heated look.

"Are you *clutching your pearls*?" She laughed again, and heat sizzled down my back.

"Of course not." I looked down at my hand, which was paused at my collar, and dropped it to my side.

Sloane walked over to the edge of the bed and hopped into it, stretching her legs before smiling up at me. "It's just a bed, Abel."

The fuck it is.

Sloane adjusted, hiking herself up to her elbows. "Look, it's really rare I get a break from making every single decision in our lives and worrying that I made the wrong one. Most days I feel like a spinning top." She exhaled and flopped flat on her back to stare at the primitive art decorating the ceiling. "I didn't realize how much I needed a little break until we showed up here. It feels good to laugh without worrying. Can we please just . . . exist here for a little while?"

It was the *please* that snagged my attention. All she was asking for was a break—a night where she didn't have to think or prepare or be strong for everyone else.

It was the simplest thing, and I had the power to give it to her.

I looked around, and my attention paused on the cave painting with stick figures in very questionable positions.

A small chuckle broke free.

"There he is." Sloane goaded as she smiled up at me. "Come on." She sat up and grinned. "Let's see what other trouble we can find at the Wild Iris."

That was the thing—I *knew* trouble, and I was staring right at her.

SIXTEEN

LEAVING our humble cave behind us, we opted to explore the Wild Iris Bed-and-Breakfast. It was delightfully ridiculous. From the outside, the Victorian-style estate was painted a soft lavender. The grand turret faced Lake Michigan, and I wondered what type of themed room it held.

Damn shame if it isn't pirates.

With a stifled giggle, I wondered if Bug understood where she had booked our stay or if she knew the Wild Iris was exactly the kind of place that would make me giggle while simultaneously annoying the hell out of her uptight nephew.

Knowing Bug's austere reputation, I suspected the latter.

Abel skulked closely behind me as I wound through the lobby and exited out the back onto the wide, open porch. Cozy chairs were arranged in groups of two or three with side tables adorned with flowers. More steps led off the back deck to a small boardwalk that directed guests to the beachfront. Near the shoreline, I spotted a bonfire pit with benches made from tree trunks split in half around it.

Waves ebbed and flowed onto the clean, sandy beaches. On the distant coastline, familiar sand dunes rose high above the water, but at our particular stretch of beach, the open shoreline was flat and inviting.

Content, I sucked in a deep breath of warm lake air. "Isn't it beautiful?"

When he didn't respond, I turned to find Abel staring at me. He shifted under my attention, clearing his throat. "Yeah. Gorgeous."

His gaze fell to my mouth, and heat flooded my cheeks in response.

"Hello!" An elderly singsong voice called from behind us. "Yoo-hoo!"

In unison, we shifted to see a woman exiting the french doors, balancing a small tray of what appeared to be a fizzy, cider-colored cocktail in champagne flutes. She waved wildly with her free hand as the glasses balanced precariously.

The woman was dressed to match the house in a flashy lavender jacket and flowing purple slacks. On top of her silver curls was a large floppy hat trimmed with lavender fringe and feathers.

"Good evening!" she called as she got closer. "Welcome to the Wild Iris. My name is Gladys. Ruby checked you in, but I just couldn't wait to meet you! We love having newly-weds stay with us. Please, try this." She moved the tray between us. "It's called Wedded Bliss."

Abel and I smiled, and each of us took a champagne flute from her tray. Each glass contained a bubbly drink, featured two slices of fig, and was garnished with a sprig of thyme.

"This looks amazing! Thank you," I said as I took a sip.

Gladys grinned. "It's got champagne, honey, orange liqueur, and apple cider. The Greeks used to prescribe honey for sexual vigor!" Her shoulders shimmied as she grinned.

I sputtered and choked on my drink. Bubbles fizzed up my nose as I gasped for air through my laughter. A hard thump landed on my back as Abel tried to help clear the drink from my system.

Gladys winked. "Happy honeymoon, you two!"

Abel awkwardly raised his champagne flute, and I dissolved into another fit of laughter as Gladys sashayed away, in search of her next unsuspecting couple—of that I was certain.

I cleared my throat again as Abel's hand softly thumped my back once more. "Thanks." I smiled and took a more careful sip. "It's good. You should try it."

He eyed the cocktail as though one sip would have us tearing at each other's clothing. Which, to be honest, wouldn't have been the worst thing in the world.

My eyes dropped to his broad chest. It would be unreal to see him completely undressed and looming over me. It was almost as if I could imagine his large hands gripping my hips, pulling them down the mattress toward him. Tiny muscles fluttered low as a throb settled between my legs and heat spread across my chest.

Abel cleared his throat and I blinked up at him, realizing I'd just been caught ogling him and thinking *very* naughty things about my pretend husband.

I stared down at the drink in my hand.

Jesus, what is in this?

A playful smirk tipped up the corner of Abel's mouth,

and I squared my shoulders to stare straight ahead at the rippling water in the distance.

The Wild Iris was fully booked, and slowly Gladys made her way around to empty her tray. We offered polite nods and tight smiles to other guests as we relaxed on the porch or took a walk down the beach.

To my surprise, I could actually relax around Abel. He was a man of few words, but the more time I spent with him, the more I realized his silence wasn't because he was just some grumpy asshole. Instead, he was thoughtful. Considerate. When he decided to contribute to a conversation, he chose his words carefully.

Abel had stopped Gladys, asking for her recommendation for a casual dinner. She pointed up the beach, assuring us that there were a few local restaurants within walking distance. We had eventually found the perfect place—one that served burgers and beer on the beach.

After our dinner, we took our time walking back toward the Wild Iris, the sunset blazing against the watery horizon. As the Wild Iris came into view, we noticed a fire had been lit in the pit on the beach.

I lifted a shoulder and looked at him. "Want to?"

His calm eyes looked down at me. "If you do."

As we approached, Gladys's voice called over the crowd. "There they are. Our newlyweds!"

I offered an awkward wave at the couples gathered by the fire. Wooden benches were arranged in a semicircle, opening to the pit and the lake beyond.

Gladys fussed and dusted sand from her hands. "There's not a lot of room, but, Mr. King, if you sit there, your wife could take your lap."

I gulped and my eyes flashed to his.

He lowered himself to the wooden bench and slapped his thigh. "Come on, Jane. Take a seat."

I liked the playful side of him and how it always seemed to catch me by surprise. Carefully, I lowered myself onto his lap. His muscular thighs were warm and wide, plenty of room for me to sit and get comfortable. His hand settled at the side of my hip, and I draped one arm across his shoulder.

He leaned in to whisper in my ear. "This okay?"

The deep rumble of his voice across the shell of my ear sent shivers down my back.

"Are you cold?" he asked, but then reached back and grabbed a rolled-up blanket from the pile behind him before I could respond. Carefully, Abel unrolled the flannel blanket and draped it across my shoulders, tucking it in at the edges to make sure it didn't slip.

I clutched the edge at my chest. "Thank you."

The conversation and crackling fire enveloped us. His eyes moved to my lips again, and I wondered if he might do it—kiss me and claim me as his wife in front of the group of strangers.

Do it.

It won't be fake this time.

I wet my lips as I stared at his mouth. Beneath me his body was warm and hard, and I fought the urge to squirm in his lap. In the firelight, I tried to memorize the slope and planes of his handsome face. His fingers drew soft circles at my hip as conversations overlapped around us.

"Do you want to go back to the room?" His words dripped with dark intention.

I lifted my chin in a jerky nod.

Abel rose, taking me with him and gently setting me on my feet. I went to remove the blanket, but Gladys stopped me. "No need, dear. Just bring it back in the morning." She winked and my stomach somersaulted. "Have fun, you two."

I turned, feeling the blush deepen in my cheeks. As we walked side by side toward the house, Abel's wide palm slipped down my arm, capturing my hand in his. His palm was wide and warm. I squeezed, loving the strength and comfort his touch provided.

When I risked a glance at his face, he leaned in. "They're still watching."

"Okay," I breathed.

When we reached our room, Abel dropped my hand to unlock the door to let us back into the Caveman Suite.

I stared at the leopard-clad bed as hope and arousal coursed through me.

Abel moved behind me and dropped the key on the small boulder-like table beside the door. "I'll take the floor."

Hope squeaked out of me like a leaking balloon. "What?"

He slipped off his boots and grabbed a pillow from the bed, dropping it to the floor. "I can sleep here."

Embarrassment flooded through me. Had a tiny part of me hoped he wasn't faking *everything* down by the fire and we might come back to the room to make a few more bad decisions?

Of course I did.

Flustered, I swiped a loose strand of hair away from my face. "Don't be ridiculous. The bed is huge. We'll just take opposite sides. It's fine."

Fully ready to argue, I was shocked when he simply said, "Okay."

"Oh. Okay." I looked around. "I'll change in the bathroom."

I scurried away, too embarrassed to even look at him as I dragged my duffel bag into the en suite bathroom with me.

Once behind a locked door, I braced myself against the sink and looked into the mirror.

What the fuck? I mouthed to myself.

I pressed my hands into my eyes and sighed. *Get your shit together.* I pointed at myself in the mirror to drive home the point that this was entirely ridiculous.

I slipped on my pajamas and quickly brushed my teeth and hair. I surveyed the simple floral shorts and matching pajama top. It wasn't overly sexy, but the shorts cut high on my thighs and made me feel feminine and pretty.

Sleep on the floor, my ass.

When I reentered the room, the lighting was dim, and I could just make out Abel's hulking frame beneath the sheets. Light danced on the cave-like walls, wrapping us in a cozy cocoon of soft, glowing light.

"I feel like Jane would cartwheel over to the bed or something," I joked.

His soft chuckle filled the darkened room. "You can try."

I smiled and pulled back the covers. The bed was large, but so was he. Abel's bare chest and black boxer briefs flashed into view.

"Oh." I quickly replaced the covers in panic.

"You okay?" he asked.

"Yep." I nodded and gulped.

I am definitely not okay.

Sliding into bed beside Abel, I lay on my back with wide eyes and a pounding heart, and I stared at the cave painting that decorated the ceiling. I didn't need to think about the fact that Abel had a body like *that* and he was inches away from me in nothing but a pair of tight boxer briefs.

I listened to the rhythmic inhale and exhale of his breathing, painfully aware of the proximity of his body to mine. I lay there, wondering about my complicated, brooding husband. Every time I thought I understood him, he revealed another complicated layer.

I sighed as I stared up. "Hell of a honeymoon."

He exhaled a tiny laugh through his nose. "Good night, wife."

I smiled in the darkness. "Good night, husband."

There were worse things in the world than lying beside the hottest man on the planet, knowing he was completely off limits.

Trouble was, I couldn't seem to think of a single one.

SEVENTEEN

ABEL

I COULD SMELL her perfume before I even opened my eyes. Hints of warm spice and subtle sweetness flooded my system and sent a throb of heat straight to my cock. Slowly waking to her scent was like being buried under a pile of blankets on a frigid winter's day and never wanting to leave.

I hiked my knees up, curling my body possessively around her and tucking my arm against her belly. My body tingled as her ass pressed against the thick shaft of my morning wood.

My eyes popped open.

Fuuuuuuck.

I couldn't believe it—sometime in the middle of the night, we'd fused together, and now I was cuddling my fake wife the morning after our sham of a honeymoon. My dick twitched against the perfect curve of her ass, and I bit back a groan.

There was no way she wasn't going to notice that.

I stilled, assessing whether Sloane was awake.

Her breathing was slow and even. The gentle rise and fall of my arm against her body told me I might be able to sneak away without her noticing the raging hard-on that forgot the whole *this isn't real* part of our arrangement.

I slowly lifted my head. Her dark lashes swooped low on her cheeks. Sloane looked peaceful. Happy.

Something pinched between my ribs at how perfectly she seemed to fit, wrapped in my arms. I adjusted myself, shifting my hips back and inching away from her, but not before indulging in one last hit of the smell of her hair.

Stop being a fucking creep, dude.

I rolled to my back and exhaled. Sunlight streamed through the window on the far wall, peeking through the animal hide curtains. A smile cracked against my cheek and I stretched, wiggling my toes and willing my cock to calm the hell down.

I couldn't remember the last time I'd gotten laid, and even if I did, I'd bet nothing would compare to being buried to the hilt in Sloane. My body hummed for her and my fingers twitched, eager to reach out and feel the softness of her skin.

Instead, I sat up and swung my legs off the side of the bed. As I stirred, Sloane groaned and rolled over. I reached for a shirt, but over my shoulder, I didn't miss the way her eyes went wide as she took in my bare back.

Fuck it.

Instead of covering up, I stood, not caring about my still-hard cock as I sauntered toward the bathroom. If I had to deal with the torture of being this close to her and not being able to do a damn thing about it, then so could she.

I felt her eyes on me the entire walk to the bathroom. By the time I finished, Sloane was up and dressed.

Her eyes were bright, and her smile pierced my heart. "Morning."

"Good morning. Ready to head out?" I asked.

She held up her toothbrush. "Just going to freshen up and I'll be all set."

I nodded, hating that the time in our little caveman bubble was so short. My eyes landed on the loincloth draped over a chair. In another life I'd toss Sloane over my shoulder and take her—leave her begging for more.

I gestured weakly around the Caveman Suite. "Was it worth it?"

"What do you mean?" Sloane swung her legs over the side of the bed and brought a glass of water to her lips.

I frowned. "Bug told me that you told Sylvie that you were really excited for a night away. That's why I agreed to come."

Sloane nearly choked on her drink as she sputtered and coughed. "Oh, wow." Her eyes went wide as she studied my face. "I mean, I am . . . glad. I had fun."

Fun.

The word rolled around in my head as I scraped a hand down my face. The pretend honeymoon was a mistake. Every time we entertained the idea that our marriage was more than just a smart business move, it became harder and harder to remind myself that our arrangement had an expiration date.

We couldn't go on faking this forever . . . especially when certain parts of me weren't getting the hint that she was totally off limits.

I nodded, letting the conversation die between us. Without waiting for a response, I grabbed our bags and loaded up the truck.

A few minutes later, Sloane's voice carried through the lobby as she gushed over how amazing our stay was, how cozy the fire was, and how we couldn't wait to return.

Gladys was thrilled at the prospect of repeat guests and slipped her a card to remember our stay by.

Like we could ever forget the Caveman Suite.

Outside, I leaned against my truck and waited for her to give one last hug to Gladys before saying goodbye.

I stared at my hand as I spun the silver band around my finger. I'd gotten used to its weight, but every time it caught my eye, I got keyed up and didn't know why.

When she was ready, I opened the truck door for her and tried not to stare at her ass as she climbed in.

I sat behind the wheel and stared out the windshield before starting the truck.

"Want me to drive?" she asked.

I glanced at her but shook my head. "No, I'm good."

Really fucking good.

The trip home was spent in companionable silence. I watched the road while Sloane fiddled with the radio and rambled on and on about whatever song happened to be playing. By the time we hit my driveway, unused energy was rattling my bones.

My thumb drummed a beat against the steering wheel. "I was thinking . . . maybe I'll make some chocolate chip cookies or something for the kids."

I parked and slicked a hand down my thigh.

Her eyes narrowed in my direction. "What's going on with you?"

"What do you mean?" I scoffed, avoiding the assessment of her striking hazel eyes. My knee bounced.

Her pointer finger made an accusatory swirl in my direction. "You're stress baking—or planning to."

My jaw flexed. "I'm not." *Of course I was.* "I just wanted to do something nice for the kids."

Her lips pursed as if she didn't believe me. "Well, let's

try something new. What is something that makes you feel better? Something that's just for you?"

I thought for a moment, unsure if anyone had ever asked me what *I* needed. "Baking."

Her playful eyes rolled. "*Besides* baking."

I peered out the windshield and felt the sting of a bright summer sun. "Gardening sometimes helps when I'm . . . I don't know—worked up."

Her eyes flashed with delight. "I love to garden!" She popped open the passenger-side door. "Let's do it!" Before I could stop her, she was out of the car and hustling toward the house. "I'm going to change. I'll meet you out there!"

I smiled, shaking my head and wondering how the hell someone with such a happy disposition had hitched themselves to me.

I stared down at the ring on my left hand. It was strange to feel as though something that had never been there before somehow felt perfectly right.

Instead of stewing over it, I rounded the house and pulled out a bucket of hand tools from the garden shed, along with a baseball cap. The gloves would be far too big on Sloane, but at least her hands would be protected. I dropped the bucket beside one of the raised garden beds and looked over the thriving herbs and vegetables.

Moments later, the back doors opened and Sloane bounded down the steps. From the shadow of my ball cap, I watched as her tits bounced and her long, smooth legs gleamed in the summer sun.

My tongue went thick and my mouth went dry as I followed the line from her ankle all the way to where her cutoff denim shorts stopped at her hip.

"Okay, boss. Where do I start?" I had to look away from the sunny smile she shot my way.

I handed her my gloves. "Put those on."

As I suspected, they were comically large, but she did as she was told. I shifted, trying to decide where to even begin. "I need to weed these beds and then check on the hops." I gestured toward the arch of the cattle panel that had long vines of hops vining up and over the top.

The breeze was gentle and the sun warmed my skin. Sloane wasted no time kneeling in the grass and gently examining the plants. "Anything in between the plants can go, right?"

I nodded. "You got it."

Seeing Sloane on her knees in front of me was a fresh hell I wasn't expecting. Instead of staring at her, slack jawed and drooling, I rounded the bed and kneeled across the corner from her. My fingertips brushed across the pepper plants, checking the leaves and making note of the fresh flower buds that were emerging.

"So I recognize the pepper plants. What else is here?" Sloane plucked weeds from beds, but the too-long fingers of my gloves were getting in her way. After only a minute, she ditched them and plopped the discarded gloves beside her.

"This bed has compact plants—mostly hot peppers like jalapeño and Hungarian wax, but also some herbs. Sage, basil, rosemary." I shrugged. "That kind of thing."

Sloane plucked a small piece of rosemary and held it to her nose. "Mmm. I love fresh rosemary." She flicked the stem with her finger. "Kind of smells like you."

I harrumphed, and she laughed before pointing to another raised garden bed a few feet over. "What's growing in there?"

I looked and said, "Yarrow, lavender. That pinkish one is heather." I pointed along a manicured section at the far side of the yard. "Over there are some juniper bushes, and

I've got some pie pumpkin vines trailing along the edge— the long vines act as a bit of insulation from the summer heat."

Sloane sat back on her heels and sighed. "Do you have plans for all these ingredients?"

I laughed. "Not really. Random ideas mostly."

Sloane continued to dig in the dirt beside me. "Tell me some of them."

I glanced up, heat blooming across my chest as I took in the slight sheen of sweat forming at her hairline. "Share my secrets? Why, so you can steal them?"

Her laugh was quick and bright. "Please. In a matter of days I'll be half owner of the brewery. I am allowed to know *all* of your secrets."

Heat prickled at the base of my skull. "Am I allowed to know yours?"

"My secrets?" She lifted an eyebrow with a sly smile. "Of course not."

I laughed and turned my hat backward. "Figures."

Sloane continued to garden with a smile on her face as I watched her from the corner of my eye. A slow, creeping sense of ease washed over my shoulders. Something about digging in the dirt with a gorgeous woman in the summer sun was a balm for my soul. I cleared my throat and decided to offer a small piece of myself to her. "That mint in those containers over there?"

I used my hand spade to point at the large pots between the craggy juniper bushes. "MJ's name is Julep, but over time it morphed into Mint Julep, and then just settled into MJ. I was thinking up a beer that's kind of a play on a mint julep cocktail." I shrugged, listening to how dumb it sounded when I actually admitted it aloud.

Sloane clicked her tongue and swiped a hand across her

cheek, leaving behind a small streak of dirt. "Aww . . . that is so sweet. I bet she'll love it."

"She doesn't know," I quietly admitted.

Sloane's big hazel eyes blinked up at me. "I won't ruin the surprise. I promise."

Without thinking, I reached up and brushed my thumb across the peak of her cheekbone, swiping away the dirt. "You couldn't ruin anything."

Sloane swallowed hard but didn't move away from my touch. My thumb danced across her cheek, and I let my fingertips trail down the side of her neck, where her pulse hummed.

Memories of the kiss we had shared in the district court judge's office flooded back—the feel of my body wrapped around her in that ridiculous room only hours before.

Sloane's hand followed mine, wiping away the small patch of dirt that had been on her delicate skin. "Thanks."

I cleared my throat, desperate to rein in the flurry of emotions I was having.

Sloane's small laugh tittered between us. "You better be careful, Abel. You keep looking at me like that, and I might forget this whole marriage is supposed to be fake."

The air around us was hot and sticky. My heart hammered beneath my ribs. "It might not all be fake."

Color rose in her cheeks. The secluded yard hid us from the rest of the world as I nearly unraveled before her.

"Oh yeah?" she finally asked, barely allowing her eyes to catch on mine. "Which parts?"

I huffed a laugh. Typical Sloane to call me out on it. I swallowed hard and gathered the guts to share yet another secret.

I allowed my eyes to steady on her beautiful face. "The

part when I kissed you in the courthouse. I meant every second of that fucking kiss."

Without hesitation, Sloane reached forward, gripping my shirt in her fist as she yanked. My mouth slammed to hers. Across the corner of the garden bed I stretched to meet her. We both rose to our knees, damning the edge of the garden bed between us. My hand gripped the back of her neck. Her tits pressed against my chest as my lips pressed against her.

She opened for me with a soft moan, and I swiped my tongue across hers. Our kiss was sweet and warm and wet. My cock surged and pressed against the fly of my jeans. Sloane's hands gripped at my T-shirt as I wound my free hand to her back and pressed her into me.

Her kiss was hot and hungry. Our tongues teased and tasted as they slid over one another. My hand moved from her back to her ass, and I squeezed.

Sloane broke the kiss, leaned back, sat on her heels, and panted. "Holy fuck."

My eyes darted away, ashamed that I had finally snapped and gone too far. "I'm sorry."

She laughed and my eyes flew to hers. "Sorry? Well, I'm not." Her hand brushed across her collarbone as she steadied her breath. "Holy hell that was hot."

Sloane stood, slightly dazed from our kiss. She looked down at me, still planted on my knees, and plucked my hat from my head before planting it on her own. "I need a lemonade or a shot of whiskey or something. Want one?"

Without waiting for my reply, she sauntered up the back steps and disappeared into the house.

EIGHTEEN

SLOANE

I'D KISSED the fuck out of Abel, and my body was screaming to do it again. I'd wanted to do that ever since this morning when I'd awoken to find his rock-hard cock pressed against my ass as he cuddled me.

Did I pretend to be sleeping and *ever so slightly* rock my hips back to feel more of it?

You're goddamned right I did.

Bracing my hands against the counter, I hung my head and tried to breathe.

What in the actual hell?

Sure, I had been tempted and grabbed him for a kiss, but *damn*. Abel made no qualms about taking control and absolutely owning me with that kiss. My clit thrummed and my nipples ached with unmet need.

My legs scissored, and I internally groaned once I realized I would definitely be needing a new pair of panties after that kiss. I glanced out the window to see Abel hunched over the garden bed and violently pulling weeds. He sat back with a sigh and raked his fingers through his tousled hair.

I giggled and pulled his hat from my head to fan myself. It was his own damn fault. How was I supposed to resist a sweaty, well-built man gardening in a backward hat? I was given zero choice and certainly did not regret that kiss.

My only hesitation was that, given the fucked-up state of my life, sleeping with Abel was for sure a terrible idea.

But oh my god it would be fun to roll around in the dirt with him.

I glanced at the kitchen clock and sighed. The twins would be finished with day camp in less than an hour, and the last thing they needed was to be confused about what was happening between Abel and me. As far as they knew, Abel and I were just friends.

I toyed with my lip and let myself daydream about his using all that masculine energy to thrust inside me while calling me his wife. My pussy fluttered and I gripped the counter.

Seriously. Get your shit together, Sloane.

I grabbed a glass from the cabinet before moving to the sink and guzzling lukewarm tap water. It did nothing to quell the fire that was building in my gut. I wanted Abel. Like, *really* wanted him.

Logically, I knew sex would only complicate and confuse things, but it had been so long, and living in his home was harder than I could have imagined. It was torture enough that he was quietly domestic and kind to my kids, but he smelled so damn good to boot.

When movement caught my eye, I jumped into action. Before Abel could enter the house, I set my glass into the sink and headed down the hall toward the primary bedroom.

I waved and called over my shoulder. "I need to get the kids in a bit. I'm taking a quick shower to clean up."

Hurrying, I escaped behind the bedroom door and tucked myself away in the en suite bathroom. Beyond the french doors, the garden mocked me. I pulled the drapes closed and turned on the water in the steam shower.

Stripping off my shorts and tee, I then pulled my hair free from its ponytail. With the water barely warm, I stepped under the spray and sighed.

In the safety of the shower, I let myself wonder what kind of lover Abel might be. Tender or rough? Demanding or slow and teasing? What would it feel like to have a man his size hover over me? I knew he was a good kisser and could only imagine what it would feel like to have his hands on me.

My nipples pinched into sharp points as I closed my eyes and pretended my touch was his.

God, I bet his dick is huge.

My fingertips brushed across my breasts and down my belly. I imagined Abel on his knees before me, licking his way up my leg to my thigh. His calloused hands would spread me open before his mouth teased and sampled. My breath came out in sharp pants as my fingers slipped between my legs, wishing they were his. I had no doubts Abel King would be a steadfast and thorough lover.

I bit back a moan as I brought myself to the edge with thoughts of his mouth and hands all over me. The moment I imagined how my pussy would stretch around his dick, I was done for.

Water flowed over my shoulders in rivulets as I came to the memory of our kiss and the picture of him easing his cock deep inside me.

Despite the steam and heat from the shower, I was more keyed up than ever. Pushing aside all thoughts of Abel, I made quick work of washing up and slipping into a fresh pair of jean shorts and a T-shirt.

Quietly, I slipped out of the house and into my car. I had the time it took to make a quick trip to and from town to figure out how the hell I was going to maintain a responsible, working friendship with Abel when every cell in my body wanted to be reckless.

"This is . . . not my favorite." Tillie pushed the roasted broccoli to the side as my eyes went wide.

"Tillie . . ." I attempted to employ my best *mom look* as I stared at her.

She shrugged. "I'm not saying it's not okay. I just don't like this dinner. It's not my favorite."

Beside me, Abel had his elbows on the table, hunched over his plate. I noticed that he ate quickly and without looking up. I wondered if his hunched shoulders were a protective way he'd learned to eat in a prison hall.

My heart ached for him.

He quietly chuckled and shook his head at Tillie's assessment of his cooking as I gritted through my teeth. "Thank you, Till, for that unsolicited opinion. Please remember that Abel took his time to make this dinner for us, and we should be appreciative of that fact."

She pushed a forkful of Rice-A-Roni around her plate as her face soured. "Sorry." She looked glumly at her plate.

"It's all right," Abel said, dismissing her blunt assessment of his cooking. "I've never really cooked for other people, so I'm still learning."

Abel sat back and looked around the dinner table.

I went to touch his arm, to reassure him, but he moved

it. Instead of making contact, I dropped my hand and fiddled with the hem of my shorts.

"Where did you learn how to cook?" Ben finally asked.

"Um . . ." Abel shifted in his seat as his eyes flicked to mine. "Actually I learned when I was . . ."

Both children looked at him with wide, innocent eyes. It was clear to me Abel was avoiding having to say where he learned to cook, when it dawned on me.

Prison.

My brain scrambled to cover for him when he cleared his throat and crossed his arms. "This guy named Willie Hampton taught me. He was an incredible cook. He could make really good food from the worst ingredients."

"I think I'd like to know how to cook one day." Ben looked hopefully at Abel, and my heart squeezed.

Abel nodded once, and my heart tripped over itself. "I can show you sometime."

Clearing the emotion from my throat, I saw my daughter's eyes brighten, and she looked at Abel. "What's the best part of your day, Abel?"

He looked between her and me.

I smiled and explained, "This is something we do at the dinner table. We all share one bright spot in our day. If you don't want to or—"

His jaw flexed, and he wiped his mouth with a napkin. "No, it's okay. I've got one." His attention was on my daughter. "Uh, I guess the best part of my day was gardening with your mom."

A prickly thrill danced up my back. The "best part of the day" conversation was something I'd done since the kids could talk. It was my way of forcing myself to remain positive and think about all the *good* in our lives. It wasn't easy sharing that with an outsider.

"Now you have to ask someone." Tillie beamed at Abel with an encouraging nod.

"Ben, what was the best part of your day?" Abel looked at my son and patiently waited for him to answer.

Ben pushed around the breaded pork chop before dunking it into apple sauce and stuffing it into his mouth. Around the food, he answered, "Probably that my friend Drew from library camp also likes the same video game and said he would friend me on there. What's the best part of your day, Mom?"

"That's exciting." I smiled. "The best part of my day was . . ."

Waking up next to Abel.

Watching him walk to the bathroom with a monster *dangling between his legs.*

Seeing him with a backward hat.

Kissing him.

Thinking of him while I was in the shower.

"Probably having this dinner with the four of us. This is so peaceful, and it makes me really happy."

Abel's dark eyes assessed me as though he was searching for the lie. He wouldn't find it. I'd always dreamed of a cozy home where family dinners were the norm. It may be Abel's home, but for now it was a sanctuary where I had quickly found myself at ease.

I smiled at my daughter. "What's the best part of your day, Tillie?"

"Abbey from camp and I decided that we're going to put on a play about space dinosaurs, and I am going to make the costumes!"

"Space dinosaurs." I laughed. "I love that idea."

The rest of dinner ebbed and flowed with a comfortable familiarity. Abel mostly stayed quiet and allowed my rambunctious twins to talk over him—and each other—as they shared about their friends, camp, and the rest of their day.

Once supper was over and the kids cleared their plates, I shooed them out of the kitchen and to the backyard with a promise of ice-cream sandwiches later if they got along.

Abel's knuckles gently tapped on the table before he rose and started clearing his plate.

I noted the misplaced gesture, curious if that was something meaningful, when I went to stop him from cleaning up. "Don't you dare." I swatted my hand toward him. "You cooked . . . *again*. I can do dishes."

He picked up his plate. "I don't mind."

I planted my hands on my hips. "Well, I do. I already feel like a little bit of a freeloader living in your house, sleeping in your bed. I won't have you cooking and cleaning."

Abel stepped forward, his chest brushing against my arm as he towered over me. His large hand grabbed the plate in mine. "I said I've got it."

The deep timbre of his voice rumbled over me, sending sparks frolicking down to my core.

I swallowed hard. "Yes, boss."

Though I hadn't meant for my voice to sound quite so breathy, I reveled in the way his body reacted. His deep eyes moved over my face and down to my mouth. I knew he was thinking about the kiss we had shared, and I loved that I wasn't the only one completely upended by it.

With a twirl, I extracted myself from his magnetic pull and moved toward the cupboard. "Wine?"

Hands full, he gestured toward the pantry. "There's some in there."

I laughed. "I know. I bought it. Would you like a glass?"

He shook his head. "I don't really drink."

Holding the bottle, I paused. "You own a brewery."

Quietly, he walked toward me. In the drawer he dug out a wine bottle opener and pulled the bottle from my hands. Without a word, he opened it and set it aside before moving back to the sink.

Abel began rinsing and stacking the dishes, the ring on his left hand glinting in the water. "I like the process of making beer and figuring out new ways to incorporate ingredients, but outside of the occasional drink, I just . . . don't, usually."

"Fair enough." I shrugged. "Is that why you didn't want to drink the Wedded Bliss?"

He nodded, and a tiny hit of relief surged through me—at least it wasn't the fact he was with *me* that had him avoiding the aphrodisiac-laced beverage.

I eyed him as he moved through the space. His frame was bulky and commanding, but he moved with the ease of a jungle cat. Every move was calculated and graceful.

Once I sipped the wine, I closed my eyes and let its flavors wash over my tongue. I thought back to our last few days together. The stress of meeting his father seemed to melt away, and despite the awkward fake honeymoon, we'd survived and had a little fun. I had zero intention of mentioning the kiss we'd shared, especially when he didn't seem to want to talk about it either.

The evening morphed into a cozy family dinner with my kids, and I didn't need to mess it up by talking about how I'd practically jumped him in the garden. "I know family dinners weren't really your thing growing up. Thanks for humoring me."

He stopped to look up at me. "I enjoy it. Kids are simple. Pure. I like hearing about their day."

I swirled my wine in the glass. "It's funny, Sylvie has told me a lot about your dad, but being in his office the other day was . . ." I allowed a dramatic shiver to shake my shoulders. "Gave me the heebie-jeebies."

Abel huffed a laugh through his nose. "Heebie-jeebies? Is that a technical term?" For a moment he stared down at the counter. "You're safer keeping your distance."

My brows furrowed. "What is that supposed to mean? Safer?"

Abel sighed and leaned against the smooth quartz of the countertop. "Has Sylvie told you much about our mother?"

I kept my eyes on him and only offered the tiniest shake of my head. Sylvie was very private and kept a lot to herself. She hadn't ever seemed like she wanted to talk about it, so I let it be. Now curiosity was eating me alive.

"My mother left my father and us when I was eleven. I was the oldest, so I have a lot of memories of her. JP and MJ hardly knew her."

It was hard to find my voice. The dim lighting in the kitchen felt as though we were in a cocoon of trust, and I didn't want to break it. "What was she like?"

I expected him to share that she was callous. Detached. How else could a mother get up and leave her six children like that? It was unfathomable to me.

"She was everything." The pain was evident in his voice as he stared at the ground. "My mother had the best laugh. She tried to find the good in every situation—even when my father was home and . . ." His eyes lifted to meet mine, and he shrugged. "Somehow it was always harder when he was home."

I pressed my lips together, unable to find the words to comfort him. "I understand."

Abel dragged a hand through his dark hair. "I don't know why I'm telling you this."

I smiled at him and took a sip of wine. "Because I'm your wife."

He nodded slowly and sucked in a breath. "Then I should probably tell you I have a private investigator looking into the disappearance of my mother."

I straightened. "Disappearance? I thought she chose to leave."

Tension clenched in his jaw. "My father said she left—that was always the story he told everyone. We have no proof she did it on her own accord."

My stomach whooshed, dread pooling in my gut. "Do you think something happened to her?"

"I do." He wrung his hands together. "Bug found a box of some of her things tucked away in the basement—things she wouldn't have left without—and none of it adds up. I've got a PI doing some digging."

Disappearing mothers and frightening exes and fake husbands. It was a lot to process, but standing in front of me was a man being open and vulnerable.

It was as though logic was irrelevant and everything inside of me was unraveling while Abel held that string and tugged.

I stepped forward and tipped my chin to look at him. "Thank you."

He frowned and looked down at me. "For what?"

My hand slid up his stomach to rest over his heart. It clunked beneath my palm. "Being open. Honest."

His fingers curled around my hip, and I melted into him. Before I could talk myself out of it, I raised onto my tiptoes. My hand found the side of his face, and I brushed my lips against the corner of his mouth.

"Is this a bad idea?" I whispered in the soft glow of the kitchen.

His fingers flexed on my hip. "I—"

A shrill shriek from the backyard broke the spell, and I quickly retreated to see that the kids were okay. Electricity and tension were at an all-time high, and I struggled to get my breath under control as I left Abel standing in the kitchen.

This is going to be a very long night.

NINETEEN

ABEL

I STOOD in the dimly lit kitchen, thankful that Ben had cried out when Tillie put him in a headlock. Sloane navigated the sibling quarrel with a firm but loving hand. She was a badass and certainly didn't need my help. Still, I quietly operated in the background, cleaning up from dinner and tidying the rest of the house to keep myself busy.

I opted to stay behind when the kids begged to take their ice-cream sandwiches and go for a walk. I needed space to breathe. Space away from Sloane and how her mere presence was making me question *everything*.

I didn't need her sunny smiles or passionate kisses or fiery looks from across a garden.

What I needed was her money.

A sick, oily feeling settled in my stomach.

Was I using her? Was I the same kind of man my father had become?

My track record was far from spotless, and I had made so many mistakes, but I couldn't imagine ever hurting her.

I'd die first.

Sloane and I had set boundaries in place, but we were

both all too eager to stomp all over them the second we had a moment alone. Thankfully, with two seven-year-olds, quiet moments alone were few and far between.

I made myself scarce the rest of the evening by watering the garden and tidying the mulch around the beds. When the soft glow from the bathroom illuminated the backyard, I safely retreated into the house, assuming Sloane was getting herself ready for bed.

From the hall closet, I pulled down the pillow and blanket I'd been using and tossed it on the couch. My back was already fucking killing me from the cramped sleeping quarters, but I had slept on worse.

The house was quiet when I removed my clothes, slipped into a pair of gray sweatpants, and stretched out on the couch. I stared at the ceiling and focused on my breathing.

In for four. Hold. Out for four.

My shoulders bunched tight as I shifted on the lumpy sofa. My feet dangled off the end as I tried to adjust and get comfortable. With my arms crossed, I stared at the ceiling.

I'd give my left nut for that fucking caveman bed right now.

Closing my eyes, I tried again.

In for four. Hold. Out for four.

A creak in a hallway floorboard snagged my attention. My eyes whipped open, but I stilled, listening to whoever might be coming down the hallway.

Soft footsteps padded down the hall toward the main living space. I strained to hear anything over my own heart-beat. In the darkness, I barely made out Sloane's shape as she came into view.

Even in the darkness, I could see her skin illuminated by the moonlight that shone through the back windows.

Dressed in only an oversize T-shirt, Sloane's smooth legs were on full display. Her hair was up in a messy knot, and my eyes devoured the smooth lines of her skin, from the top of her thighs to her bare feet.

She paused just after exiting the hallway. Her shoulders turned toward me. My eyes slammed shut and I leveled my breathing. I could hear her footsteps getting closer as I pretended to be asleep. Her soft breathing was just above me. For a moment I wasn't sure if I should open my eyes or wait to see what she was up to.

Slowly, I felt the blanket tug up my chest as Sloane rearranged it on top of me. My feet popped out of the bottom, and Sloane's soft chuckle was a lance to my ribs. With a gentle sigh, she let the blanket slip from her fingertips.

Before she could leave, I snagged her wrist.

Her soft gasp filled the living room as I gently thumbed the thin skin of her wrist.

My eyes moved to hers. "Thank you."

She smiled down at me, not pulling away from my touch. Her voice was soft and low. "You look ridiculous on this couch, and that blanket isn't big enough."

I continued to stroke her arm. "I make do." In the moonlight, Sloane was luminous. "Can't sleep?"

A single dimple winked in the low lighting. "Thirsty."

I shifted, hoisting myself to sitting as she took a step back. Bare-chested, I adjusted my sweatpants before standing and tossing the blanket onto the couch. Sloane's chin tipped up to hold my stare.

"Can I ask you something?" Her shy eyes were downcast.

"Anything."

She finally looked at me. "At dinner when you were

finished . . . Why did you knock on the table before you got up?"

I studied her face. "I didn't realize I did that." With a soft sigh, I continued, "Old habit—something I learned in prison. You knock to let others know you're just getting up to leave and not starting shit. It's also a sign of respect."

Her features went soft and she smiled. "Thank you."

As we stood in silence, I let my eyes wander and soak up the sight of her. Messy hair, sleepy eyes, and her T-shirt —*my* T-shirt—stopping dangerously high on her thighs.

I smirked. "Nice shirt."

Sloane gently tugged at the hem, which barely covered her ass. Her lips rolled. "Busted."

Shaking my head, I laughed, stifling it so I wouldn't wake the kids. I moved past her toward the kitchen. She followed as I pulled down a glass and filled it with ice water. Sliding the cup toward her, I reveled in her beauty.

Her slim fingers surrounding the glass, she held it to her lips and took a sip. "You shouldn't look at me like that."

I swallowed hard. "Like what?"

I knew *exactly* how I was looking at her.

Sloane slid the glass away, then leaned on the island. "Like you're up to no good."

I let my smile spread, slow and easy. "I'm just looking at my wife and wondering how the hell I got here."

Her hand fidgeted with a stray piece of hair. Goose bumps prickled on her forearm, and I watched as her nipples peaked beneath the loose fabric of my shirt.

I moved forward. "You like that, don't you?" I stepped into her space, keeping my voice low. "When I call you my wife?"

She swallowed and lifted her chin with a glint of mischief in her eyes. "I might."

Heat thrummed beneath my skin. My cock ached to feel her. Wanting Sloane the way I did was delusional, but there was no denying that she was standing right in front of me—a willing participant in whatever was developing between us.

It's wrong. So wrong.

But what if I want to be selfish? To have her for a little while?

My fingertips played with the hemline of the T-shirt. Her soft thighs moved under my touch. "You're my wife, Sloane." I drew circles as I indulged in the smoothness of her skin. "You're mine for as long as I can keep you."

Sloane's head tipped back and her legs scissored. I wanted nothing more than to drop to my knees to see just what waited beneath that T-shirt. Before I could, Sloane's hands planted against my chest.

With a wicked look in her eye, she walked me backward until I was pressed against the opposite countertop. Her nails gently raked across my chest and stomach, sending chills racing through me. My dick throbbed under her touch.

Never breaking eye contact, Sloane started to drop to her knees.

I gripped her elbow to stop her. "What are you doing?"

"I told you"—she licked her lips—"I am going to be the best wife you've ever had."

Sloane sank to her knees. Her fingertips toyed with the hemline of my sweatpants as my breaths sawed in and out of me. I glanced down the hallway. "The kids?"

Sloane smiled up at me, her dimples deepening. "Fast asleep. If you hear one coming, just tap me on the head or something." She quietly giggled as if that was the funniest thing she'd ever heard herself say.

My jaw clenched, and I hissed when she pulled the gray tie of my pants with her teeth. Her eyes were full of mischief as she took her time, rubbing my aching cock through the material.

Yes. Fuck, yes.

My eyes nearly rolled to the back of my head. I shifted my weight, widening my hips and settling into my stance. Achingly slowly, Sloane freed my cock.

For a moment she stared before whispering, "Holy shit."

I gripped the base, squeezing. "We don't have to do anything." It nearly killed me to get the words out, but I meant them.

Sloane's hands ran over my hips. "I want it. It's just . . . *wow*. I figured it would be big after I saw you walking to the bathroom this morning, but . . ." She rubbed her palms together, warming them. "This is going to take a team effort."

A spark of humor warmed my chest. Sloane was so different from me, never taking herself or life too seriously. I ached for her lightness. Her positivity.

A tingle ran through me when she leaned in, brushing her lips across the side of my cock. She wrapped one hand around the base of my erection and brushed the crown across her lips. Her mouth opened, and I watched intently as she dragged her tongue under the head.

My dick twitched as her mouth closed over me, teasing the tip. She moaned as she leaned in, taking more of me. The vibration rattled through me. Sloane stroked and sucked as I watched my cock move in and out of her mouth. Her lips stretched around me, and I had to focus to keep from pumping hard into her. She used her hands to keep a firm grip at my base and set a torturous pace. Wet with her spit, Sloane took me as deeply as she could, and the tip of my cock hit the back of her throat.

A rumbling moan seeped out of me.

From her knees, Sloane looked up at me with a smile. "Shh." She licked her lower lip and lifted an eyebrow. "If we're interrupted, then I have to stop."

I growled down at her. "Then don't be so fucking good at this."

With a satisfied chuckle, Sloane pulled me back into her mouth. One hand dipped between my legs, teasing my balls as she sucked and stroked. My hands gripped the counter so tightly I thought it might break. I was dangerously close to coming as she worked my cock with her hands and mouth.

Too soon.

It would be over too soon, and I wanted this moment to last.

My fingertips tangled in her hair as I palmed her face. "Hey."

Her doe eyes looked up at me. Her lips stretched around my cock as she kept me in her mouth.

"I want more," I said.

She released me. "More?"

I lifted her by the elbow and pressed her body into mine, holding her close. In her ear, I whispered, "I want you to ride my face while you choke on my cock. I want you to do it all while you stifle your screams into my pillow."

She pulled back to look at me, my hard cock pressed between us.

"Yes, boss." She took one step back, moving a hand across her chest and disappearing below the hemline of her shirt. "But if you want this, you'll have to come and get it."

Her eyebrow lifted as she took two steps back. With a

playful look, she lifted the bottom of her shirt, flashing me the tiniest glimpse of her naked body.

With a stifled squeal, she took off running down the hallway toward the primary bedroom.

Fucking brat.

I grinned and stomped after her so I could show her how a real caveman does it.

TWENTY

I DIDN'T EVEN MAKE it halfway down the hallway before Abel's arms scooped me up from behind, flipped me, and tossed me over his shoulder.

Upside down, I covered my mouth with one hand to keep from laughing too loudly and watched as his sculpted ass moved beneath the fabric of his sweatpants.

Freaking gray sweatpants. Of course they were.

Once inside the primary bedroom, Abel quietly shut the door and clicked the lock.

It didn't matter if he'd given the room to me. Once we were inside, it was clear this was every bit his domain. Abel deposited me onto the bed with a plop, but his hands didn't leave my legs. He gripped me behind the knees and dragged me to the edge.

His tawny eyes were nearly black in the dim bedroom light. A thrill zipped through me at the dark, menacing look on his face.

Desire.

"Why do you have my T-shirt, Sloane?" His eyes roamed over my legs. He settled himself between my thighs before I could close them. I watched as he lifted the hem, exposing my bare pussy.

The cool air danced over my skin as I propped myself up on my elbows. "I needed something to sleep in."

One hand moved higher up my thigh while the other palmed his cock through his sweatpants. "Try again, wife. You have pajamas. Why did you put *my* shirt on?"

My teeth sank into my lower lip. "It smelled like you. After we kissed . . . I wanted more."

The deep rumble in his throat sent shivers up my back. "I can give you more."

His thumb moved over my pussy, spreading me open to see how wet I was for him. "But first I'm going to take what I've been dying for."

Abel sank to his knees, burying his face between my legs. He moaned like a starving man getting his first meal. Sparks shot up my back as his tongue tasted and teased.

I clenched my teeth and pressed the back of my hand across my mouth to keep from crying out.

Abel's hand reached under the T-shirt to palm my breast while his other held my thigh to stretch me open. I arched into him. My hand threaded through his hair as I tugged and bucked against his mouth.

Tension built, low and deep as he drove me closer and closer to the edge. I wanted to ride that wave, to feel his mouth and tongue as he ate my pussy and I came all over his face.

"Hey," I whispered. Abel looked up from between my legs, and I grinned. "You said I could have your cock in my mouth while I came. What gives?"

He sat back on his heels, his cock gloriously jutting up from between his legs. "Are you sure?"

I nodded and swallowed back a squeal of delight. Abel

stood as I righted myself on the bed, scooting to the far side. In one quick movement, he pushed his pants down and stepped from them.

Positioning himself on his back, Abel's frame took up the majority of the bed.

I knew it.

Anticipation and excitement raced through me as I surveyed his hard cock. He reached for me. "Get that ass up here."

I obliged, straddling him and scooting my knees back so they were at either side of his head. I leaned forward, teasing his cock with my hands. My fingertip stroked up the thick vein that ran underneath, and I couldn't wait to get my mouth on him again.

"Goddamn it, wife." Abel's tongue licked up the side of my thigh toward my pussy. "You're already dripping for me. Spread these legs so I can taste you again."

Sinking down, I pressed my pussy into his face as I sucked his cock. My shirt rode up and my nipples brushed against the soft hair on his toned stomach. I worked him with my mouth and tried to concentrate on what I was doing, but his tongue was so fucking distracting.

My legs began to quiver as Abel licked and sucked and teased. His cock filled my mouth as I stroked the base with one hand. My rhythm became erratic, my hips jerking and moving on their own as I barreled toward my orgasm.

Popping his cock from my mouth, I panted. "I'm close. I think I—"

Abel's arms clamped around my thighs, pulling me down harder against his mouth. He moaned as I finally let go. Waves crashed over me as his mouth latched to my clit. Dots of bright light flashed behind my eyelids, and I gave in to the rolling orgasm.

I went limp on top of him, panting as his hard cock stood proudly beside me. A wicked grin spread on my face, and my bones turned liquid. Gathering my strength, I lifted myself up and turned, swinging my legs over him so I was straddling his stomach.

His face glistened with my cum, and a cocky smirk played on his lips. I wiggled my ass, and his hands squeezed it.

Scooting back, I teased his cock with my pussy, letting it slide between my legs. "I still want more."

Heated desire flashed across his features before his ever-present frown returned. "I don't have a condom."

I stared, indecisions coursing between us as his cock nestled against my pussy. "I have an IUD. Are you . . . ?" There was no polite way to ask someone if they were clean. Already half-drunk on each other was probably not the best time to be thinking about it, but it needed to be said.

His intensity was fierce. "I haven't been with anyone since . . . a really long time. I've been tested."

I wasn't at all surprised. I knew he wouldn't ask, so I offered the information to him. "I've been tested too." I lifted the stolen T-shirt, pulling it over my head and dropping it on the floor. "I want you—need you—to fuck me."

My knees lifted, allowing me to rise up and line his cock up with my entrance.

"Please," I pleaded as the head of his cock barely pressed against me.

His hands flexed on my hips, holding me steady. "How am I ever supposed to say no to you?"

I grinned and spread my legs, sinking him deeper. I leaned forward to whisper in his ear. "You're not."

Slowly, Abel moved his hips upward. Despite already

coming and being primed to take him, my pussy fluttered around the stretch of his thick dick.

"That's it, baby. Sink down and let me stretch that cunt." His hands massaged my thighs as I took him.

I moaned as his words played on a loop in my head. I could never have imagined that reserved, quiet Abel was hiding a seriously skilled lover. My body tensed as I adjusted to his size.

My hips began to move, setting a pace to grind my clit against the base of his dick while he filled me. Abel plucked my aching nipples, rolling each peak and tugging gently. My head rolled back and Abel adjusted, sitting up and bracing my weight on his lap. I wound my arms around his neck, and his arms banded across my back and held me close. I rocked with him, reveling in how perfectly we fit together.

Beneath me, his hips began circling, frantically chasing his own release. I arched back, providing him a full view of my tits as I braced myself behind me on the bed. His mouth came down and laved each peak with slow strokes of his tongue.

I looked at him, one hand moving to his hair and tugging. "Come for me, Abel. I want you to fill me."

On a groan, he buried his face into my neck. With slow pulses, he gave in to his release. I wound my arms and legs around him, holding him close as he finished. He may be sullen and imposing, but I know a man who needs to be held when I see one.

I wondered if anyone had ever been soft and gentle with Abel King. For long moments, he held me in the quiet depths of his darkened bedroom.

This is going to change everything.

His fingers stroked the bumps of my spine, and I toyed with the ends of his hair.

Finally, I sat back to look at him and smiled. "What did I tell you? Best. Wife. Ever."

My silliness broke the tension and eased the intensity building between us. Abel rewarded me with a rare grin. "Best one I've ever had."

I stroked the side of his face, trying to read the emotions that flickered over his features. "I'm going to get cleaned up."

I shifted, easing off him and relishing the fact I was going to be good and sore in the morning. Disappearing into the en suite bathroom, I washed up, hoping Abel would join me and we could spend the rest of the night ignoring the fact we'd just completely changed the rules of our relationship and simply *enjoy* each other.

He didn't come in.

Instead, I walked back into the bedroom to find it cold and empty.

TWENTY-ONE

ABEL

SLOANE HAD UTTERLY ROCKED my world, and the absolute last thing I wanted to do was walk out that bedroom door. It was as though from the moment we said *I do*, my primal, lizard brain went into overdrive. My thoughts were consumed by her—anticipating her needs and finding ways to make her life easier. I was a drowning man, lost and without hope, and along came Sloane, offering a solution. She was a life raft—however temporary—and I planned to hold on to it for as long as I could.

Still, walking out was the right call.

Sloane and I hadn't defined this new phase of our relationship, but I sure as fuck didn't need her kids walking in on us and finding us naked. I may not have children, but I could venture a guess that seeing us together without having talked about it would be problematic for her. So I gathered my pride and my clothing and sneaked out the door while she was showering.

She didn't need to know that I'd also lifted the pillow to my face to get one last drag of the smell of her perfume.

That night, I'd spent hours staring at the ceiling,

recalling how peaceful she looked as she slept—dreaming about what it would feel like to be wrapped around her all night in our home.

Our home.

Fuck.

Unable to sleep, I woke with the sun and started on making Sloane and the kids breakfast.

Bleary-eyed, Tillie was the first to walk out of her bedroom and pad down the hallway. I offered a quiet good-morning nod, and she climbed up onto a stool at the kitchen island.

"Morning, Abel." She rubbed her sleepy eyes with the heel of her hand.

"Hey, Till. I'm making eggs. I hope that's okay." I plucked the cooked bacon from the skillet and let it rest on a paper towel.

"Fancy breakfast on a school day?" she asked.

I glanced at her and couldn't help but smile. The small freckles across the bridge of her nose were nearly identical to Sloane's, and one dimple was the tiniest bit deeper on one side—just like her mother's. "It's not all that fancy."

She shrugged. "It's better than Pop-Tarts. Can I have orange juice too?"

"You bet." I grabbed a cup from the cabinet and moved to the fridge to pour her a cup.

I could feel Tillie's eyes on my back as she sized me up. "You're taller than my dad."

I turned slowly, doing my best to remain calm while I navigated the minefield of a conversation regarding the twins' father. What I knew about him was limited, but based on what knowledge I did have, there was no universe in which he was ever worthy of a life with Sloane or her quirky, wonderful kids.

I shrugged. "I'm taller than a lot of people."

My comments struck Tillie as funny, because she burst into a fit of giggles. "Yeah, that's true. Ben thinks you must work out a lot to get your muscles."

I laughed and kept making breakfast, wondering when the other two might appear and save me.

Tillie's eyes focused on her breakfast instead of me. "I like living here. It made me sad that Mom had to sleep on the floor of the cabin."

The floor? Jesus Christ.

I busied my hands by stirring the eggs and tried not to think of how long Sloane had spent sleeping on a bedroom floor rather than a bed.

When they were finished, I lifted the skillet full of fluffy scrambled eggs. "Eggs?" I asked.

Tillie nodded and slid her plate forward.

I plopped a hearty scoop onto the middle.

"Bacon, too, please," she said.

I smiled and moved the plate of bacon onto the island, close to her reach. Her little eyebrows scrunched. "Abel, if we stay for a long time, will you sleep on the couch forever?"

I smirked and lifted a shoulder. "Probably."

Tillie bit into a piece of bacon and frowned. "Mom said you two are friends, and friends share things, right? Maybe you and her could share the bed."

My stomach flipped on itself. It was hard to argue with simple logic, but so far the kids were in the dark about our current arrangement and its most recent developments. "You're pretty clever. You know that, kid?"

She smiled, her cheeks full of breakfast. "You should ask her. She takes sharing very seriously."

"I'll think about it." The mere thought of openly sharing a bed with Sloane was enough to send me reeling.

Lost in thought, I barely heard Tillie's whispered words. "I really like my bedroom. If you kick us out, I think I'll miss that the most."

Without even thinking, I leaned forward, certain to catch her eye and hold her attention. "Hey." I kept my voice soft, but serious. "That won't ever happen. You're always welcome here. No matter what."

Tillie stared as if she was trying to figure out whether I was simply placating her. When I didn't break eye contact, she held up her hand with her little pinkie sticking out. "Do you promise?"

Without hesitation, I hooked my pinkie with hers. "I promise to never kick you out."

A grin spread across her freckled face, and my heart clanged against my ribs.

"Something smells good." Sloane's warm voice floated into the kitchen, and I tensed, straightening and busying myself with clearing the mess. I knew as soon as I turned to see her, my heart would stop in my chest.

"Abel is making eggs and bacon and orange juice," Tillie proudly said.

"Ohh, fancy." Sloane hummed.

"That's what I said!" Tillie shouted with a giggle.

I turned and was hit with the full force of Sloane's beauty. Her hair was mussed from sleep, and she was wearing another one of my T-shirts, this time with a pair of her pajama shorts on the bottom. My heart fumbled over itself.

Sloane moved behind the island, letting her hand drag across my back as she slid into the space next to me. "Can I help?"

I shook my head. "I haven't seen Ben this morning. I've got the rest handled."

Sloane turned to her daughter. "Tillie, can you go make sure Ben is awake?" The little girl hopped off the stool and eagerly started down the hallway. "Kindly!"

Sloane turned to me. "So you left pretty quickly last night."

My jaw worked. She didn't sound mad, more playful, and it caught me off guard. I'd expected hurt and disappointment but not humor. "I figured you didn't want to confuse the kids."

She hummed and plucked a piece of bacon off the plate. "Confuse the kids or confuse yourself?"

I pinned her with a glare. *How did she know? Was she aware of the mental gymnastics I'd been performing all night?*

She raised her hands and grinned around a mouthful of bacon. "I was just asking." I grumbled and she only laughed. "Let me worry about the kids. I'll talk to them soon."

My eyes went wide. If the kids knew about our arrangement, everything would be out in the open.

I cleared the tightness in my throat. "Tillie suggested you share the bed. You know . . . to be a good friend and all."

Sloane grinned. "Is that so?"

I lifted a shoulder. "She says you take sharing very seriously."

Sloane hummed around a bite of bacon. "I'll have to keep that in mind."

Nerves simmered under my skin as my knee bounced. "How much are you—with the kids, what are you . . . ?"

She laughed again and patted my back. "Relax. I've got this. They'll know enough to not be confused, but I'm not going to tell them everything. Some secrets I'm keeping for myself." She gave my butt a quick squeeze and I jumped. Sloane stole another piece of bacon and walked back toward her bedroom before she shot a hot look over her shoulder.

I am completely fucked.

≈

AT THE BREWERY my sister Sylvie's head popped into my office, and she scowled. "You're avoiding me, and I want to know why."

I pushed back from my desk. "I'm not avoiding you."

I was absolutely avoiding her.

"Bullshit." She moved into the doorway with my nephew Gus propped on her hip. She rubbed her nose on his. "Shh. Don't tell your dad I said that in front of you."

The toddler cooed and tugged a strand of her blond hair.

I gestured toward my nephew. "Bringing the kid into this? That's unfair."

She laughed and handed him to me across the desk before crossing her arms. "I had to do something. It's been a week since the Wild Iris, and you're ignoring my texts. Royal even said he hasn't seen you skulking around town."

I frowned. "I don't skulk."

She shot me a plain look. "Sure you don't."

"Whatever." I distracted myself by bouncing Gus on my lap. "I've been busy."

"Ha!" She barked a laugh at the ceiling. "I know . . . you married my best friend, remember? Then moved her and the kids into your house. I need details."

"Isn't that what girl talk is for?" When Gus reached for a pen, I tucked it away, earning me a frustrated squeal.

Her arms were still crossed. "Maybe I want to know your intentions, that's all."

"Intentions?" I frowned at her. "You know what this is . . . my house is a temporary safe space for her and the twins while the Robinson place is rebuilt. The marriage helped her get access to her money, and she's investing in the brewery. That's it." The empty words were leaden in my gut.

"That's it, huh?" Her eyebrow raised to her hairline, and I knew that she knew it was total bullshit. "Is that why you're wearing a wedding band?"

I sighed and bounced Gus. "Things are . . . complicated. I'm just trying to keep it together."

She rounded my desk and held out her arms for her son. I hoisted him up. "Maybe don't try so hard, okay? Sometimes it's okay to just . . . be. Let things unfold naturally."

I let her words sink in and nodded. "I will try to take that advice."

Sylvie propped Gus back onto her hip. "Besides, I'm not here to see you. I'm kidnapping Sloane."

I opened my palms and shot her a *what the fuck?* look. "She's working." My sister didn't need to know that I liked having Sloane around and I didn't like the fact our time at the brewery would be cut short if she left.

Sylvie rolled her eyes. "Figure it out. She needs a new dress."

"Dress?" My brows pitched down. "For what?"

Sylvie sighed. "The Bluebirds caught wind of the impromptu wedding. They're throwing Sloane a belated wedding shower."

I nearly choked on my own tongue. The Bluebird Book Club was an unofficial organization of Outtatowner's meddling women. Ladies from all families—including Kings and Sullivans—got together to gossip and plot. I suspected they'd never discussed a single book. "A what?"

Sylvie shrugged. "It couldn't be helped. Aunt Bug and I decided it was best to not blow your cover and just go with it. This is happening."

My heart raced. "Does Sloane know?"

"That's why I'm here. I'm breaking the news." She hugged Gus close again. "His cuteness works on her too."

My nephew giggled and blew spit bubbles. I sat back, listening to the chair groan under my weight.

"Will you be gone long?" I asked.

She shrugged. "As long as it takes, I guess. Why? Keeping tabs on your girl?"

I rolled my eyes despite the fact that was exactly what I was doing. "The twins have some kind of library camp thing. Just making sure they're taken care of."

Sylvie laughed. "Bug is handling that. She and Bax are going to do a little grandchild trade-off. It's taken care of, I promise."

I grumbled, annoyed that my simple logic of using the twins as an excuse hadn't worked. With a frustrated sigh, I reached behind me and pulled out my wallet.

Resigned, I deposited several large bills onto my desk. "Don't let her pay for the dress herself. You don't have to tell her it's from me, but"—I gestured toward the money— "there you go."

Sylvie plucked the bills off the desk with a huge smile. "I knew there was a teddy bear hiding in there somewhere."

"There's not," I grumbled.

My sister turned toward the door. "If you say so. Find a different server. I'm stealing her."

With a dismissive wave I watched my sister walk away. Behind my desk, I sighed, but couldn't help the small tug at the corner of my mouth as I thought of Sylvie and Sloane having a fun afternoon on my dime.

Thankfully, the afternoon was slow, and the only impact of Sloane's absence was my crappy mood. Somewhere along the way I started to half enjoy her quippy one-liners and witty banter. Without it, the brewery felt like it was all business. It lacked her sunshine and warmth.

Rather than call someone in for her, I covered her shift myself. Forcing myself out from behind the bar, I took orders, bused tables, and genuinely tried to not scare anyone off by my mere presence, of which I was marginally successful.

When my phone buzzed in my pocket and the name John Cannon flashed across the screen, I slipped into a nearby storeroom closet to take the call.

"This is Abel."

"Abel. John Cannon. Do you have a minute?" John Cannon was a man I had hired to look into the disappearance of my mother. My siblings and I had had too many unanswered questions after my brother Whip and Bug had discovered a discarded box of her belongings. The mystery only deepened when John uncovered that there was no record of Maryann King after she left.

Nothing at all.

Unease rolled over me. "I do. What do you have for me?"

"Well." John sighed. "I don't think you're going to like this." He huffed a breath. "Shit, I don't even know how to explain it."

My stomach twisted. "Just say it."

"There is still no paper trail for a Maryann King. I haven't given up, but it's looking like a dead end. I'm looking into her extended family and seeing if there are any contacts willing to confirm she'd possibly changed her identity."

I nodded. "That seems reasonable."

John exhaled. "Well, that's not the news. Abel, there is no marriage certificate for Russell and Maryann King. There is, however, a certificate of marriage for Russell King to a woman named Elizabeth Peake."

My mind raced and struggled to succinctly connect the dots. "So what are you saying? Are you telling me that my father cheated on my mother and then married his mistress?"

"No, Abel," John continued carefully. "The marriage of Russell and Elizabeth is dated before the acknowledged marriage of him and Maryann. What I am saying is that it seems likely that your mother *was* the mistress."

The small closet closed around me. A whoosh of blood between my ears was deafening. "That's impossible. My parents were married, and it was no secret. They had six kids together."

John sighed. "I understand, and I'm looking into it. Unfortunately, having a second family isn't something that—"

"Whoa, wait. What?" I interrupted. "Second family? What the hell are you talking about?"

"Well, that's the other piece I uncovered. Russell and Elizabeth have children."

My knees wobbled. If what John was saying was true, my father was not only unfaithful to my mother, but he had a whole different family our entire lives.

Memories of long business trips, absent weekends, and flippant remarks throughout the years flashed through my mind.

How was this possible? How could we have not known?

My throat was tight. "Thanks, John. I—I have to process this."

"I understand. Do you want me to keep digging or is this enough?" he asked.

Anger churned. "No. Find out everything about this other family . . . and don't stop looking for my mother."

"You got it." John ended the call and I stared into nothingness.

For nearly thirty-six years, the life I had known was a lie. Knowing my father the way I did, it was easy to believe he was capable of this. Everything in his life was constructed around optics—being the best, looking as though you have it all. It wasn't a stretch to think he'd carefully crafted that life in order to feed his own ego.

My mother leaving him would have been a devastating blow to that ego. Dread pulled at my insides.

What other lies was my father hiding?

TWENTY-TWO

SLOANE

"WHAT ABOUT THIS ONE?" Sylvie held out the long skirt of an expensive-looking white chiffon dress on a wooden hanger.

After kidnapping me, I rode with Sylvie as she dropped her son off with her husband, Duke, and we'd made our way to a dress boutique in Kalamazoo. It was then she broke the news that the meddlesome biddies in town had negotiated a hostile takeover and demanded a wedding shower.

I had always been curious about the secretive group of women. It seemed that the Bluebirds were the heartbeat of Outtatowner and were wholly unaffected by the long-standing feud between the King and Sullivan families. I was sure they'd never take credit, but I also suspected they were the reason behind the lack of gossip regarding my best friend and her new husband.

But still . . . a wedding shower?

I had already done the expensive and draining rigama-role of show-stopping wedding events. My shower had been the social event of the season, according to my then-step-mother. Nothing about it was my own.

My fingers brushed along the soft fabrics that ranged from stark white to creamy beiges.

Everything screamed demure bridal. Nothing was flirty and fun or . . . me.

I tucked my lip between my teeth. "Maybe this was a bad idea."

"Are you kidding?" Sylvie's face looked disgusted. "We are having a shopping day to find you the perfect dress. One hundred percent funded by your husband." Sylvie's eyebrows bounced suggestively on her forehead.

"Yes, he is technically my husband, but you know the truth. It's business." I distracted myself by sliding dresses across the hanger bar.

"Mm-hmm," Sylvie said. "And you're telling me that business is the reason you moved in with him? Business is the reason you're walking around like you've floated in on a cloud? Business that Abel actually cracked a real smile when I talked to him?" She shook her head. "You can try and peddle that bullshit to someone else, but I don't buy it. I know you both too well."

I turned and looked at my friend, unable to lie. "Fine. I think I'm catching feelings."

Her eyes went wide and she scurried over to me. "I knew it! Did something happen on your honeymoon? This is so exciting!"

I shook my head. "No, I assure you . . . the honeymoon was very PG." I glanced away as my thoughts wandered to the very not-PG evening we shared.

"But it's not exciting. It's terrible. This is not supposed to be messy. Business and nothing more. But . . ." I buried my face in my hands. "I can't believe I'm telling you this, but I have no one else to tell, and it's literally killing me." I peeked out from behind my hands. "We had sex."

A noise I am certain had never before left the stoic Sylvie King echoed through the boutique, drawing the attention of nearby customers. "Are you serious? Oh. My. God."

I laughed, confirming it was true.

Sylvie was bubbling with energy. "Look, I don't want the details because that's my brother and—gross—but I am really, really happy for you!"

She shook my shoulders and a laugh escaped me. "Thank you. I'm happy too. But, like, also confused? I don't know what this means, if it'll happen again, what exactly I should tell the kids, if he likes me, too, or what. It's all very chaotic up here." I gestured wildly at my head.

There weren't words to accurately describe the toil of emotions rolling through me at any given moment. It was clear Tillie already suspected something was happening between Abel and me, but even I couldn't quite pinpoint what was developing between us.

What would happen once the brewery was acquired and the farmhouse rebuilt? The thought of staying married was ridiculous, but anytime I allowed myself to think of life after Abel and I called it quits, my stomach tightened and I wanted to vomit.

How had this all gotten so messy so quickly?

Sylvie's hands squeezed my shoulders in reassurance. "You'll figure it out. You always do. In the meantime, can I make a suggestion?"

I looked her in the eye and nodded, pleading for the right answers.

"Take it as it comes. Abe's been through a lot and doesn't ever open up to people. If he has, in any capacity, opened up to you, it means he trusts you. If he really is catching feelings, too, that's a big deal. No matter how this pans out, I know that you'll be fine, because you're strong and resilient and a badass. He may not look it, but Abel is much more fragile. Just . . . be careful with his heart, okay?"

A lump lodged in my throat. I never imagined I would be the one responsible for protecting Abel's heart, and that responsibility felt massive. "Okay," I squeaked out, and it was all I could manage.

"Good. Thank you." My best friend smiled at me. "One more thing . . . you're going to have to break the news to him that he's expected to show up at the shower."

I squawked. "What?"

Sylvie's laugh filled the boutique, and she raised her hands. "Hey, don't shoot the messenger. Aunt Bug told me he needs to be there, and I am certainly not going to be the one to tell him that."

"Well, why do I have to tell him?" I crossed my arms like a petulant child.

She grinned and shook her head. "He's your husband."

I chewed my lip. Abel was not going to be happy about this.

Damn it.

"Fair enough," I grumbled. "I'll tell him tonight."

Sylvie came up behind me and gave my shoulders a quick squeeze. "Thank you. Now let's find you something that screams *I'm a hot wife* so he doesn't stay mad at you."

Sylvie's attention was drawn to a row of short white dresses nearby. I moved with her, hoping to ignore the ache that nestled itself into my chest.

"How about this one?" With wide, hopeful eyes, Sylvie held out the perfect dress.

It was a white mini dress in a fit and flare style that nipped in at the waist and flared out with a short tulle skirt. The top had a plunging neckline and had large, loose bows to tie the straps together. Small pearls along the bodice and skirt added a touch of romance and femininity.

The dress was an absolute showstopper.

Excited, I smiled and eagerly nodded and headed for the dressing room.

Once I stepped into the party dress, I stared at the woman looking back at me from the mirror. Sure, it was me, but she was somehow different.

I ran my hands across the delicate fabric. It fit perfectly and was a stark contrast to the sensible jeans and sweaters I'd adopted since becoming a single mom. I may have experienced luxury growing up, but making it on my own with two amazing kids relying on me was no easy feat.

Escaping life with Jared meant leaving everything I knew behind. I had never regretted it—not once. Still, standing in a bridal suite with a pretty white dress on, I felt like a little girl playing dress-up.

With Abel, I got to be a brand-new version of me. The version where my kids were the center of the universe, and he never questioned that. Instead, he acted as though pretending to be a partner in our day-to-day lives was the easiest thing in the world. He accepted my children, accepted me, without question.

Sure, Abel and I agreed that being husband and wife was nothing more than a business arrangement, but it was downright scary how much I was starting to like being his wife.

Later that afternoon, I'd gotten a text from Granddad that the pickup of Ben and Tillie from Bug had gone smoothly. They planned to get supper together, and I was eager to hug my babies.

Pulling down the secluded driveway to the Robinson property was eerie. It no longer felt like home. Instead, I drove past the burned-out shell of the farmhouse and relived the familiar ache of sadness and loss.

It was a very real possibility that Jared had either arranged for someone to burn down the farmhouse or done the dirty work himself. There had been no further sign of him, but I hadn't let my guard down. Not when I had my two kids to worry about.

Pulling up to the cabin, I noted the excessive number of security cameras and chuckled. Apparently when Abel committed to something, he went all in.

Without knocking I opened the cabin door and entered. Ben, Tillie, and Granddad were sitting around the table with Uno cards in their hands. I paused, surprised to see Bug King sitting with them.

"Oh, hey, Bug." I waved.

She smiled and nodded. "Sloane." Then she triumphantly placed a wild card down. "That's four, Bax."

My granddad grinned at Bug and winked. "Ruthless. Just the way I like 'em."

Wait. What is happening? Is he . . . flirting?

"Uh . . ." I moved deeper into the room. "Hey, chickens. Having fun?"

Tillie nodded, a smear of rogue chocolate still staining the corner of her mouth. "Granddad invited Ms. Bug to get hot dogs and ice cream down at the café. Then we came here and she is dominating at Uno."

"Yeah, she's not letting him win like you do," Ben chimed in.

A tittering laugh escaped me as my grandfather

frowned in my direction. I smiled brightly. "Great. I'll get comfy. Deal me in to the next round?"

Ben scooted in his chair and patted the spot beside him. "Sit with me, Mama."

Affection bloomed in my chest as I ruffled his hair and dropped a kiss on top of his head. "I'll sit right here." I took the open chair next to Ben and leaned toward him. "That way you can't look at my cards like the little cheat you are!"

Ben laughed and dramatically pretended to peek over at me. I surveyed my grandfather. He looked younger and more content than I'd ever seen him. Moving out had been the right call—the man needed his privacy, and I was right to assume that a little distance from me and the children meant he had to step outside his comfort zone and be a tiny bit more social.

Apparently that included socializing with Bug King. I secretly looked at her and wondered about the mysterious matriarch of the King family. Sylvie adored her, and I'd never heard an ill word spoken about her. She was known to be a bit tough and no-nonsense, but there was no question that she was revered in Outtatowner.

She appeared to be a few years younger than my grand-dad. Her face had aged gracefully, and strands of silver were beautifully incorporated into her soft brown hair. Her eyes were Kings'—a myriad of darks and tans—but in the presence of my little family, they were expressive and kind.

After two rounds of Uno, the kids begged to play outside. I was nervous to let them go alone, but Granddad reassured me that Abel had done more than enough to make sure the cabin was "safer than Fort Knox." I watched as Granddad fussed over Bug, offering her coffee and a few cookies, to which she obliged.

While he brewed the coffee, I eyed Bug carefully.

"Sylvie questioned my intentions on Abel's behalf today, but now I'm wondering if I don't need to do the same with you."

Bug laughed and fluffed her hair with a dismissive flick of her wrist. "Why, I don't have a clue what you're talking about."

My lips pursed as I hid my amusement. "Mm-hmm."

Bug lifted her shoulder. "I've known your grandfather for a very long time. Bax and I went to school together, though he was a few years older."

From across the small kitchen, Granddad whistled. "So you're . . . friends?"

Bug's eyes slid to mine. "I suppose we're as much friends as you and Abel. I take it your evening at the Wild Iris went well?"

I didn't miss the slight tug at the corner of her mouth.

"Abel and I are—we're—" I cleared my throat. "You see, things—"

Shit.

Somehow Bug knew that my relationship with her nephew was changing, and given the fact he'd absolutely owned me last night, I didn't have a leg to stand on.

Bug simply lifted an eyebrow.

I smiled softly and settled on, "I'm glad Granddad has a friend."

Bug smiled. "Me too. And I'm pleasantly surprised you've been able to wear Abel down. He's suffered so much by his own hand, and it's not an easy thing for someone to get to know the real man he hides beneath the surface."

I glanced down, tingling warmth filling my chest. "That's funny. I don't think he's all that hard to figure out."

Her chin dipped slightly. "That's precisely my point. But I might suggest that whatever happens between the two of you . . . perhaps keep it close to the chest until you know for sure. For his sake."

Who was this woman? She was far too insightful to deny my growing feelings for Abel and the complications they brought. "Agreed. I would ask you to please do the same for my grandfather."

Bug smiled and offered a small nod.

My grandfather placed a small coffee cup in front of her, and I pinched the bridge of my nose to release the sting of emotion building there. "Okay, then. Can we never speak of this again?"

Confused, Granddad looked between us. "Speak of what?"

"Nothing!" Bug and I said in unison and laughed.

TWENTY-THREE

ABEL

"How many wedding showers have you ever been to?"
Sloane's question was shouted down the hallway from the
open door of her bedroom.

I looked at my charcoal-gray slacks and brown leather
shoes. My hand smoothed down the buttons of my shirt.
"Exactly zero," I answered.

Her laugh floated down the hall. "That's what I figured.
So . . . you should know that you'll be wishing you were
fishing with Granddad and the kids. These things—I don't
know . . . they can be kind of boring."

I mulled over her unexpected words. "Boring?"

Clattering noises came from the bedroom, and while I
wanted to see if she needed anything, I stayed where I was
against the kitchen island, my hands stuffed into my pockets. My thoughts drifted briefly to my mother and whether
she'd had a wedding shower, or if she knew my father had
already been married. If she were still here, would this have
been the type of thing she would attend?

None of that matters now.

Barefoot, Sloane appeared in the hallway. My heart

stopped and my thoughts evaporated. Her hand was planted against her chest, holding up a scrap of a dress. I could see it was white, with delicate bows on the shoulders, but her arms hid much of the rest of it. The short skirt landed high on her tanned thighs.

"Can you zip me up?" Sloane made it to the end of the hallway and turned around. "I tried and I can't get it."

I moved toward her. Sloane's hair was done up in a delicate knot, allowing full access to the smooth skin of her neck and shoulders. Her back was bare, the dress hanging open.

My fingers brushed against her soft skin as I worked my way down to the zipper pull. Goose bumps erupted across her skin as I took my time pulling her dress closed. When I closed the button at the top, my hands rested on her shoulders.

Sloane turned, smiling at me. "What do you think?"

Her hazel eyes shone up at me, the milky caramels and greenish browns melting together in the afternoon sunlight.

Without looking at the dress, I said, "You're perfect."

Her dimples deepened as she playfully rolled her eyes. "You didn't even look at it!"

With a laugh, Sloane stepped back and swished her hips, sending the skirt of her dress in motion. It was perfectly short, showing off her long, tanned legs. The V in the front was dangerously low, and a ripple of desire shot through me. The subtle pearls sewn onto the dress caught the sunlight and added a soft, feminine touch.

The corner of my mouth lifted. "Like I said . . . perfect."

She held up her finger. "I just have to get my heels and I'll be ready. Thanks again for doing this. Apparently the groom being at the shower is a thing now."

I shrugged. It really hadn't mattered all that much when

Sloane asked me to attend. If it made her happy, I would show up and do what she needed.

After more clatters and muttered curses from the bedroom, Sloane reappeared in pale-pink pointed-toe heels that made her legs impossibly long. Sandpaper coated my throat as my mouth went completely dry.

I stared at her and she frowned. "Are you okay?"

I shrugged. "Fine."

Her mouth twisted as if she didn't believe me. Her head tipped. "Are you sure? If this is too much, I can come up with some kind of excuse. I can—"

I shook my head to stop her. "It's not too much." I sighed. "I got news from the PI, and I think I'm still reeling from it a little."

Her hazel eyes went wide, her voice barely a whisper. "What did he say?"

I shook my head. I still couldn't believe it myself. "He didn't find out much about Mom, but he did find out some things about my father." Sloane looked at me with expectant eyes, so I continued: "Turns out Russell King isn't just a ruthless businessman. He's a liar and a cheat. He was married before my mother. Has a whole family . . . only we are the secret bastard children."

Sloane's mouth dropped into a shocked little O as her hand covered her mouth. "Abel, that's . . . oh my god."

I swallowed hard. It wasn't any easier saying it aloud. "Yeah, it's . . . a lot."

Her eyes searched mine as her questions tumbled out in rapid succession. "Did you confront him? Demand answers? What are you going to do? Does Sylvie know? Oh my god, she'll be so shocked. Did your mom know?"

Her questions were valid but only intensified the throb at the base of my skull. "There's still a lot we don't know." I frowned down at her, my eyes landing on her plush lips. "You're the first person I've told."

Her eyes softened. "Oh."

"Listen, I don't really want to think about any of that right now. Today is about putting on a happy face for the Bluebirds. They really want to celebrate you, and you should let them."

"Are you sure?"

Fuck, why did she have to be so pretty?

"I'm sure." I nodded with confidence. "If we're late, I'm sure one of the Bluebirds is going to come pounding on the door in search of us. We should probably get going before we skip over fashionably late and are just *late* late."

A tendril of soft brown hair slipped from her updo. She sighed and flipped it away, but it dropped right back into place. "I still can't believe we're doing this."

I clasped my hands in front of me. "It's part of the show, right? Making people believe this is real?"

She swallowed and nodded. "Yeah." Seconds stretched between us as we stared at one another. Finally, Sloane gently cleared her throat. "Do you think we should . . . practice?"

Flashes of Sloane's skin, dewy and slicked with sweat, as my cock pumped into her raced through my mind. "Practice?"

She shrugged. "People expect us to be comfortable around each other. We are married, after all." Her nose scrunched. "I don't know . . . don't you think it will be weird to kiss in front of everyone?"

I frowned. I hadn't thought about having to kiss Sloane in public. So far, outside of the actual ceremony at the courthouse, any affection between Sloane and me had been very,

very private. Touching her—kissing her—in public seemed extremely dangerous.

I managed only a weak, noncommittal shoulder jerk.

Sloane exhaled. "What if we try once? Right now. Just to make sure we don't seem awkward around each other."

My blood hummed. "You want me to kiss you right now?"

Her tongue darted out, wetting her lips, and she nodded.

I stepped forward, crowding her space as she peered up at me. Even in heels, I towered over her slight frame. Testing the boundaries, I brushed the back of my fingertips down her bare arm. "Is this okay?"

"Yes." Her single-word response—throaty and full of desire—shot through me.

I clasped her hand and the wrist. "And this?" Slowly I pulled her hand to my mouth, brushing my lips across her knuckles.

She nodded. "Yes."

Dropping her hand, I traced the lines of her neck with my fingertips before encircling her throat. My hips moved forward, pressing into her as my dick twitched behind my zipper. Sloane melted into my touch. "Can I tell you a secret?"

Her throat moved beneath my hand, and she nodded, her eyelashes fluttering down as she closed her eyes.

I leaned forward, my lips brushing against the shell of her ear. "I don't think I will have any issues kissing my wife."

Before she could respond, I pulled her mouth to mine. She opened for me with a soft moan, allowing our tongues to tangle and brush against one another. My other arm wrapped around her as I deepened the kiss, delving into her mouth and savoring her. One leg moved against me, desperate and needy for more.

Had it not been for remembering how drop-dead gorgeous she looked, I would have hiked that fucking skirt up and railed her against the kitchen island without a second thought.

Sloane deserves more.

With a tug of my teeth on her lower lip, I released her before I let that kiss carry us too far. My fingertips toyed with the loose strand of brown hair as Sloane stared up at me with wide, curious eyes.

A smile formed on my lips when I realized our kiss had stunned her silent. "Do you think that will do?"

Her voice was breathy and light. "That should do it."

I popped a playful kiss on her lips and walked toward the door, feeling a unique and unfamiliar sense of lightness. "Perfect. Let's go."

WEDDING SHOWERS WERE a fascinating study in female relationships. While the Bluebirds had organized it, women from all over town were present. I knew Sloane didn't have family outside of her grandfather Bax, but you would never have known that.

Bug had opened the King family estate to host the afternoon garden party. Sloane had informed me that the bride and groom were supposed to arrive fashionably late, so by the time we drove up to the house, cars lined the driveway. A massive floral swag with white and pale-pink flowers hung at the front door, welcoming the guests.

From beyond the door, we could hear soft chatter and

laughter. Sloane stared at the massive oak front door, then turned to me. "Ready?"

I slid my hand down her arm, twining her fingers with mine. "Ready."

Together we walked into my aunt's home. Music played softly in the background, and lively chatter grew louder as we made our way through the home. At the back of the house, the solarium was nothing but warm, afternoon light streaming through floor-to-ceiling glass windows. Women spilled out of the back entrance and into the beautifully landscaped backyard. Champagne and juice stood next to a tray of fruit on decorative wood skewers.

Bug and the Bluebirds had gone all out for Sloane, and affection for my aunt rolled through me. I placed my hand on the small of Sloane's back and leaned in. "This is all for you, wife."

She smiled up at me, but the edges wobbled. "It feels like too much," she whispered as her wide eyes took in the massive floral arrangements that decorated the tables.

"I promise, for you, it's not." I lifted her hand, and my lips brushed across her knuckles.

"Aww! Aren't you two the cutest!" My little sister MJ's voice broke through the crowd as she moved between two women I didn't know. Behind her, Emily Ward, my brother Whip's girlfriend, followed.

I offered a small wave. "Hey, MJ. Emily."

MJ smiled at me but moved straight for Sloane, wrapping her in a tight hug. "Oh my god. You look so good! Sylvie told me your dress was killer, but this is amazing!" She held Sloane's hand out so she could take in her outfit. "You're like Bridal Barbie but hot!"

MJ looked at me, her eyebrows bouncing suggestively. "Nice going, bro."

Emily and Sloane embraced. I'd watched their friendship slowly bloom whenever Emily and Whip visited the brewery. She was the local librarian and the perfect complement to my younger brother's wild streak. Somehow they just fit. I wondered whether people looked at Sloane and me and thought the same thing.

I shook my head and sucked a steadying breath into my lungs.

Of course they didn't. People looked at us and wondered what in the hell Sloane saw in a monster like me.

Sloane clutched MJ's hand and allowed her to lead us into the fray. Women oohed and aahed over Sloane. Casual questions tumbled over each other—*How long had we been secretly together? When did we know there was something more between us? How did the kids take the news?*

My ears buzzed.

I found solace in Sloane's steady and sure answers.

We'd been together in secret for a long time—there was just no fighting those feelings!

We knew right away there was something special between us.

The kids are thrilled.

I moved like a wooden doll, lurking behind Sloane like some dark shadow, hoping no one would actually speak to me. I didn't want to fuck this up for her.

"Here." Sylvie came up behind me with a champagne flute. "Looks like you need this."

I grabbed the drink and downed it in one gulp. "Thanks."

Sloane was being walked out of the enclosed porch by MJ and Emily and led into the sunny backyard when she turned and caught my eye. *You okay?* she mouthed.

I smiled and nodded. Delight sparkled in her eyes, and

the joy that radiated from her made this whole circus worth it.

"Abel," my aunt called. "It's time for the first game."

Beside me, Sylvie barked out a laugh that she tried to cover with a sip of champagne as I nearly growled. "Game?"

Bug scoffed. "Yes, of course. Come on." She gestured with her hand. "Hop to."

Sylvie pushed me forward, and I begrudgingly made my way outside. Two chairs were placed in front of a semicircle of tables. Women from all over my small town sat at the tables with small plates of finger foods and champagne. Sloane sat in one of the two chairs.

The walk to the seat next to her felt like a death march. All eyes were on us, and my skin itched beneath my collar.

When I sat, Sloane leaned over. "Relax. You look like your head's about to pop off."

I didn't look at her. "Maybe it feels like it."

Her hand patted my thigh, and I warmed at her touch. My eyes lifted to hers as she smiled. "We got this." With her gentle squeeze on my leg, I relaxed into the chair.

Bug handed each of us a small dry-erase board and marker. "We're going to play a little game where we ask questions and the bride and groom answer."

Well, fuck.

Bug smiled at the eager women. "The guest with the most points at the end will win a special 'date night in' basket. It'll be a fun little game to see how well the couple knows each other."

Double fuck.

Beside me, Sloane laughed, and the soft tinkling sound helped me relax and lean into the ridiculousness of it all. If this made her happy, I could put up with the charade for her.

"First question," Bug called out. "Where did you meet?"
Easy.

I scribbled down my answer. At Bug's command, Sloane and I turned the boards to reveal our answers.

Bug looked at our answers and smiled. "If you said the brewery, give yourself a point. Next question . . . how did the proposal happen?"

My blood tingled. *Do we tell the truth? Do I make something up?*

My eyes flashed to Sloane, but she was already writing something down. Unsure what to do, I scribbled my answer: *Sloane proposed to me.*

After we turned our boards, Bug laughed, and I sagged in relief. "That's right, Sloane proposed!" A variety of swoony awws and polite claps moved through the small group of women keeping score.

I looked at Sloane and she winked.

"What is the bride's favorite color?" Bug asked.

I considered my options, my hand hesitating over the white board before scribbling the first answer that felt right. Rosy pinkish.

I turned the board over, and Sloane leaned to see my answer. Her face split into a grin, and she tipped her board so I could see.

Dusty rose.

I winked back at her, feeling more confident as the game wore on.

"Okay, here's a doozy," Bug warned. "What is the bride's shoe size?"

Without hesitation, I scribbled my answer.

Getting into the game, I found my shoulders relaxing. It didn't matter that eyes were watching us. With Sloane it didn't feel as though I was on display—it was more like I was part of the group, celebrating with people who cared for Sloane.

Questions varied from my middle name to Sloane's first job to her favorite band. I nailed them all. When Ms. Tiny was announced as the winner, she accepted her gift basket prize with a rare smile. When Ms. Mabel peered over to look at its contents, the ornery old woman snatched it from her view.

Sloane was radiant. Elegance shone through her smile and the poised manner in which she carried herself. She was warm and engaging, and I stood in awe of her.

At my side, she leaned in. "How did you know all those answers? I didn't know half of the ones about myself." She laughed.

I wound my arm around her waist, pulling her close. "I pay attention."

Her hazel eyes danced with delight as she whispered, "Best. Husband. Ever."

With a sense of ease and without an ounce of hesitation, I pulled her into me and openly kissed my wife in front of the whole damn town.

TWENTY-FOUR

SLOANE

AFTER THE WHIRLWIND of the wedding shower, I was happy to slip off my high heels and trade the elegant party dress for a cozy pair of leggings. I smiled as I slid the white dress onto a hanger and hung it in Abel's closet. My fingers toyed with a shimmery pearl, and I sighed.

It really was a great party.

Sometime during the wedding shower, I had stopped worrying about people realizing my marriage to Abel was a farce, and I simply tried to enjoy myself. Outtatowner had such an inviting way about it that it was easy to forget that it was all pretend.

With Abel beside me, I found the pretending easy.

Too easy.

"Mama! Mom! I caught a huge fish today!" Ben's voice bounced down the hallway as the front door slammed open. I cringed as the door rattled the nearby bookshelf. I was sure Abel never expected his life to be so upturned by two small children and their hot-mess mother.

"In here!" I called, pulling a cardigan around the vintage T-shirt I'd chosen.

But when they didn't come to find me, I walked into the hallway to see Ben taking Granddad's phone and shoving it in Abel's face. "Do you see how big it is?"

Abel grabbed the phone and nodded, his attention solely on my son. "Wow. That's impressive. Paw Paw Springs?"

"I caught some too!" Tillie complained.

"You did," Granddad agreed. "And, yes, I took them down to Paw Paw—the creek was hopping."

"Hey there, chickens." Loving affection warmed my chest as I watched their conversations tumble over one another. "I missed you today."

I walked up to Tillie and pulled her into a hug before ruffling Ben's hair and dropping a kiss on top.

"Your hair is so fancy." Tillie's eyes moved over my sleek chignon, which I hadn't yet undone.

My hand gently pressed against the twist. "We had a party today, and it took forever to get it right. I didn't have the heart to take it down yet."

"It's really pretty." Tillie's eyes sparkled with feminine appreciation.

I cupped my sweet, tenderhearted daughter's face. "Thanks, baby." I turned to my granddad, who was showing Abel more pictures from the day's fishing adventures. "The kids were good for you?"

Granddad scoffed. "Of course."

Ben smiled at me, uncontained energy buzzing from his every pore. "We brought a picnic, but then Granddad had candies and we got dinner and then ice cream, and he let me get a triple scoop!"

I shot my granddad a pointed glare as my son rattled like a boiling kettle from his sugar high.

"What?" His hands raised in feigned innocence. "It's the land of yes when they're with me. You know that."

Unable to argue with his grandfatherly logic, I simply gave up and changed the subject. "I got some news today. The money is officially ready to be spent. We just have to make a decision on which builders we go with to renovate the house." I toyed with the inside of my lip. "Sylvie recommended Kate and Beckett."

"Kate Sullivan?" Abel grumbled.

I knew tensions between the Sullivans and Kings had lessened since Sylvie and Duke got together, but it had never quite gone away. "I think it's Kate Miller now, but —yeah."

Abel grunted a noncommittal noise.

"I reached out to her, and she was really excited to talk about it. Given the historical nature of the farmhouse, she said they might even consider it for a spot on their show. Isn't that something?"

I still couldn't believe that Kate and Beckett Miller from the popular *Home Again* show were even considering taking on the farmhouse build. Not only was their love story incredibly hot—he was Kate's ex-boyfriend's older brother and her brother's best friend—but they'd made national headlines restoring historic homes all around Lake Michigan. I was positively giddy at the thought of them taking on the renovation.

Granddad shrugged. "Whatever you think is best."

I frowned at my grandfather. I had expected him to be more enthusiastic about rebuilding his childhood home. "Well, this is for you . . . I only want you to be happy. It's your home."

"I'm not going to live forever, Sloaney." Granddad

sighed, and a twinge of emotion pierced my chest. "You do what you think is best."

Tears stung behind my eyelids, and emotion clogged my throat.

Sensing the tension, Abel's gaze bounced between my grandfather and me. "Hey, Bax." Abel's hand landed softly on his shoulder. "Can you stay for dinner or do you have plans?"

"Oh," Granddad answered, a sly smile tugging at his lips. "Actually, I do have plans. Your aunt Bug and I are sharing a meal."

Relief flooded through me at the swift change of subject, allowing me to compose myself. If Abel was surprised that his aunt and my grandfather were getting dinner together, he didn't let it show.

"Next time, then." Abel smiled and patted Granddad's shoulder.

After a few more hugs from the kids, I walked my grandfather to the door, and we said our goodbyes.

I turned to Abel and sighed. "Thanks for the assist. I hate when he talks about not being around. Sometimes it just catches me off guard."

"I think he just likes to see you happy." Abel's shoulders always seemed to carry the weight of the world. He offered a quiet half smile. "But you're lucky, you know."

My throat felt tight. I knew enough to know that love like my granddad so freely offered me wasn't at all what Abel had experienced from his own family. Thankfully, it seemed as though his siblings were trying to stay connected despite their complicated relationships with their father.

I clasped my hands in front of me. "How do you feel about a low-key movie night? After today, I could use some downtime."

"Movie night!" Cheers erupted behind me as the kids clambered onto the couch. After fighting over the remote control and taking forever to decide what to watch, the kids settled on a fantasy adventure film about a riverboat captain in search of treasure.

Abel moved to the kitchen. "Hey, Ben. Want to learn how to make BLTs?"

My son scrambled to his feet. "What's a BLT?"

Abel looked at me and shook his head in disbelief before returning his attention to Ben. "Bacon, lettuce, and tomato sandwiches, but we can make them fun." He gestured to the sink. "Come on. Wash up and I'll show you."

I sat on the couch, fighting emotion as I watched Abel patiently speak with my rambunctious son. Together they looked through the refrigerator, pulling out options to uplevel the simple sandwiches. Ben giggled through taking our requests—Tillie wanted avocado, but no tomato, Ben chose no mayo. Abel and I wanted the works.

"Let's make a quick salad." Abel began chopping lettuce.

"Rabbit food? Gross." Ben's face twisted.

Abel laughed and continued chopping. "Trust me, kid, with the amount of bacon I'm going to put in this, you'll barely notice."

Heat spread through my chest as I remained a silent observer. Abel smiled with ease and laughed when Ben got silly. He redirected him with a firm but kind hand. Ben listened and nodded as though making a BLT was the most interesting thing in the world.

When they brought the food to the living room, I quickly reined in my emotions. Tillie and Ben sat on the floor, eating their sandwiches and some potato chips on the living room coffee table.

"What's the best part of your day, Mama?" Tillie asked me as we got settled.

I smiled. "The party was really lovely. I had fun." My eyes flicked to Abel, and I wondered if he could tell I was remembering our kiss. "What's the best part of your day, Abel?"

His eyes flicked to my mouth, and my skin tingled. He licked his lips. "Probably . . . cooking with my new sous chef. How about you, Benny?"

Ben's face split into a grin. "Definitely cooking with Abel. Or the big fish. I don't know. Can I have two best parts?"

I laughed. "You sure can." I tipped my head toward Tillie to remind Ben to ask her.

"What's the best part of your day, Till?" Ben asked.

"The picnic with Granddad. And ice cream before dinner."

I smiled at my little girl, and we all settled in to watch the movie.

I sat cross-legged on one end of the small sofa and perched my plate in my lap. Despite the playful and raucous opening theme music of the movie, I was painfully aware of Abel sitting on the opposite end of the couch.

His wide frame took up the majority of the space, his spread legs creeping over to my side. I kept my legs tucked under me and leaned into the armrest as I ate. The living room was dark, except for the flashes of light coming from the television.

When I finished, I gathered my plate, along with Ben and Tillie's discarded sandwiches. With one arm full of dishes, I reached out for Abel's plate.

He immediately started to rise when I shook my head. "I've got it. Relax."

His brows pinched down, but he settled back into the couch, and I walked toward the kitchen with a grin on my face. Abel was so quick to try to take care of everything around the house that it felt nice to be able to beat him to the punch for once. After quickly rinsing and stacking the plates in the dishwasher, I made my way back to the movie.

I stopped short when I saw Ben tucked into Abel's side. Tillie was standing in front of them. "I wanted to sit by Abel!" Her lower lip jutted out in a ferocious pout that never worked on me.

Abel looked around at the couch, and then he and Ben scooted over. "You can take this side."

Sucker.

From the sidelines, I watched as my twins cuddled Abel on the too-small couch. Tightness seized my chest. His arms spread across the back of the couch like it was the most natural thing in the world to watch a silly movie with my kids.

This is what Jared has to live without.

He may never realize it, but my ex didn't deserve their love.

Abel did. He was patient and kind and accepting of them, just as they were. A swell of happy tears threatened to spill over my lashes, and I had never been more grateful for the darkness of a living room.

"Sit here, Mama!" Ben patted the small sliver of couch where my seat used to be.

I smiled. "Are you sure there's room?"

The kids wiggled, sandwiching Abel between them. I barked a laugh at the ridiculousness of it. "If you say so."

The film was surprisingly heartwarming and fun—at least the parts I could pay attention to. Despite Ben between us, I was painfully aware of Abel's proximity. His muscular arm stretched across the back of the couch, and the warmth of his hand radiated to the back of my neck. When a well-timed jump scare happened, we all laughed, and I felt the soft brush of his fingertips at the nape of my neck.

I swallowed hard, leaning into his touch. His fingers twined with the tiny hairs that had fallen from my updo. The pads of his fingers stroked my skin until I felt as if I would burst into flames. I couldn't think—couldn't breathe —for half the movie. All I could think about was how much warmth and comfort I found in his touch.

Feeling brave, I peeked across the couch at him. His dark eyes were forward, focusing on the movie as the swash-buckling hero courageously led his team into a dangerous cave. I studied Abel's strong profile—his high cheeks, his straight nose, the stubble on his jaw.

Tingles rushed through me as I recalled the delicious scrape of that stubble across my inner thigh. His fingertips were toying with me, and my insides began to unravel. Something so simple and wonderfully domestic as a family movie with the kids hit me in the chest.

It could always be like this.

I swallowed down the ridiculous thought and spent the rest of the movie ignoring the hum of my blood whenever Abel touched me.

TWENTY-FIVE

ABEL

How was it that, even in leggings and a cardigan, Sloane was so damn pretty?

I should have kept my hands to myself, but in the cover of darkness in the living room, it felt safe to let my hands wander a bit. Her skin under my fingertips calmed me in a way I couldn't really explain. The slow, steady breathing of her kids at my side was an unexpected comfort. The twins took pure, unbridled joy in the adventures on screen, and I caught myself laughing with them at the silly puns and obvious jokes.

By the time the movie ended, Tillie was out—her mouth open and the sound of soft snores—a strong giveaway that she'd missed the entire ending of the movie.

Sloane patted Ben's back and whispered. "Okay, bud. Let's get you to bed."

Ben gave a slow, bleary-eyed blink. "I'm not tired."

The look she gave Ben was full of maternal affection. I could still remember that same look from my own mother. Sloane smiled at me over Ben's head, and my heart rolled.

It would be so easy to let myself fall for you.

She rubbed slow, patient circles on Ben's back. "I know. Let's walk that way anyway."

Sloane shifted, helping Ben to his feet. She then leaned over me, placing her hand on Tillie's shoulder.

I stopped her as I stood, careful not to jostle the sleeping girl. "It's okay. I can get her."

Sloane frowned. "Are you sure?"

I scooped up Tillie, and when she didn't seem to notice, I nodded toward the bedrooms. "After you."

Sloane guided Ben back to his room, and I quietly followed behind them. His padded footsteps flopped against the hardwoods, and I watched as he tipped forward and landed face-first on top of his bedsheets with a plop.

Sloane laughed and began to work him under the covers. I turned and carried Tillie across the few steps toward her bedroom. In the few weeks they'd been there, she'd made it her own—decorating the walls with doodles. My current favorite was a drawing of a cat with a hot dog body. It was weird and oddly cute. Something akin to pride moved through me. She was a blossoming young artist, and I wondered where she got that talent from.

With one arm, I moved her blankets out of the way and gently set her in bed. After tucking her legs beneath the covers, I made sure the blankets were right. Before I turned to leave, I looked down at her sleeping face.

She looked so much like her mom. Without thinking, I bent down and dropped a kiss on the top of her hair. I stood and turned toward the door to see Sloane leaning against the doorjamb, watching me.

Had I overstepped a boundary? Fuck. I had no right.

Nerves raced through me. "I, uh—"

"Shh." Sloane smiled. She motioned toward the hallway with her head and whispered, "Come on."

Unable to resist her, I silently followed her into the hall-way. Racked with unease, I stopped. "Sloane, I'm sorry I—"

Sloane's hand reached out and gripped my shirt, pulling me toward her. Her mouth moved over mine in a quick, chaste kiss that left me aching for more. "Shut up."

I nodded. "Yes, ma'am."

A grin spread across her face as her sultry voice filled my head. "Oh, I like that."

I moved forward, bracing one hand against the hallway wall and caging her in. "Is that right?"

Sloane licked her lips and nodded as she smoothed her hands up my chest. "I do like it. I also like that you care about my kids." Her wide eyes searched mine. "Thank you for showing them kindness and affection. I do my best, but sometimes I know it's not enough."

My hand cupped her face. "You are an incredible mother, and they're lucky to have you. I promise it's enough."

Her eyes flicked down. "Thank you."

I stayed where I was, enjoying the way her sweet perfume floated between us. My thumb brushed across her cheekbone as I committed every line and curve to memory.

I leaned down, brushing my lips across her brow, peppering soft kisses around her eye and across her cheek-bone. Every kiss was a silent promise to protect her.

Her hazel eyes slid to mine. "Abel, what are you doing?"

I took her face in my hands. "I am giving you the kind-ness and affection that you deserve." My lips brushed hers. "Is this all right?"

Her breath was like a whispered promise in the dark-ness. "It's more than all right."

My mouth crashed to hers, a plea for her to also feel whatever it was that was building inside me. Her soft moan moved through my chest. I pressed my hips against hers, and one leg hitched beside my hip. My palm grabbed her leg, grazing the outside of her thigh, and I squeezed.

I lifted Sloane, wrapping her legs around my waist. We fumbled and kissed as I made my way in the darkness toward her bedroom. Behind the closed door, I walked toward the bed and gently set her down. Sloane removed her cardigan and whipped the T-shirt over her head. Her nipples puckered beneath a sheer black bra, and my mouth watered. I slid her leggings down her thighs and deposited them on the ground beside the bed.

My world stopped when her legs spread to show off her bare pussy. I removed my shirt and palmed her breast. Sloane's head tipped back, and my mouth found the thumping pulse of her heartbeat at her neck. I licked and sucked at her pulse point as my cock hardened in my jeans.

At the edge of the bed, Sloane watched me remove my jeans and slide my black boxer briefs to the floor. My cock jutted from between my legs, hard and ready for her.

I slid my fingers into my mouth to wet them. "Look at me," I demanded.

Her eyes whipped up as I slid two fingers into her hot, wet cunt. She gasped and spread her legs wide, and her hips began to move.

I stepped between her legs, planting a hand at her chest and pressing her back into the bed. "That's it, beautiful, look at me while I warm you up."

She swallowed and shook her head. "Don't—don't call me that."

I slowly dragged my fingers in and out of her as I stroked my cock. "You don't want me to call you beautiful?"

"No, it's fine. I just . . ." Her eyes flicked away. "I want you to call me your wife." A pink blush swept across her cheeks. I fucking loved that she was shy and unsure, but still willing to tell me exactly what she needed.

I pinched her pert nipple through the flimsy fabric of her bra before gliding my hand to encircle her throat. I gently squeezed—a question.

"Yes." Sloane squirmed beneath me. "Yes, please."

I slid my fingers from her pussy and used my free hand to guide my cock to her entrance. With my hand still around her throat, I leaned down to whisper in her ear. "I will always protect you. You're mine. My wife." On *my wife* I slid into her, stretching her open and prompting a moan of pleasure to rip from her throat. I silenced it with a kiss.

My cock thickened, and her walls clamped around me. With her back on the bed, I reveled in the way her tits bounced as I pounded into her. Sloane's sleek bun nearly unraveled as I continued fucking her.

With muffled moans and stifled grunts, I pounded into her. My thighs burned and my cock ached for release, but I wouldn't quit—not until I pulled every ounce of pleasure from her. Her fingers clenched the bedsheets, her jaw clamped closed to keep from screaming out. I reached between us, briefly feeling the way my cock disappeared inside her, before using my thumb to circle her clit.

She bucked as I drew her closer and closer to the edge. My hips slapped against her as I relentlessly drove into her. Her pussy gripped tighter. "That's it. Come for me. Show your husband whose cock you can't get enough of."

Sensing she was moments away from completely falling apart, I tightened my grip on her throat, only fractionally. It was enough to send her reeling. Tiny pulses of her inner walls and quivers of her thighs were immediately followed by a rush of her cum. I pumped again, leaning my weight into her as she came on my cock. My own release pumped into her as I moaned.

Slack and smiling on the bed, Sloane hummed. I left my cock inside her, reveling in her warmth.

An entire lifetime would never be enough.

Sloane was flushed and slicked with sweat. She beamed up at me. "Thank you."

I smiled down at her, carefully examining her neck to ensure I hadn't left marks. While I certainly wouldn't have minded leaving behind evidence of whom she belonged to, Sloane didn't need the questioning looks from nosy neighbors.

I brushed my fingertips across her cheek. "You really are beautiful."

Sloane's arms stretched above her. "And you are constantly surprising me."

I slid out of her and stepped back before helping Sloane to sit up. "Surprising?"

She stood, wrapping her arms around me, and cuddled into me. My arms wound around her back, and I held her close. "You're tender."

I laughed. I had just had my hand around her throat, and she was calling me tender?

"I'm serious." Sloane laughed with me, batting at my chest. "Not gentle—thank god—but you have a tenderness. I always feel safe with you."

I peered down at her, brushing away the strand of hair that covered her eye. "You are safe with me. Always."

Sloane grabbed my hand and led me to the bathroom. When she bypassed the shower, I paused.

Sloane pointed at the claw-foot bathtub and smirked. "I'm still not convinced you fit in this thing. Care to prove me wrong?"

I smiled. "I'd love to."

After scrounging up some bath salts and lighting a candle, I filled the tub with hot water, and the bathroom quickly filled with steam. I slipped into the bath first, nearly taking up the entire thing as Sloane covered her laugh with the back of one hand.

I playfully rolled my eyes and held out my hand to her. "Get your ass in here."

I let the hot water soak into me as I relaxed against the porcelain. Sloane was right, of course. I barely fit, and my knees popped above the surface of the water. Despite the close quarters, Sloane leaned her back on my front, and I held her. Using a loofah, I scrubbed her back and shoulders while I listened to her talk. She shared about drama at the brewery between servers that I had no idea was happening, how she worried about her granddad, and her excitement over the farmhouse build.

She never seemed to mind that my responses were a mix of nods and grunts and hums. She never once asked me to change or open up or be better for her. Only, she didn't realize that for her, I would do it.

Determined to show her, after washing and conditioning her hair, I wrapped my arms around her and held her once more. I rested my chin on her shoulder. "I noticed Tillie is a really good artist. Does she come by that naturally?"

Sloane laughed. "Well, she doesn't get it from me, that much I can assure you."

I let a water droplet fall from my fingertip onto her shoulder and watched as it slid down her arm and disappeared into the hot water. "She's talented. I've been reaching out to local artists to design some new labels, so I have seen a lot of drawings lately. I think, especially at her age, she's got skill."

Sloane considered. "Maybe I need to enroll her in some art classes or something . . . now that I have the money."

I chuckled. "Now that you're a rich lady, you can do whatever you want."

My joke didn't seem to land, and Sloane grew quiet. In the small tub, she maneuvered to face me. "The money won't change me. I'm still the same person."

I studied her face, curious as to where this was coming from. "I know that."

Her arms rested on the top of mine, and she looked me in the eye. "I'm serious. Nothing's changed."

I only managed a nod.

Nothing's changed? Are you fucking kidding me?

Everything has changed.

TWENTY-SIX

SLOANE

THE EARLY SUMMER sun heated my shoulders as I walked across the blackened shell of what used to be my granddad's living room. Taking it all in was surprisingly cathartic. After all the times I'd driven past the shell of our former safe haven, I had learned to ignore it. I had shoved down the fear and the heartache. Now there was no ignoring the acrid smell of burned plastic and wood and the hint of rot after the home had been exposed to the elements.

We all need a fresh start.

"Be careful of your footing," Beckett Miller warned me and his wife, Kate, as we surveyed the property. Much of the debris had been cleared during the investigation, and only a few walls were still upright.

I nodded and carefully stepped over a burned-up lump of something. "The fire department and police cleared the scene, but it's kind of an explore-at-your-own-risk situation."

My toe kicked a partially metal frame that used to contain a picture of me holding the twins. My stomach soured.

"The assessment from the structural engineer came

back." Based on Beckett's soft tone, I assumed it wasn't good news. "Unfortunately, the home is going to have to be considered a total loss." He looked at me with sad eyes. "I'm sorry, Sloane."

I swallowed past the lump in my throat. I wasn't really surprised by the news, but I'd still held out a shred of hope. "I understand."

Kate pointed to a far wall that had remained standing despite the fire. "What about the brick?"

Beckett nodded. "That's our silver lining. If we take on the project, I believe there are several aspects of the original structure that we can use in a new build." Excitement built in his eyes as he gestured toward a small table outside on the lawn, and we followed him out. "I dug into the archives at the Remington County Historical Association."

Once we reached the table, Beckett fingered through a few sheets of paper, bringing forward several black-and-white photos. He pointed at a picture of my granddad's farmhouse, only it looked slightly different. "It was an impressive home. For the time, it would have been a gorgeous estate."

Kate sighed, her finger sweeping across the covered porch that wrapped around the building. "Look at that porch. It wraps all the way around for a double entrance. And the scallop details on the roof fascia paired with the wood-slat soffit? Stunning."

I looked closely at the photograph. "The porch wasn't as big. It had two smaller staircases to the entrances." I pointed to the small crumbling, burned staircase that remained. "That led to a little vestibule or something, and the other led to the kitchen."

Kate nodded. "It was common in the eighties and nineties to separate everything. Split levels were all the rage at that time and, unfortunately, older homes like these were hacked apart to fit the aesthetic. I'm sure the interior was similarly remodeled."

"Here's what I'm thinking." Beckett's evident enthusiasm captured our attention. "We have a real opportunity to return this home to its former glory. While we will never be able to give you back the house that is gone, we can provide a home that feels as though it was built in the eighteen hundreds—only with updated touches and modern conveniences. Kate and I will work to incorporate any salvageable parts of the original house, but create your family something that is completely new. Yours. It will be something that will stand the test of time for future generations."

I held my breath as his words sank in. I looked out to the burned remains of the farmhouse. The idea that anyone could take something so damaged—so ruined—and see past the rubble to the beauty at its core was arresting. He may not have realized it, but it was the perfect parallel to my own life and what I was desperately trying to do for my children.

There was still a chance to take bits and pieces of my past and rebuild them into something magical—something better than I could have ever hoped for.

Kate gripped her husband's arm. It was clear they were both excited about the prospect of taking on this job. I took a split second to check in with my gut and grinned.

I stuck my hand out between them. "Mr. and Mrs. Miller . . . you're hired!"

Kate grabbed my hand and pulled me into a hug with a delighted squeal. "I am so excited about this! I have so many ideas."

Tears pricked my eyes. If it weren't for Abel agreeing to

marry me, I could never have accessed my trust fund. I knew I had to find a way to make it up to him—to make the lie worth it in the end.

This is really happening.

I glanced across the yard. The cabin was barely visible down the path and through the trees, but my heart ached. It was going to take work to pick up the pieces after the fire, but I could do this for my granddad and prove to myself that Jared could knock me down, but I would always stand back up.

Beckett began shuffling the paperwork on the table as he packed to leave. "If it's official, I can start drafting plans."

Kate wrapped her arm around my shoulder, and my heart clunked. "So, Sloane, how do you feel about being on television?"

∽

ABEL

You're late for work.

Am I fired?

Yes.

Fantastic. My boss was the WORST.

That's not what you told him last night.

I GRINNED down at my phone and scrambled through Abel's house to find my keys and purse. He'd known my meeting with the Millers might make me late for my shift, but it still made my tummy flutter that he cared enough to keep tabs on me.

Maybe it meant that he missed me. I missed him too.

We were still waiting on JP to draw up the paperwork for the brewery acquisition, and I knew Abel was getting antsy. Neither of us knew why his brother was dragging his feet with the deal. Most days, I didn't let it bother me, because it meant more time in our little bubble pretending.

Nothing's changed.

It had been weeks since those words slipped past my lips, and I still regretted them. Sure, what I had meant was that going from broke and desperate to a literal trust fund baby didn't change who I was on the inside. The immediate hurt that had flashed across Abel's face haunted me. In the heat of the moment, he'd stuffed it down, but there was no denying that it had been there.

Since then, I was still too chickenshit to admit that I was falling in love with my husband. After the deal went through and the brewery was his, there was no need to continue tying himself to me. Once our agreement was satisfied, I didn't want him to feel guilt or shame or beholden to me in any way.

Still, I didn't know how I was going to ever let him go.

Flying through the house, I put those thoughts on a shelf and would have to deal with them later. I was already late. I breezed past the table and into the kitchen. Abel and I had spent another night tangled in the bedsheets, and my ass was dragging. A coffee to go was the only way I was going to make it through my afternoon shift at the brewery without falling asleep in someone's beer.

I yanked open the cabinet and pulled down a ceramic travel mug and lid. I made quick work of dumping in too much creamer and popping in a new pod of coffee before pressing the button to start the brew. Hurrying down the hallway, I had planned to check my makeup one last time when something in the hall bathroom caught my attention.

I stopped, facing forward, unable to make myself look into the bathroom. I swallowed hard and turned my head. My vision narrowed and a whooshing sound filled my ears, my heart thundering. Breaths sawed in and out of me as I stared at the open shower curtain.

Isn't it better to have them open? You never know if someone's hiding behind it.

The hair on my neck stood on end, and my fingertips tingled as I listened to the silence of the empty house. I stepped forward, my eyes never leaving the portion of the tub still covered by the shower curtain. I walked into the bathroom, my pulse thrumming at the base of my neck. My ears pricked, but I heard nothing. My eyes scanned the tub. I prayed it was empty and that my imagination was simply running wild.

When I reached the tub, I reached my hand out and gripped the shower curtain, clamping my teeth together as I checked to find the tub empty. The scrape of metal across the bar shrieked as I yanked the curtain closed.

Surely one of the kids had left it open after their showers last night, and I simply hadn't noticed. Kids did that shit all the time.

Right?

Unease rolled through me. Suddenly my safe haven, with its large windows and long backyard, felt isolated yet exposed.

Secluded.

Forgetting my coffee, I dashed toward the unlocked front door, then threw it open and yanked it closed behind me. I fumbled with my keys to unlock my car, and I raced toward it at lightning speed. The early-afternoon sun beat down on me as I tugged on my seat belt and peeled out of the driveway.

In the rearview, Abel's sweet little ranch faded into the background. By the time I hit Main Street, my breaths had evened out, and I had almost convinced myself I was imagining things. Surely there was no way Jared would have somehow entered Abel's house and then left the shower curtain open just to mess with me.

It was ridiculous.

Still, nerves simmered under my skin for the rest of the afternoon. I dropped a glass, got orders wrong, and searched the faces of our customers—all without being able to shake the feeling I was being watched.

Dark clouds seemed to hang over Abel's head as he grumbled behind the bar, and it assured me I was doing a shit job of holding myself together. I kept myself busy with customers and avoided him as best as I could.

Before I could sneak away to the employee bathroom, Abel found me in the back hall. "You okay?"

I looked around. "Me?"

He stared at me with a blank look. Of course he meant me. "Oh, I'm good. Just a weird day, I think."

Softness overtook his grumpy features. "Is it about the farmhouse?"

I offered a noncommittal hum.

I wasn't ready to tell him that my ex may or may not have been in his house. I still wasn't convinced it wasn't simply my mind playing tricks on me or a tiny case of misplaced paranoia.

Abel wrapped me in a hug. "It'll be okay. I promise."

I wanted to believe him, so I closed my eyes tight and hugged him fiercely.

"Okay, lovebirds." Reina wagged a finger in our direction. "Are you going to be disappearing on me all shift?"

I smiled. "Nope! Someone else is your problem tonight.

I'm headed out." I turned toward Abel. "Are you staying late?"

His dark eyes softened. "Meatball and I have some work in the back, but I shouldn't be too late. Wait up for me?"

I batted my lashes. "I guess." When I turned, Abel rewarded me with a smack on the ass. I yelped and laughed, our playful banter setting me at ease for the first time all afternoon.

"Oh, and Sloane?" I turned to see Abel smiling shyly and stuffing his hands into his pockets. "Give the kids a hug for me, will you?"

TWENTY-SEVEN

ABEL

It irked me that something was bothering Sloane and she hadn't yet confided in me. I'd thought we were a team—in this thing together. Instead, she'd spent her entire shift acting jumpy and out of sorts. Once the front of the brewery was running smoothly, I found solace in the back with Meatball. The heat and the loud hum of equipment calmed my nerves.

"Hey, boss." He greeted me and I grumbled, missing the way those same words rolled off Sloane's tongue. "Been a while since I've seen you back here."

I offered a noncommittal grunt as guilt worked through me. My hand gripped the back of my neck and squeezed. "I know . . . things have been . . . kind of hectic."

A grin spread across his face. "I heard you got hitched. Congratulations, man."

Meatball held out his hand, and I took it. "Thanks."

Not wanting to spend any more time than necessary talking about myself, I pointed toward one of the kettles. "Everything running smoothly back here?"

He shrugged. "Nothing we can't fix." He kicked off his desk and walked toward me.

I waited, knowing Meatball would spell it out for me so we could fix whatever issues had come up.

"Something went sideways with the mash tun on this one. When it went to the kettle, it needed a ton of water. Now look at it." He handed me a glass with a beautiful brown liquid in it. Definitely not the black coloring of the well-brewed stout we were aiming for.

"Well, fuck." I sighed and swirled the glass, noting the silky texture.

"Yep." He took the glass from me and knocked it back and exhaled. "Doesn't taste half-bad. A little underwhelming maybe."

I crossed my arms and considered our options. "All the extra water affected the coloring and diluted the flavor." I scraped a hand across my jaw. "Do the pH and gravity still look good?"

He nodded. "They're perfect."

My brain ticked through the options. "Let's try adding plum in the final stages to boost the flavor profile. Come up with a name that's a play on a brown plum porter or something."

His eyebrows creased, and his face fell. "I was going for a stout."

I nodded, empathizing with his frustration and disappointment. He was learning the hard way, like we all had to do. "Congratulations, you successfully brewed your first porter."

He shook my hand and let it roll off his shoulders. The stout was an easy save—unlike the time he forgot to sterilize and there were enough microbes from previous brews in the kettle to introduce Enterobacter. That mistake was twelve hundred dollars down the drain, but the worst of it was the fact it was in the pipes, and the entire brewhouse smelled like baby vomit for a week.

That was the thing.

In this business, if you couldn't problem-solve on your feet, you were sunk. I suppose it was part of the appeal of running a brewery—the ability to think on my feet and fix things. A true brewer would do almost anything to avoid dumping barrels.

He waved a hand in dismissal. "Maybe I should have done a single barrel."

I shook my head. We didn't have an official pilot program for new beers. Nine times out of ten we developed a recipe and let it rip at full scale. The only time I took the painstaking steps for a sample barrel was to ensure it was perfect.

Meatball followed my attention to the small batch that was nearly finished and grinned. "You are going to want to try this one. I think you're finally onto something, man."

Meatball poured a sample into a tasting glass. He passed it to me, and I peered into the amber ale. Its color was inviting, with rich and warm orange tones with hints of deep ruby. I sniffed the beer, pleased with the caramel notes that had already developed. I took a tentative sip.

My eyes flew to Meatball as he nodded and grinned, excitement dancing around the edges of his slim frame. Toasty malt flavors mingled with smooth caramel. Subtle bread-like hints shone through the sweetness of the beer.

It was fucking perfect.

I looked at the glass again, reining in my excitement. "ABV?"

Meatball looked over his notes, scribbled in a notebook. "It should be just under seven percent alcohol by volume."

I swirled the glass and cracked a tiny smile before taking another sample. "It's pretty good."

Meatball's fingertips came to his temples before he gestured toward me in disbelief. "Pretty good? Are you fucking serious? It's amazing."

I smiled down at the new beer. After seven iterations, the recipe I'd developed to perfectly capture the subtle notes of biscuit and honey, which reminded me of my wife, was a slam dunk.

"What are you going to call it?" he asked.

I watched the last bubbles of foamy carbonation cling to the sides of the glass. "Still figuring that one out."

He nodded. "Well, if we agree it's a winner, I can start bulk ordering what we need to begin large-scale production and get it on the calendar."

Everything about it felt right. "Let's do it."

I sat, hunched over my desk, with my notes for a blood orange ale I was looking forward to brewing. Plucking a few books from the shelf, I flipped through. I scribbled a few ideas regarding hops varieties or herbs I could try, and in the end decided to go with a malt that would balance out the natural bitterness of the orange pith.

My ears pricked when something felt off. I sat up and listened. Meatball had also noticed. Your body got used to the hum and thump of the equipment, but when any little thing changed, you noticed.

I listened again. "A pump turned off."

Meatball offered a salute. "On it." He pushed away from his desk to investigate.

Frustrated with my inability to focus, I tossed my pencil onto my desk and leaned back in my chair. The heels of my hands pressed into my eye sockets. So much of my life had been upended, and while I normally found solace in the precise and scientific nature of brewing and developing new recipes, I couldn't stop my mind from spinning.

I was too distracted—my thoughts bounced between whatever was bothering Sloane, the information about my mother, my father's secret life, all of it.

I dragged a hand through my hair and sighed, gaining Meatball's attention as he walked back. "I can't do this tonight."

His eyes narrowed. "Everything okay?"

Not really, no.

"Yeah." I looked away and exhaled. "I don't fucking know."

He lifted a shoulder. "All right. You know I've got it covered here. Just do what you need to do."

I nodded, grateful for my devoted employee, and pulled my phone from my pocket to send a group message to my siblings.

It was time to have a serious talk.

> We need to meet . . . all of us. I wouldn't ask if it wasn't important.

MJ

Brewery?

> Somewhere private. Royal, can we meet at your place?

One by one my siblings agreed to meet at Royal's house that evening. Unable to sit still, I gathered my things and decided to head straight to Royal's place. The walk was only about two miles out of town and, given the gorgeous sunny weather and cool breeze, I could clear my head before I faced my family.

By the time I arrived at Royal's house, the sun was

sagging low in the western sky. His neighborhood was a quiet mix between dated historical houses and newly built summer homes. His driveway was straight and tidy and led to a cobalt-blue home with a rounded arch-top front door.

I shook my head as I followed the path up to his front door. Only Royal could pull off the white picket fence and dormers—complete with flower boxes—considering their contrast to the devil-may-care, heavily inked persona my brother put out into the world. Part of me suspected he liked being a nonconformist.

I climbed the steps, and my knuckles landed on the door with heavy knocks. After a moment, Royal opened the door with a grin, stepping aside to invite me in.

"Hi, come on in. JP is already inside. Whip and the girls are on their way," he said.

I dipped my chin and slinked past him. His home was bright and clean, and for the first time, I realized how incredibly tidy he was, but chalked it up to being a bachelor who worked odd hours. My thoughts briefly flicked to the constant cleanup of snack wrappers, socks, and rogue marker caps that had started filling my own home.

One by one, my siblings arrived, with our littlest sister, MJ, arriving last. She swept into his house without knocking and immediately propped herself on top of the kitchen island.

She pointed across the space into the living room. "What's with the tripod?"

Tucked into the corner was a tall black tripod with a ring light. All eyes slanted toward Royal, who shifted in his boots and scoffed. "It's nothing. Just filming some tattoo ideas. Doodles."

"In the living room? There's not even a table to sketch on." MJ's eyes narrowed into little slits. "That's weird."

He took a breath and released it with a huff. "I use a sketch pad. The lighting is better in there. Why am I having to explain myself to you?"

I eyed him, noting the large picture windows in the kitchen and the late-day summer sun streaming in. I saw through his bullshit, but what he did in his own house was none of my business.

MJ seemed to buy his excuse, and she rolled her eyes at his impatient, brotherly tone. "Whatever." She turned to me. "So what gives, Abel? Your texts are freaking me out."

I stuffed my hands into my pockets. "I have information from John Cannon, the private investigator. It's . . . well, the information he had was disturbing."

In near silence, we stared at each other as I let the seriousness of my tone sink in.

MJ looked at each of us with soft, worried eyes. Sylvie had found her quiet confidence, and her chin was raised, ready to withstand whatever reason I had called us all together. Whip paced, seemingly unable to contain the energy that danced through him. Royal stood with his tattooed arms crossed over his chest and waited while JP's hands were tucked into the pockets of his slacks.

It wasn't often all six King siblings were in a room together. Over the years it became apparent that it was easier for my father to control us if we were isolated, even from each other.

But that's over now.

"There's news, and also a little speculation." I glanced at each of my siblings. "But I need to know we're in this together. That we can trust each other, because after tonight, things are going to change."

My eyes landed on JP, cautiously watching his reaction. His hard eyes were level, and he nodded.

"Right now it looks like our father was married before Mom. In fact, he had a family." Murmurs rippled through the group, but I forged ahead. "There is no evidence that his marriage to our mother was ever legitimate. I don't know how much Mom knew . . . but I think either she found out about his wife or maybe gave him an ultimatum of some kind. I don't know. I think Mom pushed him too far, and he made the problem go away."

Sylvie took a small step forward, horror shining in her eyes. "What do you mean, he made the problem go away?"

My gut churned. I hated having to give voice to my darkest thoughts. "I think there is a very real possibility that he killed her."

"Whoa!" JP raised his hands as various levels of shock rippled through my siblings. "Are you kidding me? That's a serious accusation, Abel. You have no evidence."

"We have her driver's license," Royal corrected.

"She wouldn't have left, not without us." Sylvie's arms wrapped around her middle. "As a mother, I can guarantee that. She would have found a way to take us with her if she'd been given a choice."

MJ looked at us, sadness weighing down her shoulders. "Maybe he didn't give her a choice. Maybe he scared her enough to make her think we were safer if she left on her own. She could still be out there."

"It's possible," I conceded. We had all experienced the wrath of my father at one point or another. Perhaps his threats were enough to force her hand.

"What do we do?" MJ asked.

Royal stepped forward. "I think we'd all be safer if we distanced ourselves from Dad. Just until we have more information and figure a few things out."

A disgusted scoff rattled the back of Sylvie's throat. "That's not a problem."

Our sister had been all but banished from the King family after her relationship with Duke Sullivan was outed. Our father couldn't fathom choosing them over us. Still, we stood behind Sylvie in silent support, much to his disgust.

"John is still tracking down a few leads. If there is any new information, you will all be the first to know," I said.

JP nodded slowly, as though he was carefully gathering his resolve. "I can reach out to Veda Bauer. When it comes to business, there's no one more skilled—or ruthless—than her. If shit hits the fan, we need to be protected. I wouldn't put it past Dad to leverage everything he has to save face. If he finds out we're going behind his back, he'll be out for blood."

We all stared at JP with a mixture of shock and awe. In all his years, he'd never spoken in opposition to our father. If anything, he was the wild card I was half-convinced would turn against us. If anyone would tip our hand to Dad, I suspected it would be him.

"How much do you think Aunt Bug knows?" MJ's sad eyes nearly gutted me.

Whip frowned and shook his head. "She doesn't know about this. All our lives Bug has put herself in his path to keep us safe. She never really wanted to work with him or take part in any of the family business, but she did it to keep us close. I can't imagine she would have known all this and not done or said anything about it. She loved our mother."

She also loved this town. Bug was as tied to Outta-towner as any of us.

Sylvie frowned. "She's his sister. She might know more than she has let on."

A smirk tugged at Royal's lips. "You don't know everything I've been up to."

Collectively, our heads whipped to Royal. He stood tall, realizing he'd spoken aloud, and cleared his throat. "What? All I am saying is that people can have secrets. It's possible Bug didn't know."

"Fair enough." Whip nodded. "For what it's worth, I can confidently say that when Bug discovered the box of Mom's things, she was visibly upset. I think she knows there was something very, very wrong about those items being left in the basement."

I mulled over that information. At some point, we'd likely have to bring our aunt into this. If not for more information, but also for her protection from our father.

"So we agree?" I looked each of my siblings in the eyes. "We're in this together until we get to the bottom of it?"

"Together," Whip said.

Royal nodded. "I'm in."

Sylvie leaned into him. "Me too."

"Yeah," JP said.

"Same." MJ was near tears, but JP patted her knee, and she offered him a watery smile.

And just like that, the King siblings found themselves unified for the first time in decades.

TWENTY-EIGHT

SLOANE

SUNSHINE BEAT down on my face as I dug my fingers into the dirt of the backyard garden bed. I swiped the sweat from my brow and squinted into the sunshine.

I couldn't imagine life getting much better than this.

It had been a week since I'd scared myself silly, thinking Jared was somewhere lurking in the shadows. I didn't have the heart to tell Abel my fears, since things with him seemed to be going so well. There was a lightness about him that I'd never seen before, and a tiny part of me hoped it came from me and the kids.

Since my mini freak-out, there had been no other signs —real or imaginary—that my ex was anywhere near Outta-towner. No one mentioned seeing him, and I hadn't gotten the creepy-crawly feeling that had prickled the base of my skull since that day with the shower curtain.

So life went on.

When I wasn't working, I spent my time discussing the farmhouse renovation and soaking in the simple, small-town life with my children. We lay on the beach, climbed impossibly high sand dunes, and ate way too much ice cream on the lighthouse pier. I always offered an out, but more often than not, Abel chose to join us. He'd even found a drive-in movie theater about twenty miles from Outtatowner, and neither Ben nor Tillie made it through the double feature. Abel held my hand the entire time.

Major swoon.

I sat back on my heels and exhaled. The ache in my shoulder was a welcome reminder of how good my body felt with a little physical labor. I smiled down at the happy little herbs and plants that swayed in the gentle breeze.

When my father was alive, all I knew was life in a bustling city. Parties and events and being seen. Abel made me feel seen in a completely different way. Sometimes he looked at me, and it seemed like whatever had blossomed between us was beautiful and exciting, and real.

The first stage of the farmhouse renovation was underway, and I had hired a lawyer to look over the proposal JP had sent us. Abel assured me that we could trust his brother, and we all wanted the paperwork signed before Russell King got wind that his children were investigating the disappearance of their mother.

I looked across the yard at Abel, who was fussing with the hops plants vining up a cattle panel.

My heart ached for all of them, but mostly for Abel. He had shared with me that he had been days away from his twelfth birthday when his mother disappeared. He knew her and loved her. Abel remembered her in a way the others didn't, and I could tell by the pinch in his shoulders that he still carried her loss with him.

He'd endured so much, but it hadn't hardened him. He didn't allow enough people in for them to see he was so much more than his brooding, towering exterior.

I watched him carefully fuss with his plants and smiled. Little by little, he'd let me in.

My phone rang beside me, causing me to jump and laugh at myself. *Outtatowner Public Library* flashed across the screen, and I noted that there was still nearly a half hour before I was due to pick up Ben and Tillie from their camp.

I tapped my phone and pressed it to my ear. "Hello?"

"Sloane? This is Emily." Her voice was a hushed whisper, and the hair on the back of my neck stood on end.

"Hey, Emily. Are the kids okay? I thought camp ended at three." I stood, dusting my dirt-caked hands across my denim shorts.

"It does. They're okay, but . . . a man tried to pick them up early, and I just had a bad feeling. Something was off and I—"

"What? Who? Emily, who picked up my children?" My voice started to rise as panic gripped my chest.

"No. I'm sorry." Emily's voice was clear and calm, but it did nothing to settle my nerves. "I wouldn't release the children to him. The man is claiming to be their father. He's pretty mad that I wouldn't let him take them. He's making a scene."

"I'm on my way!" I practically shouted into the phone as I ended the call and took off across the backyard.

By the time I'd found my purse in the house and flown out the front door, Abel was standing by the car. "What's going on?"

My mind was spinning. "I don't know. Emily called and said someone tried to pick up the kids. I think it's him." I yanked open the driver's-side door without waiting for Abel to answer.

He leaned in close, gently holding my arm as he peered down at me. "I'm going with you. I'll drive."

My heart pounded as my mind tripped over the fact I knew that with Abel's history, driving made him anxious. Still, I didn't have time to argue with him, so I rounded the car and climbed into the passenger seat.

Abel threw the car into drive and headed into town. Thankfully, there was a parking space in the lot. The tires squealed as he slammed on the brakes, then threw the car into park. With anxious steps, I marched toward the library without bothering to see whether Abel was following behind me.

"Sloane. Slow down," Abel called behind me, and I whipped to face him.

"I can handle this." *Couldn't I?*

He held up his hands in surrender. "I know. Just tell me what you need me to do."

I scanned his body. What I wanted was to curl into him and trust that the kids and I were safe. I raised my chin. "I'm going to confront whoever was trying to take my children without my permission. If it's Jared, he's getting a piece of my mind. I'll be fine."

I didn't look back as I stomped through the automatic sliding glass door. As soon as I entered the library, I followed the raised voices behind the circulation desk.

Jared immediately came into view, and my blood ran cold. His cheeks were ruddy, and he was pointing an angry finger at Bug King. She looked thoroughly unimpressed. Emily stood beside her with her chin raised and arms crossed.

I stormed toward them. "What the hell is going on?"

All three heads whipped in my direction. An oily smile spread across Jared's face. "Hi, Lolo."

I planted my hands on my hips despite the wobble in

my knees. "Don't call me that. What are you doing here, Jared?"

His hands spread as he feigned innocence. "I just wanted to see the kids"—he gestured toward the women—"but these two are keeping them under lock and key."

"I have an order of protection. You're not allowed to be here." My words were sure, but the wobble in my voice betrayed me.

Jared scoffed and raised a finger. "Correction. You have a protective order in California. It's valid in Michigan if and when you register it. But you didn't, did you, Lolo?"

Blood drained from my face. *Fuck.*

I was under the impression that my order of protection was a federal document and would automatically protect us —it was what my lawyer in California had told me.

"Look at you, Lolo." His hand flicked in my direction. "Covered in dirt and living in this shithole town. You need to be taken care of . . . you know that."

My stomach soured. Jared always had a cunning way of cutting me down and making me feel weak. I swiped my dirt-stained hands down my jean shorts, struggling to find strength in my voice.

His sickening smile widened, knowing he was already breaking me down. "I think"—he stepped forward, crowding my face as his hand wrapped around my biceps—"maybe you didn't register the protective order because, deep down, you knew I would find you, and after some time, we would work everything out. Just like last time."

His stale breath floated across my face as I tugged to free myself from his grip.

"If you want to keep that arm, I suggest you get your hands off my fucking wife." The boom of Abel's voice behind me sent shivers crawling down my back.

All eyes turned his way, and I froze. I had never seen Abel look as dark and menacing as he did standing in the library, staring at my ex-husband. Barely contained fury radiated from his pores as his fists clenched and his shoulders bunched.

If looks could kill, Jared would be a dead man.

With an aggressive flick, Jared released my arm, and I took a step back, rubbing the spot his hand had gripped me too tightly.

"You stupid bitch." Venom spewed from Jared's mouth. "I heard the rumors and thought, 'No. She wouldn't ever be that dumb.' Guess I was wrong."

"I'm calling the police." Emily already had the telephone to her ear and was dialing.

My eyes bounced between the men. Abel didn't need any trouble, and if things escalated, he could be in a seriously sticky situation, given his past. "No, it's okay."

"Mama!" Tillie's sunny voice broke through the tension as she and the rest of the campers bounded down the stairs. She ran forward but came up short when her attention landed on Jared. Her eyes went wide with fear.

Jared crouched in front of her. "Hi, Tillie." He gestured toward himself. "Come say hi to your dad, baby."

Tillie took a tentative step backward before tucking herself into Abel's side. Rage built in Jared's eyes as he stood and watched Abel's protective hand rub down Tillie's back.

Ben emerged from between the group of children Emily had herded away from the scene. I opened my arms. "Come here, Benny. It's okay."

With wooden steps and frightened eyes, Ben came to me.

"I have a right to see my children." Jared's teeth ground together as he pointed at me. "This isn't over."

Abel stepped forward, placing the twins and me behind him in one fluid movement. "Do you want to end it right now?"

I reached forward, gripping his rock-hard biceps. "Abel." My voice was a harsh whisper.

A warning.

A plea.

His nostrils flared as he tensed with indecision. "You stay away from my wife and kids. If I so much as hear a whisper of your name in this town, you're a fucking dead man."

Through the doorway, Amy King and another police officer entered. "Outtatowner Police Department. What seems to be the trouble, cousin?" Amy's sharp and assessing eyes took in the tense situation despite her casual tone.

Jared pointed a finger at Abel. "This man—a felon, mind you—just threatened my life. You heard it!" He gestured wildly around him. "You all heard it."

Amy shrugged. "I didn't hear a thing." She looked past Jared to Bug. "Did you?"

"I think Abel was just giving the man directions out of town." Bug smiled and lifted a shoulder. "At least, that's what I heard."

Amy's lips pursed. "Makes perfect sense to me." She gestured toward her partner, then looked at Jared. "If you'll come with us, sir."

Surrounded by Outtatowner residents, Jared must have known he was fucked. With fury in his eyes, he slinked forward as the other officer escorted him outside.

Amy patted Abel's shoulder. "Keep your cool, cuz. We'll take out the trash."

Abel offered only a terse nod.

"Can we go home, Mama?" Tillie's voice cracked as she looked up at me.

"Yeah." My laugh was watery as I gestured toward my dirty hands and mud-streaked thigh. "Look at me. I'm a mess."

My hands found my little boy's face. "Are you okay, Benny? I know that was unexpected."

My son's shoulders straightened. "I'm okay. I'm not afraid when Abel can keep us safe."

My heart rolled as I looked at my husband. "Okay. Let's go home."

ONCE WE WERE BACK HOME, I encouraged the kids to play in the backyard so I could slip into the bedroom to have a private conversation with their therapist. She assured me that kids are resilient and, in the end, we kept them safe and reassured them. Still, the plan was to have additional sessions later in the week to ensure the kids were coping with the newest development with my ex-husband.

My second call was to the Remington County Courthouse to register my protective order in the state of Michigan. I was still beating myself up over the oversight. I had assumed that my protective order would stretch beyond state lines. A quick Google search assured me that it would be enforced—I only had to be sure the state was aware of it.

I walked through the rest of the afternoon like a wooden doll. I hugged the kids, smiled though I felt like crying, and did everything I could to create a calm and peaceful evening. When it came to bedtime tuck-ins, I inhaled sharply, pushing past the sting in my nose and hoping to make it through without crying.

I gently knocked on Tillie's door before entering. She smiled up sweetly from beneath her covers. I returned the smile and sat next to her on the bed. When I reached my arm across her to give her a hug, I felt a hard object, hidden beneath her comforter.

"What's this?" I asked, patting the hard lump.

Tillie smiled and whispered, "I was doodling."

"Can I see?"

Tillie sat up, pulling her thick sketch pad out from under the covers. She tipped the page toward me. "It's us."

Tears filled my eyes. It was us. In the cartoon style she'd adopted lately, I could clearly make out Ben, Tillie, me, and Abel. Side by side we smiled up from her drawing—all except for Abel. She hadn't drawn him smiling, but rather perfectly captured a tiny, reluctant smirk at the corner of his mouth.

I shook my head. "You amaze me. This is so cool." My fingertips floated over the details she'd incorporated.

"Mama, are you and Abel married?"

I searched her face, but she didn't look me in the eye. Rather, her gaze was fixed on the drawing.

I exhaled. She deserved the truth. "Yes, baby. Abel and I decided to get married to help each other out. It's a little complicated . . . kind of adult things."

She shrugged. "Okay."

A small laugh bubbled in my chest. "Okay? That's it?" I noted her tiny frown. "You don't look too happy about it."

Tillie's brow furrowed. "Well . . . I just would have wanted to go too. I would have worn a party dress."

My heart swelled, and I stroked a hand down her hair. "If it makes you feel any better, I didn't wear a dress either."

She looked at me in horrified disbelief. "Why not?"

"Remember when I said that friends help each other

out? Well . . . our marriage was mostly to help each other." I swallowed past the lump that expanded in my throat.

"But you love him." Her words were so sure.

With a small laugh, I rearranged her covers. "Okay, chicken. Let's get you to bed."

Tillie scooted until she was lying back on her pillow with her covers tucked under her chin.

I kissed her nose and she smiled up at me. "He loves you, too, you know."

The simple confidence of her statement gave me pause, and I studied her heavy eyes and sleepy smile as I stroked her hair. "What makes you think that?"

Tillie didn't even hesitate. "He watches you. He watches you and he smiles."

Heat bloomed across my chest. "Huh," I choked out. "I guess I never noticed that." I tried to breathe, and it was nearly impossible.

Tillie closed her sleepy eyes and cuddled deeper into her bedsheets. "I'm glad he's our new dad. Benny is too. We already talked about it."

I stared down at my sweet little girl as though she hadn't just upended my entire universe. My hand gripped over my mouth to muffle the sob that threatened to escape.

Feeling brave, I leaned close to her ear. "Can you keep a secret?"

Her eyes widened as she nodded.

"I do love him," I whispered. "I just haven't told him yet."

Tillie grinned. "I knew it."

"Okay. Bedtime, baby." I patted her back as she finally closed her eyes and cuddled into the warm bed. Her view of the world was so simple and pure. She was too innocent to know anything about fake marriages and complicated, not-so-fake feelings.

He watches you and smiles.

A lump formed in my throat as the threat of tears tingled my nose. I watched Tillie's body relax as she drifted off to sleep, hoping that somewhere in her innocent view of love, there was a thread of truth, and he really did love me back.

TWENTY-NINE

ABEL

THE DAY NEEDED to just fucking *end*.

I rubbed a kink out of my shoulder as I looked over the cases of freshly bottled barrel-aged whiskey. The Michigan market was running without any hitches, thanks to my team and our hard work. The company's sights were set on expanding to Illinois—Chicagoland, specifically—and it took a hell of a lot of work to prime the market and be ready to distribute.

But we'd done it.

I looked over the slip and triple-checked it against the sheet on my clipboard. All seventeen pallets would be hauled out in the morning and travel from Kalamazoo to Chicago-area bars, restaurants, and liquor stores. Another twenty-five still needed to be packed, labeled, and shipped by the week's end, but at least we'd squeaked by and would have the first shipment ready by morning.

All it took was seven brutal hours of overtime.

"We got it," I called to the employees. "Let's wrap it up and get the hell out of here."

Half-hearted cheers echoed through the distribution

center. I helped shut down equipment and tidy up before flipping off the warehouse lights.

A hand landed on my shoulder. "Abe, a few of us are heading to Remy's for a beer. You in?"

Behind him a cheer rang out. "Let's fucking go!"

I shook my head. "Count me out tonight." Sandpaper coated my eyelids as I pinched the bridge of my nose. I just wanted to collect my check and go home. It was no secret that this job was simply a means to an end.

"If you say so." My faceless employee glanced at his watch and scoffed. "See you in five hours."

My teeth ground together. This job was fucking killing me.

In the parking lot, I waved over my shoulder to the men leaving the warehouse and climbed into my truck. I exhaled as the engine turned over and rumbled to life. The shine of my headlights seared into my brain, and I groaned against the sharp light.

I pulled out of the parking lot and headed toward home. The highway was desolate and eerily quiet. I yawned and adjusted in my seat. My eyes burned.

Shaking off another yawn, I rolled down the driver's-side window and took a gulp of the fresh predawn air. I glanced out the windshield into the inky sky—not a star in sight.

Highway 131 rolled past me. I stared at the lines as they morphed from four lanes to a rural two-lane highway. Every mile was closer to home. To my bed.

I eased into the seat and adjusted my grip on the wheel as music droned in the background. My tires created a rhythmic thump as I rolled down the road.

My head jerked.

A flash of light.

I yanked the wheel to the right to avoid it.

My body crumpled as I felt the weight of the impact.

The shrieking groan of twisted metal filled my ears.

I bounced as my truck swerved, and I struggled to maintain control. Finally, the front bumper slammed against the ditch, and my body flung forward at the sudden stop. Pain radiated through my shoulder, and my mind raced to catch up to what had just happened.

Lights flashed in my dashboard, and the smell of chemicals floated on the night air as plumes of thick smoke rose from beneath the hood of my truck.

With a groan, I unbuckled. My shoulder was certainly fucked—I could barely unbuckle my seat belt. It took considerable force to push the door open, and when it finally gave, I tumbled to the ground.

The dirt and gravel bit into my knees as I tried to orient myself. When I looked up, desperately trying to figure out what had happened, I saw it.

A small blue car on my side of the highway.

Upside down.

One wheel spun as I stared.

I got to one knee, then pushed myself to standing. Black tire marks marred the surface of the highway. To my right, I saw her.

A woman's body was askew in the grass. Her face tipped toward the full moon. Her long hair fanned out around her head and was already matted with blood. When I reached her, my knees buckled.

Sloane.

This isn't right. No. This isn't how it happened. Please, no.

"Sloane! Fuck. Please. No. No, no, no, no, no." Afraid to touch her, my hands hovered over her broken body.

The woman I loved stared up at me, a tear slipping from her eye. Her voice was barely a whisper as she rasped, "Please. Save them. Please."

My gut churned.

This isn't possible. This isn't how it went.

My attention swept past the overturned car and onto the outline of a small shoe poking up from the tall grass.

I raced toward the figure and fell to my knees when I realized Ben and Tillie were together, holding hands in the grass, eyes closed.

I was too late.

Again.

I did this.

Again.

An anguished cry tore through my chest. I sobbed uncontrollably as the sharp bite of metal handcuffs closed around my wrists.

"Abel!" Sloane's panicked voice slammed me into reality. I jolted—disoriented, sweaty, and confused.

Her voice softened as I scrambled to my feet. "Abel, shhh. It's okay."

I watched in confusion as Sloane crawled to her knees in the middle of the bed. I looked around, assessing my surroundings.

My house.

My bed.

My woman.

Clarity broke through my confusion as I realized the horrific scene I'd experienced was a nightmare—a reliving of the accident, only this time with Sloane and the kids. My stomach curled, and I had to breathe through the wave of nausea that tore through me.

Sloane's hazel eyes were wide, and she had her hands up. "It's okay. It's okay. I think you had a bad dream."

I surged forward with tears in my eyes and clasped her face. I took a fraction of a second to study her concerned features before my mouth crashed to hers.

My heart thundered as breaths sawed in and out of me. I pressed my forehead to hers. "You're okay. The twins are okay."

Her hand rubbed up and down the outside of my arms. "We're okay. They're asleep in their rooms. I'm here with you. You're safe."

My eyes searched hers. I held her at arm's length, looking over her body to assure myself she wasn't broken— that I hadn't harmed her.

Satisfied that it really had been a dream, I exhaled a shaky breath. "I'm so sorry."

"You're okay," Sloane reassured. "You were tossing and turning and then . . . you made this sound." She swallowed hard and shook her head. "I've never heard anything so heartbreaking."

"I'm okay." I breathed through a fresh wave of panic. "If you're okay, I'm okay."

Sloane moved out of the center of the bed and pulled back the covers. "Come on. Lay with me."

Without a word, I did as she said and slid into bed beside her.

Her fingers made gentle strokes down my arm as I stared at her precious face. "Do you want to talk about it?"

I didn't.

My throat was lined with hot coals as I swallowed. "It was the accident. Sometimes I dream about it, only . . . only this time it was different. Instead of the mother and her son, it was you and the kids."

Her face pinched. "Oh, Abel. I'm so sorry." Her fingers stroked the sides of my face, and I closed my eyes. "I promise we're okay. We're safe with you."

I wanted to believe it. I needed to believe that I could keep Sloane and Ben and Tillie safe from harm. I couldn't lose control—that was when everything went to shit, but my past was haunting us in more ways than one. First the nightmare, but also with Jared.

My chest ached. "I'm worried," I finally admitted.

"About what?"

"He knows—about my conviction. He made an offhand comment about it in the library. He was already pissed about our relationship, but what if he uses my past to—"

"Shh. It's okay." Sloane's eyes bore into mine without wavering. "It doesn't matter. I promise."

Her words were sure, but worry gnawed at my gut. Jared didn't appear like the kind of man to let things slide. He reminded me of my father in that way—willing to do whatever it took to win.

My arms wrapped around her frame, pulling her into me. I buried my face in her hair and breathed her in.

I need you.

I can't let you go.

Emotion tore at me. Everything I never thought was possible was encircled in my arms. Sloane had given me everything despite the fact I didn't deserve it.

My hands moved down her back. She'd stolen another one of my T-shirts to act as pajamas, and I teased the hem. Her legs moved between mine as she moaned softly. Her soft lips pressed against my neck, and I hummed with pleasure.

I shifted, moving Sloane beneath me so I could see her. Feel her.

With my weight pressing her into the mattress, I stared down at her. Her soft hair fanned around her head as she peered up at me.

My hand slid down her side, molding to her every curve. My cock thickened as I pressed my hips into her. I moved the shirt up and over her head, leaving her bare beneath me. Her skin glowed in the soft moonlight. "You are radiant."

My fingertips barely brushed across her belly and down her thigh. Her hips tipped up, silently pleading for more. "Abel."

My heart clanged as I memorized every hill and valley of her body, every place I wanted to disappear to explore. I cupped her breast, gently squeezing as her nipple pebbled beneath my palm. I worked my way up, achingly slowly. I freed my cock and let the heat of her pussy warm me. My hard length pressed against her without entering. I throbbed against her heat, my cock begging for more.

My palm slid over her neck and gently held her face, willing her to look at me.

Her long lashes swooped down, then up as her gaze found mine. "I don't deserve this life with you. I know that . . ." Her lips parted to argue, but I forged ahead. "I don't. But I need you to know that I will fight for you. My right to happiness—the light in my soul—died on that dark highway, but somehow, you brought me back to life."

I swallowed hard and fought to find the courage to tell her exactly what I was desperately trying to convey. "I love you."

Sloane gasped as I shifted and drove into her hot, wet cunt. She clamped around me as I moved in and out of her, pistoning my hips and reveling in the way her arms and legs held me closer.

I worshipped her in every way that she deserved, bringing her to the peak before grinding my hips against her and giving her everything she needed to come. Sloane cried out and pulled me closer.

With her limbs wrapped around me, I pumped my release into her, filling her until my cum seeped past my cock and down her thigh. My heart hammered in time with hers as our chests, slicked with sweat, pressed against each other.

Sated and soaring, I lifted my weight from her and peered down at her gorgeous face. A soft smile teased her lips, and her eyes were closed. I studied my wife, adoring every freckle and pore.

A silent tear slipped past her closed lashes. My thumb darted out to sweep it away as panic tingled my spine. "Hey. Baby, why are you crying? Did I hurt you? What's going on?"

Her head jerked to the side. "Not at all. I just . . . I love you too. *A lot.*" Her eyes opened and searched mine. "I just really don't want to divorce you." Her watery laugh filled the dark room and my hold tightened.

The tender bruise of my heart throbbed as I held her. "You're my wife. If I get my way, nothing is going to change that."

My words rang true, despite the titter of uncertainty that scratched in my brain. My intuition told me that nothing in my life was meant to be this easy. This pure or simple. It was only a matter of time before the hammer swung, and my past took it all away.

THIRTY

SLOANE

Warm morning sunshine beamed through the kitchen windows. I looked across the kitchen island at Abel, who was busy plating breakfast for the kids. Ben and Tillie were sitting at the island, Tillie with her sketch pad beside her, Ben chattering away as Abel pulled slices of french toast off the griddle.

I looked down at the Abel's Brewery logo on my T-shirt and smiled. Today the ownership of Abel's Brewery would be official. By the end of the business day, Russell King would no longer control Abel's business.

We did it.

"Morning!" I chirped with a sunny smile.

"Hi, Mom." Tillie didn't look up from her sketch, and Ben continued his one-sided conversation as Abel listened.

When he turned, Abel stopped and stared.

Heat and passion flared in his eyes. I was in a simple T-shirt and black leggings, but Abel made me feel as though I was the prettiest woman he'd ever seen. A warm blush crept up my cheeks.

My eyes swooped down and back up again, only to find

him still looking at me. I rounded the counter and popped a kiss on his cheek. We'd never been openly affectionate, and it stopped Abel in his tracks.

"Morning." I smiled up at him and turned to grab myself a plate to keep my blush from deepening.

My chaste kiss didn't seem to register with the kids. Tillie kept drawing, and Ben was reliving the slightly scary movie I'd reluctantly agreed to let them watch last night.

He bumped his sister's arm. "Remember the witch? Man, she was gross . . ."

"I don't want to talk about it," Tillie complained. "I don't really like scary movies."

"Did you have a nightmare?" I asked my daughter, brushing a strand of hair from her face.

She shook her head and continued quietly working on shading her drawing.

"Do you ever have nightmares, Abel?" Ben asked during his stream of consciousness.

The loaded question hung in the air as I looked at Abel. He'd stopped plating the french toast, and a deep line formed between his eyebrows.

He nodded slowly as he looked at Ben. "Yeah, I do." He lifted a shoulder. "Sometimes."

"What are they about?" Ben asked.

"Ben," I scolded. I knew what Abel's nightmares were about and that he certainly didn't want to rehash them to a nosy seven-year-old over breakfast.

"It's okay," Abel said, turning to Ben. "I was in an accident once and a woman got hurt. Her little boy died. Usually if I have a nightmare, it's about that."

Ben's wide, innocent eyes were pinned to Abel as though he knew he'd done something wrong by bringing it up. "Oh."

Abel reached across the island to squeeze Ben's shoulder and reassure him that he hadn't done anything wrong by being curious. "It's okay, buddy. You're allowed to ask me things. And I will always be honest with you."

Comforted, Ben's eyes flicked to me, and I offered a soft smile and nod of reassurance.

Abel slid a plate in front of Ben and another near Tillie.

Ben took a huge bite, and syrup dribbled onto the plate. Around his bite, he continued, "My therapist says that bad dreams are normal and our brain's way of dealing with things. Is that what your therapist says?"

Abel made me a plate and deposited it in front of me before dropping a soft kiss on my forehead. "Uh . . . I don't have a therapist, bud."

Ben hummed as he frowned over his food. "Oh . . . well, maybe you should."

A shotgun burst of laughter escaped me as I mused over the directness of my child. My hand covered my mouth, and I apologetically looked at Abel.

As though he was totally unfazed, a smile hooked at the corner of his mouth. "You might be right. Maybe I should talk to someone." He forked a mouthful of french toast before gesturing toward Ben's plate. "Eat up and you can tell me what you like about it."

Abel glanced at me and winked. My ovaries nearly exploded as I watched how at ease he was with my kids. Somehow we'd formed a warm little cocoon, and I never wanted to leave. My eyes moved to his lips when he smiled and mouthed *love you*.

My heart tumbled over itself. Abel was full of surprises.

"Eat up. Your mom and I have a big day today. I'm thinking tonight we can celebrate." He turned to me.

"Maybe we can let them horse around the farm for a little while."

He had plans later in the morning to meet with JP and finalize everything with the business. It poked at a tender spot in my chest that Abel wanted to share it with his sister.

I smiled. "I'll call Sylvie and set it up."

It made my heart so happy that things were finally falling into place for the King children. Sylvie had always wished her siblings had a normal upbringing with stable parents. At least we could do that with our kids.

Ours.

It was painfully easy to see a life with Abel unfolding in front of me. Part of me wondered if he ever wanted his own children. I rarely let my mind daydream, but as I watched him share a casual breakfast with my kids, I couldn't help but wonder what he would look like with our baby in his arms.

Floating on a cloud, the morning couldn't have been more mundane.

It was absolutely perfect.

By lunchtime, Abel still hadn't returned from his meeting with JP, and I was dying of curiosity. My attorney had assured us that the process was pretty painless, and with the proper paperwork filed, everything should go off without a hitch.

Still, I was anxious to see Abel and have him confirm that it all went well.

Distracted, I seated a few patrons interested in ordering lunch. A solo woman walked in and found a spot at a high-top table near the bar.

I smiled politely and slid the lunch menu toward her. "Welcome to Abel's Brewery. I'm Sloane, and I'll be your server today. Can I get a drink started for you or are we waiting on any others?"

The woman had dark hair and ice-blue eyes. Though her features were severe, there was a softness at the edges when she smiled. "Miss Robinson?"

"Oh, you can call me Sloane." I smiled brightly, but only to cover the tiny alarm bell dinging in my head. How does this stranger know my last name? "What can I get started for you?"

The woman stood. "Are you Sloane Robinson?"

"That's me." She gave me a once-over, taking in my branded T-shirt and simple leggings. A flash of something crossed her face—pity, maybe? The woman slipped a thick manila envelope from her leather bag and placed it in my hands. "You've been served."

The weight of the envelope was heavy in my hands. I stared at the woman as she slipped on a pair of sunglasses and strode out of the brewery without looking back.

The words *Personal and Confidential* were stamped in red ink on the front.

"Everything okay?" Reina asked from behind the bar as her hand moved in rhythmic circles across the wooden top to clean it.

"Yep." My gaze flicked to her briefly before returning to the envelope. "I think so."

I carefully slipped my finger under the seal to open it. I slid the stack of papers free from the envelope and stared down at the thick, blocky letters. My eyes scanned the legal document as my heart ticked and panic rose in my throat.

Due to legitimate changes in circumstance, which include

those as set forth below, modification of the present custody provision is warranted and father JARED HANSEN should be awarded sole, primary physical custody of the minor children.

Blood drained from my face as the information failed to process. My eyes darted across the pages, trying to make sense of the mass of legal jargon in front of me.

In support of JARED HANSEN's petition for issuance of a Temporary Order of Change of Custody, JARED HANSEN states:
a.The minor children were subjected to a relocation from their family home in California to a one-bedroom cabin in Outtatowner, Michigan, in which they shared with their mother and an unknown, non-relative male.
b.The minor children were then subjected to an additional relocation when mother SLOANE ROBINSON entered into a marriage with an unknown male, Abel King, for whom she worked. [Exhibit A]
c.The mother and minor children remain in the home of Abel King, despite the felony conviction which is a part of his violent and negligent criminal history. [Exhibit B]
I blanched as the clicking of glasses and the grainy smell of the brewery got closer, and black seeped in at the edges. Blood hummed between my ears as I read the papers over and over again.
Sole, primary physical custody of the minor children.

None of this seemed real.

Petitioner Plaintiff Father JARED HANSEN is currently employed, can provide the minor children a more suitable

*home, better schooling and education, better financial
support and stability, and better supervision and guidance
over the minor children if custody was modified to provide
the Petitioner with physical custody over the minor children.
Plaintiff father is requesting that this matter be referred to the
Friend of the Court for investigation and recommendation.*

He was coming after my children.
My knees buckled and I began to tumble.

THIRTY-ONE

ABEL

I couldn't imagine life getting much better. Hell, it was already giving me more than I ever deserved.

Once JP and I finalized the paperwork, it was official. Abel's Brewery was mine.

Well, technically Sloane was a silent partner with the majority ownership, but I had paid my debt to King Equities. I couldn't have done it without Sloane, and I fully planned to do everything in my power to make that up to her—financially and otherwise.

I owed Russell King nothing.

I was free.

After leaving JP's office, I took a detour down Main Street. Birds chirped happy songs as my long strides pounded on the sidewalk. A trio of women stood outside of a clothing boutique. One looked up at me with wide eyes, and instead of turning inward, I simply touched my fingers to the brim of my ball cap. "Ma'am."

Behind me, giggles and whispers erupted. I clenched my jaw to fight a smile. For years, it felt as though I carried my past around like a brand. Everyone knew what I had done, and they feared me.

Judged me.

For the longest time, I felt as though I deserved their skeptical whispers and wary glances, but slowly, I was feeling the shift. A tiny spark of hope bloomed in my chest that perhaps I wasn't as shunned as I once thought. Maybe if I wasn't quite so closed off, the people of my town would see me differently.

I glanced up to see the fearful eyes of an elderly woman track my movements.

Well, maybe not.

Undeterred, I wound my way around tourists and townies as I enjoyed my walk through downtown. As I passed King Tattoo, I peered in the large storefront window to see Royal behind the counter and my little sister MJ sitting on top of it with her legs dangling as she talked his ear off. I turned and entered the tattoo parlor.

Their heads rose in unison, and I offered a smile in greeting.

"What's wrong with your face?" Royal immediately asked.

The back of MJ's hand landed on his chest with a thwack. "Shut up. He's smiling, you idiot."

"Oh, yeah." Royal grinned and nodded. "Nice."

I cleared my throat and fixed my face. "Hi."

MJ laughed. "Hello, brother. You look like you're having a good day."

I nodded and spread my hands. "It's official. Abel's Brewery is no longer controlled by King Equities."

MJ threw a fist in the air and whooped as she hopped off the counter. Royal rounded the front desk and stuck a hand out. "Congrats, man."

"Thank you." I shook his hand, and an uncomfortable warmth settled in my chest.

MJ squinted at me. "Oh my god, I know that look." She pointed a finger toward my face. "It's not just the brewery. You're in love!" She squealed as I rolled my eyes, dodging her accusation. "I knew it! Does Sylvie know? I cannot wait to tell her!"

I brushed off my little sister as she danced around me. "Don't you work?"

MJ beamed up at me with a smile and then stuck out her tongue, which reminded me how young and innocent she really was. "As a matter of fact, I do and I'm late. I want to check in on Red Sullivan before my shift."

Red was the Sullivans' dad, and he suffered from early-onset dementia, which required him to live at the assisted-living facility where she worked. MJ had always had a soft spot for him, though she seemed to have a soft spot for everyone.

I glanced over my shoulder as she flounced toward the door. "Julep, it's . . . it's kind of new, so maybe let Sloane tell Sylvie."

"You got it," she singsonged, with a salute over her shoulder.

Once she left I exhaled and dragged a hand down my face. I made a mental note to add a little sweetness to the beer recipe I was testing for her.

Royal's hand clamped over my shoulder and squeezed. "I'm happy for you."

I looked at my younger brother. "Thanks. I kind of feel like I have no idea what I'm doing, but I'm trying."

He lifted a shoulder. "I think that's probably all that counts." His eyes gave me a once-over. "So, no issues with Dad?"

I shook my head. "We timed things right. He's out of town, and JP pushed the paperwork through. As far as we know, there are no issues, but I suspect that will change if more comes to light about Mom."

Royal grew sullen as he nodded. "You're damn right about that."

I looked around the tattoo parlor. "What about this place?"

"I own the business outright, but Dad owns the building. I guess I'll just take the hits as they come." His eyebrows bounced. "If they come."

I nodded. "Knowing Dad, they will." I stuck out my hand again. "But we're in it together now."

With a smirk, my brother shook my hand, and I squeezed. It was more than a friendly handshake.

It was a promise.

Eager to find Sloane, I made my way past the marina and headed toward the brewery. I entered the back and quickly double-checked the kettle temperatures, ensuring things were running smoothly. When I made my way to the front, the brewery was buzzing with families coming in off the beach and people enjoying a late lunch.

I scanned the floor, pausing when I noticed Reina bussing tables instead of working behind the bar. The brewery wasn't overflowing with customers, so it didn't make sense she was tending bar and bussing.

I stomped toward her, relieving her of the plastic tub she had planted on her hip. "What's going on?" I looked around, realizing I hadn't noticed Sloane either. A sinking feeling settled in my gut.

Reina leaned in to whisper, and my stomach pinched. "Sloane was served legal papers today. She didn't say what

they said, but she was rattled. She's in the staff bathroom, I
think."

I nodded, leaving Reina to handle the front of the brewery. I only stopped at the kitchen to dump the tub into the
sink. I didn't bother acknowledging the staff working and
instead tore off in the direction of the staff bathroom.

I had raised my fist to pound on the door when I heard
soft, muffled sobs. My palm flattened against the door.
"Sloane. Baby, it's me. Open up."

The door handle rattled, and I impatiently pushed
through the doorway. Huddled in the corner on the floor,
Sloane looked up at me with red, puffy eyes.

She swiped a hand under her nose. "I'm sorry."

Worry and panic gripped my chest as I moved to her.
"Hey, hey. It's okay. What's going on?" I crouched in front
of her, placing my palm at the side of her face. Her eyes
wouldn't meet mine, and fresh tears clung to her wet lashes.

Beside her, she picked up a thick manila envelope and
shoved it between us. "He wants—" Her voice hitched as
emotion snagged her words. "He doesn't even love them.
He just wants to hurt me."

I grabbed the envelope, but my attention stayed locked
on her face. "Sloane. Tell me what's going on."

"It's him!" Her voice wobbled as it rose. "He wants to take
Ben and Tillie from me, simply because he thinks he can."

It was disturbing how quickly murderous rage filled my
lungs. "He can't. He won't."

Her hand jutted toward the envelope in anger. "He's
already trying. My trust fund is nothing compared to the
family money he has backing him. He is cruel and vindictive and an asshole. He'll use that money to fight, and everything I had is now tied up in the house and the brewery."

I scoffed. Fuck him and his family money. "You have an order of protection against him. No judge in their right mind would ever entertain the idea of giving him custody after that. He has no grounds. He would have to prove you're an unfit mother, which you are not. You have a stable job. You care for their needs. You're married and living with—"

Her eyes flew to mine when realization hit me like a freight train. The truth expanded in my throat, cutting off my air supply.

"—with a felon." The words were acid on my tongue. "He's using me against you, isn't he?"

A fresh sob racked out of her, confirming my fears.

I stood to my full height, fury radiating from every pore.

That son of a bitch. This cannot be happening.

I stared at her for one last beat before I yanked the door open.

Sloane scrambled to her feet behind me. "Abel, wait!" She had to jog to keep up with me as I stalked down the hallway, rage seeping from every pore.

She rounded me, planting her hands on my chest. "Please. Please don't do anything stupid."

I looked down at her precious face. My entire future—the one where Sloane and the kids were at the center of my universe—flashed before me.

There was no fucking way her piece-of-shit ex was taking that from me. I'd rather rot in prison for the rest of my life, knowing the twins were safe with her.

Red seeped into my vision at the mere thought of Sloane without her children. "Sloane, call your lawyer. Now. You can handle it your way, but I'm handling it mine."

I moved past her and sailed out the door. The engine to

my truck roared to life, and I jerked it into drive. It took no time to make my way through town and come to an abrupt halt in front of King Tattoo. I slammed my foot on the brake and threw the truck into park. I didn't give a fuck if I got a ticket for double-parking.

A horn honked behind me, and I turned, fists clenched, and stared at the driver. His eyes went wide as he slowly drove around me.

Heat coursed through my veins—my blood thick and hot with fury. I pulled open the door and stormed into King Tattoo, disrupting the peace inside the shop. Royal's laugh faded as he turned to me.

I stared at him. "Get your shit. I need you to have my back." I pointed at the floor. "Right now."

Excitement danced in Royal's eyes. He nodded to Luna, King Tattoo's resident piercer, and immediately followed me out of the shop. "Are we fucking someone up tonight?"

I pushed open the door, spilling late-afternoon sunlight into the shop. I made my way toward my truck. "Probably," I ground out.

Giddy energy zipped through him as he jumped and shot a fist into the air.

"Yes," he shouted through gritted teeth.

I glanced at my little brother as I climbed into my truck and shook my head. "Will you please calm the hell down? The last thing I need is you getting a violence boner."

A slow grin spread across his face, and I exhaled. "I'm serious, Royal. Sloane's ex is trying to take the kids from her. I've been paying Bootsy to keep tabs on him, and right now we're going to have a conversation."

Royal's tattooed hands rubbed together as he geared up for what was about to unfold. I headed out of town, my mind flipping through our options. Jared was going to learn the hard way that when you fucked with a King, it was your last mistake.

My leg bounced. If things went sideways, I would have to take the fall. This wasn't Royal's mess, and if the worst-case scenario played out, he'd need help.

"Fuck." My hand slammed against the steering wheel as I drove. "Whip's working."

"Do we need one more?" Royal asked, unlocking his phone.

I shrugged and shifted in the seat, unable to sit still. "It would help."

Royal nodded and immediately began dialing. I looked over at him, but he stared ahead and said, "Duke."

My head whipped to him. "A Sullivan? Are you serious?"

Royal lowered the phone. "You want help or what? He can just stand in the back and look scary, but we're fucking doing this."

I clenched my jaw and conceded with a firm nod.

It looked as though the Kings and Sullivans were coming together to send a message that no one fucks with us and gets away with it.

THIRTY-TWO

ABEL

I PULLED my truck down the long driveway toward Sullivan Farms. Duke's three-legged hound dog shot out of the tree line and chased my truck, making circles and barking as I got closer to the farmhouse.

I dodged the dog and looked behind it. "Is that a . . . duck?"

Royal flicked his hand. "Apparently they're a bonded pair. Cute, right?"

I ignored my brother as the truck came to a stop. On the steps of my sister's farmhouse, Duke Sullivan stood, his arms across his chest, and stared. His brother Lee was beside him with a wide grin.

I opened my door and stood on the floorboard, looking at them over the roof of the truck. "Get in. I'll explain on the way."

The two nodded and climbed into the back seat without another word. In any other scenario, it would have been comical to see the four of us crammed into my truck.

Duke sensed my unease, and his fist clenched. "Are we

calling in the cavalry? I can have Beckett and Wyatt here in five."

I shook my head. "This is enough. We're not doing anything stupid—I don't think—just making sure someone understands who he's fucking with."

"Who is it?" Duke asked.

"My money is on the prick who burned Sloane's house down and nearly killed her kid." Anger clung to the edges of Lee's words as he stared out the window.

My eyes flew to him in the rearview mirror. Lee had been there the night Bax's farmhouse burned to the ground. He saved Ben when the boy had panicked and hid in a closet.

Fear and anguish clutched my chest.

I didn't realize it before now, but I fucking owed Lee.

"Do you know that it was him who caused the fire?" Duke asked, always the voice of reason.

"We don't know for sure," I answered. "I have my suspicions, and I'm getting answers. I still have a contact from prison that can probably do some digging for me. A guy like her ex doesn't do his own dirty work."

"So what the hell are we doing?" Duke asked.

Royal shifted in his seat. "Delivering a message. Sloane's asshole ex is going after the kids." He shook his head. "After everything she's been through."

We drove up the highway, and I pulled the truck to a stop in front of the Grand Harbor Hotel.

Lee whistled as he looked up at the wide, arching windows. "Fancy."

With lakefront views and private villas, the Grand Harbor was a boutique waterfront hotel. It oozed old money and dripped with the kind of quiet luxury that only the wealthy experienced when vacationing in Western

Michigan. After Sloane had spotted Jared in town, I had paid Bootsy to keep a lookout. Within days he had gotten wind that Jared hadn't gone far and was hiding out at the Grand Harbor.

No more hiding.

When we exited my truck, we paused and stared up at the hotel. "What's the plan?" Royal asked.

I steadied my voice. "I'm having a conversation." I slammed my door closed and headed into the lobby.

As luck would have it, Sloane's piece-of-shit ex was standing, dumbfounded, near the reception desk as the four of us walked in. I took in his drab khakis and crisply pressed button-down. He looked more suited for a symposium discussing the riveting topic of corporate tax code revisions than an upscale destination hotel.

I pointed at him and surged forward. "Get the fuck outside."

The receptionist's eyes bounced between Jared and the wall of men standing behind me. Her hand hovered over the telephone, but Royal smiled at her and gently shook his head. "Nope."

Her unsteady hand slowly retreated and disappeared behind the desk.

Panic flashed in Jared's eyes. He was stuck—trapped like a rat with no way out. He squared his shoulders. "I'm not going anywhere with you."

I lifted my chin. "You walk your ass outside and we talk, or we can have this conversation with all these eyes on you." I swirled my finger in the air, and Jared took in the gaping stares and whispering voices from the other hotel guests and workers.

He shifted and straightened his shirt. "I'm not afraid of you."

He was.

I could feel it.

Jared's chin jutted into the air. "You lay one finger on me and I'll personally send you straight back to prison. You'll never see the light of day again if I have anything to do with it."

My molars ground together. "Outside."

I turned, walking through Duke, Lee, and Royal to stand on the entryway outside of the hotel. Jared followed with the three of them in tow.

Before he could open his mouth, I jabbed a finger into Jared's chest. "You listen to me, you motherfucker. I know what you did. I'll prove it if it's the last fucking thing I do. In the meantime, you leave town. If you don't, I will find out about it. You don't talk to her. You don't look at her. You don't breathe the same air as her. Stay the fuck away from my wife."

A slick smile spread over his face. "It doesn't matter if I leave or not. You really think a judge isn't going to have reservations about her moving the kids in with a convicted murderer?"

A ripple of shame hummed through my blood as it ran cold. I couldn't change what happened on that dark, lonely stretch of highway. Now it was haunting me and threatened to take away the very thing that had brought me back to life.

My fist clenched and my arm reared back.

Before my punch could land, Lee's fist landed with a crack against Jared's jaw.

"Oh, fuck!" Lee shook his hand and laughed.

Fucking laughed.

Jared howled as he crumpled to the ground in pain.

I stared at Lee Sullivan in shock as he bounced on his heels and looked down at Jared. "You almost got your own son killed, you selfish prick." He shook his hand again and looked at Duke. "Fuck, that hurt!"

Royal gripped Lee's shoulder and guided him toward my truck. "Come on. Let's get some ice."

Duke spat on the ground next to Jared, glaring down at him. "You picked the wrong family to fuck with. You're common enemy number one now."

Surprised appreciation barely registered as Duke gestured with a nod for us to get going. We left Jared struggling to get to his knees as we climbed into my truck. From behind me, Lee squeezed my shoulder.

"Sorry I stole your thunder, but I've been wanting to do that since the fire, and I figured it probably isn't a good idea for you to assault anyone."

"Thank you." I looked around the truck. "Seriously. I appreciate you being here."

Duke nodded. "Don't mention it. Now let's get back before we have to explain to the cops what we're all doing here."

Without another word, I pulled out of the parking space and headed away from the hotel. My brain ran through what happened over and over again. Still, not all the pieces fit.

I was nearly silent when we dropped Duke and Lee back off at Sullivan Farms. As Duke opened his door, I leaned over. "Tell my sister I'm sorry to have dragged you into this."

He glanced at his house with a soft smile. "I have a feeling I might get a pass on this one." He tapped the side of the truck and closed the door.

Back on the road toward town, Royal broke the tense silence. "I think he got the message, don't you?"

My jaw tightened. "I sure hope so." Frustration bubbled

inside me. *I should have fucking hit him.* "He knew about the accident and my time in prison. Dad did his best to kill the story in the local papers, but it was all still public record. It's what he's using against Sloane."

Royal shrugged. "I guess it wouldn't be unusual for him to dig it up, then." I could feel my brother's assessing eyes on me as I drove. "What else has got you doing mental gymnastics?" His finger looped in circles next to his ear. "I know it's more than just a shitty ex digging up dirt."

I sighed, not sure where to even begin to explain the odd, unsettling feeling I had. "I need to make a few calls and see if he has contacts on the inside. Someone feeding information or maybe even someone who was willing to do his bidding. If I can prove he was behind the fire, he'll leave her alone for good."

My hand scraped over my jaw. "Did you see what he was wearing? A man wearing boat loafers and no socks doesn't burn down houses and risk the lives of their own children. They use their money and power to do it for them."

It was scary how easily I could have been talking about my own father instead of Sloane's ex-husband.

Royal frowned. "Prison calls are recorded. Any contact with the inside doesn't look good for you. Didn't your parole officer recommend you cut all ties?"

Frustrated, my hands tightened on the steering wheel. "I can't just sit around and do nothing." I glanced at my brother. "I know a guy on the outside I can talk to. It's worth the risk."

The rest of the trip back to Royal's tattoo parlor was spent in strained silence. It would be only a matter of time before the news of what happened spread like wildfire through our small town. It wasn't every day the Sullivans and Kings rallied together and got into a fight with someone else.

When Royal exited the truck, I sat in painful, tortured silence. I weighed my options. Finally, I unlocked my phone and typed in a number from memory.

> I need information.

UNKNOWN NUMBER
'Bout time.

> Now?

I sat back against the seat. My head throbbed. I pressed my thumbs into my eye sockets and willed the pressure to release. When my phone buzzed, I glanced at the message and sighed. The meetup was happening.

I sent Oliver the location, then flipped my phone onto the passenger seat and left Outtatowner fading in my rearview mirror. On the outskirts of our quiet little town, I pulled to a stop near a hidden clearing nestled within the dense thicket. Impatiently, I waited for my unexpected reunion with the past I thought I'd left behind.

The setting sun slanted golden light over the tall grass. The air hummed with the soft whispers of the wind. I had chosen this secluded spot to escape prying eyes and communicate without judgment. The scent of pine mingled with the earthy fragrance of damp soil.

The crunch of gravel under tires announced the arrival of my former cellmate, a man I once shared a confined space with, but never truly knew. Dressed in unassuming gray slacks and a white button-down shirt, Oliver appeared more suited for a corporate boardroom than the depths of a prison cell. His slender frame moved with an agile grace, the setting sun revealing sharp features. A cascade of dark hair fell over his forehead, framing a pair of intense blue eyes that betrayed the man beneath the polished facade. It was no wonder that at one time, he was practically the mayor of the Muskegon Correctional Facility.

Despite the time spent apart, his handshake carried the same controlled strength, a silent testament to the resilience we both clung to in our separate worlds.

He leaned against my truck. "What do you need?"

I leaned next to him, looking out onto the open field, and exhaled. "There's this woman . . ."

Oliver's barking laugh cracked through the air. "It's always a woman, my friend."

I shrugged him off. "We've got some issues with her ex."

"Need him to disappear?" The seriousness in his tone was chilling. I looked at Oliver as he grinned.

I shook my head. "Jesus. No. I need information. A while back the house she was living in burned down. An investigation ruled it arson. Trouble is, this guy—her ex-husband—isn't really the hands-on type. I have a theory that he hired someone—someone willing to take the fall if the price was right."

Oliver dragged a hand across his clean-shaven jaw. "I got you. That would be a lot of money. A payday like that is hard to keep quiet."

I nodded. "Exactly what I was thinking."

Oliver kicked off my truck and faced me. "Well, you're in luck. I can ask some questions personally. I'm headed back."

I frowned at him. "Again?"

He rolled his eyes as if going back to prison was simply interrupting his weekend plans. "I got pinched for inten-tionally damaging by knowing transmission. Apparently putting a tiny little bug on a public official's personal computer to prove he's into kiddie porn is frowned upon."

His exaggerated eye roll and air quotes were almost comical if it weren't for the fact he wasn't taking his upcoming sentencing seriously.

He leveled me with his steely stare. "I tried to stay straight, but those bills don't pay themselves, you know what I mean?"

I held out my hand. "Call me when you know anything. And when you get out, I'll have a job at the brewery waiting for you." I pointed at him. "I expect to hear from you."

He nodded rhythmically, and his lips pressed together in a small smile. "You will. You will."

I pulled him in for a quick hug. "Be safe and be smart."

Oliver sauntered back to his car like he didn't have a care in the world. I only hoped his contacts on the inside proved insightful. If we could prove Jared was behind the fire, we just might have a fighting chance, but if Sloane lost her kids . . . *fuck*.

We would lose everything.

THIRTY-THREE

SLOANE

I PACED BACK and forth across the hardwood floors and drilled holes into the front door with my stare.

Where is he?

I glanced at the envelope on the kitchen island and worry gnawed at my insides. When Abel stomped out of the brewery and tore out of the parking lot, I knew in my bones that something bad was going to happen. Somehow I managed to dry my tears and compose myself enough to call a server and beg for her to cover my shift.

A car pulled down the driveway, and a tiny knot of tension unfurled in my stomach when I saw Granddad's car pulling up to the house. Ben and Tillie climbed out of the car, and I opened my arms. They hugged me and I squeezed them so tightly they both groaned and wiggled away. When I released them, they ran past me and into the house.

My grandfather walked up to the front door and looked at me with soft eyes. "What's on your mind, Sloaney? Your face looks like a punching bag."

A watery laugh escaped me as I swiped under my swollen eyes. "Thanks."

His hand found my shoulder and squeezed.

I tipped my head toward the sky and groaned. "Ugh, I don't want to get into it again because I'll start crying. Jared is coming after the kids."

He shook his head, a fierce line forming between his white eyebrows. "That won't happen."

I nodded, trying to make myself believe it. "I know. I know . . . but then Abel found out and left the brewery in a rampage. I'm worried about him."

"He's a good man with a smart head on his shoulders. He wouldn't do anything to mess up what he's got here." My granddad's reassuring words settled over me.

My voice was tiny when I looked at him. "I hope you're right."

Granddad patted my arm. "I'm always right. Now I'm off to see if Bug wants to join me for a movie."

My eyes went wide. "Another date?"

His hand smoothed down his shirt. "I'm too old to date. I just enjoy her company, that's all."

As he turned, I smiled at his back. He deserved this happiness. I watched him walk to his car and turn down the road that led away from the house. I worried my lip as the sun sank lower and lower behind the trees.

"Mom, can we play in the back?" Ben shouted from inside the house.

I nodded and lifted my hand, unable to clear the emotion that expanded in my throat.

I sat on the front stoop, willing his truck to turn down the driveway. I checked—and rechecked—my phone.

Fresh tears prickled behind my eyelids as I watched the sun sink lower and waited.

Finally, his truck came into view, and I stood. My heart squeezed, relieved that he was safe and home.

Abel climbed out of his truck and paused.

He took one look at my red-rimmed eyes and splotchy face before his long strides ate up the distance between us. With his hands on the sides of my face, threading through my hair, his mouth crashed to mine. I opened for him, my gasp swallowed by his demanding kiss.

This.

This is everything.

In the distance, muted shrieks from the kids playing in the backyard rang through the air, dragging us back to reality.

His voice cracked through the haze. "I love you."

I gulped. The riot of emotions I'd experienced in the last few hours was utterly draining. "I know. I love you too."

His dark eyes were intense as he smoothed the hair from my face.

"Where did you go?" I asked.

He stepped back so I could look at him. His eyes shifted to the side, and my stomach tilted with a nauseating flop. "Jared never left the area. I'd been keeping tabs on him, so today I sought him out and made sure he knew who he was dealing with. His days of scaring you just because he thinks he can are over."

My eyes went wide as my thoughts jumbled together. "Did you . . . hurt him?"

His jaw tensed. "I wanted to fucking kill him. I almost lost my cool and pummeled him without thinking twice, but thankfully I had some help."

My brows pinched together. "Your brother?"

Abel nodded. "Royal was there, but it was actually Lee Sullivan who beat the shit out of him with one punch."

Surprise pulled a laugh from me. "Lee?"

Abel wound an arm around my shoulders and pulled

me into him. "That guy's got a surprisingly effective right hook."

Abel turned and led me into the house.

Our home.

"Right now I just want a normal night with the kids." He looked down at me, affection and reassurance shining in his eyes. "We can talk about our next steps later. Can we do that?"

"Yeah." I squeezed his middle and leaned into his comforting warmth. "We can do that."

Two WEEKS WENT by without a word from Jared or his lawyers. I contacted a family law attorney and laid everything out in the open. She assured me that she would fight tooth and nail for us. Given Jared's past history with aggressive behavior and my previous order of protection, she was confident I wouldn't lose the kids—it was my only thread of hope.

I leaned into that nugget of relief as we all tried to squeeze out the last drops of fun as summer started to wane. I also realized that Abel's comment about having a normal night turned out to be painfully accurate.

After that night, something had shifted—he was quieter and more intense than before. Something was weighing on him, but he wasn't letting me past his walls to figure out exactly what it was.

On the back patio, Abel was grilling hamburgers while Ben and Tillie played a rowdy game of tag. When I looked out the back window, I watched as smoke billowed out from the grill.

I popped my head out the door. "Hey! I think your burgers are burning."

Abel jolted and looked at the grill. "Shit." He fumbled to move the patties away from the flames and salvage our dinner.

Lately, despite the lawyer's reassurances, I would often find Abel staring into space. A pinch poked behind my ribs.

I walked outside and set the platter of burger toppings on the table. My hand found his back. "Lost in thought?"

He frowned at the blackened food. "Something like that."

I watched him and worried. Whenever I had asked him about what was weighing so heavily on his mind, he simply smiled softly and said that it was nothing. His stress baking told me otherwise—we'd had more cookies, pies, and brownies in the last two weeks than we could eat.

"The salad is ready and lemonade is freshly poured." I infused my voice with brightness to try to lighten the mood.

He only nodded and scrubbed a hand against his face.

"Chickens!" I called to the kids. "Dinner's ready. Time to wash up."

Ben chased his sister, making her giggle, and they made their way into the house.

"These burgers are shit," Abel complained as he scowled at the overdone patties.

"Are you kidding?" I slapped a black patty on a bun with a smile. "I love that perfectly charred crust."

He shot me a flat look, and when I gave a cheesy smile, he cracked.

Reaching his hand behind my neck, he pulled his mouth to mine. "I don't deserve you, woman."

I winked at him. "Well, that's true. I am pretty awesome."

He laughed and shook his head as the kids bounded down the steps and clambered to the table. I leaned over to make their plates as they got settled.

"Abel, what's the best part of your day?" Ben asked between pants.

He smiled at my little boy. "Well . . . probably watching you two—"

A pounding knock sounded at the front door. Abel and I exchanged a glance as he stood.

"Are you expecting anyone?" he asked.

Silently, I shook my head. I glanced at the kids and smiled. "We'll be right back. You can keep eating."

I followed behind Abel as he walked through the house. When he opened the front door, fear gripped my chest. Two police officers stood at the front door with serious expressions. Abel angled his body to block the kids and me from view.

"Mr. King? We need you to come with us," one officer said.

"Dusty." Abel tapped his own chest. "You know me. What's this about?"

The man's serious expression didn't waver. "We'd really like to have this conversation at the station."

I shouldered past Abel. "What conversation?"

The blond officer spared me only a glance before looking down at his notebook. "Mr. King, we have some questions in regards to your altercation with Jared Hansen at the Grand Harbor Hotel."

Abel's arms crossed. "What about it? The guy can't take a beating like a man?"

The second officer's eyes narrowed. "So you're openly admitting to a battery?"

"Abel." I straightened and placed a hand on his arm.

"Stop talking." I lifted my chin toward the officers. "He's not admitting anything, and he is not going anywhere with you."

"Mr. Hansen has been reported missing. Recently his vehicle was found abandoned. You and the men you were with were the last known interaction shortly before his disappearance. We'd like to talk to you about that. We would like you to come with us right now."

I didn't miss the way the officer's fingertips brushed his handcuffs. The gesture spoke volumes.

"No!" I shouted. Panic zipped through me.

Abel shook his head. "Sloane, it's fine. I'll go with them." He looked between the officers. "They just want to talk."

The second officer stepped forward. "This way."

I watched in horror as shame consumed the man I loved. Before my own eyes, he was transformed.

My eyes bounced between his, desperately trying to understand what was happening.

From behind, Ben pushed past me, clinging to Abel's leg. "Stop! Please. Please don't go!"

Abel's eyes pleaded with me. "Ben. This is just a misunderstanding. I'm going to talk with them. It's going to be okay."

Ben cried out and tightened his grip.

I carefully pried my wailing son from Abel's leg. "I'm calling the lawyer. Just don't say anything. We'll figure this out."

Abel only nodded.

In his truck, he followed behind the squad car, and I watched in horror as they drove away.

THIRTY-FOUR

ABEL

THE INTERROGATION ROOM of the Remington County Sheriff's Office was cramped and cold. The air hung heavy with the acrid smell of stale coffee and lemon-scented cleaner. The harsh, fluorescent lighting cast a murky pallor over the worn-out linoleum floor, where I counted the scuff marks beneath the table. The cold bite of handcuffs against my wrists was the only distraction from the unforgiving metal chair.

After walking me to the interrogation room at the back of the police station, they'd deposited me into the chair and started asking questions. I offered a half-truth that Jared had been punched, and I allowed them to believe it was me who'd done it.

They determined that that made me a threat, and I was unceremoniously handcuffed and left while they figured out their next move.

I assumed making me wait was only part of their interrogation tactics.

The muted whir of a distant air conditioner provided a feeble attempt at comfort, but the oppressive atmosphere clung to the room like a heavy fog. My every breath seemed amplified in the small space, each inhale bringing with it the musky odor of anxiety. The oppressive weight of the room pressed on me as I waited, handcuffed and vulnerable.

The look on Ben's face as they walked me away from my home played on a loop in my mind. I shifted in the uncomfortable chair, an ache settling between my ribs.

Sloane didn't deserve this. None of them do.

Shame coursed through me as the metal hinges of the door groaned and a detective in an ill-fitting, shit-colored suit walked in.

"Mr. King." He nodded once and looked down at the file folder in his hands.

My jaw clenched. "Am I a suspect? Am I being charged?"

His eyebrows popped up. "A suspect?" His head tilted. "For which crime, exactly?"

Fuck.

Sloane's plea to keep my mouth shut echoed through my mind. I had the sinking feeling that something bad had happened, and I was public enemy number one. Only, this time I hadn't actually done anything, yet it didn't seem to make any difference at all.

I gathered my breath. "I would like to speak with my lawyer."

The detective chuffed. "I'm sure you would."

My brows scrunched down as I raised my head to look at him. My stomach pitched as his gaze communicated that, to him, I was nothing more than a common criminal breathing his air and taking up his space.

The room's cold beige walls seemed to close in on me, suffocating, as if they held secrets whispered between the peeling paint and the microscopic cracks. The one-way mirror mocked my every move, a silent spectator to the tension that electrified the room. The taste of dread clung to my senses like the damp chill that permeated the air.

I had fucked up by willingly walking into the station and running my mouth. Now I was no longer able to leave on my own accord.

The electric click of the door lock drew our attention as a second officer entered. She leaned in and whispered something to the detective as he stared at me. Annoyance flickered over his features, and his gaze swept me up and down.

"You're sure?" he asked the officer. She nodded before silently exiting. The detective slapped the folder onto the table in frustration. "Well, Mr. King . . ." The detective rounded my seat, towering over me. He reached down, slipped his hand under my biceps and yanked upward. A pinch in my shoulder screamed as I stood, my arms still locked behind my back.

At my full height, I looked down at him over my shoulder. He shook his head and reached into his pocket to pull out a set of keys. "Looks like today is your lucky day."

Without tenderness, he jostled my arm and yanked on my handcuffs to release me. Once I was freed, I rubbed my raw wrist with my other hand.

"You're free to go." He gestured toward the door, but paused. "For now."

Unease rolled through me, but I was not about to look a gift horse in the mouth. He led me down the hall toward the precinct's lobby.

My steps faltered when it was not Sloane standing by the reception desk, but rather my father.

Without a hair out of place, Russell King stood eerily still, his hands clasped in front of him.

I blinked. "You're here."

"Of course I'm here." He turned to the detective. "Thank you, sir—for your duty and care of my son."

I watched in shock as my father shook hands and charmed everyone in the office of the police station.

He turned to me. "Let's get you home, son." His hand landed in a hard thump on my shoulder as he pulled me toward the door.

I moved with wooden steps, and we walked into the sunlight. Dad's car and driver were waiting for us. Russell King climbed in and I followed, sitting next to him in the back seat of the luxury car.

The mood shifted as soon as the door to the outside world slammed shut. "These messes of yours, Abel . . . they're really getting to be an inconvenience."

"I'm sorry." My apology was so automatic it made me sick. I swallowed past the pebbles in my throat. "It was a misunderstanding. Sloane's ex-husband was giving her and the kids some trouble. I only had a conversation with him, but—I'm working it out."

My father laughed. "Harassing a man in a public place with the help of Sullivans? You're better than that and you know it. We have to be smart about this, son."

I lifted a noncommittal shoulder. I didn't trust my father and wasn't about to divulge my suspicions that Jared was behind the fire at the Robinson place. I was already looking into it, and knew it was going to take some time. My father was undeterred by my stony silence.

The car wove down county roads in the direction of our hometown. The closer we got, the more a hot ball of tension pinched behind my shoulder blades.

"No more outsiders, son." It was clear from his tone that my father's words were a warning.

I stared at my calloused hands.

His disappointed, long-suffering sigh was so familiar I could recall it in my sleep. "Did you really think a half-rate criminal like Oliver Pendergrass was going to take care of things for us?" Disdain rolled off his tongue as he scoffed. "Please."

How the fuck did he know about Oliver?

I struggled to maintain my composure. "I am doing what I can to figure it out. But now her ex is missing, and they're looking at me, apparently."

He waved a hand in the air. "He won't be an issue anymore."

I stared at the side of my father's face as the car rolled down the street. "What did you do?"

My father adjusted his shirtsleeves beneath his suit jacket. "What I always do. I took care of the problem. Stop asking questions, Abel."

Ice ran through my veins.

Like you took care of my mother?

I opened my mouth to ask—to accuse—when he stopped me.

His heavy sigh dripped with parental disappointment. "I assumed you would have learned your lesson the first time."

My blood ran cold. "My lesson?"

Dad shifted against the leather seat. "My children don't seem to appreciate all I do for them—the lessons I have taught. That's my cross to bear, I suppose." A chilling smile spread across his face. "But you learned, didn't you? I knew a little time away would prove to you where you belong. This new, unfortunate development was just a blip, and it's taken care of. Tell me you've finally learned your lesson, Abel."

Dread and sweat prickled my hairline as realization

settled over me. "It was you. You were the reason the judge was so harsh at my sentencing?"

"Harsh?" he chuffed. "You killed a child. Do you know how bad that looks?"

I blinked, unwilling to accept the truth scratching at my brain. "I fell asleep. It was an accident."

The words felt foreign, and I waited for the inevitable shame to seep in, reminding me that I was truly a monster. Only . . . there was nothing. The pain and guilt never really subsided, but for the first time, I was starting to accept that what happened was truly an accident.

"True. It was very unfortunate." He swallowed the word as if holding back his disgust. With a sigh, he spread his hands. "But look at you now. You're home, running a successful business." His shoulder bumped into mine. "You're a King and finally acting like it—thanks to me. Though we still have to talk about your little stunt with Sloane's trust fund. If it were anyone else who'd done that to me, things would have gone very differently, but you are my son."

My nostrils flared. "Leave my wife out of this."

Russell tsked his tongue. "Wife." The word spat from his mouth like venom. "Are you still putting on that charade?" He shook his head and sighed. "As an unlikely couple, you two are pretty convincing, I'll give you that. You've fully seduced Bug into thinking the marriage is real."

My heart hammered against my ribs. "It is real. My feelings for Sloane are very real."

My father sighed and pinched the bridge of his nose. "I swear, when will my children learn to stop moving through life tethered by their heartstrings?"

I barely recognized the man sitting next to me. His navy

bespoke suit was a stark contrast to my simple jeans and scuffed work boots.

He sucked in a deep breath through his nose and exhaled. "To be honest, I'm quite proud. You found a way to pull the brewery out from under me." His wink sent an oily shiver down my back. "Maybe there's hope for you to live up to my name yet."

Reeling, I sat against the black leather interior with closed eyes and let painful realization wash over me.

Everything in my life was made of tinder, and Russell King had lit a match.

THIRTY-FIVE

SLOANE

Abel returned home a fractured man.

He painted a small smile on his face and reassured the kids that his conversation with the police was not a big deal. The red marks around his wrists told me differently.

I knew deep down that his brave face was a facade to not scare my children, and while I deeply appreciated that, I couldn't help but feel discouraged that he'd shut me out too.

If he looked at me one more time with sad eyes and said *I'm fine*, I was going to scream.

Over the next few days, Abel buried himself in work, leaving to check or recheck temperatures, filters, and pumps. We were living in his house without him, and his absence left my emotions feeling raw.

Frazzled, I jolted when my phone rang. Clutching my throat, I let out a relieved laugh at how jumpy I'd been lately. Recognizing my lawyer's number, I painted a smile on my face and attempted to sound cheery. "Hello?"

"Sloane? Laura Michaels. Is now a good time?" I had

learned to appreciate my lawyer's directness. She had come highly recommended and was a respected family law attorney.

"Hey, Laura. Thanks." I checked my watch. "It's fine. What's up?"

"A small update. We've submitted a statement disagreeing to each point in your ex-husband's complaint on your behalf. We have also filed a counterclaim. The next step is a meeting with the friends of the court case manager. Given the past domestic nature of your relationship, those meetings will be held separately. Although it seems the plaintiff's attorney has had some difficulty contacting their client."

My mind raced back to finding the shower curtain open. I knew that just because Jared was quiet, it didn't mean he was gone.

"I know Jared. He will put up a fight." I hated knowing the truth in my words.

"I would assume so based on the aggressive nature of his complaint." Her words were harsh, but honest. "I do have to tell you . . ."

My heart hammered. "What is it?"

"The complaint was well drafted and brings to light some very difficult issues, particularly the short nature of your relationship and the criminal history of your current spouse."

The air swirled around me, and I was stunned into silence. This was supposed to be a slam dunk.

"If you stay with him," she continued, "there is a very real possibility that your ex-husband will gain custody of the children, depending on the judge."

The truth stabbed like a driven nail. My hands shook. "I

can't lose my children." My voice cracked, and I was barely holding it together.

"We are doing everything we can to ensure that doesn't happen. However, if we cannot mediate a custody and visitation agreement with the FOC, it will go in front of a judge, who will be forced to make a final ruling in what he or she believes is in the best interest of the children."

My knees shook, and I sank to the floor. My voice was barely a whisper. "I understand."

My attorney politely ended the call, and I stared into nothingness. I couldn't seem to wrap my brain around the fact that I could accept a custody agreement that allowed my dangerous ex-husband access to our children or fight and risk losing them altogether.

It wasn't only Jared using Abel's conviction against him, just as he'd feared. It was a heartbreaking realization that his past was a brand that he would always wear. So few were willing to look past it to see the man he was—the man he had worked so hard to become.

Despair seeped into my bones until I was left with two impossible outcomes—I could end my marriage to the man I had fallen in love with, or risk the safety of my children.

"You're quiet." Sylvie's voice was soft and concerned.

I pressed my lips together in a strained smile. "I'm sorry."

My best friend's arm wrapped around me as we sat on a blanket by the beach and watched our children play—hers on a towel in front of us and mine splashing in Lake Michigan with Abel and Duke. The men took turns growling and chasing the squealing twins and propping them on their shoulders for a game of chicken.

Sylvie's head rested on my shoulder. She was so good at holding space for me. I could tell her everything or nothing, and she would understand. I looked across the sandy beach at her brother.

But how could I tell her this?

Sylvie had asked me to be careful with Abel's heart. I'd learned just what she meant about the sensitive nature he tried so hard to keep hidden. It was one of the many reasons I'd fallen madly and completely in love with him.

Abel had been transformed from a sullen grump on the fringes of our town to frolicking on the beach with a Sullivan, playing a game of tag with my kids. He scooped Ben into his arms and swung him in a circle as his laugh rang out above the rolling waves.

Our love did that.

And one decision could completely destroy him.

"Any more news from the lawyers?" Sylvie's attention was on Gus, so she didn't see me swallow back the bile that had risen in my throat.

"Not much. I had my appointment with the friends of the court and gave them the rocky history of my relationship with Jared. We talked about how Abel and I met and fell for each other. I highlighted how well the kids are doing here—Tillie with her clubs and artwork and Ben making new friends and having less incidents with his anxiety. I told the woman how the children are in therapy and really bonding with Abel." I shrugged. "She took a lot of notes."

"You've changed him, Sloane." She gestured toward her brother. "I mean look at him. He's a dad."

Unshed tears stung my nose as I planted my tongue on

the roof of my mouth and watched Abel be silly and play with the twins. I nodded and let out a watery laugh. "Yeah . . ." I swiped under my eyes. "Yeah, I guess he is."

Duke walked up and plopped onto the blanket next to Sylvie, kicking up sand. "Sorry," he offered before scooping Gus up and bouncing him on his lap. "Pretty soon I'll be chasing you across the beach, huh, big guy?"

Gus babbled at his dad as I watched the scene unfold. Behind him, a group of women gestured toward our group with curious eyes and hushed whispers.

I jutted out my chin. "Looks like you and Abel have caused quite a stir."

Duke didn't bother looking behind him, but Sylvie laughed when she saw the group of women tittering and shielding hushed words behind their hands.

"If they think Duke and I getting together caused a stir" —she giggled—"you can imagine the gossip now that people think we're all friends."

Duke scoffed as though it was still an insult to be considered the friend of a King, and I smiled at him. "Aren't you?"

He rolled his eyes and looked at Abel. "I guess."

The tension fizzled as Sylvie and I laughed.

"Men are so dumb," Sylvie joked. "Don't think I don't know about the text thread."

I perked up. "Text thread?"

Sylvie grinned. "After the incident at the Grand Harbor Hotel, Lee started up a group chat. Someone even titled it Nemesis Nucleus."

I chuckled. "Let me guess . . . Royal?"

The corner of Duke's mouth twitched. "That man's a fool. Reminds me too much of Lee."

My heart squeezed. Perhaps if there was a world in

which Kings and Sullivans were friends in Outtatowner, there was a way things could work out for me.

I shielded my eyes from the sun and watched Abel stand between my children, holding their hands as they walked toward us.

I'm not ready to let this go.

THIRTY-SIX

ABEL

I HAD THOUGHT an afternoon on the beach would be what Sloane needed. Something was off, and I couldn't quite put my finger on it. My own thoughts had been consumed by the conversation with my father. I carried with me a sinking feeling that he had something to do with Jared not showing up for his friends of the court meeting.

In fact, Sloane's ex hadn't been spotted anywhere, and his disappearance was still under investigation.

I drove my truck past the marina, through town, and down a quiet road toward home. It amazed me how Sloane and the kids had turned a cold, empty house into a home.

Our home.

My eyes flicked to the rearview mirror. Ben was curled into his seat, the seat belt acting as a makeshift headrest as he dozed. Tillie's head was back, mouth open, and already snoring.

Beside me, Sloane's gaze floated dreamily over the passing buildings and blueberry fields as we made our way out of town.

I no longer felt tense and frazzled with them in the car. Behind the wheel I was in control. They were safe.

They would always be safe with me.

My right hand found Sloane's arm, brushing down her soft skin to capture her hand. I pulled her knuckles to my lips and nestled her hand against my chest as I drove. Late-afternoon sunlight slanted through the window, high-lighting the swirls of browns and greens in her eyes, but it didn't hide the sadness. Just beyond the edges of her small smile, I could see it.

"I love you," I whispered, kissing her knuckles once more.

I watched the small muscles of her neck work as she swallowed. "I love you too."

I held her hand and focused on the drive. We would get through this. We had to. In my mind, there was no other option. I may have been content merely existing before Sloane and the kids, but now? I couldn't fathom a world in which we weren't together.

As I parked, I pressed a finger to my lips and gestured toward the quiet back seat. "I've got them."

After opening the back door, I scooped Ben into my arms. His deadweight was heavy, but as I jostled him, he curled into my shoulder. "Hey, bud, we're just going inside."

He mumbled something but didn't wake. Sloane moved toward Tillie's door, and I shook my head. "I can get her if you grab the towels."

She smiled and agreed. After carrying Ben to the living room and depositing him gently onto the couch, I returned for Tillie. She was still snoring when I reached across to unbuckle her seat belt.

Once she was secured in my arms, I straightened and turned toward the door. "Thanks, Dad."

Pressure bloomed in my chest.

I stared down at her little freckled face. She was dreaming, but I held her closer, holding back tears. "No problem, kiddo."

My heart raced. I had fallen for these damn kids before I even fell in love with their mother. It was too late now—I was sunk. I wouldn't stand for a life without them in it, and it was about time I made that clear with Sloane.

Tillie had roused by the time I'd made it in the house with her, so I set her onto her feet. She dragged a hand across her tired eyes. "I think I'm going to relax in my room before dinner."

Sloane smiled and guided her down the hallway. "That's a good idea, hon."

With Ben still sleeping on the couch, Sloane met me in the kitchen. Worry creased her forehead, and I moved to her. "Hey, are you okay?"

Unshed tears swam in her eyes as she looked up at me. I cupped her cheeks. "What is it?"

She could barely look at me as her chin wobbled and she finally crumpled. "He's just so vindictive and cruel. He'll use every penny he has to punish me."

My nostrils flared. I hated that her ex-husband wielded his wealth to cause pain and instill fear in the woman I loved. The answer was clear, so I lifted my chin. "We sell."

Her eyes searched mine. "What?"

I crossed my arms. "We can sell the brewery to my father and use that money to fight this. Whatever it takes."

A pit opened in my stomach when a single tear slipped from under her lashes. "It's not about the money, not really.

I'm just so scared, Abel. I can't lose them. I don't want to lose you."

"Hey, hey." I softened and dotted light kisses across her face. "You aren't going to lose them . . . or me."

A silent sob racked out of her as she folded herself into my embrace. I held her tightly, unsure of where this flood of emotion was coming from.

"I have to choose," she sobbed. "That's the problem. Because he did this, I have to choose between you or them—between my calling as a mother and my heart's desire as a woman."

Her words cracked through my skull.

She thought she had to choose.

The hard callus that had been slowly peeling away because of their love re-formed in an instant. I held the woman I loved. "Look at me."

Sloane's head lifted. Her face was splotchy, and tears streamed down her cheeks. "There isn't a choice. You already know that."

Her eyes searched mine. "He's using you against me. If I don't agree to joint custody, the case will go in front of a judge. The judge could take them away forever. My attorney—she said that our relationship—"

She could barely get the words out, but I understood.

I had known from the moment Jared tipped his hand that he would use my past to hurt Sloane. In the depths of my soul, I had already known it would come to this.

Though I didn't anticipate how deeply it would hurt.

My back ached and my chest burned. My jaw clenched tightly as I swallowed past the lump that had expanded in my throat. "Sloane," I ground out, holding her precious face and willing her to listen to the words I needed to say. "There isn't a choice."

Her lip quivered. "I know."

She knew, just as I have always known.

A shuddered breath coursed through me. I was going to fall apart in front of her if she kept looking at me with those soft, sad eyes.

"There isn't a choice," I said again, more firmly. "When it comes down to it, it's them."

Her grip on my shirt tightened as she whispered, "I don't want this to end."

I stared over her head at a spot on the wall to keep from crumpling. "I know. You're doing this for them. It's the right call."

She stepped back, finding her resolve and lifting her chin. "Where does that leave us?"

My hands rubbed down her arms. "Right now, nothing changes. We can cross that bridge when we come to it."

"Nothing changes?" She looked at me with hopeful eyes, and I wanted to hold her and reassure her.

Instead, I cleared my throat. "Maybe a few things need to change." I dragged a hand across the back of my head, sinking lower as the reality of our situation became clearer. "I should probably leave . . . stay with one of my brothers, or hell . . . maybe Bax will let me rent the other room in the cabin."

Her hazel eyes searched mine. "You want to go?"

I held her shoulders. "Hell no, I don't want to go, but the less ammunition we give Jared, the better. If I'm not around or involved in your life, he can't use that against you."

"Isn't there any other way?" she pleaded.

I shook my head. I wish there was literally anything I could do, but that was it. "I can't erase my past, and you can't pick a different ex-husband. For now it's all we have."

Her eyes swept over Ben, sleeping on the couch. "They're going to be so heartbroken."

I steeled my spine. I'd made my mistakes—this was the bed I'd made. I knew the entire time I didn't deserve a life with Sloane and the twins.

It was always going to have to come to this.

For long, heavy moments, I silently held Sloane in our kitchen. I had no words to reassure her that didn't feel like a lie. Instead, my resolve hardened, and I made a silent promise.

I will always love you and do what needs to be done to keep my family safe.

THIRTY-SEVEN

SLOANE

THE CONVERSATION with Abel left my insides raw.

I knew he loved me, and my love for him nestled deep into my soul. I also knew the legal system couldn't care less about my feelings for Abel. On paper, my decision to uproot my children and relocate to Michigan, then marry a felon and move in with him wasn't a good look. At best, I appeared impulsive, and at worst, like I had a disregard for my children's safety.

But they don't know him.

Deep sadness unfolded in my chest as I stood in my lawyer's office, staring down at the pile of paperwork, hating the lies they held.

Jared had the money to hire the country's best attorney. He knew the children were the perfect way to punish me for leaving, and he had no qualms about using them against me.

Dissolution of our marriage wasn't something that could happen overnight, but my attorney had started the process of severing my ties to Abel.

Optics, she called it.

Initially, I had balked at Abel's suggestion for me and the twins to stay at the house while he slept at the cabin with Granddad. However, my attorney agreed that the optics of my separation with Abel would only work in our favor.

Every signature I scrawled was laced with regret.

My lawyer looked at me with kind eyes as my hand froze in the air. "This is simply to counter the points your ex-husband will inevitably use against you. Once this custody battle is behind you, you're free to spend your time with whomever you choose."

Her words were hollow and grim, offering no comfort to the ache in my stomach. Without looking, I scrawled my signature—Sloane Robinson—across the line.

I hadn't even had the chance to take his name.

The thought was ridiculous. Even I knew we had started our relationship as a ruse. It shouldn't have hurt so badly to end it, but every swipe of my signature felt like a betrayal—against him, against my heart.

By the time I was finished, my soul was drained. For now, it was a waiting game until the court hearing. I offered a weak goodbye and folded myself into my car. As soon as the door closed beside me, I burst into tears. Hard, aching sobs racked from my body as I hunched over the steering wheel.

How had I messed things up so badly?

All I had ever wanted was to feel safe. In Abel, I had found that plus so much more, and now it was being pulled out from under me. Like he had so many times before, Jared was controlling the narrative.

Sadness gave way to anger. I fucking hated him and everything he had put us through. I gripped the steering wheel and screamed at the windshield until my voice was raw.

I sat in silence, my angered howl still ringing in my ears as my breaths sawed in and out of me.

My phone rang and my chest tugged into a knot.

I didn't recognize the number, but I swiped my fingers under my eyes and cleared my throat. "Hello?" I croaked.

"Sloane. This is Russell King. Are you all right?"

I swallowed and tried to sound normal. Nervousness rang through my body with a sharp edge. "I'm fine. Is something wrong? Is Abel okay?"

Russell chuckled on the other end. "As far as I understand, my son is doing very well—thanks to you, young lady. I'm calling because I heard a rumor that you might be in a spot of trouble, and I thought I could help."

Unease rolled through me. Abel didn't trust his father, and my alarm bells were ringing.

"Oh," I said. "Thank you, but I think we have it handled."

"Hmm." Disappointment dripped through the phone. "Still . . . I'd like you to come by the house. Could you do that for me?"

My fingers twitched as I glanced at the clock. Abel was working at the brewery, and since he wasn't staying at the house, I wanted to steal a few moments with him. Still, I knew Russell King was a powerful man, and if there was any way he might be able to help me, I'd be a fool not to take it.

Right?

Indecision gnawed at me.

"How about some lemonade and cookies? I won't keep you long." There was a softness in his request I wasn't expecting.

"Um . . . okay. Sure." I swallowed past the regret.

"Wonderful. I'll be expecting you." Russell King ended the call, and my stomach flopped over.

The drive to the King estate was short. Pulling down the long driveway, I was reminded of my first meeting with Abel's father. I had been so nervous that he would suspect the marriage between Abel and me was fake. Now, I knew it was real and, still, the looming house filled me with unease.

I knocked, and Russell opened the door with a wide smile. He was dressed in a collared knit shirt, beige dress pants, and loafers. If I squinted hard enough, it reminded me of what Jared might grow to look like in a few decades.

"Sloane." He stepped aside to open the door and stretched out his arms. "Please, come in."

I ducked through the doorway, sidestepping him to avoid an awkward embrace. His hand landed softly on my back.

"Please, come this way. The office can be so stuffy. I have refreshments in the solarium."

I followed behind him, taking in the grandeur and opulence of the King estate.

The interior was pristine. Sunlight danced through the floor-to-ceiling windows, casting a golden glow over the tastefully arranged furniture. Every corner exuded a sense of sophistication, with delicate lighting hanging from the high ceilings, and thick drapes cascading gracefully down the windows.

"This way, you remember," he said. "It may not be as lovely as the wedding shower Bug decorated for, but I always enjoy a sunny spot."

Together we walked to the back of the house, toward the solarium. Sunlight streamed through the floor-to-ceiling glass. Without the wedding shower decorations, the windows provided an unobstructed view of the sprawling backyard. The home may have been nestled amid lush greenery and picturesque surroundings, but it stood as a testament to the King family's wealth and opulence. It lacked the warmth and coziness of the home Abel had carved out for himself.

My soul ached at the mere thought of my husband.

Russell gestured toward a small tray with a plate of cookies and two tall glasses of iced lemonade.

I forced a smile. "It's lovely. Thank you."

Carefully, I sat down, and Russell took the seat next to me. A small table with our refreshments stood between us. He slid it in my direction. "Please. Enjoy."

The glass was cool in my hands. I placed it against my lips and took a small sip. The lemonade was the perfect balance of sweet and sour. "Thank you."

Russell did not move toward his glass, but rather folded his hands in his lap. A gold pinkie ring with a small diamond winked in the sunlight. "Outtatowner is a hidden gem, don't you think?"

I smiled. "It's perfect."

He leaned back. "I thought so too. Nestled against the Western Michigan shores, you've got beauty and grandeur. I'm able to maintain my business and travel to Chicago when needed, but outside of our little town, very few people have heard of it. It's quiet. Secluded."

I stared down at my lemonade. "I think that's why I chose here. I needed a fresh start, and my granddad was here. It seemed too good to be true."

Russell nodded. "Bax Robinson is a good man. I've known him for many years." His hand ran the length of his thigh. "Bit of a shame about his farmhouse—though I hear you've started rebuilding."

I nodded. "Home Again Designs are taking on the renovation. It's going to be really beautiful."

He hummed, disgust laced in the single sound.

Russell King was known to hold grudges, and it was clear he did not like that I was associating with Kate Sullivan and the design company she ran with her husband.

He leaned against the armrest. "I don't want you to worry, my dear. That's why I asked you to come."

I tipped my chin toward him, and my brows cinched down.

"Many people tell me many things in this town. I have to apologize for not letting on earlier, but I know about the heartache you and my son are enduring." He exhaled a heavy sigh. "Now, I have to admit, when he paraded you in here the first time, I thought you were both lying to me. However, I have come to realize that you do care a great deal for my son—and he for you. Which is why I want you to know that you no longer need to worry about your ex-husband meddling with our family."

I looked at him. "Sir?"

A slick grin spread across his face. He liked that I called him *sir*, and it made my stomach bunch.

Above all else, Russell King craved power.

He scoffed. "No one contends with a King and wins, my dear."

I swallowed hard. My mind flipped across dangerous whisperings of Abel's mother and Jared's disappearance.

My eyes went wide. Russell took note of my fear, and his laugh rang out as his meaty palm patted my hand. "No need to be frightened. I simply want to reassure you that the problem has been silenced indefinitely."

Why was he telling me this? What could he possibly gain

from me knowing that he was responsible for something happening to Jared?

Blood drained from my face. "If my children ever ask about visiting their father . . ."

His icy eyes bore into me. "That is not an option, my dear."

I blinked up at him, trying to buy some time so I could figure out what the hell to do, my heart rate spiking. "Thank you, sir."

He laughed, sinking back into his chair and winking. "Now there's a woman who knows her place. Abel sure picked a good one."

I looked down at the simple silver band on my finger.

Abel's mother.

I sucked in a breath and infused sweetness into my voice. "I'm surprised a man as benevolent and charming as yourself never remarried."

"Ah." His eyes glittered over my fawning. "I, like you, have not always had the best fortune in relationships."

"Like Abel's mother," I offered innocently.

"Precisely. I tried for years to give her everything, and it was never enough." His voice held wistful memories. "You aren't the only person in this family who's needed a problem to go away. I assure you, those are two inconveniences that won't ever be found." A twitch near his eye nearly gave him away. I was certain he hadn't meant for that last bit to slip out, but he smiled to recover. "But we can keep that little tidbit between us. Is that a deal, my dear?"

Any deal with Russell King was a deal with the devil.

Abel's words rattled around my brain.

"Of course." I glanced at my watch as my brain screamed for an escape. "Oh, I'm so sorry. I need to get the kids soon." I rose and he stood beside me. "Thank you—for everything."

He walked me to the front door but stopped before opening it. His hand gripped my shoulder. "There's safety in knowing your place. Don't forget that."

My lips formed a flat smile. "I won't. Thank you, sir."

Pacified, Russell released his grip, and I moved as quickly as my feet could carry me without running down the front steps and across the front lawn to my car.

I raised my hand in farewell and shut myself inside the safety of my car before watching Russell enclose himself inside his fortress.

A guttural exhale filled my car. My hands shook as I started the vehicle and backed out of the driveway.

One thing I knew for certain:

Russell King disappeared my ex-husband . . . just like he'd done with Abel's mother.

THIRTY-EIGHT

ABEL

HOLY HELL, this bed sucks.

I stared up at the ceiling of the small room in Bax's cabin, wondering how Sloane and the kids had managed to live here for so long. The wood-planked ceilings were drafty, there was a weird stain in the corner, and the mattress was like sleeping on a pile of rocks.

I missed the couch. I missed my bed, waking wrapped around my wife and pulling her pliant body into me.

My fingers dragged across my eyes as I sat up and swung my legs over the edge of the bed. I sat and sighed, soaking in the moment before pushing to my feet and getting on with the day.

Another day surviving without them.

When I walked into the small kitchen, Bax was in his recliner. He glanced my way and scoffed. "You're walking around like a beaten dog."

I nodded. *Accurate.*

Bax shook his head. "Damn shame. I thought you had more fight in you."

My attention turned to him. My brows furrowed.

He raised an eyebrow and lifted a shoulder in dismissal. "One bump in the road and you're giving up."

Bump in the road? Sloane's ex-husband was actively trying to dismantle her life, and he thought it was a bump?

I shook my head. "It's complicated."

Bax crossed his arms. "Doesn't seem all that complicated to me. You love her, don't you?"

I stared at the old man. "I do."

"And the kids?" He gestured toward me.

My arms crossed in defense. "Like my own."

Bax scoffed and pushed himself to standing. "Ah, see. I knew it. You love them, so it's up to you to work it out."

"It's not that simple. My past conviction, I—" I exhaled.

Bax swatted the air. "Don't come at me with that. People make mistakes all the time. Few pay their penance, but you did. Water under the bridge."

My shoulders slumped, defeated. "I wish it were that easy."

"Nothing worth having was ever easy." He pointed a finger in my direction. "That I know for a fact."

I stared at the peeling linoleum floor. The truth came out in a whisper. "She deserves more."

Beside me, Bax placed his hand on my shoulder and stared down at the same spot. "Then you give it to her, son." He sighed. "I can venture a guess who made you feel so unworthy, and it's a damn shame."

Bax's clear eyes bore into me. "You're good for her. You light her up. The kids too." He circled a finger around his head. "You figure out how to wrestle the demons in here, and I'm betting you'll realize it too."

I swallowed hard. "I don't know how to do that," I admitted.

"Gotta square up with the past if you want to have a

future." After two heavy thumps on my back, Bax swiped a muffin off the counter and returned to his recliner.

I sucked in a breath.

Maybe Bax was right.

I needed to get my shit together. I owed it to Sloane, but I owed it to Ben and Tillie too.

THE AIR-CONDITIONING in the library hit me as the automatic doors opened. I walked past the main circulation desk and up the stairs toward the children and teen section. Emily sat behind a desk, doing something on the computer.

When I caught her attention, she smiled and stood. "Hi, Abel. Picking up the kids early today?"

I scratched a spot behind my head. "Um, no, but I do need to talk with Ben for a minute. Would that be okay?"

She smiled. "You've got great timing. Right now the kids are having a snack before we head outside. I'll grab him."

Emily rounded her desk and disappeared behind a tall stack of books. I looked around and folded myself into a too-small chair and waited. My palms were sweaty, so I swiped them down the thighs of my jeans.

Moments later, Ben appeared at Emily's side. When he saw me, his eyes lit up and an arrow snagged my chest.

"Hi!" He waved and Emily resumed her position behind the circulation desk.

"Hey, bud." I gestured to the seat beside me. "Why don't you sit down."

Ben frowned as he lowered himself into the seat. "Am I in trouble?"

I leaned forward and rested my hand on his shoulder. "Not at all."

His eyes were downcast. "Are you here to say goodbye?"

Blood drained from my face. "I know it's hard, but your mom and I agreed that me staying at the cabin for a while is a good idea. It's got nothing to do with you."

He nodded but wouldn't look me in the eye. I gave his shoulder a gentle squeeze. "Really, I came to see you because I need a pep talk."

He looked up. "What's a pep talk?"

I considered how to put it for a seven-year-old to understand. "Well, it's kind of like when a coach talks to his players before a big game. He reminds them to play hard and lets them know he believes in them."

"Are you playing a game?" Ben asked.

My heart ached for this sweet little boy. I shook my head. "No. But, I remember you told me that I should talk with a therapist. I listened and found someone to set up an appointment with." I glanced at the clock above his shoulder. "He's probably already waiting for me." I leaned in to look Ben in the eye. "The thing is . . . I'm feeling a little nervous."

"Oh . . ." Ben nodded, holding my stare with serious eyes. "But therapy is fun. You play with toys and talk about your feelings, and sometimes she'll tell you little tricks to feel better when you're scared."

I ached for his simple worldview. "Talking about my feelings is hard sometimes."

Ben's hand landed on my shoulder with a thump. "Harder than keeping them inside?"

Emotion rose in my chest as I pulled him into a hug. "No, I guess you're right, bud." I patted his back as he squeezed me.

Emotion banded across my chest. "Thank you." I stood

and cleared my throat. "Sorry to interrupt camp. You should head back. Give Tillie a hug from me."

"I believe in you, Abel." Ben waved before smiling at Emily and disappearing around the corner.

Behind the circulation desk, Emily's hands were clutched in front of her, tears swimming in her eyes.

I nodded and stomped away.

THIRTY-NINE

ABEL

BEN'S PEP talk was exactly what I needed. That kid was stronger than he realized, and if he believed in me, then maybe I could too. I let myself sink into that feeling on the drive to my appointment.

When I got there, the office was unlike that of any therapist I'd imagined. Instead of a sterile office building, Dr. Alexander Bennet opted to see his patients from the comfort of his own home. When I pulled up the driveway just before my appointment time, he was waiting for me on the porch in a pair of jeans and a T-shirt.

"Mr. King." He stood with a smile, reaching out his hand to shake mine. "It's nice to finally meet in person. I'm Alex."

I gritted my teeth and nodded. "Abel."

Dr. Bennet laughed and turned, opening the door to his modern home. Through a set of glass double doors, he led me to his office. It was decorated with sleek, no-nonsense furniture. The desk in the center was simple, black, and free of clutter. A pair of wingback chairs were tucked into the corner. I eyeballed the small sofa on the opposite end.

Dr. Bennet laughed and gestured toward the chairs. "How about we sit here?"

Without a word, I folded myself into the chair and clamped my hands together and looked around the office.

Maybe coming here was another mistake.

"Coffee? Tea? Whiskey?" he asked.

An eyebrow shot up at his offer of booze. *What the hell kind of therapist is this?* "I'm good."

"I'm glad to hear that." He settled into the chair beside me and exhaled.

I waited, hoping he'd have some way to break the ice. When the silence stretched on, I cleared my throat. "Dr. Bennet, aren't you going to ask me why I'm here?"

"You can call me Alex." He shrugged. "I thought we might get to know each other a bit first, but if that's what you want to talk about, we can dive right in."

Frustrated and feeling foolish, I braced my hands on my knees and began to stand. "Look, I think this was a mistake."

Alex stood with me, unfazed by my abrupt demeanor. He held out a hand. "It took balls to come here in the first place." He nodded when I shook his hand. "It is nice to meet you, Abel."

I frowned, looking him over.

Was this some sort of therapist Jedi mind trick?

My boots stomped across the rug in his office, and I turned, pacing back toward him. "Look. I don't know what I'm doing here. All I know is there's a lot of shit going on up here"—I gestured toward my head—"and I need to figure it out."

A grin spread across his face. "We can do that."

I exhaled, relieved that the weight of my statement wasn't enough to scare him off just yet.

There was a lot to unpack, so I figured I could start with

something tangible. "I've been having these nightmares . . . they're like a replay of a memory, only they're different. Worse."

I recounted the accident, my sentencing, and a brief overview of life after prison, including my relationship with Sloane. Dr. Bennet nodded and listened without offering judgment or his opinion. I shared how recently the dreams had shifted to the accident involving Sloane and the twins.

When I looked at him expectantly, hoping he'd offer some suggestions for making the dreams stop, he only sat back. "What do you think the dream means?"

I blew out a stream of breath. "Getting behind the wheel that night is my greatest regret. It haunts me. The only thing worse is if something were to happen to Sloane and the kids."

"Something by your own hand." Dr. Bennet confirmed my darkest fear.

"Exactly. I wouldn't survive that." My jaw ached from grinding my teeth.

"We've only just met, but I get the sense that you're a protector. Maybe you fear losing control because you've had firsthand experience with that, and now the stakes are even higher. Right now it seems as though you're carrying your shame like a badge of honor instead of allowing yourself to feel forgiveness."

I scoffed. "I don't need forgiveness. The mother already claimed to forgive me, though I don't understand how that would be possible."

His eyebrows raised. "Have you asked her?"

"What?" I stared at my feet.

He gestured toward me. "Have you asked the mother why she forgave you?"

I mulled over his words. "Not exactly."

"Perhaps if you understood how she could find forgiveness, you may begin to forgive yourself." He shrugged. "Just a thought."

Just a thought, my ass.

After an hour, Dr. Bennet shifted topics to end our time together, but I couldn't let go of what he said. Sure, the mother claimed to forgive me, but I had always assumed that was bullshit. It was incomprehensible that she could ever truly feel anything other than hatred toward me.

Still, instead of turning toward home, I headed east and out of town.

THE SMALL TWO-STORY home was painted white, and each window was decorated with a planter box full of flowers. The neighborhood was bigger and more active than Outta-towner, but still maintained a bit of small-town charm. The hour drive gave me plenty of time to think, and rethink, how to even begin the conversation.

Before I could back out, my fist landed with a hard knock on the sunny, yellow front door. Seconds later, a woman pulled it open and stared up at me.

It was her. She was several years older, but I could never forget her face.

I sucked in a deep breath. "Good afternoon, ma'am. I'm sorry to bother you, but I'm—"

"Abel King." The woman stared up at me. "I know who you are."

I nodded like the fool I was. "I'm sorry. I shouldn't have come."

I had taken one step in retreat when she walked onto

the small porch and closed the door behind her. "Wait. Please."

I turned to see her offering a soft smile. "I'm glad you came." She gestured toward her home. "Would you please come in?"

My tongue was thick and motionless. I nodded and followed the woman into her home. It was homey, and windows allowed bright light to stream in and make the space feel open and airy.

She gestured toward the sofa. "Can I get you something to drink?"

I shook my head, and she sat in a chair next to me. With my hands clasped in front of me, I stared at the floor. "Ma'am, I came here to say . . . I needed to—" Adequate words escaped me. Emotion rose in my chest and stung the bridge of my nose.

"Please, call me Rebecca." Her gentle hand rested on my forearm. "May I go first?"

I glanced up to see her soft blue eyes staring at me. I nodded.

"I want you to know that I do not hate you, Abel King."

My frown deepened. I couldn't understand. "How could you not hate me for what I did? What I took from you?"

Rebecca sighed and looked at me with pity. "I hate what happened. I hate that we lost Chase and that nothing will ever be the same. I hate that you went to prison for something that was so clearly an accident. I hate that I chose the highway instead of the back roads because I assumed it was safer. I hate knowing I was partly responsible, but let you take all of the blame."

I shook my head as my mind swirled. "I don't understand."

Fresh tears swam in her eyes. "I told them. When the police came to the hospital and asked me what happened, I told them what I knew . . . Chase and I were in the car, driving home. It was late. And dark. Something on the side of the road caught my eye—a deer, I think. It darted in front of us, and I swerved."

Her eyes went glassy, and she shook her head as if she were reliving that night in her mind. "I think I overcorrected. Got too close to the center line when I crossed it. It was at that moment you must have dozed off, and it just . . . happened. It was horrible, perfect, devastating timing."

My breath was ragged. I could barely comprehend what I was hearing.

My car never crossed the center line? It was why, after the crash, her car ended up in my lane instead of the other way around.

As I stared, she continued: "I was mourning my son. I was hurt and angry and in a really bad place. Later, my lawyer told me that if I mentioned the deer again, I could get into trouble myself, so I didn't."

Understanding washed over me, and my eyes lifted to meet hers. "It was removed from the police report."

She swallowed and nodded. "I don't know how or why, but yes."

My father.

He may not have had enough pull to sway a judge, but he certainly had enough power to convince an officer to leave out a few details in the investigation, ensuring a harsher sentencing for me . . . to teach me a lesson.

"I realized too late that it was an accident," she said. "The only way I knew to help was to speak at your trial."

I felt sick. Everything I'd carried, every night I'd lie awake wishing it was me instead of Chase came flooding back. "It was still my fault. I was overly tired. My reaction time was delayed."

Her hand was gentle on my arm. "You don't carry the weight of this alone. There are so many things that I hate about that night, but you are not one of them. I only ask that you forgive me for not being strong enough to do more."

Forgive her?

She had told the truth, and my father manipulated the situation to suit his needs. I spent five years in prison because he wanted to teach me a lesson and allowed a mother to feel guilt and shame for not doing more.

I hated him.

My jaw clenched. "You were grieving. You had just lost a child. I—"

"Abel . . . you held his hand when I couldn't. I never thanked you for that."

My eyes flew to hers. A tear slipped from beneath her lashes, and my anger melted away. Neither of us could change the past.

Her words were true and stung the deepest parts of my soul.

After the accident, she was too injured to move, and when I found the boy, I had held his hand and talked to him until help arrived. It was only later that I learned that he'd gone into cardiac arrest in the ambulance and died from his injuries.

The memories that flooded back broke me. "I'm—I'm so sorry." I crumpled in on myself, openly sobbing in her living room.

Her grip on my forearm tightened and, together, we cried for Chase, for the tiny micro-decisions that led us both to that quiet stretch of highway, for fate that brought us together in such a tragic way.

We cried until we were both wrung out.

FORTY

"Good morning." Judge Tamara Barnes smiled down from her bench as my attorney silently guided me toward the small table at the front of the room. "I appreciate everyone being with us today. We'll start in one minute so that we can stay on schedule throughout the day."

I adjusted the hem of my top and put on a brave smile as I faced the judge.

"Today's hearing is for the child custody case number 27842—this is the matter of custody concerning the minor children, Ben and Tillie Hansen, between Jared Hansen, the plaintiff, and Sloane Robinson, the defendant. Counsel, please state your appearances for the record."

My attorney exuded quiet confidence while I stood with wobbly knees and a hopeful heart. "Your Honor, Laura Michaels appearing on behalf of the defendant, Sloane Robinson."

The judge scribbled something with a pen. "Thank you, Ms. Michaels. And for the plaintiff?"

She looked up at the empty space near the opposing

counsel. "Well . . . Mr. Hansen appears to be absent." She gestured at the attorney with her pen. "Are you representing on his behalf?"

Jared's attorney smiled, but tension clung to his shoulders. "Aiden Waxman, Your Honor, appearing on behalf of the plaintiff, Jared Hansen."

The judge made another note on paper. "Thank you, Mr. Waxman. Can you provide any insight into your client's absence?"

"Your Honor, I believe there is an ongoing investigation as to the whereabouts of my client. At present, he is . . . not in attendance."

My heart sank. Though I didn't want to believe it, there was no denying that Abel's father was somehow behind the mysterious disappearance of my ex-husband.

My stomach churned. Just because I wanted Jared's volatility far, far away from me and my children, it didn't mean I wanted him dead.

My mind still couldn't wrap itself around the idea that Jared was still missing.

My attorney touched my elbow, and when my eyes met hers, I exhaled the breath I'd been holding.

One worry at a time.

Judge Barnes sighed lightly. "I see." The judge flipped through a few sheets of paper in front of her. "It appears as though stirring up trouble and then disappearing is a recurring theme for Mr. Hansen."

The attorney shifted in his buffed, wingtip shoes but didn't respond.

"Very well," the judge said. "Let the record reflect the absence of the plaintiff. Mr. Waxman, would you like to proceed with your case?"

Attorney Waxman slicked a hand down his tie. "Your Honor, we request that all evidence previously submitted be considered with the weight it deserves. However, we will rely on the court's discretion in this matter."

My attorney leaned to whisper in my ear. "They are choosing not to call any character witnesses against you. This is very good for us."

A shiny spot of hope bloomed in my chest.

Judge Barnes nodded. "Very well. Let the record reflect that the plaintiff calls no witnesses. Ms. Michaels, would you like to proceed with your case?"

My attorney smiled. "Yes, Your Honor. We are prepared to proceed. I would like to call the listed witnesses to testify on behalf of the defendant."

Judge Barnes gestured to the space in front of the bench. "Please proceed."

Laura nodded and faced the courtroom. "I call Norman 'Bax' Robinson to the stand."

My heart swelled to see my dear, sweet grandfather, dressed in an ill-fitting, rumpled suit, walk to the witness stand. He confidently placed his hand on the Bible to be sworn in.

My attorney gently talked him through a series of questions in which he shared his experiences with my children. My throat went tight when he looked at me and smiled as he told the court how proud he was of me and my ability to care for my children despite our recent bouts of bad luck. He spoke of how happy the kids were and how life near the lake was good for all of us.

When he was finished, he winked at me from the stand, and I mouthed *I love you*.

Judge Barnes then asked, "Any cross-examination, Mr. Waxman?"

Jared's attorney shook his head and tapped his pen. "None, Your Honor."

"Very well. You may call your next witness, Ms. Michaels."

One by one, my lawyer called friends and neighbors to the stand—Granddad, Bug, Sylvie, Emily, even Bootsy stood on the stand and spoke of the kindness and politeness of my children, to which he credited my parenting skills.

Each of them had nothing but kindness and support for me and my children. I blinked back tears at how they chose to show up for us in such a big way.

My hands clamped together in my lap, and I fought back grateful tears.

My lawyer dropped a folded piece of paper in front of me before resuming her position at the front of the court.

I unfolded it and read *Do not react*.

My brows furrowed as I watched her. "I would like to call my final witness, Abel King."

My mouth dropped open, and I shot a look at my lawyer. Unfazed, she didn't spare a glance in my direction. I clamped my lips together.

From the last row of seats, Abel stood. I don't know how I could have missed him. Dressed in the same bespoke charcoal suit he'd married me in, Abel walked with cool, unhurried strides. The expensive material stretched across his strong chest, and his tailored pants exuded a sumptuous confidence.

If ever there was a King, Abel was it.

His eyes stayed level, focused ahead at the witness stand as the rest of the courtroom collectively tracked his movements with their eyes.

He was strong and powerful and painfully beautiful.

Just as he passed my seat, I felt a soft brush of his finger along the back of my arm. Heat erupted in my chest, and I fought back tears.

He was here. Fighting for me. Fighting for us.

After Abel was sworn in, I stared as he focused his attention on the questions presented by my attorney. She probed about our working relationship, which Abel proclaimed had slowly developed into a romantic one. Her questioning focused primarily on my relationship with my children and his observations during our time together.

"Sloane is a dedicated and loving mother. I have watched her make every single decision from the sole place of loving and providing for her children. In truth, she is the type of mother I wish I had the opportunity to know as a child."

My heart ached for the poor, sweet little boy he'd once been. Abel had been robbed of his mother and saw in me the kind of woman strong enough to lovingly raise happy children. A tear slipped from the corner of my eye, and I quickly swiped it away.

My thumb fingered the simple silver band on my finger.

My attorney nodded. "Thank you, Mr. King. No further questions, Your Honor."

The judge moved a paper from the stack in front of her. "I have a few questions for you, Mr. King."

My heart thumped as he nodded. "Of course, Your Honor."

"The court is aware of your prior conviction." Judge Barnes's cool expression gave nothing away.

My eyes bounced between my lawyer, Abel, and the judge.

He nodded. "Yes, ma'am."

The judge's hands clasped together. "Tell me . . . what has life been like since your release?"

Abel considered for a moment. For the tiniest second, his eyes swept over me before darting away. "In many ways, difficult."

My chest squeezed.

"Living in a small town where everyone knows you have demons can be difficult," he continued. "For a while, it was easier to live on the fringe of our community. I'm a bit of an outcast, you can say." His guileless scoff was a dagger to my heart. "But that all changed when Sloane came into my life."

His eyes lifted to mine. "Through her, I realized that bad things happen to all kinds of people. We make mistakes and we have to pay for them, but continually punishing ourselves may not always be the right answer. She allowed me to finally see that."

"So you've forgiven yourself then?" Judge Barnes asked.

The corner of Abel's mouth lifted. "No, Your Honor, but I'm trying. I've started therapy—for myself, but also for Sloane and the kids. In fact, it was Ben who'd given me the reassurance I needed to find the strength to even go. I know he got that resilience from his mom. And Tillie?" Abel smiled. "Tillie's laugh rings out and gets you right here, you know?" He tapped his chest. "She's a good kid. A happy kid, with a lot of talent. They love their mom, and she loves them—with everything she's got."

Judge Barnes didn't react but simply lifted an eyebrow at Abel. "Ms. Robinson filed paperwork for an uncontested divorce in which you signed. Is that correct?"

"It's true." Abel sat tall. "I will do whatever it takes for Sloane and her children to be together. If that means removing myself so that a judge who knows nothing about me can sleep better at night, then so be it. But she will always be my wife." He thunked a finger against his chest. "Right here."

The judge set down her pen and flattened her hands against the desk. "Well, that is a very bold and impassioned speech, Mr. King."

My heart raced as I watched the scene unfold. Abel never wavered under her quiet assessment. My attorney stood next to me, unmoving.

"Mr. King, I have been a judge for many years. In that time I have had women and men, not so unlike yourself, stand before me and make proclamations—claims they've changed, that their criminal history was simply a blip. Promises to never skirt the law again. In that time, I've learned to suss the liars and the cheats with a fair bit of accuracy." Her cool gaze stared down at Abel from her bench, and my chest squeezed. "Do you believe me, Mr. King?"

He nodded. "Yes, ma'am. I do."

Judge Barnes's expression was unreadable. "Very well." She looked at my attorney. "Does the defense rest?"

A confident grin split across Laura's face. "Yes, Your Honor."

Judge Barnes nodded. "Considering the evidence presented and the absence of the plaintiff, I believe the best outcome to this case is clear. This court will submit a default judgment against plaintiff Jared Hansen."

She looked at attorney Waxman. "Counselor, once the issue of his whereabouts is resolved, your client is free to re-petition the court, but as of today, I award sole custody to Ms. Robinson, *without* visitation. I urge you to speak to your client about the seriousness of the current order of protection for Ms. Robinson. He can expect strict consequences if he chooses to be in violation of that order, especially if it comes across my desk again."

With a grim nod, Jared's attorney simply said, "Understood, Your Honor."

"Very well." The judge turned to me and smiled. "Congratulations, Ms. Robinson. Case dismissed." The gavel struck her block, and I let out a cry of relief.

It was really over.

Cheers erupted behind me as the swell of support from my friends and family—my town—rolled over me.

My hands came up, burying my face and stifling the sob of relief. I swallowed back the hard ball of emotion as I watched our attorneys shake hands.

Laura turned to me. "Congratulations, Sloane. You earned this."

I stood and pulled her into a tight hug. "Thank you. Thank you so much."

She held me at arm's length and smiled. "You're welcome. I'm sorry for the surprise witness." She winked. "He reached out and pleaded his case to speak on the stand on your behalf, and I have to admit . . . that man is something else."

My eyes slid to Abel, who was standing near the front of the courtroom. "He sure is."

When she stepped away, Abel moved forward, stealing the space between us and scooping me into his arms. I buried my face in his chest as he lifted my toes from the ground.

"Thank you. Thank—"

My words were smothered by Abel's warm, soft kiss. I gasped into him, pouring my gratitude and love into that kiss. His tongue slid over mine, deepening the kiss, and my arms pulled him closer.

I melted into him.

"Mr. King." The judge's gavel sounded behind us. "Mr. King."

We turned to peek at Judge Barnes. One discerning eyebrow lifted as she flicked her head. "Outside of my courtroom."

I blushed and buried my face into him, stifling a laugh.

He cleared his throat and nodded grimly. "Yes, Your Honor."

Abel's arm wrapped around me as the rumble of his deep voice tickled the shell of my ear. "Let's go, wife. We've got some celebrating to do."

THE PARKING LOT to Abel's Brewery was packed full as we pulled up.

"What's all this?" I asked, turning in my seat to face Abel.

He lifted a shoulder. "Just a few friends getting together to celebrate your big win."

My eyes were wide. "But we didn't know we'd win before . . ."

Abel winked and my stomach somersaulted. "I did." He popped his head to the side as he exited the driver's seat. "Just come on. Stop being a pain in the ass."

"Okay, boss." I scoffed a laugh and got out. "I'm glad to see you're still a grump."

Abel pulled me into him, wrapping an arm around my shoulders. He kissed my hair and leaned in close. "I have to keep up appearances. I can't let everyone know I've gone soft because of you."

My fingertips grazed down the front of his shirt, teasing

the front of his jeans. "Trust me, there's nothing soft about you."

He growled and walked us forward toward the brewery's entrance. "I knew you were trouble."

Once inside, cheers erupted from the front of the brewery. The garage-style doors were open to let a breeze through, and friends and family spilled out onto the patio as twinkle lights illuminated the outside space. In the corner, Layna was strumming her guitar and providing live acoustic music while a few of the Bluebirds were decorating the space with flowers and balloons.

"Abel! This is too much!" I laughed and hugged my way through the entrance as people moved forward to embrace me.

Once I got through the crowd, Meatball came up and shook Abel's hand. "He hasn't even shown you the best part." Meatball handed me a frosted pint glass full of a rich, golden beer. "Here. Try this."

I glanced at Abel but took a tentative sip. It was rich and toasty with a hint of sweetness. "Mmm! That's so good." I smiled at Meatball. "Did you brew this?"

He grinned and shook his head before gesturing to Abel. "Nope. This is Abel's baby."

I looked at him. "It's really good." I sipped again.

Abel exhaled in relief. "I'm glad you like it. It's yours."

I lifted my glass in salute. "Thanks."

Both men laughed, and Meatball shook his head. "Yes, the glass is yours, but the brew is yours too. Abel made it for you."

My eyes went wide as I looked at Abel. The man had the audacity to look away and blush. "Are you serious?"

He smiled at me, letting his fingertips smooth down a

strand of my long hair. "Warm notes of biscuit and honey. Just like you."

I was floored. He'd created something just for me, and it was incredible. "I thought you were creating something new for MJ."

A sheepish smile curled the corner of his lip. "I still am." He lifted a shoulder and looked across the room at his little sister, who was chatting with a group of friends. "Hers is more of a winter brew. This one is just for you."

Meatball nodded. "Right on, man. Tell her the best part." He slid the bottle across the table, and I picked it up. "Look at the artwork."

Brewer's Wife was across the front of the label, but I recognized the illustration style immediately. My eyes flew to Abel's. "Did Tillie draw this?"

On cue, my daughter collided with my leg, hugging my middle with her brother following behind her. "Mom!"

"Hey!" I squeezed her tightly. "Did you see this? It's amazing, Till!"

She beamed up at me. "Abel said it was a surprise. Isn't it cool?"

At the bottom of the design was a honeybee in Tillie's quirky, cartoon style.

"I said to put flowers on it," Ben added.

I hugged my twins. "It's perfect."

Tillie looked up at me. "Granddad said we can hurl ourselves down the sand dunes, and he and Miss Bug will judge us. Can we? Please?"

I laughed at their wide-eyed pleading. "Of course. Just please stay out of trouble."

Without even hearing my plea, they were off, weaving through people to find my granddad. I looked at the bottle again. "Brewer's Wife?"

Abel's dark eyes were intense. "If she'll still have me."

I leaned into him. "I guess this means we're still married."

His face grew serious, and he shook his head. "I'm sorry, but no. The paperwork was filed, and my lawyer said it'll still go through."

Confused and hurt, I scrunched my brow. When he grinned, I narrowed my eyes and looked up at him.

Abel widened his palms. "Look, I promised Tillie a new wedding so she can wear a fancy dress. My hands are tied."

A shocked laugh burst out of me. "You're going to let the State of Michigan grant us a divorce just so you can appease a seven-year-old?"

Abel's grin widened. "Not entirely."

He stepped back and reached into his pocket and pulled out a small square box. My hand flew to my mouth.

"Sloane Robinson. My wife. When you found me, I was a broken man, but you weren't afraid to scoop up the pieces and show me how they could fit back together into something entirely new. Your love gave me the courage to look inside myself. To get better. I promise to love Ben and Tillie as fiercely as I would my own. I promise to love you forever."

Abel dropped to one knee in front of our friends and family. He opened the small box, revealing the most gorgeous ring I'd ever seen. The cushion cut solitaire danced with fire. "Will you marry me . . . again?"

Tears flowed down my cheeks as I clutched my left hand to my chest. "But I love the ring I have."

Abel smiled and shook his head. "You'll keep it. My mother was the first woman I ever loved, and you'll be the last. Her ring belongs to you. The diamond is just because you deserve some sparkle."

I flung myself at Abel, wrapping my arms around him. "Yes. Oh, Abel, yes!"

He laughed—the sweetest-sounding rumble in the world—and stood, taking me with him as everyone in the brewery clapped, whistled, and cheered behind us.

The man I'd fallen for was grumpy, brooding, and head over heels in love with me.

. . . And, really, that's just my luck.

EPILOGUE

Abel

"You nervous?" Royal's hand clamped over my shoulder as I shifted in my suit.

"Nah." *I was.*

Royal's laugh rang out. "You're so full of shit." He looked around as we stood just inside the brewery, looking out onto the sand dune cliffs where Sloane and I would be married.

The golden sun dipped low on the horizon, casting a warm glow over the sandy cliffs. We'd briefly discussed being married at a church or different venue, but Sloane had insisted she wanted to get married at the brewery.

"I'm happy for you."

I shook my brother's hand. "Thank you."

Side by side, we watched as our guests took their seats. Chase's mother, Rebecca, sat with her husband near the back. She smiled politely when I caught her eye, and I nodded with a pressed, heartfelt smile.

It amazed me how much could change in such a short

amount of time. It wasn't all that long ago that I was an outsider—shunned and whispered about. Feared for what I'd done.

All that had changed when Sloane blew into my life.

Duke Sullivan sat with my nephew on his lap. His brothers and their spouses sat around him. Over the past few months, I'd gotten to know Kate and Beckett Miller as they worked on the farmhouse. Construction was going well, and Sloane had invited them to dinner on several occasions. It pained me to admit that they weren't all that bad.

I laughed and shook my head.

"What is it?" Royal asked.

"Just this." I gestured toward the guests. "You think anyone would have believed Sullivans and Kings would be in the same room, but be practically family? It's wild."

He scoffed. "It is pretty fucked up." His eyes narrowed. "I think I'll toilet paper Lee's truck to make up for it."

I shook my head. "You are such a child."

As we waited, I watched as Royal scanned the crowd. When his eyes fell on Veda Bauer, he smirked. She must have felt his attention on her, because when she looked over her shoulder, her stare could have frozen the depths of hell.

"Yikes," I said. "What the hell did you do to her?"

Royal's grin spread. "I don't know . . . I don't think she likes me."

My face scrunched. "Why are you smiling like that?"

Royal's shoulders bounced. "I kind of like them feisty."

I pinched the bridge of my nose. "Jesus. Do not mess with the one woman who's helping us out of Dad's mess. That woman looks like she would crush your balls and smile about it."

I checked my watch and steadied my breathing. It was almost time.

Off to the side, Bug fussed with the bow on Tillie's frilly, dusty rose dress. I caught her eye and winked at my daughter.

My daughter.

I had never envisioned myself as a father figure, but with Sloane by my side, I felt ready to embrace the role. Ben and Tillie made it easy.

Royal's chin lifted as he smiled. "There he is." He gestured for Ben to come closer. "Your best man looks pretty good, Abel."

I placed a hand on Ben's shoulder, and he smiled up at me. "He sure does. You ready, kid?"

Ben nodded and grinned as I stepped behind him. Without fuss, JP, Royal, Whip, and Ben lined up in front of me, ready to walk down the aisle. Beside them, MJ, Sylvie, Layna, and Tillie smiled, holding small bouquets of wild-flowers.

It was time, and I was more than ready to marry my wife.

Again.

I GRIPPED Sloane's waist as we stared up at the Wild Iris Bed-and-Breakfast. We couldn't think of a better place to spend our wedding night. At the wedding, Gladys was over-joyed to hand us the keys to the turret suite.

We trekked up the circular staircase to our room.

"It was so sweet that you cried." Sloane smiled up at me.

I frowned. "I did not cry. A bit of sand blew into my eye."

She bit back a smile before stopping in front of the door.

"Mm-hmm." She patted my chest. "Keep telling yourself that, tough guy."

"You were right, though," I admitted.

Her eyebrows pitched down, and I smiled as I toyed with her hair. "You were the best wife I've ever had."

She batted her lashes. "I told you." Her sigh was soft and satisfied. "It really was the perfect day."

When we reached the room, instead of opening the door, she paused. "Do you still think you made the right decision to not have your dad there?"

My face turned to stone, and I answered without hesitation. "Absolutely."

"He scares me." Her lower lip tucked between her teeth. "I'm nervous about what'll happen."

I held her closer, soaking in her warmth and letting her perfume wash over me. When Sloane told me about her meeting with my father and her suspicions he was behind Jared's disappearance, I was livid. There was no doubt in my mind that his calling on her was a thinly veiled threat to keep her in line. I seethed with rage anytime I thought about her being alone with him.

I squeezed her, in part to remind myself she was here and safe with me. "You don't have to worry about anything. I won't let him hurt my family anymore."

Sloane toyed with her lip. "So what's the next move?"

"We know he's involved—how much or how little, we're still figuring out. JP is working with Veda behind the scenes to ensure my father doesn't make any moves, but for now . . . we wait." I brushed a strand of hair from her face as I held her.

Her fingertips stroked down the side of my jaw. "I'm proud of you."

My chest ached, as it always did when she reaffirmed me.

I unlocked the door to our suite and shoved it open. Our eyes went wide.

"I knew it!" Sloane laughed as I scooped her up into my arms and carried her into the room. I dropped her onto the bed and pointed. "Don't. Move."

I dragged our suitcase into the room and dropped my bag beside the bed. Crawling over her, I pinned Sloane to her back. "Right now, I don't want to talk about anyone but my wife."

She shifted beneath me, allowing my hips to settle against her. "Is that so, boss?"

I raised an eyebrow. "Boss? Look around. I'm the captain now."

A peal of laughter echoed through the turret suite of the Wild Iris, which was, of course, pirate themed. Swatches of fabric hung from the ceiling in swags, mimicking a ship's billowing sails. Small circular windows that looked like portholes dotted the wall. There was even a cannon and treasure chest in the corner of the room.

I pulled a soft strip of fuzzy fabric from my bag beside the bed and dragged it across her chest. "I'm the captain and you're my prisoner. Arms above your head."

"Is that . . . ?" Desire and delight swirled in her eyes. "Did you keep my robe tie all this time?"

I smiled as she held her arms above her head, her hands gripping the ship-shaped headboard. "Are you kidding? Of course I kept it. I stashed it in my desk drawer. It was my first glimpse of what you were hiding beneath that ridiculous robe. Your tits haunted me for weeks."

Sloane smiled and arched into me as I secured her hands and attached them to the headboard.

With an aching slowness, I unbuttoned her sundress, exposing her to me.

"Fuck." My hand moved across her throat, down her chest to her pussy. "You're fucking perfect."

She hummed and squirmed beneath me.

"Easy, girl." My hand squeezed her hip. "I'm going to take my time with you."

I dragged out long, hungry kisses across her belly and lower. Across her hip until my nose was buried against her hot, wet cunt. I inhaled, savoring her scent as I teased her. I had plans for my wife, and she was going to be reminded of exactly what it meant to be married to a man like me.

NEED MORE SLOANE & Abel? Read an exclusive bonus scene here: https://www.lenahendrix.com/get-abel-and-sloanes-bonus-scene

SNEAK PEEK OF JUST BETWEEN US

Royal King is pure mischief wrapped in a cocky smirk and a heated stare.

Five minutes in his small town and I knew he was going to be nothing but trouble. He's an arrogant, tattooed playboy with a secret and I'm the woman tasked with quietly cleaning up his family's mess.

I never dreamed he could be the mysterious stranger behind my hidden, late-night messages.

It doesn't matter what he says or how hard he tries to get under my skin, I won't break. Not for him. Not for anyone . . . but when our secrets are exposed, **all bets are off.**

He knows the rules—just a little fun exploration. Nothing more. But one lesson leads to another . . . and another, and soon I realize that he's set out to break every rule I've ever put into place.

I refuse to find myself melting under his gaze or swooning at the way he makes the noise around us quieter.

I can handle men like him.

Everything will be fine, as long as we can keep this ***just between us.***

～

Pre-Order JUST BETWEEN US here:
https://geni.us/lenaJBU

ACKNOWLEDGMENTS

My first thank you has to be to you, dear reader! Abel King has intrigued me since he first started lurking around in the Sullivan series and I am so thankful that you gave him a chance. I always hoped you would grow to love the broody, complicated man just as much as I did!

To Rachel and AJ Blume: I have a million and one thank yous for taking the time to answer all of my beer brewing questions. I now know more about enterobacter than I ever thought possible. In reality, you brought Abel's Brewery to life. I am so excited to see where your next adventure takes you. First round's on me!

To my husband who never thought twice about the fact that I was a single mother when we met and loved my son as your own. You won my heart when you wholly accept us, just as we were.

To Kandi and Elsie - you keep me sane and motivated. You make the good days great and the hard days a hell of a lot more fun.

To Paula, you make workshopping a story idea so damn fun! Thank you for making tiny suggestions that add another level of sparkle to my stories. I love the way your brain works and I am so thankful to work with you!

James, I would be LOST without you. You don't seem to mind that timelines are my nemesis and commas don't exist. Thank you for your thoughtfulness and patience with each book we work on together.

Anna and Trinity, your beta reading always adds another layer of richness to these crazy stories. Thank you for flagging spicy quotes and swoon-worthy moments. I love you!

HENDRIX HEARTTHROBS

Want to connect? Come hang out with the Hendrix Heartthrobs on Facebook to laugh & chat with Lena! Special sneak peeks, announcements, exclusive content, & general shenanigans all happen there.

Come join us!
https://www.facebook.com/groups/
lenahendrixreadergroup

ABOUT THE AUTHOR

Lena Hendrix is an Amazon Top 10 bestselling contemporary romance author living in the Midwest. Her love for romance stared with sneaking racy Harlequin paperbacks and now she writes her own hot-as-sin small town romance novels. Lena has a soft spot for strong alphas with marshmallow insides, heroines who clap back, and sizzling tension. Her novels pack in small town heart with a whole lotta heat.

When she's not writing or devouring new novels, you can find her hiking, camping, fishing, and sipping a spicy margarita!

Want to hang out? Find Lena on Tiktok or IG!

ALSO BY LENA HENDRIX

Chikalu Falls

Finding You

Keeping You

Protecting You

Choosing You (origin novella)

Redemption Ranch

The Badge

The Alias

The Rebel

The Target

The Sullivans

One Look

One Touch

One Chance

One Night

One Taste (prequel novella)

The Kings

Just This Once

Just My Luck

Just Between Us

Just Like That

Just Say Yes

Printed in Great Britain
by Amazon